Bandrovic stared at her with narrowed eyes. "This is it? This is the great Healer Dione? The ghost of the forest? The Gray Wolf of Randonnen? The Heart of Ariye? Where is your fight, woman? Where is your fire?"

He hit her then, hard, on the cheek. Her head rocked back, but there was no sound except the smack of his hand on her face. It was calm, calculating, and the raider's expression was intent, as if he judged her will by her lack of reaction. He hit her again. The third time, she raised her head from his blows and spat blood on his boots.

He eyed her almost curiously. "No cursing, no crying. No fury of the Gray Ones . . . Where is the fighter who refused to die? Where is the legend I've followed? Or do you simply face your path to hell with the stoicism of a stone?"

By Tara K. Harper
Published by Ballantine Books:

Tales of the Wolves
WOLFWALKER
SHADOW LEADER
STORM RUNNER
GRAYHEART
WOLF'S BANE

LIGHTWING
CAT SCRATCH FEVER
CATARACT

WOLF'S BANE

Tara K. Harper

A Del Rey® Book
BALLANTINE BOOKS • NEW YORK

In memory of my mother

A Del Rey® Book
Published by Ballantine Books
Copyright © 1997 by Tara K. Harper

http://www.randomhouse.com

Library of Congress Catalog Number: 97-92491

ISBN 0-345-40634-6

Manufactured in the United States of America

First Edition: November 1997

10 9 8 7 6 5 4 3 2 1

To those who have generously given
of their invaluable time and advice,
many thanks:

Ed Godshalk
Marc Wells
Howard Davidson, Ph.D., Sun Microsystems
Thomas Moore, University of Arizona
Ernest V. Curto, Ph.D., University of Alabama, Birmingham
Matthew Beckman, Ph.D., University of Alabama, Birmingham
William C. Haneberg, Ph.D., New Mexico Bureau of Mines
Yehudah Werner, Ph.D.
Garry Mayner
Nick Landau
Chip Gardes
Toby Tyrel
and the crew of *USGS Polar Star*

Also, special thanks to:
Dan Harper, Kevin Harper, Richard Jarvis, Colleen Gaobois,
Kris Hasson, and Sandra Keen

I

*In the night, the roads are different. The roots stretch out like
white-skinned arms; the moons are eyes that do not blink.
The air is thick with sounds that gather silently to watch you pass.
And you kick your dnu to a faster gait, while fear hangs on your
back like a worlag clawing at your courage. But you ride,
because the lives of your family ride with you. You ride
the black road, because your speed is the difference
between life and death.*

—From Riding the Black Road, *by Merai Karrliamo maKaira*

She came out of the night like a wraith. One moment, there
had been only darkness, with six of the nine moons waning and
the woods sounds quavering like ghosts in the wind. Then a
wisp of movement breathed in the trees. Brush snapped. Something large and menacing leaped the barrier bushes. His heart
jerked. The next instant, a whirlwind struck the road.

He shouted, kicking his riding beast into a charge. From the
side of her vision, she caught the dark movement. One fluid,
half-rearing motion, and she twisted her six-legged dnu midrush.
Then she spurred the beast back at him.

Black hair whipped around her face in a halo of urgent violence. Her dark eyes gleamed with the light of the yellow-white
moons. The gray shadow on the ground—the wolf with its yellow
eyes—bunched its body to fling itself after the woman.

The dnu thundered straight for him, its six hooves frantic
with speed. Too fast! By the moons, she would kill them both.
He should turn—*she* should turn—but she didn't slacken her
pace. Desperately, he leaned out, away from his own riding
beast. The dark woman leaned in. Her face, a blur in the night,
was hollowed out by shadow. A howling seemed to hit him.
Then his arm slapped hers, and their hands dug into each other's
musculature. Her body came free of the saddle. She snapped like
a rope across the gap of pounding hooves, letting her dnu race
free in the night. Then her body struck him.

One leg caught against his dnu; her chest hit his ribs. Her

1

weight, slight as it was, nearly lost him his seat even with his heavy grip on the double pommel. Then her other leg was over, and her body melted against his broad back as she slid into the rhythm of riding, her free arm seeking his waist.

"On?" he shouted.

"Set," she shouted back. She was grinning, but beneath the six moons that hung in the sky, the expression was feral and sharp.

He threw his right leg over the pommel. For a moment, he hung on the saddle and the strength of her arms. Then he hit the road running. Hooves pounded as she picked up speed. The gray wolf flashed beside her. She was gone, and only the scent of her hair and the sweat of her ride remained for him to taste.

He walked, limping, after the other dnu, which had finally stopped on the road. The sides of its bloated, segmented belly heaved with breathlessness, and its eyes rolled in its head. The odor of fear was upon it. There was a dark patch on its flanks, but he couldn't tell what it was. Then the creature shifted nervously out from under the rootroad trees and into the white-bright moonlight. He stepped closer, and the riding beast grunted its warning, stamping its middle legs. No wonder the wolfwalker had not simply moved away from him like a relay runner and slowed to let him catch up. She must have barely been able to control the beast, frightened as it was. Had he tried to ride up from behind, the dnu would have panicked into the barrier bushes like a hare from a hungry worlag.

He moved again, slowly soothing the creature until he could get his hands on the reins and examine the patch more clearly. The ragged gashes that had bled out on its flanks were deep and dark. He felt their warmth—they were hardly clotted yet—and rubbed his fingers together. The scent of the blood mixed with the beast's sweat, and again he heard the howling. His voice was low as he looked after her. "Ride with the moons, Dione."

* * *

Menedi heard the hooves of the riding beast first. "Quick now. Look sharp," she snapped at the two youths. She was already half out the door.

"Is she here—the healer?" The younger boy's voice was thin with excitement.

Menedi didn't bother to nod back over her shoulder. The boy would hear for himself in the next few seconds. "Get the dnu loose and ready. Culli, make sure the reins of the two trailing beasts won't tangle."

Hurrying to the woman's side, the tall youth cocked his head. "She's coming in fast."

"And be glad that she is. It's your uncle who's out on that venge."

"I know it, ma'am." He checked the reins of the dnu, then glanced back through the doorway to the table where his second meatroll lay untouched. Another glance up the road told him the rider was not yet in sight. He thrust the reins of the relay dnu at the younger boy and dashed inside, grabbing up the food. There was no napkin to wrap it in. Running back out, he yanked a bandanna from his pocket and slapped it around the meatroll. He had time only to thrust the small bundle in the saddlebag before Menedi swung up on the lead dnu and started the other two relay beasts out at a slow trot.

Menedi's three dnu—the one she rode and the two relay beasts she led—strung out like a crude chain. Gradually, they picked up their pace. Then, from the road behind them the incoming rider's shadow separated itself from the night. The wolfwalker was hunched low over her dnu's neck, rolling with its six-legged gait as if she were part of its muscles, not simply a rider racing the dark. Culli caught his breath as he glimpsed the smaller loping shape—the wolf that sped before Dione as she urged her riding beast to catch up to Menedi. Maybe this time he'd be close enough to catch that yellow gaze. Perhaps this once he'd hear the packsong himself. But the wolf flashed by, and an instant later, Dione pounded past.

Involuntarily, Culli stepped out after the racing pair, nearly tripping on the other boy. He steadied his friend and stared after the wolfwalker. She had caught up with Menedi now, and her switch from one saddle to the next was so smooth in the dark that it took him a moment to realize it was done. Menedi dropped back with the single, exhausted dnu, letting the tired animal slow itself. With a flash of steel-white hooves, the extra beast reined to Dione's new mount trailed her into the dark.

The smaller boy stared after the rider. "She didn't even slow down."

Culli's voice was superior. "She's a wolfwalker."

But he too stared down the road. The gray wolf had barely turned its head when it had passed him, but the wet-musk scent it left behind seemed thick in the cold night air. Culli sucked it in. Then he vaulted into his own dnu's saddle and raced for the relay tower.

* * *

Ember Dione's thighs were numb. Her fingers were dull and cramped around the reins, and the thin, spring mist that rose from the draws climbed through her skin like venom. In spite of the effort it took to ride, her sweat had chilled and her skin was cold. The brief respite of switching saddles merely made her aware of the ache she'd soon feel in her buttocks. She had almost missed that last switch, and the adrenaline rush of her mistake had snapped her awake far better than any sweet-sharp mug of rou. Even at that, it took her a moment to realize that something was flapping with the dnu's smoothed-out stride; the saddlebag was loose. She put her hand down to the latchflap and felt the faint heat of the bag.

She pulled out a steaming bundle, wrapped in a bandanna. "Bless Menedi," she murmured. The meatrolls were small, but she didn't care. She had barely come in from the Black Gullies when the venge request hit her scouting station, and she'd had no time for dinner. She could have refused the call—there were two other healers who could have taken the ride—but this ride was not just for the venge, but for herself as well: It would bring her home to Aranur four days early. If the scouting went quickly and the raiders were close, she'd have extra time with her sons.

She almost sighed with the first bite she took from the meatroll. There would be a trail meal on the dnu that waited for her at Kitman, but that was six relay switches away. This simple snack, with its heat and energy, brought for the first time that night a smile to her dark, tired face.

* * *

Daws was idly whittling at a figurine when the signal mirror caught his attention. Instantly, he snapped from drowsy to alert. The figurine went in the bin by his chair; the knife went into the loose sheath. Quickly, he tipped the lantern to the pile of magnesium in the signal bowl and watched the metal flare. Ignoring the ominous creak of the wood, he rocked his chair back to call sharply at the sleeping ring-carver. This time of night, a relay could only be urgent. As the woman sat up, he opened the fuse straw so that the flames were drawn through to the flash pile in the signal oven. By the time he was ready to retransmit the incoming message, the rest of the fuel would be fired up and bright-hot as a kettle of devils.

He glanced out the window as he shifted in the chair. In the valley below, the mist had gathered thickly like puddles of moonlight, hiding the village message tower. The spring chill that came in with the light merely heightened his sense of alarm. It was a raider fog for sure, he thought, and worlag moons above it.

The ring-carver had awakened silently, her long arm snaking out from under her blankets even before she threw off the cloth. Now, as Daws picked up a pen and set it to the top presspad, the woman dragged her bag of tools and paints over to her pallet.

She grabbed three sticks of different sizes from the neat pile beside her bed. Hoops, sticks—they were both called message rings, but the hoops were for details: death notices, trade negotiations, and other things one had time to carve with sensitivity. Sticks were for quick messages: raider strikes, venges, urgent missives from the Lloroi. Stick handles were easier to braid and knot, their straight edges good for fast carving. On top of that, the lengths of each stick were divided into shorthand sections: the relay list, action or venge details, casualties, and so on. Since the standard sectioning had been approved two years ago, shorthand carving had been sped up by almost 20 percent, and speed-painting by half of that.

Now the woman waited for Daws to dictate the urgency so she could choose the best stick for the message. Her hands hovered like wings over water, not touching, but ready to dive.

"Begin. Begin. Begin." Daws muttered the words automatically to the ring-carver as he signaled his readiness to the other relay tower. Then he paused to read the flashing lights. "Strike." His voice held a sudden sharpness. "Raider strike."

The ring-carver grabbed the largest stick and kicked the runner alarm at her feet. By the time the alarm stopped ringing in the next room, her fingers had already slashed the strike symbol into the wood.

"Raiders on the northwest roads," Daws said. "Relay to Xinia, then Forthut and Stone Gate." He marked the relay stations and message on his own presspad as the woman slashed their symbols onto her stick. "Eight raiders struck the mining-worm train on Willow Road at dusk. One raider dead. Remaining raiders continued north along Willow Road; did not ride through Bogton. Presumed to have taken Red Wolf Road northwest toward Ramaj Eilif. Presumed to be waiting out the night." He paused. "Venge details: Venge of eight fighters gathering out of Tetgore. Aranur leads. Request for Forthut: Venge-trained tracker, four more fighters, one healer. Will ride at dawn. Expect to engage raiders two hours after dawn." He paused. "Strike details: Three miners dead. One wounded critically. Five wounded lightly. Healer Kelven on site. Request wagon for transport of wounded." He paused again. "Cargo details: Mining worms loose. Projected recovery: Forty percent or less. Relay warning to road crews at Stone Gate. End. End. End."

The large man was silent for a moment as his thick fingers flashed acknowledgment through the arrangement of lenses and mirrors. He didn't glance toward the ring-carver. The woman was young—and surprisingly pretty—not the type of relay carver he usually got for a partner. This was only her second month on the relay towers. But her slender fingers were deft as a fastbird's beak; he knew the message being carved and painted onto the stick would be as clear as his own curt words.

He held silent, reading the flashing light from the western distance station. "Second relay," he warned the ring-carver. "Second relay," he repeated as she grabbed another stick, and he another presspad. "Begin. Begin. Begin. Relaying in from Crowell. Relay on to Ontai, Carston, and Kitman. Details: Healer Yamai with patients. Healer Boccio unable to travel. Healer Brye down with spring fever. Healer Dione riding in from Black Gullies as tracker and healer for the venge. Dione requires the following: Relay of fast dnu along northern route to Kitman. Single-rider escort from Ontai to Carston for shortcut across Zaidi Ridge. Two extra healer kits and two fighters as escort from

Kitman through to the venge. Dione requests a healer intern if available. End. End. End."

He acknowledged the message. But he still wasn't finished. "Third relay," he warned. "Third relay. Begin. Begin. Begin. Relaying in from Menedi. Dione just passed Menedi station. En route to Ontai. Will make Shortstop in forty minutes; will make Ontai by fourth moonrise. End. End. End. Relay out. Relay out."

He flashed his acknowledgment back to the other relay station, then dragged his chair around so that he faced the northeast window. The second of the three sets of mirrors were already aimed at the next station in the east-west line, and he barely checked the alignments before switching open the lenses. Scant seconds later, he focused the warning light toward the ridge between Baton and Ontai.

* * *

The Kitman alarm rang in Merai's ears as she tumbled from her bunk. *Urgent,* it screamed. *Urgent!* Her heart answered with a race of blood.

"Hurry," Pacceli snapped at her as she grabbed her tunic and boots. The night-rider was already buckling on his sword, and she hadn't even found her socks. Pacceli cast a single disparaging look over his shoulder as he strode from the small Kitman dormer, and she could have cried as she heard his voice reporting his readiness. Late, always late, Merai. She gave up on the socks and thrust her bare feet into her cold boots, her skin shrinking from the clammy, sweat-dampened leather. Her curse would have surprised even Pacceli.

She had barely skidded into the Kitman relay room when the ring-carver, a stocky man with dark gray hair, thrust the first stick of the three message rings into her grip. "The fog is thick in the valley, and we can't reach the town tower by light," Wolt said without preamble, his manner flat and brusque. "The message rings are urgent. Ride straight to Elder Willet's house. He's on call tonight—has the postings for this ninan." The stocky man didn't wait for her answer. Instead, while she fumbled the first stick onto her right loop, he strapped the second one into her left belt loop and lashed the third stick beside it. As her fingers slid along the last piece of wood, the harsh slashes caught at her skin, and she felt part of the message. She caught her breath in excitement: the Wolfwalker Dione was riding the black road tonight—riding this very line. She couldn't tell if the sliver of tension that seemed to pierce her chest was eagerness or fear.

But Wolt's voice was professional, flat, and his words cut like a wire saw as he noticed her eager flush. "Raiders struck northeast of here—a mining train, Merai."

Merai looked up sharply, suddenly wary. Wolt's blue eyes, which earlier that day had been warm, were now like chips of ice. He had changed, she realized, as though a switch had clicked inside him. And now he looked like the weapons master he once had been—like a man who had spent too much time on the road, with too many blades in his hands. Even as she eyed him, his fingers kept flicking back to his belt as if to find a sword, not the short carving tools he wore; and his feet shifted in what seemed a nervous twitch until she realized that his muscles were clenching a riding beast he was not astride. This was not the same man who showed her each morning how to carve and read the message rings. This was not the man who had walked her through the relay drills for ninans, or taught her the difference between riding the black road—with urgency and maybe even death on her heels—and just riding the night track with a message ring. This Wolt was ready to fight—to kill—not to sit and wait for relays. She found herself backing away from him as much as from his voice.

She fumbled the securing straps as she eyed Wolt's expression. The burden of being a protector was easily shouldered, but not easily set aside—Wolt had said that to her once. He had ridden the venges for twelve decades before he gave up his blade to save what was left of his soul. But even after two years on the relays, his hands were clenched at word of the raiders, and his eyes darkened like night. Merai's fingers pressed into the message rings. The wolfwalker Dione—she was young now, but if she kept riding the black road as the elders asked, she would someday look like this man: eyes dark and cold, and hands like twisted wire, while trying to shoulder the burden that the elders set upon her. Merai wondered suddenly how much weight it took to kill a wolfwalker's soul.

Wolt's hands finished checking the message rings, and he

caught the expression on her face. His voice was as harsh as her thoughts. "This is not a drill, Merai. Three miners died, and six others were wounded. There's a venge already gathering to cut off the raiders, and Dione is riding in fast to join them."

"There are three other healers closer." She yanked on the straps to make sure they would hold.

"Yamai's tending a dozen who are down with pogus flu. Boccio still can't use his left arm, and Brye nePentonald is sick himself with spring fever." He pushed her toward the downpole that led to the stable, but her feet didn't move. Wolt was suddenly closer, his voice as sharp as a slap. "You're young, Merai, and this is your first time riding the black road, but you know the way by heart." He put his hand on one of the message rings. "This is what you're here for, girl. Not to practice ring-carving, or to moon after Pacceli, or to dream about bonding with wolves, like Dione. We need healing kits and two fighters ready when Dione rides through in three hours. The road crews this side of Stone Gate must be warned, and the Willow Road site must be guarded. This is not the night to drag feet, Merai. You've a job to do. Now do it." Her cheeks paled, then burned at his words, and he nodded, a curt, sharp movement. "You've an instinct, Merai, to ride like the wind and run like a fire in a grass field. It's time to show your paces." Abruptly he set his palm against her sternum. "Ride safe," he said.

Her lips moved, and she heard her voice choke. "With the moons." Then she found her hands on the wooden downpole, and slid out of sight toward the stable.

Pacceli had already saddled his dnu by the time she ran to the stalls. Late, always late, Merai . . . He was at the stable door while she tightened her cinch. Late, always late, Merai . . . At the courtyard gate while she ducked through the doorway. And out on the track toward Morble Road before she had crossed the courtyard. Dione was riding in like a wolf, and Pacceli was out there before her. Angrily, she urged her dnu. It leaped eagerly for the road.

But Pacceli's hands flashed a warning before she could spur her dnu past him. "Me first," he said. "Till we reach Morble Road. Then you can ride like the wind." He didn't wait for her answer. Instead, he loped ahead onto the relay tower track, letting his mount warm itself up into the wary, smooth, six-legged pace of an escort while the ringrunner stewed behind.

* * *

"Sixth moon's set, and fourth moon is nearly up." The elder's voice was eager, sharp. Her pale blue eyes peered down the road from the porch of the brightly lit house. The village of Ontai was dark except for a few late lights, and her house would stand out like a beacon for the rider coming in.

Royce nodded shortly, but his dark eyes smoldered; rather than trust his voice to answer, he checked his bowstring again.

"Stop fidgeting," she said impatiently. "This is an honor for you. It could gain you a great deal of notice from the healer, and so then from her mate. It's not every day you get a chance to ride out on a venge with a man like Aranur—especially not a venge that guards our mining and metal trains."

"It shouldn't be my chance at all," he muttered. "Not yet, on my own, at least."

The elder rounded on him. "You'd shame yourself—you'd shame *me*—in front of the Healer Dione? Of all the things you could protect in this county, the metals are the most precious." She stared him up and down. "Centuries, Royce. That's what those metals represent. For centuries, we've been hiding our metalwork and sciences from those moons-damned alien birdbeasts. Working steadily, quietly toward the goal of reaching back to OldEarth, and space, and the stars ... But you, the son of an elder yourself, are not willing to help protect that? That's not just juvenile shortsightedness, Royce, that's a betrayal of everything this county has stood for for more than eight hundred years. How many counties have the burden and the goal of returning to the stars? Ariye. Only Ariye. No other county—even Randonnen, though they help," she conceded shortly, "has the dedication that we do—"

"Gama," he broke in irritably, "I didn't say I didn't want to protect the miners. It's just that I'm not yet certified—"

"No more, Royce," she snapped. "If I say you're ready to ride escort, then by all the moons, you're ready. You fought off that worlag by yourself last month when Cliff fell off his dnu and broke his leg in the bargain. You spent three and a half ninans—

practically a month—riding guard to the salt pools and back. Nulia had high praise for the way you handled your shifts." She looked him up and down in sharp satisfaction. "The route from here to Carston is short, and the venge will be just beyond it."

The young man's words were carefully measured, but deliberate for all that. "Distance doesn't define danger, Gama."

Her expression changed. "Royce—" Her voice was suddenly hard. "If your own father hadn't died just two months ago with the others in the council, I'd—I'd—"

"Have sent Tentran or Jonn in my place, or woken Nulia to go with me."

Her face tightened. "I am the lead elder now. I can make those decisions alone."

"For now," he agreed. He didn't say the words that hung on his lips—that the council was reconsidering her interim leadership already. She had been an elder before, but not a lead elder. Her temporary responsibility had merely been an attempt to keep his father's knowledge alive. Once someone else understood his father's work, there would be another elder in charge. As it was, she might not even hold on to her secondary council seat now that his father was dead. It wasn't something that his gama awaited with anything akin to pleasure. Even now, her face tightened at his lack of response, and he wondered if someday her skin would split across her aged cheekbones. He asked quickly, to forestall her, "What if Dione asks why a youth is her escort?"

"We have no fighters more capable than you."

His lips set thin and stubbornly. He was tall for his age, his shoulders already filling out, and he was strong as a dnu, he acknowledged. But there were five fighters in this village as good as he in either sword or bow—three that were better—and every one of them still talked about one-armed Tule, the man who now herb-farmed the lower Lull Fields but who had once fought like a moonwarrior, fast and fierce. They said he had faced a dozen worlags, just like the wolfwalker Dione. Another time, he had climbed out on a rockslide to carry back a wounded miner just before the slide had loosened and cascaded over a cliff. They said he had even seen Aiueven, the aliens who lived in the north. Royce's lips thinned further. Even that one-armed herb-farmer would be a better escort.

Royce stared bitterly at the older woman. The only reason it was he who would ride at the wolfwalker's side—and without his mentor, Nulia—was that he was the elder's great-grandson. That, and his gama had told the relay stablemen to stand down and then had refused to notify the others of the task. Roused too late to ride for Jonn or the others, there was only he to protest.

Movement caught the corner of his eye, and he glanced back over his shoulder. His sister hovered behind the door frame, her brown eyes peeking out. Royce caught her hero gaze full-blast. Quickly, he decided.

"Where are you going?" The elder's voice was sharp as he turned back to the house.

"I forgot my boot knives."

"Moons save us from our children," she snapped. "Get them quickly. I think that's the healer on the upper road."

He didn't answer as he ducked back into the house. Instead, he beckoned to his sister. Hesitantly, Anji stepped toward him. His voice was low as he said rather than asked, "You know the healer rides in."

She nodded solemnly.

"She needs a fighter to ride with her north, across Zaidi Ridge."

Anji's eyes caught the light off his newly woven warcap. "You're a fighter, Royce." The pride in her voice made him wince.

"But not experienced enough to be justified in taking Jonn or Bogie or Tentran's place—not this time, anyway. I'm not the right one for this ride." He glanced quickly over his shoulder, then back at Anji. "What about you? Are you brave enough to go on an errand yourself?"

"I'm as brave as you are." Her eyes flickered with excitement.

"Right now?"

She looked over his shoulder. The front-lit shape of the elder was stooped and sinister against the inky blackness, and in spite of the girl's eagerness, her voice was hesitant. "It's dark, Royce."

"It is," he agreed. "But you'll be on the roads and inside the barrier bushes. The bushes are thickly grown here." He took her small hands in his. "Ride for Tule. Tell him Healer Dione needs him, and the elder thinks to send me in his place. Bogie's out on the night crews, Nulia's home is in the outer fields, and none of the others will stand up to Gama if she insists that I go alone. Tell Tule that I ask it. I'll ride as his student or stay behind, as he chooses."

She hesitated again. "Does it have to be Tule?"

Royce's lips stretched in a humorless smile. "He's mean as a starving lepa, and you don't like him—I know that. But he is closest, he's experienced, and he is the one who's needed. He's also the only one you have a chance of reaching before Healer Dione arrives. And if Dione is riding the black road on a night of worlag moons, you know that it's important."

The girl hesitated, then nodded. She turned to go, and Royce touched her shoulder. "Ride quickly, Anji. Gama will try to talk with the wolfwalker. That will give you some time, but not much."

"Not much is enough to get Tule." She flashed a sly look over her shoulder, and Royce suddenly realized his sister was not as young as he thought.

"The fledgling tries her wings," he said softly to himself. A moment later he heard the hooves of a dnu pounding out of the stable. He turned and went back to the elder.

"Well?" she said sharply. "Are you finally ready?"

He forced himself to nod. Anji did not appear in the light, and the faint sound of hooves was already almost completely gone. He flushed slowly. She'd taken the back road, which led around the village proper—something he should have warned her to do but that she'd thought of herself. Of what use would he be to the wolfwalker, when he couldn't even think to keep his own sister out of sight?

He fingered his bow irritably, letting his grip slide and stick, slip and stick on the fresh varnish. His gama had ordered it detailed with inked drawings of Aiueven, as if those images could give him the alien perception and farsight that had kept humans down and away from the stars for so long. Aiueven could see kilometers through skies dark or light, but Royce was just a human. No carvings would change his eyesight or make his bow arm stronger. He had never seen a real scout with paintings on his weapons. Not even Tule, retired last year, decorated the weapons that still hung on his walls. Royce couldn't help glancing up the road. One-armed or not, he thought, Tule still kept his sword sharp as a razor. And if Tule was as good as they said he had been, the man would be out of bed at the first sound of hooves and running for his weapons.

The older woman grasped his shoulder. "There—look there. That has to be the wolfwalker, crossing the black-grain fields. She'll be here in ten minutes." Like claws, her hands turned him toward the light. "Let me check your tunic. Straight for once, thank the moons. And your sword—is it polished? Show me. Good, good. I'll have no rust ride with Ember Dione. She saved the Lloroi's son, you know. She has influence with all the elders."

"The Heart of Ariye," Royce said, more to himself than her.

But his gama heard. "It's not for nothing that they call her that," the older woman said sharply. "Dione is the reason the wolves came back to Ariye: She Called them, and they Answered, and now we have more wolfwalkers than any county except Randonnen."

"It's not a competition, Gama."

She snorted. "Everything is competition, Royce. And the sooner you learn that, the better off you'll be. This escort ride is a chance to show what you can do—to bring you to the attention of the weapons masters so that you can get that position in Pillarton. I've worked hard to get you this opportunity. I won't have you discard it." She glanced at the upper road and just caught the expression he made. Her features tightened. "By the seventh moon, Royce, if you don't get that scowl off your face, I'll scrub it off myself."

He carefully blanked his expression.

"Move the dnu out into the light," she said curtly. "She'll want to see them as soon as she arrives."

"Our dnu aren't the fastest, Gama. She ought to have the relay dnu."

The elder's voice was suddenly cutting. "We've gone over this twice, Royce. The healer Dione deserves the best. There's not a man or woman here who argues that our dnu are the finest in the village."

"But not the fastest—"

"You'd rather she rode one of the relay ronyons? Those dnu have more scars and mange than a whole pack of wild cur."

He shrugged eloquently.

The ringing slap of his great-grandmother's hand left his cheek bright red and smarting. For a moment, neither one moved. Then, urgently, "Royce—"

He turned away.

She caught at his arm. "Royce—darling—"

His voice was flat and strangely adult. "Leave it be, Elder Lea."

Had he seen the expression on her face, he might have softened his tone; but as it was, he left her alone, as her sons and their sons had done, and strode coldly out to the road.

* * *

Dion thundered toward an Ontai hub that was dark as the ebony grain. Baton, Menedi, Ontai, Mandalay; then Carston, Allegro, and Kitman . . . The litany of relay stops was a chant that tickled her brain. Behind it was a constant whisper in the back of her head—the mental voices of the wolves. Howling, growling, the packsong was a constant drone. It seeped into the back of her skull like water from under a door. Right now Dion held her bond with Hishn tight, ignoring the other wolves, so that the only images that were clear in her head were those she received from Gray Hishn.

Ahead of her, the gray wolf flashed like a thought, nearly unseen in the night. Dion didn't have to use her eyes to know where Gray Hishn was; the invisible link between their minds locked them together like the sea to the sand. Ancient engineering had accentuated the natural lupine bonds so that humans and wolves could be mental, not just physical, partners in exploring new colony worlds. That same engineering had mutated some of the humans, linking them in turn to the Gray Ones. And in the eight hundred years since the Ancients had landed, the wolves had grown and spread across the planet. Now they were a constant noise—a rich packsong in each other's minds, and a pull on the wolfwalkers with whom they bonded. No simple thread of mental gray linked Dion to those wolves. The longer she lived with the bond in her head, the thicker grew the howling.

She wondered whether, if she had not grown up so isolated in that small Randonnen village, she would have bonded to the wolves so strongly. "Closer to Gray Ones than to humans," they said, "was Wolfwalker Ember Dione. And closer to the moons than the world itself, was the moonmaid Ember Dione." She had heard those lines just last month at a puppet show. The puppeteer, when he saw her, coerced her out of the audience to speak the voice of the wolfwalker doll. He had been clever to use her: He had earned more silver that night than in five previous nights of work. And as for what he had said about her: closer to wolves than to humans . . . At the time, flushing and flustered, she hadn't argued the puppeteer's point. But now, with the world dark and quiet as death, she wondered if it was true. She didn't even have to stretch to feel the wolf like herself. Her bond with the Gray One was close as family, and the constant din of the lupine voices was never absent from the back of her mind. Hishn was friend, packmate, wolf pup . . . The Gray One had taught Dion more about mothering than any human she had known, since her own mother had died soon after childbirth, and Hishn had had several litters now. To Hishn, Dion was packleader and friend, hunting partner and family. A double bond, between them.

As she rode closer to the town, Dion let her senses flow through the yellow lupine eyes. The mental wolf voice strengthened immediately. Movement became sharper to Dion's eyes, and contrast increased. An instinctual joy spread through her. She felt the fog on her teeth. She threw her head back silently. The howl that tried to burst through her lips made no sound in the night, but it echoed far into the graysong. Instantly, lupine howls returned. Hishn's voice was clearest, but there were others in that mental fog: Gray Rishte, Gray Elshe, Gray Barjan, Gray Koursh . . . The touch of each wolf in the pack was light, like a feather against her hand.

Sonorously, in her mind, the voices soared. Rising, then falling, falling, falling. From the depths of Dion's mind, the graysong felt her, surrounded her, howled at her presence. Through Hishn's mind, the wolves stretched back. Night flavors touched the tip of Dion's tongue. Night sounds hit her ears. She reached out, as if she could capture the images and save them for her sons. Thirteen years with Aranur . . . Their sons were now eight and nine; and Tomi, her adopted son, had just Promised himself in mating. Dion let herself read the packsong for the sense of her family. Like Hishn longing for Gray Yoshi, the female wolf's lupine mate, Dion reached for Aranur and the boys. Soon, she thought, she would see her sons. Soon she would feel Aranur's hands on her skin, his strong touch on her slender shoulders . . .

Distant light caught Hishn's eyes, and the gray wolf's mental voice changed. Dion shivered out of the packsong. She focused so that she saw the pinpoints of light from Ontai. "Hishn?" she asked softly, over the hooves of the dnu. She could have spoken mentally, but she needed the sound of her voice to anchor her in her own world and outside of the howling packsong.

Wolfwalker! Hishn returned.

The wolf further opened the link between them until Dion was swamped with the Gray One's senses. She peered through both Hishn's eyes and her own, but she saw lights on in only five homes up ahead. There was nothing more than a front light at the relay stable itself. She frowned, slowing as the line of rootroad trees hid the village again.

Wolfwalker? The wolf's voice rang in her head. It hadn't been a human word that was sent, rather the image Gray Hishn had of her. But fifteen years with the wolf in her head, and Dion couldn't help but know how to interpret the lupine images. The only thing she wished was that she had the perception of the alien birdmen. Legend told that the Aiueven were able to see into human brains, not just into lupine minds. For Dion, being able to tell the difference between raider and Ariyen would have been a useful trait.

"Stay with me, Hishn." Her voice was soft with unease. "There were two dnu by that second house. Maybe they've moved the relay beasts over for some reason."

There are no hunters here or ahead, the wolf returned. *The dens here smell of stale food and sleep sweat.*

Absently, Dion bit her lip. Hishn's senses were tuned to the wilderness, and her predator sense was strong. If the Gray One said there was no danger here, Dion was inclined to believe it. She shifted to a rolling post as the six-legged dnu slowed itself further and fell into its scuttling gait. This close to the village proper, the clouds of gnats that hovered above the road hit her like tufts of smoke. She blinked and snorted and spit them out as they fluttered into her face. "The ice fevers hit this village hard," she said, covering her mouth with one hand. "Nine died in this village, including three in the council. Perhaps this is part of those changes."

The gray wolf snorted softly. *Fevers burn change into all of us.*

Dion gave the wolf a sharp look. The image sent had not been recent, but old, as though the wolf had tapped into a memory of disease. The gleam of yellow eyes that looked into her mind seemed layered with other, older, foreign eyes. Dion started to follow that thought back into the Gray One's mind, but the shiver she felt at the echo of death made her withdraw. She could not ignore her chill of recognition. The memory of fever the wolf had pushed to her mind was of plague, not winter death.

It had been years since Dion had felt that fever herself, but her own images of it were sharp. What had decimated the Ancients eight centuries ago had almost killed her too, and she could still feel the touch of aliens behind the minds of the wolves. Still feel the sense of those foreign minds that had sent the plague to the humans. From their peaks in the north, Aiueven still watched the humans and kept them from the stars. And what had once been a tentative colony world had become an earthbound prison. No human had returned to the stars in over eight hundred years. She bit her lip as that sense of time remained in Hishn's mind. It had been too long—those centuries without the sciences of the Ancients. Aranur's goal, his county's goals to return to the technology of long ago—they were blind hopes. The aliens who had lived here first would not allow any more human progression. So the domes of the Ancients were still ridden with plague, and the wolves, who had helped to colonize this world, still carried their own seeds of disease.

Hishn howled, low in her mind, and the sound was echoed through the packsong. A hundred voices came softly back. None of them pushed, none of them pressed her, but she felt their need like a pressure on her chest. How could she not, when half the cubs birthed were stillborn on the ground? The alien plague had affected the wolves far longer than it had the humans, and Dion had made a promise to the wolves about the Aiueven disease.

It had been thirteen years, and that promise hung unfulfilled in her head, suspended in the work that she did each month and never quite finished. Each semicure she thought she found went nowhere when tested out. And the other work—the immediate work—of healing, of teaching in Ariyen clinics, of making her scouting runs . . . That work seemed to press in on her life. What time she had left went to her sons, not to quiet, frustrating labs.

She took a long, slow breath, letting the night air clear her lungs of the stench of ancient plague. The wolves were as patient as winter demons. Their memories would not fade with time— neither those of plague nor of her promise to cure it. And she was only thirty-eight. Raiders and worlags and lepa and work might postpone her duty, but they could not destroy it. She had two hundred years and more to find the cause of the alien death. To heal the wolves . . . To see them bring forth living litters instead of so many stillborn cubs . . . Aranur dreamed of the Ancients' stars, but Dion dreamed of thwarting death.

Gray Hishn looked back at her from the road, and Dion felt the impact of those yellow eyes as their minds blended thoughts and words. *You think of your promise. Of your bond to us.*

Her answer was a projection, her voice a set of ringing images in the gray creature's mind. *You saved my brother. Saved Aranur and his family. I want that same salvation for you—freedom from death, from the plague. It is my dream for you as much as Aranur's dream of the future is for his people.*

Dreams are like threads, returned the wolf. *They weave themselves into the packsong. They will not end till they die with you.*

"Aye," Dion said softly, as she turned beneath an arbor. The trees arched overhead into a canopy that splintered the moonlight against the road. "But what dreams die that cannot be recovered?"

Hishn heard her voice, not over the sounds of the dnu's drumming hooves, but as another mental projection. *A dream is a howl that lifts to the moons,* the massive wolf returned. *The silence of the stars is our answer. There is no end to either—the howl or the silence. What you dream and what you promise—they are forever in the packsong.*

"They might be forever in your packsong, Hishn, but my memory is short. I have in my head only what I have lived or dreamed of, not all the lives that you remember. And if I fail in my promise to you, I cannot simply pass on my memories as you do."

Then I will pass them on for you to your wolf cubs and your wolf cub's cubs.

The image of her two younger sons was clear—her oldest, Tomi, had never been comfortable with wolves—but Dion didn't answer. The cure she had promised to search for—that was hers to find. And she could not forget it. Each voice of the Gray Ones that touched her mind was tainted with alien plague. The history that was memory to Hishn was killing the wolves off slowly. To find that . . . To find a cure was a goal that Dion had set. She might be a grandmother ten times over before she found that cure, but she'd be damned to all nine hells of the moons before she would quit that work.

She felt her jaw tense and looked down. Her hands were almost clenched on the reins, as if her determination was set in her fingers as much as in her mind. She laughed wryly, and relaxed back in the saddle. Hishn glanced back, eyes gleaming.

Dion came out from under the arbor barely a kay away from the village, but she did not see the figures of the relay men she expected in front of the relay station. Unconsciously, her hand strayed to the hilt of her sword. She stretched her mind through the senses of the wolf to see the buildings more clearly. Her human sense of shape fed the wolf more specifics than the lupine black-and-white night vision, while the Gray One's sense of movement and contrast merged with hers to create a fuller mental picture.

Now she could see them—the three men at the stable, right there on the edge of town. But they merely stood, watching, and there were no dnu nearby. It wasn't until she rounded the last corner and entered the village proper that she saw again the elder's house where the relay dnu stood instead.

The two people who waited in the light from the elder's house were not mounted; neither made a move to get in the saddle or bring the dnu up to speed for her to switch mounts while riding. If one of them was her escort, he didn't seem inclined to ride. Dion slowed further. Still neither of the two villagers moved, and finally, having no choice, she pulled to a stop.

"Healer Dione." The elder stepped slightly out of the light so that her thin silhouette grew more reedy. "We are honored by your visit."

Warily, Dion eyed the older woman. "I'm honored by your greeting this night, Elder Lea," she said, not quite so swiftly as to be rude. "However," she added, "I'm riding the black road, not visiting. I need a new mount, my escort, and both quickly." She cast a brief, appraising glance at the youth, then looked at the riding beasts. "Are those the relay dnu?"

The elder preened. "These are much better than the normal relay dnu, Healer Dione." She stepped forward and petted the neck of one of the dnu. The beast skittered nervously. "Their coats shine like oil on water, and their temperaments are gentle yet still spirited. No bulging temple veins in these pretties—their heads are finely shaped." Her voice held obvious pride. "They're from my own stable."

Dion tried to see beyond the breeding to the meat of the animals. The dnu looked well-fed and glossy, sure enough, but their legs were dainty, not muscle-lanky, and their necks showed the fat, shapely thickness of short exercise rather than the leanness of long running. "They look like fine dnu," she started, "but—"

"They're the very best in the village," the elder assured, missing the glint in Dion's eyes at the deliberate interruption.

Hishn skirted the dnu and sniffed their haunches so that their eyes rolled back skittishly. *They are like mice in a meadow—easy to frighten, easy to catch. I could run them down before they reached the forest.*

Dion shot the wolf a mental warning. *Don't unsettle them.*

But Hishn's low growl was already rising. The Gray One's automatic challenge brought a roughness to Dion's own voice, and she struggled to smooth her words before speaking. "Elder," she began again, "I appreciate the offer of dnu from your own stables, but I don't need pretty and gentle in a beast. I need only speed and endurance. I prefer something trail wise. Where are the relay dnu?"

"Surely you're not suggesting that we allow you to ride out on the mangiest beasts we have—"

"If they're fast enough, yes," the wolfwalker said, her voice just an edge short of sharp. "I'm not afraid of mange."

The youth at the elder's side made a sound suspiciously like a snort. The elder shot him a look before spreading her hands in a shrug. "But Healer—"

Hishn growled clearly now, and Dion, aching and numb from her ride, forgot to keep her voice calm. "By the moons, elder, I've told you what I need in a dnu—speed and endurance. Nothing else. I don't care what kind of coats or tails or fat-shaped necks they have. If they don't get me to the venge by dawn, some of our people could die." Unconsciously, she tightened her knees in irritation, and her own mount, tired as it was, chittered and stamped its middle legs.

The three stablemen, emboldened by Dion's words, crossed the street to hear more clearly. Lights went on in another house, and two faces appeared at a window. Gray Hishn's ears flicked, and the faint sound of pounding hooves filtered into Dion's head through the wolf. "Who's coming now?" she demanded.

"Just one of the farmers," the youth said casually.

Hishn was already moving away from the dnu to eye the approaching rider and beasts. *One man, three dnu,* the gray wolf sent. *They are fresh from the stable, and he is fresh from his bed. They smell of sleep-sweat and eagerness.*

Dion, her ears tuned to the nuance of emotion as Hishn's were to the breathing of prey, did not bother to watch the incoming rider. Instead, she let Hishn watch them approach while she turned her attention to the youth. He was tall and carried a sword that looked too new to have been used. His bow was bright with varnish, rather than oiled and dull as a scout would have left it. He stood confidently, but he made no move to join her. "You are my escort?" she asked sharply.

"If you wish it, Wolfwalker."

Something more in his voice gave her pause. "You're trained?"

"Trained, yes," he returned, with such a slight emphasis on the first word that Dion hesitated again.

"Experienced?"

"No, Wolfwalker."

Dion caught the anger that flashed in the elder's eyes, then realized the resemblance of the elder's aged features to those of the youth. No wonder the young man had done as he had, warning her of his status without speaking of it at all. Her own anger, fed by exhaustion and Hishn's rising aggression, swamped her. It wasn't about the venge, she realized, it was about respect for others' lives. She worked so hard to save those she could . . . Aranur drove her to it by example, the council by request; but she believed in what she did. To be confronted with an elder who had such a lack of consideration for others that she could cause Ariyens to die—and have no better excuse for it than a desire to look important . . . Dion fought to form words, not fists. "And there are no more experienced fighters in this village? What happened to Bogie and Jonn?"

"They are—" the elder began.

"Asleep, Wolfwalker," the youth cut in blandly. "Or out of the village boundaries. At best, they are half an hour away."

Dion tried to bite off her anger, but it clipped her words so that they hit the air like cracks of a whip. "Elder Lea, my relay request for a riding beast and escort should have reached you an hour ago. I've got to make Carston by the seventh moonrise, and I've got to hit Kitman by dawn. The Zaidi shortcut is the only route that will get me there on time. It is not a ride for the inexperienced. We'll be outside the barrier bushes for over fifteen kays. The moons are high, so any predator will catch the glints even from our eyes. There's fog to hide the road from our hooves, and the worlag packs are hunting nightly. Yet you hand me a grain-fed dnu for a mount and an escort who has yet to earn his sword."

The elder broke in. "Healer, Royce is from my own family. We're simply trying to honor your presence with our best—"

"My presence be damned. I'm here as a relay rider, and I need a relay dnu. I don't need a beast whose strength peters out after the first hill. I need a dnu with endurance. More, I need a beast that has seen enough trail riding that it doesn't jump off the road with every intimation of danger." She glared at the elder. "Have you or haven't you such a beast?"

"These, Healer—"

Dion snarled suddenly, and the sound was too much like a wolf. "Damn it to the seventh hell." Her anger brought a tightness to the gray wolf's throat. Yellow eyes gleamed at the elder, and involuntarily, the old woman stepped back to the light, leaving Dion, in the dark, a somehow menacing shadow. At the edge of the village proper, the approaching rider, trailing two riderless dnu, rounded the street corner and pounded loudly toward the growing group.

In front of the wolfwalker, Royce felt his stomach tense. That third beast—that was for him. So he'd ride with Dione after all. His hands were suddenly nervous, and his feet itched in their boots. Gray Hishn's eyes gleamed at him, but only the wolf-walker noticed.

"Healer Dione." One of the stablemen caught her suddenly sharp attention.

She half wheeled her mount to face him. "What is it?"

The short man cast a cautious look at the elder. "There are relay dnu if you wish one, but it will take us some time to get them."

By now there were a dozen people on the street, but Dion ignored them. "Do it," she said to the man. "Please," she added belatedly.

The elder's pride snapped out. "They are my stables, Healer. I choose the mounts that are to be used for relay, just as I select those who work in my stables." She gestured sharply to the man who had unwisely spoken. "Those dnu are not fit for you. Take these or take nothing."

Slowly, Dion cursed under her breath. Shortcut or no, she couldn't make it to Carston, let alone Kitman, on the worn-out dnu she now sat—it was tired as a winter worlag. And weary as she herself had become, she'd been careless again with her words. She'd escalated a challenge of the elder's leadership, and with it, gods help her, she'd put the lives of her mate and his men at stake. For a long moment, she stared at the elder. Then her anger hardened into a coal, igniting a slow burn in her gut. She didn't give a damn if she offended this woman or not, she realized. The long ride had left her no patience.

"You would put my people—our people's—lives in danger for the sake of your pride?" Her voice was low and steady, but hard as steel in the air. "How many of your own men and women have ridden out on a venge trusting that their elders had the judgment to send the fastest and most experienced to help? Do you think they'd trust your dnu on such a ride?" There was an

ugly murmur in the small crowd. Dion's hand crept toward the
hilt of her sword, but the sound had not been directed at her.

The incoming rider pulled up his dnu, and the elder glanced
at him, then glared as she recognized the one-armed figure.
"Tule? What are you doing here? Go back to your fields. You
have no business with me this night."

The hulking man didn't bother looking at the elder. Instead,
he gave Dion an appraising look then maneuvered one of his
extra dnu close to her tired beast. The others gave way like water,
but the elder placed herself between Tule's dnu and Dion's.
"Get your ronyons away from here, Tule." She grabbed at the
reins. "They aren't fit for her to ride."

The elder came close to Dion's dnu, and Gray Hishn was
there instantly, snarling as she glared at the elder. The woman
gasped and stumbled back.

Hishn, Dion snapped. *Back down.*

The gray wolf's eyes gleamed. *Wolfwalker,* the creature acknowledged. But Hishn slunk only slowly from the elder.

Tule eyed Dion. The anger that tautened the shoulders of the
wolfwalker was palpable even in the darkness. He hid a humorless grin. Had it been he, not the wolfwalker, who dealt with the
elder, there would have been blows flying between them by
now. The wolfwalker was still trying to talk—if one could call
that near-growl talking—and he eyed her curiously. Dione was
as he'd heard her described: slender, dark-haired, lean as a wolf.
Her clothes were drab and stained in patterns that melted into
the background; the silver healer's circlet he knew she wore
was hidden beneath a dull warcap. The hilt of her sword was
wrapped with worn leather, and her bow and quiver were dark.
Even her boot knives were barely visible against her legs.
Nothing glinted; nothing reflected light except her teeth—white
and sharp as she bit her words out to the elder—and those
flashing violet eyes. "Healer Dione?" he asked without preamble.

Dion nodded curtly, returning his look with one of her own.
With Hishn's aggression coloring her words, her voice was as
low as Tule's, though his was as gravelly and bitter as if he'd
drunk too much grog on a cold day. His words held a slight tone
of irony. In the faint light from the elder's house, she could see
that the man's tunic was not that of a scout or fighter, but the

heavier fabric of a farmer; yet his warcap and jerkin, obviously old, were well stitched and well worn, still supple for his movements. On one side his wide shoulders ended abruptly in a shortened sleeve, but the sword that hung down his back showed which hand he now used in a fight. He didn't bother with the reins that were looped loosely around the saddle horn; instead, he controlled his dnu with his knees.

Dion nodded almost imperceptibly to herself. The beast this man rode was as lean as a dnu could get, its eyes small and mean, and its neck barely more than bone in its hardness. The second beast was nearly as lean, scarred across its rump and back, with its tail twisted and raggedly cut as if it had been broken twice. Its neck had the barest shape, as if the fat layers had begun to shape up last ninan, but the definition on its hammer-like head spoke of long-distance endurance. The third beast, lean as the others, was marked with half-patches and stripes. The size of the third dnu's saddle spoke of someone other than Dion, and she raised her eyebrows at Tule. He nodded slightly at the youth.

The elder, seeing the bare relief in the wolfwalker's manner, missed Tule's motion toward her great-grandson, and angrily gestured at Tule. "He has only one arm!" The old woman spat toward Dion. "Royce at least has two! He's more than qualified to ride as your escort—"

"As student, not escort." Tule's voice, harsh and cold, cut the elder into silence. "Or he'll ride not at all. The fighting rings have their own authority, Elder Lea. It's not you who decides who's ready to ride out on a raider venge. The day Nulia releases your great-grandson is the day Royce can ride out alone. Till then, he will ride with me." He glanced at Dion. "With your permission, Healer Dione."

Dion looked at the youth. The expression on the young man's face was not that of anger, but of eagerness. It was the elder, not Royce, who objected to the one-armed man. For an instant, time seemed to stand still, and she saw not Royce's face, but those of her own sons. Someday, Olarun and Danton would stand like that—as eager to ride out as this youth. And someday, if the moons willed it, they would be ready to run with the Gray

Ones—to hear the packsong in their heads, not just human song in their ears.

"I'd be honored," she said to the one-armed man, including the youth in her answer. She threw her leg over her saddle and slid to the ground, her numbed thighs refusing her weight. She barely caught herself on the stirrup before Royce's hand steadied her arm.

"It's an honor for me also, Healer Dione," he said quietly.

She saw he meant it. She nodded. "Dion," she corrected, giving him her nickname.

The young man drew himself up, his pride almost palpable. When he withdrew his arm, Dion forced her legs to work, pushed past the elder, and mounted the second dnu. The youth vaulted onto the third animal's saddle, and Dion envied his energy. Then Tule wheeled his beast and flashed into a canter. A few minutes later, they were swallowed by forest as dark as the elder's rage.

*   *   *

With the moons overhead for a guide, Pacceli and Merai worked their way warily down the track. The rootroad was new and still growing, barely hardened and still filled with gaps. Rounded roots and soft potholes tripped up their dnu so that there were few places they could ride faster than a lope no matter how well they knew the way. That and the fog kept them from anything but a slow trot.

Merai couldn't help the look she cast at the line of rootroad trees. They were not yet full-grown, and their spindly trunks were like sticks, not bands of reassurance. Behind them, outlining the new road, the line of barrier bushes had sprouted but was thin and patchy. The shrubs wouldn't thicken up for years. Merai swallowed and tried to force her eyes back to the track, but the unevenness of that thorny wall gave it uncomfortable humps so that it looked like a line of waiting worlags hunched against the ground. The moonlight glinting off glossy thorns gave the impression of squinting eyes, while the pale white roots over which they rode were like skinny white arms in the dark.

Something cried out to Merai's left, and she started, jerking at the reins. Her dnu skittered, and she soothed it automatically, though her own voice was not calm or steady. Her hand clenched one of the message rings until the wolfwalker's name rang out in her mind. Dione, the healer. Wolfwalker Dione, riding in like the wind. No night-beast sounds would frighten that one from the woods. Merai rubbed the slashes of the healer's name and straightened her back and shoulders. She had signed on to ride the black road, and no beast sound would scare her either. If she were Dione, she told herself, she'd pass Pacelli and ride on like a wolf. If she were a wolfwalker herself . . .

The sharp forest cry came again, and her bravado abruptly fled. She felt the sweat start on her brow. "Pacelli?" she asked softly.

His voice was confident and curt. "Night-beating birds."

But his sword, she saw, was loose in its sheath, the holding thong gone, and his hand didn't stray from its hilt. "Are you sure?" she blurted out before she could bite at her tongue.

"More sure than you are that you're ready to ride the black road." He glanced back. "For someone who wants to be like Wolfwalker Dione, you startle like a city girl."

She knew he was just teasing her to make her less afraid, and she opened her mouth to retort. Then the sound came again, and she was suddenly crowding his dnu. It skittered slightly; the young man cursed over his shoulder. "Moonworms, Merai. What are you trying to do? Bolt my dnu off the road?"

She reined in too hard, and her own dnu grunted sharply. Apologetically, she soothed it. The riding beast was fast, but skittish—like her this night, she admitted. She dropped back again to lope just off Pacelli's flanks, grinding her teeth as though the bit were in her mouth, not in that of her dnu.

Inside her boots, her feet had begun to sweat as the clammy leather warmed up with the ride. But the chill that hit her as the night-beating birds cried out crawled down her legs to her heels. Night-beasting birds? Or bihwadi? The question echoed in her head while her mind conjured up a nightmare vision of those doglike predators. Pink, slitted eyes guided sharp, curved fangs that could tear through leather as easily as skin. She'd seen them twice in the northern meadow last ninan, up behind the tower. They had been moving fast, like wolves on the hunt, but nastier and lower. They hadn't loped—they'd slunk through the grass, leaving it somehow dirty. The second time she had seen them there, the bihwadi had stopped at the treeline, turned, and looked right at her. Even at that distance she'd felt their gaze, the speculation in it. Like looking a six-legged rast in the eye, she had thought, and had quickly stepped back from the window.

Now the night-beating birds cried out again, and Pacceli's dnu snorted softly. He soothed it, then said over his shoulder, "It's all right, Merai—it's just the birds. We're only a kay away from the road."

She didn't answer, but her dnu felt her uneasiness and began to fight the reins. She cursed herself and urged the beast forward, struggling with herself to do it. Her right hand closed on one of the message sticks so that the wooden edges cut into her hand. Raider strike, and they needed fighters, and Wolfwalker Dione was coming . . .

But the barrier bushes, scrawny and thin, seemed to move on the road beside her. The shadows, which pooled like the mist in the gullies, almost seemed to breathe. "Pacceli," she whispered.

He didn't hear.

"Pacceli," she tried again, louder.

And then the road erupted.

Merai screamed. Her dnu half reared. Its front legs flailed out against the shadows that leaped from the dark. The middle legs kicked out, humping its back in the middle. Merai screamed again and realized that her throat was clenched tight with terror, and it was Pacceli's voice, not hers, that she heard. Something slammed into her riding beast's neck; something else yanked hard on her foot, unseating her from the saddle. She caught the pommel with one hand, her other hand tangling in the reins. Her dnu whirled, striking out with its hooves. The weight on her foot was suddenly gone. A pair of slitted eyes flashed in front of her, missing her midflight. Pacceli screamed again. His dnu, riderless, screamed with him and bolted into a patch of moonlight. Merai caught a glimpse of bloated shadows clinging to its flesh. Pacceli was on the ground, staggering, and there was moonlight on his sword, then none, as blood covered his blade.

Merai's dnu staggered, and she lost her grip on the pommel, falling beneath the hooves. She hit the road hard on her back. Her breath slammed out. Hooves flashed above her head. Then something pink and slitted stared into her eyes. She couldn't move. Its fangs spread out and lashed down toward her throat—

And suddenly it was gone, torn from her as it would have torn her throat. Pacceli was dragging her up, yanking his sword free of the beast, and hauling her at a dead run up the road. He staggered, half turned as he ran, his sword arm heavy as he tried to keep the blade up and pointed out. Merai's legs didn't seem to be working—she couldn't keep up at all. She didn't notice Pacceli's fingers digging through her shoulder; she didn't see the blood on his face. She grabbed the message sticks and pressed them close to her side. Her other hand found the hilt of her knife and yanked the steel from the sheath. As she was dragged back from the dnu, from the feeding bihwadi, she held the blade out like a sword between her and the snarling darkness.

* * *

The gray wolf prowled the small clearing, then disappeared into the forest while they watered their dnu at the well. The riding beasts needed the five-minute breather; they had run hard the first half of the ridge route. To the east, the cold air falling from the cliffs brought with it the smell of yarrow. There were no barrier bushes here. No rootroad trees either—both barriers and rootroads had petered out three kays ago; this road was solid rock, not root. She stretched her ears through those of Gray Hishn and heard the owldeer hooting. Down the valley, a herd of eerin bolted away through the trees. The herd was spooked, and their pace was swift; even Royce caught the sound of their hooves.

"The night is restless," Tule murmured, taking his turn at the well.

"Raider fog and worlag moons," Dion agreed softly. "Everything is out hunting."

"Yes, but hunting us or other game?"

"Does it matter?"

"I'd like to think it does."

Dion chuckled, a soft, low sound, and swung back up in the saddle. "Thinking gives you an edge only when you've had time to do it, Tule. In the night, life is simple: It's hunt or be hunted, as it has been throughout time. Of all that we learned from the Ancients, there was this first: We'd be less than we are without the stimulus of survival."

"Philosophy in the moonlight—now that's something, Healer Dione, that I hadn't heard about you."

"Dion," she corrected automatically. "I don't ride on formality."

He glanced over his shoulder toward Royce, who was waiting for them at the road. "I noticed," he returned dryly.

This time, Dion didn't smile. "I've a reputation I can't fight, Tule—I'm learning to live with that. But I won't allow my presence to be used as a status symbol by anyone, elder or not. I won't carry that weight as well."

"A job is a job, eh? No matter who does it that day? And you'll be treated like any other rider?"

Dion gave him a sharp look. "You disagree?"

He gave her a one-armed shrug. "I think it's foolish to deny the way people think of you when you're different—to deny the effect you have on those who are around you."

"People want a legend," she said shortly. "Not a human being."

"You think that makes a difference? You're a figurehead for a dozen stories. Those stories have to be based on some sort of truth or they wouldn't have been told in the first place."

She snorted. "Truth is the first thing that gets lost in the translation from history to story. You heighten this emotion and indulge that fantasy for your listeners, and suddenly, you have a fable with heroes and heroines and not much room for real people. Reputations are expectations, not realities."

Tule patted his dnu as it finished drinking, then mounted in a single smooth motion. "And what is your reality, Wolfwalker?"

"That I'm far too simple to be the stuff of legends."

"Simple? Temper and drive can appear simple in themselves, but judging by the quantity in which they appear in you, they mask something more complex."

"I think," Dion said with a slow smile, "I'll take that as a compliment."

He chuckled. "I'm not sure it was meant that way." He gestured for her to lead them back onto the road.

"I'm sure of that," she tossed back. "All I am is too damn blunt, too prone to act before I think, and moonwormed lucky to be alive. Everything else is window dressing—" Her voice broke off. A wolf howled far up the ridge, and Hishn's mental projection caught her at the same moment the faint sound hit her ears.

"Healer?" Tule's voice was low and sharp, and his sword was already out of its sheath. He'd heard nothing, seen nothing, but he felt her alarm as clearly as if she had shouted.

"We need speed," she said shortly. "Now," she snapped, glancing at Royce. She tightened her knees. The relay beast responded, leaping forward. Dion's face was suddenly whipped by fog. Something burst out on the road behind Royce, and he, startled, fumbled the reins.

"Sprint it!" Dion yelled.

A crude roar—an *ayah-chuh-chuh* sound—hit their ears. A massive shape flowed over the road. Tule hunched low, his one-armed torso a blur as he matched Dion's pace. Behind them, Royce leaned in like Dion until he was almost flat against his beast. Dion didn't have to look back—the image in the Gray One's head was as clear as day to her sight. The badgerbear, spring-starved like a raider's slave, cried out its challenge again. It flowed across the stones, its claws glinting blackly in the night. It gained at the curve, then gained again on the flat, and Gray Hishn's snarl filled Dion's head so that she felt as if she were running like the wolf, not riding on top of a dnu.

Another curve, and the badgerbear was suddenly only ten meters back from Royce's dnu. The harsh predator cry that filled their ears brought a cringe to all three necks. Its fur, a red-tipped brown in daylight hours, made the badgerbear a blackened demon at night. Its sharp, pointed teeth gleamed like tiny lanterns, catching at their urgent vision. Its limbs were loose and intent. And its heavy breathing was suddenly far too close to Royce. The young man, panicked, viciously spurred his dnu. The animal surged ahead.

And then they were suddenly alone on the road. The badgerbear was gone. Royce began to slow. Dion glanced back, saw him, and cursed at him to keep up. The hooves of their dnu pounded the road like their hearts, but they did not slacken their pace until they had raced another kay. By then the badgerbear was far enough behind that it would not follow even when they dropped back to the distance lope.

Tule pulled his dnu back beside Dion's and gave her a thoughtful glance. Her warning had been all that had saved them. Without it, at least one of them would have gone down when the badgerbear attacked. His voice was dry in the fog. "Window dressing," he called to her ears. "I see what you mean, Wolfwalker."

Dion didn't answer.

* * *

Carston was barely a blur in the night. "Message came through half an hour ago," the stablewoman told Dion as the wolfwalker dismounted. Dion nodded and stamped her legs to get her blood moving. "A bit brief," the stablewoman added dryly.

"My fault," Dion said shortly. "I offended one of the elders."

"I heard. Yet you made off with her grandson, so it couldn't have been all that bad." The woman handed Dion the reins.

Dion cast a glance over her shoulder. "You know him?"

"Royce? He's young, but he'll do, if that's what you're asking."

Dion smiled faintly. "I wasn't, but I was. Thanks." She swung up on the new relay beast, feeling the dnu's muscles bunch as it skittered awkwardly sideways. In the distance, waiting in the shadow, Gray Hishn began to move. Dion felt the wolf lope just off the center of the road. Barely visible, Hishn touched the edges of shadow and extended them with her lupine shape.

The stablewoman caught the unfocused expression on Dion's face and watched the wolfwalker with interest. "This dnu's fast and headstrong. Don't let him run your arms off, Dione, or the legs off your gray wolf."

Dion's gaze sharpened. She looked down at the woman. "Considering what's been on the trails in this fog, I might be glad of his speed in spite of the ache on my arms tonight."

"Raider fog," the woman agreed. "Ride safe."

"With the moons," Dion returned. She reined the dnu in a tight circle and spurred the creature forward. Within seconds, its hooves struck a sharp rhythm from the stone road. The sounds doubled, then tripled, as the two other beasts matched its pace. Dion knew who rode behind her. "Ontai is the other way," she shouted over her shoulder.

"I think you can assume that we know that," Tule called back across the sound of the hooves.

"I've an escort waiting for me in Kitman."

"And this one to get you there."

"It's a long ride you're taking, Tule."

"Aye."

She glanced at his face, then back, meaningfully, at the young man who rode behind them. "It'll be a dark dawn for Royce to ride into."

"It's time," Tule called back.

"Time?"

"For him to see dawn for what it is."

Dion's eyes flickered to the black horizon. To see dawn for what it was—a bloody sky reflected on land? A morning of death on a world that was theirs by birth, but not by breeding? Her lean jaw tightened. Aranur might be able to look beyond the dawn to see the stars, but for Dion, whose mind was already filling with the lust of the lupine hunt, the morning heralded a bloody dream, not one of moons and freedom.

Night had progressed, and only four of those moons now rode in the sky. Their light gave that blue-blackened expanse a purity she knew was false. In two hours, the chill she felt now would be full of dawn shadow, and the now-bright moonlight would be a faint sky and gray. There would be wolves in her mind, pushing the hunt, while her human side held herself back, and the mist would cling like a shroud to the trees where it hid raider swords and death. In the end, she knew, when the steel was still, it would be blood, not rain, that made mud of the ground; and it would be youth that was sacrificed. Swords, she thought bitterly. After starships and sky cars and tethers to space, they settled their violence with steel. And all because of an alien plague that turned the ground into graves. Her fingers tightened spasmodically. By plague, by steel . . . It didn't matter. Blood, she thought. Always blood on her hands. And no moonlight could wash it away. She stiffened the walls of her darkening heart and braced herself for the dawn.

* * *

They were early into Kitman. Their dnu had been fast and eager to run, and the moonlight bright enough to urge them on.

But even though the Kitman relay had had hours to prepare for the riders, the Kitman stables were not ready. Men and women were still saddling up as Dion, Tule, and Royce pounded in, and there was a rush of people back and forth on the street, like a marketplace in the dark. Hishn took one look at the bustle, snarled like a badgerbear, and fled back into the night. Dion grimaced after her.

Tule's voice was amused. "No escape for the wolfwalker? Only the wolf?"

"That's the truth," she returned. She slowed to avoid hitting one of the running men. "What's going on?" she called out as she slid off her dnu.

Someone grabbed the reins from her hands. At the same time a woman took her arm, pulling her away from the dnu almost before she had time to release the reins to the hostler. "Healer Dione—this way," the woman said urgently, propelling Dion before her. "They'll get your dnu ready for you." The woman's hands were tight on Dion's arm. "Through here, Healer."

Dion knew that tone of voice: the edge of urgency, the careful control, the unvoiced need to run rather than walk. She didn't resist. Instead, she shouted over the noise, "Tule, Royce, make sure there's enough gear for all three of us for at least four days—just in case. I'll be a few minutes here."

"Thank the moons you're early," the woman worried, ignoring Dion's shout to Tule and Royce. "There's time to see them before you ride out on the venge. No, not that way, Wolfwalker. They're in the elder's house. We've got spring fever in the clinic."

"What happened?" Dion asked as she ducked into a small side street.

"The ringrunner and her escort were riding the black road—I mean, they were bringing the message rings in—when they were attacked by bihwadi. Through here, Healer. It happened up on the track from the relay tower to town. You know the one? The barrier bushes are still new up there—this way, Healer— and the line of shrubs won't be grown in for a decade. Merai— she's the ringrunner—and Pacceli went over the bushes to avoid the bihwadi on the trail. The thorns tore them up something awful. Pacceli—he took fierce wounds from the bihwadi, and then the barrier thorns cut him more. He's lost too much blood. He doesn't even move. Merai, I think, will be blind."

"Brye's down with spring fever, isn't he?"

"Aye. He daren't go near Pacceli's open wounds. The clinic nurse treated Merai and Pacceli."

Dion nodded, forgetting that, in the dark, the motion was lost on the woman. But they were already at the door to the elder's home, and the other woman pushed her through the brightly lit coralline doorway and into another man's grasp before she could answer out loud.

"This way," the man said to Dion. "In here." He let go of her arm only after pushing her into the sickroom. She took no offense. Instead, her gaze went to the beds.

One figure lay still, swathed in bandages. The nurse, an older man, sat beside the youth, holding onto the limp wrist. "Pacceli?" Dion asked quietly. The man nodded without speaking. On the other bed was the young woman who had been the ringrunner that night. Merai clenched her bandaged hands at her sides to keep from tearing at the bloody cloths that hid her face and eyes. Dion touched her briefly on the arm, then went to the young man who lay still.

The nurse moved only reluctantly aside for Dion, but the wolfwalker took his place without comment. For a long time, she held Pacceli's wrist with one hand and let the other rest on his chest, her eyes unfocused and dull. Then she rose. "He'll be all right," she told the nurse. "The pressure of fluid on his spine paralyzed him temporarily. He'll be weak for several ninans—a lot of blood lost, as you said—but his wounds are clean, and his blood will build back naturally." She indicated the woman who had brought her to the house. "Give him two or three days, then move him to a better location—someplace where he can rest for a few ninans."

The nurse frowned. "Healer . . ."

"Heartbeats can tell you many things if you listen long enough." Dion fielded his unspoken question. She turned to the ringrunner. "Merai, is it?" she asked gently.

The young woman caught her breath through torn lips. "Healer Dione?"

"Yes," she answered. "May I?" she asked the nurse, although

she was already sitting on the bed. The ringrunner shuddered as her weight shifted, then lay still, and Dion peeled back the bandages, her body shielding Merai's face from the others who waited near the door.

"Your eyes, Merai—how were they hurt?" Dion asked, not because she needed the answer, but to give the ringrunner something to do while she examined the wounds.

Merai fought to steady her voice. "The thorns, Wolfwalker. I was trying to get Pacceli over the bushes before the bihwadi attacked again. The bushes weren't thick enough to support our weight, and we fell through. Pacceli was caught, and I—oh, moons—I hurt him more getting him out—and my eyes were gouged."

The last bandage came free. Dion didn't flinch, but she suddenly looked tired. She forced her voice to be light. "Merai," she said briskly, "your face is a mess."

"I know, Wolfwalker."

"I think, after the venge, I'll come back to see you again."

"I am blind then."

The young voice was strangely adult, and Dion was silent, the words she would have spoken caught in her throat.

"Wolfwalker?"

"I'm here, Merai."

On the edge of town, Gray Hishn howled. For a long moment, Dion fingered the bandages in her hand. The blood that had soaked them was starting to dry, stiffening the threadlike strands of beaten bark that made up half of the gauze fiber. She could smell the bark in the fabric; she could smell the openness of the ragged tears in Merai's face. The torn and swollen tissues gave no hint of the young woman's features, but the ringrunner's voice was steady, and her hands obeyed the nurse and stayed at her sides instead of clawing at those raw, burning eyes. Dion stared down. She could feel the strength of will in Merai as the girl heard what Dion didn't say. Dion rubbed the bark gauze between her fingers again. The healing chemicals that were part of the bark would help those gashes heal quickly into scars, but no simple ointment or touch of salve would repair the thorn-torn eyes.

The Ancients had known how to heal such wounds before the

aliens killed them. Their technology paired with the internal alien arts so that healings were simple and quick. If the aliens ever found out how determined the Ariyens were to recover those sciences, she didn't think they would continue to be absent from these northern Ariyen skies. She shivered. She had heard the voices of Aiueven herself—in the packsong of the wolves. She had followed those harmonies back through the time layered in the Gray Ones' minds until she reached the earliest memories: wolves, new as babes on this world. The first landing of the colonists. And Ovousibas, the healing art that the aliens traded the Ancients . . .

An art that was partly now her own. Absently, Dion chewed her lip. But it was an art that was without most of its knowledge: the details of the body that the Ancients had known and been able to manipulate, to mutate, to engineer . . . What Dion could do was only a shadow of the original skills. And until they could reclaim the Ancient domes and ships and relearn the Ancient knowledge, it was all she was likely to be able to work with. She glanced at Pacceli. What she knew had been enough for him: His wounds were deep, but simple. But the ringrunner . . . She studied Merai's torn eyes.

"Wolfwalker?" the ringrunner asked, her young voice barely a whisper. "They say that you can heal people. They say your patients don't die."

Dion glanced at the nurse, but he hadn't heard Merai's words. Her own voice was soft in answer. "My patients die as often as those of other healers. I do what I can. That's all."

"I'm not a child, Wolfwalker."

Even without the use of her eyes, the young woman's voice was expressive. A faint smile touched Dion's lips. "I understand," she said.

"You said Pacceli will be all right."

"Yes."

Her voice dropped even lower. "You healed him."

Dion hesitated.

In the distance, Gray Hishn howled. "That wolf," the ringrunner managed. "Is that Gray Hishn?"

Dion looked up, toward the window. "Aye."

The ringrunner paused. Then, "Wolfwalker?"

"Yes, Merai."

The young woman's lips moved, but no sound came out, and the bed trembled. Dion lightly touched her cheek. If Merai had still had eyes, they would be glistening; if she had had tear ducts, she would cry. Hope warred with fear in the ringrunner's body, and Dion could feel both. She closed her own eyes for a moment. The darkness was filled with the sense of the wolves, and she hardly remembered what it was like anymore to be without the Gray Ones. But Merai didn't have a wolf in her head; her mind was alone in its darkness.

Slowly, Dion opened her eyes. "Merai," Dion said softly, "I'm going to examine your eyes more closely now. This might feel odd, and it will probably hurt, but I need for you to lie still."

Merai forced the words out. "Yes, Wolfwalker." She couldn't quite hide her hope.

Dion let her fingers explore the wounds, her unfocused gaze on Merai's face. The young woman jerked, then went still, then twitched again. Then Dion touched the bruised cheek gently. "You will lose the sight of one eye, Merai. There is nothing I can do to help that."

Merai's chin seemed to stiffen. "And my other eye?"

"Your other eye, I can save."

"Tonight?"

"No. It will be a long process, Merai. I can start that process so that your own healer can continue it, but I cannot do that in the few minutes I have left before I ride out again."

For a moment, the ringrunner was silent. "The venge," she finally said.

"It's your eye or their lives," Dion agreed quietly.

The young woman struggled to control her breathing. When she spoke again, her voice was carefully steady. "Ride with the moons, Wolfwalker."

Dion set her hand back on the bed. "I'll be back in a few days." She rose from the bed, swayed, and caught the nurse's arm.

"Healer?" the man asked quickly, supporting her. "You're not well?"

"I'm fine." Dion straightened. "It's just been a long night," she managed.

He nodded, worried, but she gently shook him off. "You've

done a good job with Pacceli," she said instead. "As for Merai, salve and bandage all the wounds as you have been doing except for her good eye—the right one. Do not treat her right eye with anything but original. If your healer—Brye—has a question about that, assure him that I mean what I say. Original only, until I return. I'll be back as soon as possible. It might be the whole ninan, but venges this far north don't usually last nine days. I expect to return before then, perhaps in two or three days."

"Original will keep the wound from healing," he commented as he handed Dion some wet cloths to clean the blood from her hands.

She nodded her thanks as she reassured him. "That is what is needed. If, before I return, her eye begins to form scar tissue, she'll have no sight at all except perhaps that of distinguishing day from night." She glanced at the ringrunner. "Do you understand that, Merai?"

The young woman tried to nod.

"It will be painful, and it will feel as if the pain gets worse every time the nurse applies the original. But you've got to stand it if you want to see again." She handed the towels back to the nurse.

"I understand, Wolfwalker," she repeated.

Dion eyed the ringrunner as the nurse rewrapped the bandages. "It was a brave thing to do, Merai, to bring Pacceli with you."

"No," Merai said flatly. "I was scared as a hare in a lepa den. It was Pacceli who saved me, not the other way around. He pulled the bihwadi off me and got us away from the pack. And when he realized he couldn't run, he tried to stay behind to stall the bihwadi so that I had time to escape. He made me keep going, even when my eyes were torn and he could hardly stand."

"Brave as his father," the nurse agreed, gentling his touch further as he rewrapped the ringrunner's eyes.

"Healer," said the woman who had waited at the doorway. "I'll show you back to the stables."

Dion nodded, and followed the woman from the elder's house.

"Merai—she was every bit as brave as Pacceli," the woman

said. "Slight as she is, she dragged that young man down the hill till they found one of the barrier channels and crossed back onto the road. Moons alone know how many times she fell—her knees are like pulp, and her feet are badly blistered. When she reached Mac neBanyon's house, she didn't have breath left to rouse anyone. It was Mac's dog that woke everyone up. Mac came down with his blade ready for a raider and found her, blind as a glacier worm on his porch. Said she handed him Pacceli, then told him he had to reach you, to get you the fighters and healing kits. She practically ordered him to ride in." They were in sight of the stable now, and the woman hesitated before releasing Dion to the crowd that was even now mounting up. "What you said to her—you can help her see again?"

"Yes—if her eye remains unhealed till I get back."

"She's a good child, Wolfwalker. She deserves to see again."

Dion's eyes were suddenly distant. "I've never noticed the moons to give out what was deserved."

"No," the other woman agreed. "That's why we have healers like you."

Dion didn't answer. Something heavy settled onto her frame, and she shrugged as if it could be shifted from her shoulders. But there was nothing there. She rubbed absently at the silver circlet covered by her warcap. Gray Hishn, on the other side of the city, caught the edge of her mind and howled again, deep into her thoughts.

"I hear you, Gray One," she murmured.

The hunt gathers, Wolfwalker. It is time to run down the moons. Hishn's eagerness was aggressive and hot, dispelling the shiver she felt.

Dion glanced ahead. The other riders were waiting. "Soon," she murmured. "I come to you." She put Merai from her mind.

Then she turned and moved toward the dnu that Royce was holding for her. Tule nodded at her, called out to the other fighters, and gestured a question at Dion, to see if she wanted to lead. She shook her head. A few moments later, with the hub behind them, the gray shadows filled her mind. The sky became flat, and the forest filled with movement as they began to race the blood dawn.

II

What you think you can see
 Is not real.
What you think not to feel is
 Real.
What you think to hold on to
 Is illusion.
What you think to escape
 Is yourself.

—*From the fourth chapter of* The Book of Abis

The night whistled in her ears, and the sky was filled with fog-chilled air. Her thighs clung automatically to the saddle, and she dozed as she rode, as she had earlier that night when she had reached the protected stretches. They hit a long, straight section thick with puddles, and Dion was jarred awake as the road-soiled rain flung itself at her. The healer intern, Monteverdi, was near the end of the group, and after a while, Dion dropped back to ride beside him. They had met eight years ago when he had entered a kayak race determined to place against his older brother. Monteverdi had lost the race, but not his determination. Now he was taller, even more scrawny looking, his hair even more cowlicked and awkward. But his hands were as sensitive as the hairs on a caterpillar, and even though he had not bonded with a wolf, he could hear the Gray Ones like Dion. This was his last year as an intern. Next summer he'd be on Journey, and his Promised, Sena, would go with him.

Dion caught the half smile on his face and wondered if he was thinking of his Promised now. The intern had been sharing Kum-jan with Sena for months, the two of them sneaking off in the night or late afternoon. And now they were Promised. Her smile twisted wryly. Ariye was so formal compared to her own county. In Randonnen, one would simply choose to find a private place to be together. Here in Ariye, intimacy between friends was Kum-jan, intimacy between two Promised people

42

was Kum-kala; and intimacy between two mates was Kum-
vani. According to Ariyen custom—and much to her own
brother's chagrin—she and Aranur had shared two of those intimacies before she knew their formalities. Her brother had not
cared about the formalities as much as he had—at that time—
distrusted Aranur. Aranur, however, had assumed Dion knew the
differences between Ariyen intimacies. It was an ignorance he
had swiftly corrected when he took her back with him to Ariye.

She fingered the reins as if she could feel Aranur's hands, not
leather against her skin. This last scouting assignment had taken
her far west of their home, and she was as eager to get back as
her dnu was to run. It was not enough to get a message ring
from her mate, or to hear his voice through Hishn. The faint link
that had grown between them, as happened with many wolfwalkers and their partners, was not enough for her. This ride
was as much an excuse to go home as it was to ride as venge
healer.

Yellow eyes gleamed, and Dion shook herself in the saddle.
She cut herself off from the link. The predawn was cold enough
without longing to compound it.

Half an hour out of the Kitman hub the fog was left behind in
the lower valley, and a thin breeze crept over the hill. It dissipated her weariness like a soft alarm. Gray Hishn, up the road
and out of sight, was only an echo in Dion's mind. Hooves beat,
and heads didn't nod. Hands rested loosely on hilts. No one
spoke, and the dnu didn't snort. The wary tension that filled their
arms began to cross into their shoulders.

They hit a stretch of old road where the roots, hard as stone,
had turned brown with age. The tiny streaks of new root growth
that had begun to stretch in like needles from the edge of the
road caught at Dion's mind. White walls, white light . . . The
domes of the Ancients, pale in the skies, hung in her memory
like moons. Just beyond this ridge, she knew, she'd be able to see
the mountain. Truncated by the Ancients and flattened off, it was
a landing place where the tethers came down from the stars, and
the skycars soared back up. Empty now, with vacant sailplanes
and the ever-present humming, that landing place was a taunt to
this county—a reminder of what they could try to regain, but
could never quite reach. Saturated with plague, but always within

sight . . . Someday, she thought, she would find a cure. Get rid of the alien plague. And Aranur would have his domes again, while she had the lives of the wolves.

She stared at the trees that hid the mountain. Beyond them both, to the north, were the peaks of the alien birdmen. Aiueven: the will of the moons, the eyes of the stars . . . Alien spacefarers who had settled here first and had claimed the planet for their breeding grounds. The Aiueven had not wanted humans to join them on this world. But the colonists had landed, and the aliens had coped—at first—as had the humans who began to build homes.

The Ancients had said this world was enough like OldEarth to disguise itself with treachery. Yet in the end, it had not been the world, but the Aiueven who had decimated the colonists. A plague that raced through the human-built domes, and a slow death for the wolves . . . Anything that would keep humans out of the skies, away from the alien stars.

Over time, the Gray Ones, like humans, had recovered and spread across the nine counties, but the wolves would have spread more thickly and farther had they not lost half their litters to stillbirth. That the centuries of stillborn pups were connected to the alien-sent plague—of that, Dion was sure. That there was a cure for the plague that lay dormant in the wolves—that caused those stillborn cubs—of that Dion had only hope. She stared up at the blue-dark sky as the lupine echo followed her thoughts. Had the Ancients known how much they would lose, would they have dealt with the Aiueven differently?

As though the thought triggered Gray Hishn's own memories, the wolf snarled in Dion's mind. Soft at first, the bond between them hardened into a link of steel, and the rush of howling that burst out from the back of the wolfwalker's skull struck her like a whip. Lupine memories stretched back more than eight hundred years. Opened to their history, the Gray Ones howled together. Not just Hishn's voice, but a hundred wolves sang out the images of time. New memories faded into old lines of thought; old memories fled into ancient ones. Back, and back again, through the decades, then centuries, of life the packsong wove its threads. Wolves did not forget, and what each one experienced in its life, it sang back into the packsong or passed on to its young. Now there were hundreds of years of lupine lives sewn into the distant howling.

She let part of her mind filter back through the faded harmony. It was an old exercise for her—the searching out of the Ancients' voices and the alien overtones. She had made a promise once, years ago, and the Gray Ones still remembered. Since then, when she ran the hills with them or rode the black road at night, they opened to her like a book. Distant memories, ancient songs . . . Always in the backs of their minds were the clues to the cure she sought. Yet she never quite touched it—the cure for the wolves. Never quite understood . . .

Wolfwalker, Hishn sent.

She found the single thread that was the wolf she knew and drew back from the ancient voices. She felt the windchill, cold as steel, as it hit her bared teeth, and realized she was grinning. Hishn was eager and focused. Dion shook herself. She had to remember to keep the wolf away from the fighting this time. The Gray One was growing aggressive.

But Hishn tugged at her hands, making her fingers clench on the reins. *Run with me,* the gray wolf sent. *The hunt is close. Run with us in the dawn.*

"Soon, Hishn," she murmured. "But this time, you will only scout. When the fighting starts, you stay behind."

Wolfwalker . . .

"You'll stay behind, Hishn. I mean it this time." She ignored the wolf's mental protest. "Besides, I'll be on the outskirts of the action anyway. I'll be in little danger."

The gray wolf howled beside her, and this time the sound was real. One of the other riders started, his dnu skittering away. The man gave her a wary look. She shrugged a smile and tasted the chill air like a cup of cold rou, rolling it around on her tongue. Dawn, she thought, was getting close.

Ten kays out of Kitman, they swung onto Red Wolf Road. There were fresh marks there from Aranur's group, which had come in from the east. Two kays—maybe four—Dion thought, and she'd feel Aranur himself in the song of the wolfpack. Hishn's voice would ring with his energy, and then Dion would see her mate for herself. Strong hands, stronger arms; broad shoulders and back. His face was not handsome as her brother's face was;

Aranur's cheekbones were too high and his chin too strong, his eyebrows too heavy over those gray, icy eyes. But those features caught and held the eye, as if they forced attention to them the way a magnet pulled at iron.

She stretched her mind and let the packsong float there like a mist. It was thick here, so she knew there were wolves in this rocky, mountain forest. Like layers of gauze, the distant voices overlapped until they formed a chorus of rising and falling tones. Hishn raised her own voice, and Dion felt her throat open up. She had to choke back the howl that she wanted to cry out.

How far? she asked the gray wolf in her mind.

Soon, Gray Hishn answered. *The eerin ahead were chased from their beds, and your prey has gone on beyond them.*

Aranur, or the raiders?

Your mate is close; the prey near the rocks. I hear nothing over the ridge.

Dion nodded absently. The ridge that Hishn pictured, flattened in the gray wolf's mind, was Missive Ridge. The southern side was a series of broken cliffs split by old, collapsed draws; the trail the wolf projected was of the narrow path that cut up through a split in the stone. One dnu wide, heavy with overhangs, rough with slabs of rock—it was a dangerous place to ride and a deadly place to enter if one was going after raiders. That Hishn knew raiders had not crossed the ridge meant that there were other wolves already on the heights and that those wolves had not seen humans.

Dion projected her thanks to the wolf, then urged her dnu along the line until she caught up to the leader. Dacarr spared her a glance. "News?" he asked tersely.

"I think the raiders have stopped at the cliffs."

"Then they'll face the venge there?"

She nodded.

"Well, raiders are rough, not stupid. That's good fighting ground. What about Aranur?"

"We'll see him within the next two kays."

The short man grunted his acknowledgment.

Dion dropped back past Tule and Royce. If the raiders were this close and staying on the roads, she wouldn't be needed till they reached the cliff. She looked ahead, but could see neither

Hishn nor the venge. The way was shadowed by the rootroad trees, and the dawn, barely lightening that blue-dark sky, turned the road into a muddy mess of contrasts. In the end it wasn't she who spotted Aranur, although she knew where to look. It was the man riding beside Dacarr who caught a glimpse of the riders.

No one called out, and it wasn't needed. Within minutes the two groups had merged. Aranur looked back to catch Dion's eyes, but the two rode far apart. Not until they approached the low, foggy stretch where the road began to swing by the cliffs did Aranur halt the group.

One minute, there were only men and women and riding dnu on the road. The next minute, the gray wolf had joined them. Instantly, the group's posture changed. The fighters, except for Tule and Royce, pulled away from Dion, giving the gray wolf room to join the wolfwalker. Tule, catching Dion's eye as she slid off the dnu, nodded almost imperceptibly at Royce. The youth had deliberately stood his ground when the gray wolf stalked up beside him, but the young man's eyes followed the wolf as carefully as a hare follows a worlag's teeth. Dion hid her smile.

"Ready?" Aranur asked softly, moving over to touch her arm briefly, lightly. There was an intimacy of years in that touch. Tule and Royce, with a glance at each other, moved quietly away.

Dion's ears automatically took in their footsteps, but she had eyes only for the man with the icy gray eyes. "There's a wolf pack on the heights," she said. "They have no sense of humans up there." She loosened her jacket, peeled it off, and bundled it into the small pack on the back of her saddle.

He rubbed at his chin. "They have to be close, then. If they didn't take the cliff route, I can't see them going on down the road where we could catch them on the flats. You can get close enough here to see them?"

She murmured agreement. For a moment, her scarred left hand rested on the pack. Aranur's hand covered the seamed flesh, his strong fingers rubbing along the ridges. The faint white lines on his own tanned skin made an old pattern in his flesh, and Dion's right hand covered his. Then Aranur squinted at the brightening sky. "Make it quick," he said simply.

"As the fourth moon," she promised. But she didn't move. "I miss you," she said softly.

"I'll miss you more when you go."

"I'm always going."

"Always?"

"Here, there . . . The council points, and there I go, trotting off like a dog to do their bidding."

"You wouldn't want to trade the council's bidding for that of a weapons master's bidding, would you?"

"I've heard you're a hard taskmaster."

"I've heard you're a tough scout."

His hand pressed hers. There was an instant where the gray ice of his eyes shattered into a gaze of intensity that hit her like a fist. The riders around them faded to fog. Violet eyes stared into gray. The yellow gaze that gleamed through both their minds brought a howling from the distant pack, blindingly intense.

"Soon," he promised softly.

Some of the other riders shifted as a group, catching the tall man's attention, and his expression hardened again into a distant focus. Dion dropped her right hand. Her fingers brushed against the hilt of her sword, and the chill of the steel mirrored the expression on Aranur's face. For a moment, the world tilted. A dozen years rushed by her eyesight. There were faces and ghosts that cried out in memory, only to be blinded by wolfsong. Lupine threads wove through her mind, tightening across and around her brain until she felt as if her very skull were honeycombed in gray steel. Aranur's voice was one of those threads; Aranur's hands were her anchors. And yet that touch, strong and firm, which still rested on her left hand, was a promise not yet kept. Like the one she had made so long ago to the wolves, this was one that hung between them like time on a dangling thread. He looked down again, and she heard his voice as if he had not spoken out loud, but had projected through the packsong. *Soon*, he said again.

She moved her lips to speak his name, but no sound came out. She looked at him oddly. Time, she thought, was not a friend; it was insubstantial hope. Then the voice that had ordered the riders to the venge spoke her name instead. She shook her head, then shrugged at his raised eyebrow. A moment later, she was gone, swallowed by the thin fog.

"Aranur?" one of the men asked at his elbow.

He stared after the wolfwalker. "I missed something," he said softly. "Something important."

"Dion?"

"Dion, and not Dion," he murmured, more to himself than Dacarr. "She said she missed me."

Dacarr shrugged. "She's been in the Black Gullies for a month."

"It wasn't that." Absently, Aranur rubbed his jaw, but his voice was once again firm when he said, "She's gone to check their positions. She'll send word back with the wolf."

Dacarr nodded, but neither man moved. For a moment both looked out, studying the wisps of fog that clung to the forest. Then they turned back, gathering the other riders while Aranur outlined the approach to the cliff.

Moving silently away, Dion no longer heard them. The forest had swallowed their voices as if they'd been battened with cotton, and her ears, tuned as they were to what was natural, heard only the woods' sounds now.

The underbrush was damp and cold. Dew, caught on waxy leaves, wetted Dion's sleeves and darkened her clothes in patches. Hishn's feet padded softly, making a talalike rhythm as she moved over the fallen logs and around the half-buried boulders. Morning birds, awake before dawn, were already calling shrilly, and tiny flocks of treespits swooped through the foggy canopy like bats fleeing the light. And even though she was working her way toward the rocks that would soon be bathed in raider blood, she felt a sense of freedom. There was nothing here but Hishn and her. Nothing but forest and sky. These moments were clean and cold and quiet, and she savored them like a kiss.

When she neared the cliff, Dion dropped to her knees, lowering her profile to that of the ferns around her. The dampness pressed instantly through her leggings, and the scent of the soil hit her nose. Ahead of her Gray Hishn snorted, and Dion cleared her own nostrils. A wide swath of young sticky trees were growing back from an old burn, and their sap stung like fireweed where it caught and clung to her skin. But the low branches hid her shape, and the fog hid her slight movements like music hiding a message.

They are here, Hishn projected into her mind.

I see them, she returned. Carefully, she pulled an arrow from her quiver.

She felt her mind shift from wariness to anticipation, to the heat of fear or fury. Time blurred and ceased until only her senses were left. She knew her ears caught sounds, her eyes saw movement. She felt her own feet shift as a dawn breeze rose. She caught the odor of wood smoke that clung to the raiders' clothes. The fog shifted and began to dissipate. She picked four of the raiders out from the rocks. Six, seven, nine, eleven, she counted so far—more than what they had expected.

Hishn picked up the thread of her concern. *Your pack—you need their fangs to strengthen yours. You cannot flank a herd by yourself. You need Leader to help you here.*

Hishn's image of Aranur was clear, and the wolf's concern about the raiders was thick behind that mental picture. Dion smiled without humor, her expression one of grim intent. *I don't intend to flank anyone, Gray One. I'm just the eyes of the venge. Go to Aranur, Hishn. Show him what I see, and tell him it's time to move in.*

An instant later, like a ghost in the trees, the wolf was gone.

A few minutes, and Aranur's voice touched Dion's mind, and she knew that Gray Hishn had reached him. She didn't have to see Aranur begin to move his people through the trees. With the early breeze clearing the fog, he knew enough to hurry. And with wolf eyes watching through the woods, his figure was clear in her mind. Eleven men and three women, who crept like snakes, were a wash of movement to Dion. The healer intern had stayed behind, with Hishn to guard his safety.

Dion still moved forward, low to the ground. Gray fog; gray voices. Hishn snarled in her thoughts, and Dion opened her mind to the wolf. Left behind with the dnu, the wolf snarled again, and the dnu around her snorted.

Wolfwalker! she called.

Stay. Dion's voice was firm. *This hunt is mine, not yours.*

The gray creature growled. *I am your packmate. This hunt is as much mine as you are my wolfwalker.*

No. Not when the fight is with humans, Hishn. It's not for you anymore. You know what it does to you to attack men. You cannot stay with me.

Hishn snarled again, anger and frustration thick in her mental voice, but Dion didn't weaken.

Wolfwalker! the gray creature howled.

Dion read the eagerness of the wolf for the hunt, the instinctive wariness of strange humans, and the hunger that growled in Hishn's belly. She closed herself off. The focus that Hishn had strengthened still remained in her mind, but the hot lust for blood was leeched from the intensity of seeking her prey.

Close, Aranur's people moved. From Dion's left, the outermost raider seemed to grow impatient, wondering if the venge was near. The man had barely risen from behind his rock when he went down with a bolt in his cheek. He screamed and kept screaming until the sound was abruptly cut off, and Dion knew that someone else had struck a killing blow. But the focus in her mind left her distant from the noise.

There was a rush from Aranur's men. A bracing from the raiders against the attack. A figure rose carefully in front of Dion, aiming at the Ariyens, and she knew her body moved because the man went down with her arrow in his back. He thrashed and tore the ferns and finally stopped breathing.

Dion crawled up beside him to take his warbolts after rolling his body off his quiver. She didn't look at the blood that marked her skin as her hands grasped his soaked leather jerkin.

Raider archers let fly with their bolts. Somewhere ahead, a woman cursed quietly as her bolt missed her mark, and a man beside her cursed too, but with eagerness because his bolt hit his mark straight on. Someone screamed, and Dion tuned it out. Something brushed by her knee, and she jerked back, dropping instantly behind a log. Another bolt whicked over her head. Quickly, she elbowed along the log until she reached a slight depression and could ease herself away.

She reached a root mass and crouched there for cover. Aranur was a hundred meters away, his steel flashing as he squared off with a slender raider. The raider moved like lightning—Aranur was hard-pressed to stay his ground and force the other man back. Tule had locked with a burly man, shouting to Royce as he did so. To the right of the one-armed man, from the cover of a rock pile, three Ariyens were angling their shots to catch one of the raider archers. And two raiders had dragged an Ariyen archer from his place between the boulders, grappling him to the ground. Dion grasped her bow, but did not nock an arrow. With the figures struggling as they were, she could shoot the Ariyen as easily as the raiders.

She saw it all and yet saw nothing. She saw the Ariyen archer escape, and one of the grappling raiders die; saw an Ariyen swordsman go down and another raider run. It had happened before—the warbolts flying, the flash of steel in the dawn. Distance kept her mind from the fight, and foreknowledge of the death she saw locked her emotions. There was a speed and accentuation to movement and fear, but the world itself was unreal and dimmed; the forest made of blood, not brown and green.

An arrow sliced across her forearm. Abruptly, she lost her grip on her bow. She lunged for it instinctively, but another bolt checked her motion. And a raider charged from between the trees, his bow nocked with another arrow, his dnu churning up the ferns. From back on the road, Hishn read Dion's heightened emotion and howled into her head. Dion howled back, her eyes glinting. Another arrow, and this one sliced through her leggings as she jumped for cover.

He was almost upon her. She scrambled to the side, barely regaining her feet. The raider had jammed his bow in his saddle holder and now grabbed his sword. Dion threw her own blade up. Even with the angle of her sword—steep, to let the blow slide off—the force of the man's blow was jarring. She was smashed to her knees like a nail beneath a mallet. Her warcap slipped; the silver healer's circlet showed.

Her distant focus shattered. Blue-gray eyes stared intently into hers. Some part of her mind noticed the flecks of darker blue in his eyes, the shallow lines that seamed his face. Sweat beaded the raider's brow beneath gray-peppered hair. The man's breath was suddenly harsh in his throat as he took in the silver glint of the circlet. Something changed in his eyes. Blood was suddenly real again; steel was suddenly cold. Dion thrust herself up, back to her feet.

The raider charged. She leaped aside, and the midshoulder of his dnu hit her like a mace. Tangled, she went flying over a log. She hit the ground like a sack of old shoes, her limbs flailing out. Then the sting of sap hit her neck. She scrambled to her feet.

The raider's dnu stamped its hooves, its muscles bunched beneath short, bristly fur. When the man charged, he cut Dion even farther away from the line of the fight, like an eerin from the herd. His sword was there before hers, beating her own blade down. His speed was like that of Aranur, blindingly fast. Dion felt a thread of fear lace her breathing. This man was better than she.

He spurred the dnu forward, and she had to dodge. Again he spurred the beast forward. She flung herself around a tree. Away from the rocks, from the raiders, from the others, who couldn't see her—like an animal, she was being herded. It was forceful. It was clever. It was . . . deliberate.

Wolfwalker! Hishn howled, feeling the fear grow in her gut.

Hishn, she returned quickly. *Stay away. The Ariyens will protect me. I just have to get back to their line.*

A fourth time, the raider charged. This time he twisted his dnu so that it half reared its hooves, striking out at her arms. She flung herself back, but she was at the top of a draw. The soft loamy edge crumbled away. She cursed—and went down the layered humus, half sliding through and half leaping over the meter-deep leaves and soil. Without hesitation, the raider followed.

He caught her near the bottom, slicing at her as his dnu jumped past. She parried his blow neatly and slashed at his boots. Parried again, then thrust away. Ducked. Twisted. Slipped on a moss rock and cursed under her breath as her ankle scraped nastily along it. Hishn's voice rang in her skull. The wolf's strength fed her arm, making her muscles bunch. But she barely turned the blows. The six-legged mount thundered past again, blinding her with the dirt and leaves kicked up in its wake. Like a dancer, it pivoted on two of its side legs to come back at a dead run. She cut up, catching the base of the man's boot as he jerked his leg away. But though she sliced through leather, the blade was caught by stirrup, not bone. She had to jerk it free. She barely managed to loose her throwing knife at the raider's reaching arm.

"Moons-damned pail of worlag piss," he snarled as he jerked back, not quickly enough. The knife sliced his biceps, not deeply, but enough to bloody him. He cut viciously down at her. Hishn howled, and Dion turned his blade again, but the sheer force of the blow threw her back against the half-rocky, half-muddy ground. The raider grabbed at her but got air, not tunic. Dion, out of reach, scrambled over a rock and faced him, ready to dodge as soon as he committed his rush. She knew how to take him now, she thought. His fighting moves were like Aranur's, but he was not riding for the best cuts.

He spurred forward and she dove sideways, under a log that had fallen at an angle. Soft earth and rotted splinters jammed against her cheeks and went down into her tunic. The raider's sword hit the log beside her arm. The force of it shook the dead wood like a drum.

No chips had flown; the blade had not cut at all. He had swung to batter, not kill. Dion froze. Fear was a sudden, sharp taste in her mouth. He saw her realization. For a moment, both were still, caught in the dawn tableau. Then, in a voice as soft as fog, he said, "You are mine, Dione."

It was instinct that shoved her back, away from his lightning-fast hands. His words had been like blades of glass, sliding into her chest. She felt a terror slide in with them. Death—she had faced that often enough. But capture . . . She had been beaten once, long ago, and the memory had never faded. She had seen refugees from raider-run camps. And bodies after raider capture . . . This man's eyes were intent as a wolf's. This was no raider who struck out blindly for greed; this was a man with focus. He knew her. He wanted her. And he was more skilled than she.

She felt her hand grip her hilt too hard. Her name on his lips— so steadily, so determined—it had shattered her. She had lost her evenness—her distance. Hishn howled at the rush of her fear.

He charged. Clinging to the dnu by his knees, he leaned down and made a grab for her hair. His heavy fingers caught the edge of her warcap, and she ducked frantically away, leaving the cap in his hands with a handful of hair. He flung the cap aside, and his eyes did not leave her face. He spurred the riding beast forward.

Fear coalesced into a knot of fire. The howling burst open her head. Wolves seemed to flood into her mind, leaving a wash of gray across her brain. Fear shifted to fury. Her feet were suddenly paws that dug into the soil. Her eyes flared with a lupine tint that was lost in the light of dawn. But the raider caught that hint of yellow and hesitated for an instant. His dnu pulled up; Dion flashed away, sprinting through the trees.

Ferns whipped her face and arms. The soil clung to her boots.

Long, fallen branches caught at her feet, but she leaped them like a wolf. From the other side of the rise, back by the road, Hishn was sprinting toward her. She no longer held the wolf back. The danger to Hishn from attacking the man—of losing her fear of humans and turning unexpectedly against others— was no longer Dion's concern. It was Dion's life now or his, and she could die without Hishn's strength.

And then the raider's dnu caught her. The flat of the man's blade struck the edge of her shoulder. She went down sideways, slipping in the soil, barely missed by the hooves. The raider slid off his dnu in a single movement, following her down.

As she fell, she twisted her sword between them, the long knife in her other hand coming up to meet it. The hilt of his blade caught in her crossed brace. His blow, frustrated, hung over her face in an instant of matched strength. Blood from his arm dripped onto hers.

Hishn's snarl was behind her eyes; the gray wolf's strength in her arms. The raider breathed heavily. His teeth were white and straight. His eyes were dark and piercing, like a lepa on its prey. Her back was against a rock and the soil, and one of his knees was grinding into hers. But her focus was on that heavy hilt that hung over her face and temple. And the raider eyed her with steady intensity as he began to power her back.

"Why?" she breathed.

He didn't waste his breath in answer. His weight bore down. Her shoulders strained. Her arms wavered.

"Why?" she shrieked. And gave way like the wind. The raider's hilt struck down like an ax. He buried it in the soil. "Bitch of a lepa," he cursed as she wrenched away.

He grabbed for her arm. Her knife slashed back, and he jerked away, the blade scraping again along his muscle. They scrambled, broke apart, then clashed. She was barely faster than he. His sword arm was like a mallet pounding through her guard, and her elbow was still jarred from before. Again he beat her blade skillfully aside, then lunged to strike at her head. But this time she dodged forward, into his arms, then under and away. He caught only a handful of tunic and jerkin.

It was enough. He twisted his fist, and Dion's body was flung in a tangle of limbs. The tip of her sword caught against a tree trunk, and she lost her grip on the hilt. The blade flashed out like a falling star. The raider grappled her hard, managing to catch one of her arms just above the elbow. Then her knife caught him on his hip.

He screamed, a short, brutal sound, and slammed her down. Enraged, he swung the hilt of his sword to strike her chin. But she writhed away, and his blow struck only her shoulder.

Hishn! she cried out.

I come!

She tore a rock from the ground and flung it. It missed his head by two handspans. He barely ducked. He scrambled after her, grabbing her foot, and holding on as she kicked at his face. The forest seemed to roil around them. He caught the feral glare of her teeth just as his hand closed on her knee. She bucked like a dnu, kicking and cutting at his hands. He took a slash to his wrist, one to his ribs as they twisted together and jerked back apart, another to his biceps. The last one cut through the leather. He didn't bother to curse; his breath was too harsh, and she was too quick—the Ariyens had taught her well. If he could get one of her hands, he'd have her. But he couldn't get to the tie-straps on his belt—he needed both hands just to keep her on the ground.

She slapped another blow aside and grabbed the hilt of his own blade, but he jerked it away. His weight was an advantage now.

Then the gray wolf hurtled out of the brush. Dion's eyes, tinged with yellow, warned him an instant before. He twisted, trying to bring round his sword, but the burning tearing of his flesh forced him to drop the blade. The wolf flashed past. Instinctively, with one hand clenched in Dion's jerkin, he scrambled to his feet, dragging the wolfwalker with him. His dnu skittered sideways, out of his reach. The gray wolf burst back. The raider took one look at the yellow eyes and grabbed for the saddle. Dion fought him wildly. Her fists struck his chin, not his neck, as he ducked his head against her blows. Her legs kicked the dnu as she struck out. The man caught the saddle pommel of the half-rearing beast but lost his grip on Dion's jerkin. Hishn snapped. Dion dropped like a rock. The riding beast panicked. With his weight hanging off its side and the gray wolf at its haunches, the man cursed. The dnu leaped forward, away from the wolf. The raider swung up, bouncing off the ground like a trick rider.

Dion staggered to her feet, her weight light on one leg. The raider wheeled his dnu. For an instant their eyes met again, blue-gray gaze piercing violet. There was rage in his eyes, and purpose, and hunt—like a lepa eyeing a rabbit. His hand was clamped on his hip as he stifled the blood that flowed there, and Dion's hands were pressed to her side. Her ribs felt cracked from his blows. Gray Hishn, between them, snarled deep through her throat. The raider pointed at her in silent promise. Then he wheeled the riding beast again and sprinted for the rise.

Dion grabbed her sword and ran after the raider, staggering up the side of the draw as her feet slid in the slick humus. She stopped at the top, her breath coming in gasps. She had to cling to a tree to stand. The fear was like bile on her tongue, and her heartbeat was crushing her brain. The raider was already near the other fighters, racing toward the cliff. What had seemed like hours down in the draw had been only minutes up here. Swords still flashed and people cursed, and the man who had cut Dion off from the others was now halfway through the melee. Two men staggered into his path, and the raider slammed into them both, throwing the Ariyen free and trampling his own man under his dnu. Then he was through. Of the three bolts that followed him to the cliff, only one hit near its mark. Like a weak tail, that bolt stuck in the raider's saddle, snapping back and forth as the man spurred his mount up the pass.

Dion followed him through Hishn's senses as much as through her own. The sounds of his hooves, his breathing, his curse . . . The raider barely kept his seat as the dnu's front legs jolted onto the steep path. The sides of the pass closed in. Two more arrows hit the rock beside him, flinging stone chips into his face. He didn't flinch. Instead, he wrenched his shoulders sideways as the dnu plunged beneath a wicked overhang. And when he passed the second ledge, he reached out to the rocky wall. A moment later, the thunder of falling rocks blocked the route behind him.

III

It is dark, and in this darkness
  is the cry of hungry death;
It is cold, and with this icy breath
  of steel comes fearful chill;
It is silent now, and in this quiet
  dawn lie bodies still;
It is over now, and still I stand
  and feel the tears that freeze my cheeks,
  and search for life that once had been.
For now the steel is fed again,
  but when shall the silver shine?

—*Second refrain,* Lament of the Healer Dione, I

Dion forced herself to move toward the fight. Hishn's eyes saw the movement of the bow raised in her direction before she did, and the howl that hit her mind flung her to the ground. She dropped behind a tree just as the bolt whished through the ferns. A moment later the archer was killed, and Dion saw that too, through Hishn's eyes.

There were six raiders on the ground; two still grappling with Ariyens. Two more fought viciously near the cliff, and one last archer hid in the boulders. Another swordsman went down, and the Ariyens shifted their attack. Aranur was over there, his back to a boulder, fighting a raider coldly, viciously. Dion stumbled forward, still trying to catch her breath. Her elbow still rang as if jammed, and her shoulder was wrenched where she'd taken the brunt of the raider's strength. Her ribs were not cracked, she knew, only bruised, but her breathing was painful and thin. She felt again those fists, that hilt ... The man's voice echoing back in her mind ... Urgency. Purpose. What had she become in Ariye, that a raider wanted her? The shudder that caught her was almost shocking in its depth.

Hishn caught her leggings in lupine teeth. *Stay. You are hurt. It is nothing.*

Hishn growled at her. *Your fangs are weak as old Neysha's. Your mate does not need your help.*

Dion glared at the wolf, but those yellow eyes gleamed with unrelenting truth. Her bow had been lost somewhere to her right. Her quiver was empty—the arrows had been lost in the draw. Her sword in that melee would simply be one more weapon in Aranur's way. She nodded shortly, jerkily. Besides, there was something wrong with her hands. They were shaking like the ferns.

She fumbled at her belt pouches for the small healer's kit. "I'll need Monteverdi," she muttered to the wolf.

Your packmate is already here.

She looked up. The lanky man had just ridden into sight on the road. The intern looked anxious, glancing nervously from side to side as he neared the fighting. But he slid quickly enough from his dnu to kneel beside one of the Ariyens. The man pushed him irritably away, pointing to another man lying nearby. A moment later, Dion joined them. "He's dead," she said flatly, as Monteverdi tried to find a pulse on the body.

Monteverdi's face shuttered. "All right," he said. He straightened up, glanced at her, then took her arm firmly. "Dion—"

Absently, she looked down. The slash that had split the edge of the leather tunic had split skin as well, and blood now soaked her arm. Annoyed, she shook off Monteverdi's grip.

The tall intern asked something, taking her arm again, but she couldn't answer. Something about blood, he was saying, and shock. She shook her head. It was not shock she felt, but something else, deep and gripping and cold. This blood was not from a wound meant to kill her, but one from a stunning blow. And it was not the sight of her own blood that chilled her now, but the words she had heard from that raider.

Stubbornly, Monteverdi hung onto her arm. Hishn snarled at him, but the intern snapped, "Back off, Gray One. I'm helping, not hurting her."

Wolfwalker— Hishn's voice was caught between protecting Dion and her instinctive fear of humans. The wolf recognized the intern, but Dion's need for protection colored her response so that she stayed and snarled instead of slinking away.

Back down, Hishn, Dion projected. *Ease off now.*

But the wolf's projection was strong, and Dion was drowning with the sensation of lupine muscles, seeing foggily through two sets of eyes. Some part of her mind tried to draw back from that strength, pulling away from the gray bond. She took a deep breath and finally swallowed the eagerness that threatened her and the urge to spring away. How much of her mind was her own anymore? Had that puppet master been right? She wrapped her arms around herself and hugged herself till she quelled the violence. By the moons, she whispered to herself, was she more woman or wolf?

Your heart is gray as mine, said Hishn, baring her teeth at Dion. *You fight with the fangs of the pack.*

She tried to concentrate on her shaking hands as the violence worked its way out of the set of her teeth. *I run with the pack, Hishn,* she acknowledged. *But I've grown too used to your bloodlust. You swamp me with emotions that I must control.*

Violence is the way of life. You cannot hunt without it.

Dion's hands clenched. *Peace is also a way of life. And you can hunt from necessity, not violence, and still find your prey with your fangs.*

The wolf seemed to shrug. Gray thoughts blended with others until a mixed song filled Dion's head. *Violence, peace . . .* the gray wolf said. *Each defines the other.*

Dion shook her head, and Monteverdi misunderstood. "Dion—" He tried again to catch her arm.

"It's his blood," she forced herself to say. "Not mine—"

"Some of this is from you," he said stubbornly. He ignored her half-hearted gesture. Quickly, efficiently, he tugged a cloth from a pouch and wrapped it expertly around the light gash. By the time he had finished, Dion was pulling away, her mind again clear, her hands already reaching for one of the healer's kits he had brought. They moved quickly toward the other wounded Ariyens.

"Extra bandages are in here," he told her, jamming a bundle into her hands.

"Extra salve?"

"Couldn't get it. The lab workers are down with spring fever." He stopped and knelt by another wounded man.

A hard voice cut into their words. "Where's the Healer?"

"Over there—by the cliff," another voice responded.

Dion moved quickly through the figures who stood strangely isolated now, after the fight. There were bodies—some sprawled, some huddled, some like lumps of dough on the ground. One man half crawled toward another; one thrashed against the branches that, like hands, caught the last of his blood. A woman sat on her knees, trying to breathe, while another archer felt along her arm for the break they knew was there. But even the figures beside each other seemed somehow separated. Dion's chest seemed suddenly heavy, and the distance closed again over her eyes so that she wondered absently if there was something wrong with her bond to the wolves that she was having trouble with her vision. But she could see the tight expression on Tule's face clearly enough as the man beside him waved urgently for her attention.

It wasn't Tule who was hurt—or Royce, she realized in relief. Then she cursed under her breath as she saw the woman, Mjau, who lay behind one of the boulders.

Aranur was beside the archer, speaking steadily into the woman's wild, unfocused eyes, while Tule's single hand captured some of the guts that had spilled from the woman's split belly. The stain of fluids had washed across Mjau's jerkin, darkening it like paint; and the dawn mist was gathering on both the leather and the woman's gray-white hair like tiny stars. Mjau was barely conscious, but her hands cupped desperately around Tule's single hand, holding her own entrails.

Aranur didn't look up as he heard Dion shout for the intern. Instead, he kept his eyes on the archer. "Keep conscious, Mjau," he said firmly. "That's it. No—look at me, woman, not at your stupid belly. Don't close your eyes!" he said sharply. "Look at me. Look at me," he repeated urgently. He barely shifted as Dion dropped to the ground beside him. "Stay with me, Mjau. Keep your eyes open."

Quickly, Dion broke open the healer's kit. Gray Hishn sniffed Mjau's torso, then sat expectantly across the body from Dion. Her yellow eyes gleamed as she followed the wolfwalker's movements.

Dion looked up at the other three fighters who sheltered the downed archer from the falling mist. "Leave us," she said curtly, and they fell back without comment, their place taken by the intern. "Edan, wait," Dion called after them. "Bring a bota of water, and—" She tossed the short man a vial. "—mix this in it when you do." She turned back to Tule and Aranur. "Is this her only wound?"

The one-armed man didn't move his hand from the archer's guts. "There are two scratches on her leg, but both superficial. She took a clubbing blow to the upper back, but there was no blood on her jerkin, and she still moved fairly well after it."

Mjau still stared at the guts that pooled and slid in her hands. Dion thrust the tools at the intern and took the bota from the man who scrambled back over the boulders. "Mjau," she said to the archer as she poured the solution over her hands. "It's me, Dion. I'm with you."

The woman sucked in a ragged breath. Her lips moved. "Wolfwal—" Mjau's eyes rolled wildly. "Dio—"

"I hear you, Mjau." Beside her, Monteverdi grabbed the bota and, after rinsing his own hands, began to bathe the entrails. Swiftly, Dion began repacking the archer's guts. The white-haired woman burbled a scream, and only Aranur's hands on the woman's shoulders kept her down on the ground. Monteverdi froze at Mjau's hoarse cry, and Dion snapped. "Get the ointment on the rest of her skin."

He reached for one of the vials, and Dion elbowed his hand away. "Not that one. Not yet."

"Are you . . ." He glanced at Tule, and his question trailed off. But Dion answered tersely, "Yes."

In an instant, Monteverdi's manner changed. He put away two herb packets and reached for others. His hands, still gentle, seemed also suddenly eager. Tule watched the intern without speaking, but when Dion had set the last of Mjau's guts back in her belly and gestured for the one-armed man to leave, he merely sat back on his heels.

Dion, already pinching the edges of the wound together and clamping them in place, didn't glance up. "It would be easier for me if you stepped away, Tule."

The one-armed man nodded. "Easier," he agreed. But he didn't move. Aranur looked up and met the other man's eyes, and Tule shrugged. "Heard some interesting stories about the way Wolf-walker Dione works. Thought I'd see some of it for myself."

Dion snorted, her hands working quickly as she crimped the

clamps into semipermanent clasps. "It's window dressing, Tule. Remember?"

"*I* remember," he said meaningfully.

She looked up then. Aranur made to get up, but Dion made a small sign with her hands.

"Dion," Aranur said softly, for her ears alone. "It's too many people."

She spoke as quietly, projecting her words through the wolf so that Aranur heard her voice as a faint echo in the back of his head. *He's already seen the damage up close,* she whispered into his mind. *He'll be more danger with suspicions and questions than he will be with a few straight answers.*

"You don't know him."

"No." Her hands stilled for a moment. "But Hishn does."

Aranur eyed the wolf, then the wolfwalker. Hishn's yellow eyes gleamed. The Gray One's lips parted to show the white teeth against blood-pink gums, and Aranur shivered as a faint sense of howling drowned out Dion's voice in his mind. Abruptly, he nodded.

Tule had watched their exchange without comment, but now he added his own voice. "How can I help?"

Dion's answer was terse. "Be ready to take Aranur's place."

"And do what?"

"Do what he does. Keep your hands on my shoulders, your eyes shut, and be quiet. Don't fight me, no matter what happens. I will do the rest." She thrust the crimping tools aside. "Monteverdi, are you ready?" The intern nodded and placed his hands over hers so that he could follow her movements. "All right, then." She looked up. "Aranur—"

He placed his hands on Dion's shoulders.

"I'm going to need to go in fast," she said softly.

He nodded.

She looked down into the archer's still-wild, barely focused eyes. "Mjau, listen to me. Listen to my voice. I'm here. I won't leave you. Just close your eyes and trust me. You've known me many years, Mjau. You know what I can do."

She reached mentally to feel the presence of the wolf. *Hishn?*

Growling, the wolf's yellow eyes met Dion's violet gaze. *She is close to the moons. Her breath is weak; her blood too quick in her belly.*

Dion nodded and spread her hands over the wound, not quite touching the half-stitched gash. Beside her, Aranur's hands felt cold on her shoulder, but beneath his grip she felt a chill all her own. What she was doing was not of the Ancients and not of the human science that had brought the Ancients to this world. What she was doing was alien, from the heart of the Aiueven. Here, human and not-human met through the mind of the wolf. And the lupine memories of what had once been a gift of the aliens were the only guides she had.

What science the humans had managed to keep was theory without technology. Technology meant activity; visible advances beyond growing houses and roads were a guarantee of death from the watchful alien eyes. But Dion's teachers had been old lupine memories locked into the packsong, not the old technology. And the medical theory she had learned all her years was suddenly life in her hands.

For more than a decade, she had been experimenting and manipulating chemical patterns. She had learned to recognize the feel of different kinds of energy. Once she understood it, she began teaching others to push a patient's heart, to seal tissues, to melt and mend shards of bone. And through the years, she had grown in strength and sensitivity. She was so sensitive now that Mjau's blood flow was like ten thousand threads in her fingers. She gathered those threads, let herself feel where the pulse was strong or weak. Let herself reach out for the woman's heartbeat. Then she looked up into the yellow eyes of the wolf.

Take me in, Gray One.

Then run with me, Wolfwalker.

Between them, the thread of gray thought became sharp. Dion let her mind flow along that thread until her consciousness sank into the mind of the wolf. Odors filled her mind and nose; colors shifted in her eyes. The sickly sweet scent of blood and bile almost overwhelmed her. Automatically, she blocked both off.

Hishn growled in her head. Then her mind was caught in a sudden wrench. Her vision rushed inside, to the left, spun dizzyingly, and dropped. And then the wounded woman's body opened up before her.

Mjau's pulse became hers, the ragged breaths her own. She steadied herself against the shock of the archer's pain. She could feel every aspect of the woman's body, every inch of flesh and bone. The wolf blanketed her senses with Aranur's strength until their presence was a thick, gray, pain-killing fog—a shield against the agony that wracked the archer's torso. She could feel Monteverdi's presence too, but it was as an observer, not as part of that fog. And in Mjau, she felt the blood. Bile. Muscle contractions. Raw edges of tissue that had pulled apart.

Lower. Farther. Deeper. In. She sank her consciousness lightly into the slashed belly. Sound faded from her ears—now she felt, deep in her own bones, the throbbing heartbeat of another life. Bone, tissue, fluid, blood . . . all became one with her consciousness. She followed the flow of life through the wound as blood spurted from severed blood vessels and fluids spilled into the torso. Blood, bile, white cells, pollens . . . On OldEarth, the pollens stayed in the lungs; but here they could force their way into blood vessels before they were broken down. In a healthy person, the body could compensate; but the tiny holes they tore in Mjau's body would make this healing worse. Dion followed the blood, calling more white cells to her, breaking down pollens, and forcing the spills and leaks of bile into tiny, stable pockets. She touched vessels, drew edges together so that the blood flowed smoothly again. She bound the breaks tightly against the pressure that threatened to break through their new, unstrengthened walls. Then, as the vessels set, she began to reach farther to the severed threads of tissue. She touched, then bunched the intestinal tubes so that they nestled together again. The tiny threads of supporting tissue were woven back into place. Not strong enough yet to hold the woman's jumbled guts, the tiny threads lay flaccid against the movements from Mjau's quick and shallow breathing. But Dion pulled at the tissues, melting and melding them together until thin membranes formed to hold the shape of the organs. Piece by piece and strand by strand of tissue she wove and placed and secured the archer's body. Mjau's lungs breathed with hers; Dion's pulse pushed blood for both of them. And slowly, gradually, the archer's heartbeat strengthened enough to stand by itself again.

Dion's focus began to slow. Around her the gray fog thinned.

There was energy lost to the archer's body that had come dangerously out of hers. She weakened, and the wolf urged her out. Aranur's voice pushed behind the wolf, tugging at her brain. The strain pulled at her concentration like taffy. The pain-killing barrier thinned. She could feel the ache in her mind that signaled the start of deep weariness. Long before she lost herself to exhaustion, long before the fog could form hands to yank her from the body, she let herself be drawn away, drawn back. Her consciousness began to withdraw, feeling Mjau's body again as a layer of threads, not as something within herself. Her pulse split into two: hers and Mjau's; her breathing was once again her own.

She opened her eyes. For a moment she was disoriented. The fog swirled at the edges of her vision, and the chill she felt was like the end of strength. Then her sight cleared, and she realized that the fog was in the Gray One's mind, and the chill was merely the cold touch of moisture that had settled on her skin.

Monteverdi caught her glance. "Is it enough?"

She nodded.

Aranur absently chafed Dion's hands, checking on their temperature. The wolfwalker's tunic was damp with dew, mud, and blood, and her hands were colder than they had been before. "All right?" he asked softly.

She nodded again. Aranur got to his feet, giving Tule a significant look. "I'll get her a cloak. Watch her for a few minutes."

The one-armed man nodded. As Aranur left, Tule eyed Dion thoughtfully. To his gaze, the wolfwalker looked no different than before. But he had felt the energy she had drained from his own body. When, for a few minutes, his hand had taken the place of Aranur's, that pull had been sharp as a hook. And the howling that had echoed on the inside of his skull had been like an eerie song. He had heard the wolf packs singing late at night to the distant moons. But this had been different—it was as if he had been drawn into something that lay behind the howling. Wolf voices had spent their words in his head; wolf tones had caught at his mind. Wolf limbs had stretched along trails he didn't even know. For the first time since he had lost his right arm, he'd felt the weight of one hang from his shoulder. "Moons," he said under his breath.

Dion glanced up.

He shook his head silently. He had seen no change in the archer's body, but Mjau now breathed with more ease. The woman's heartbeat was stronger too—he could see the pulse in her pale neck—and when Mjau's eyes finally opened, they were pain-filled, but calm instead of wild with fear. The raw, crimped gash in the archer's belly being bandaged by the intern spoke of a dangerous wound. But the woman lay quietly on the ground, and it was the wolfwalker who shivered.

His voice was uneven, and he steadied it carefully. "Your jacket's back at the road; Aranur's bringing a cloak."

Dion nodded. "Any others this bad?" Her voice sounded flat to her ears, and she forced herself to put more energy in it, bringing it back to the steady, brisk tone she had used before.

"Not that I saw. One broken arm, one gashed leg that's already been bandaged. Scrapes and cuts. One dead."

She didn't ask who. She had seen the dead man with Monteverdi.

Tule watched her eyes, but the glaze he saw there was not exhaustion, he realized, but distance, as though the wolfwalker was pulling back and away. Her face seemed suddenly remote, and he felt as if he studied a mask. "Dione," he said sharply.

She looked at him, but her eyes were not focused.

He grabbed her arm. "Wolfwalker—"

She looked down, but he didn't remove his grip, and he saw the anger build in her eyes. The wolf, who had moved away, was suddenly back beside her, its yellow eyes gleaming into his.

"Don't," he said softly.

Dion just looked at him. Abruptly, her eyes focused.

The one-armed man released her. "Don't stop feeling," he said softly. "Don't remove yourself like that."

"You don't know what I feel, Tule."

"I can see it in your eyes."

"See what?" she asked sharply.

"That you've been too long on the trail, Wolfwalker Dione. Too long behind the steel."

"Aranur needs me with him."

"Then he can need someone else."

"He is my *mate*, Tule."

"That doesn't change what's happening to you." He nodded

at her. "I've seen that expression on others. You need to back off from all of this. You've carried enough life and death for your years. It's time to put it aside."

Dion stared at him, then almost laughed. "Put it aside? With the elders calling me to scout every other month? With the council adding healing jobs every other ninan? I stay out of more venges than I ride on, Tule, and I try to stay back from the action."

"But you don't really stay back, do you, Dione? If you were truly only a scout, you would mark the position then fall back to the road. But you stay to make sure Aranur—or someone else— doesn't need you. You carry steel to kill, not just heal. And each time you do kill, even if it is in defense or protection, it's still a piece of your soul. You only have so much in you, Dione. Don't throw away what's left."

She had listened to him, her face still. When she spoke, her voice was low. "Saying no to the elders when there is a need for my skills, when people could die without them . . . Could you live with yourself if you did that?"

He met her question frankly, and she was surprised to see the depth of pain that writhed within his gaze. His voice was equally soft. "What good are your skills if you kill yourself carrying such burdens? No one can ride forever, Dione. Not even the Gray Wolf of Randonnen. Step aside, Wolfwalker. Let someone else bear the weight. There has always been and will always be a need for people like you. Your turn will come again."

She looked at Hishn and let the gray voice wash over her mind. "You think it's the elders, the burdens, the fighting? It is and it isn't, Tule. The wolves pull me and make me as much as I make myself." Yellow eyes gleamed, and Dion felt Hishn's protectiveness surround and engulf her. "I don't know if *they* would let me go. Or if I can let go of them." She looked up at him then, and the shadows in their eyes seemed to meet and merge. "What do I do then, Tule—if neither Hishn nor I can let go?"

He touched her scarred hand with his single one. "Find something beyond yourself, something stronger than the wolves to pull you. And leave this if you can. You weren't made for this— weren't raised for this the way your mate was raised to lead and protect his people. There is joy in you, not just duty. But you'll kill that joy if you stay in the violence for the sake of duty alone."

She began to shake her head, but Tule cut her off. "Spend time with your mate and your sons, Dione. Stay away from the venges and swords. I know what I'm saying, Wolfwalker. I've lost an arm, but you—you've lost a part of your heart. Yours is the harder loss."

Aranur returned then, to wrap a heavy cloak around her shoulders and help her to her feet. His gray eyes looked deeply into hers. Then, unobtrusively, he pressed a packet of food into her hand. He was away again in a moment, striding toward a small knot of men and women, pausing only briefly to drop his hand reassuringly on Royce's shoulder where the young man knelt vomiting in the dirt.

Dion followed him with her eyes as she slowly unwrapped the meatroll. Her ears, still sensitive through the wolf, heard his quiet words clearly.

"Some people say you shouldn't look," Aranur murmured to the young man in the dirt. "I say look, and look well. Know what you've done to that man, and why. He attacked, he robbed, and he killed for greed. Now he won't do it again. Stay sick, stay angry if you must, but keep your guilt at bay."

Weakly, Royce nodded.

"And get yourself a different bow," he added. "Details like that stand out and catch the eye. They'll make you more of a target."

Aranur motioned sharply to another man, who was wiping his hands continually on his leggings as if to scrape off blood he could no longer see. "Ibriam." Aranur broke the man's abstraction. "Gather the loose weapons, then go with Tehena to get the dnu."

In the morning chill, Aranur's gray eyes were shadowed, and his dark hair lifted slightly with the wind as he gave his orders. The bodies of the raiders were carried to one side and thrown into a shallow depression. Branches and debris were tossed on top. The boughs gave a rude protection to the dead, but no words were spoken over that scant grave before it was lit on fire. Within the hour, the mountain men and women had cleaned the trail and packed their gear to move to a temporary camp. They spoke little as they lashed the body of their own dead man onto a funeral pyre. They built it hot so that the flames forced them back, away from the smell of flesh. It was Aranur who finally spoke the Words of the Dead, and his voice seemed to blend into the raging fire so that the words rose with the smoke to guide neHendar's soul.

Half of them rode carefully to the campsite with Mjau and the other wounded. Dion, Aranur, and five others stayed at the cliff to scout for the raiders' trail. But with the pass blocked up to the ridgetop, there was little else to see. By the time Dion confirmed that, the insect scavengers were already at work near the burial pyres, and clouds of daybats, attracted by the smoke, had gathered overhead.

Aranur joined Dion at her dnu. He gave her a hand checking the cinch while she packed the healing kits back into her saddle-bags. She caught his glance at her bandaged arm. "It's just a scratch," she said.

"Dacarr said you were limping."

"Scraped my ankle again. It's just bruised."

"I didn't see you until after we had taken most of them down."

"I know." She paused in what she was doing. "I was cut off."

His gaze sharpened. "Cut off—deliberately?"

She nodded.

"To keep you out of the action?"

"At first, that's what I thought."

"But then?"

She shook her head, more to herself than to him. "There was only one raider," she said. "But he was highly skilled—as good as you and Gamon. He had to be a master in Abis, if not in other arts also. Knives, swords, hand-to-hand . . . For a while, I thought I could hold my own until I got help, but it was he, not I, who controlled the fight."

"What do you mean?"

"He cut me off, Aranur. He pushed me back, chased me down into the draws so that you couldn't see me. Every time I tried to move, he was there before me. Every strike—he could see it coming. He was fast. Deceptive. Intent . . ."

"Intent?"

She nodded. "There was a moment when we simply faced each other. He looked at me as if I were a goal. As though he would go through whatever defense I had to get me."

"Dion . . ."

"He didn't want to kill me, Aranur. He wanted to capture me— take me alive. He wanted *me*, not just any Ariyen."

Aranur's voice, when he spoke, was low, so that only she could hear. "Are you sure?"

She glanced over her shoulder and kept her own voice quiet. "His blows were flat, not lunging."

"He knew who you were?"

"He spoke my name."

Aranur was silent for a moment. Then he nodded curtly. But his hand was gentle as he touched her cheek before he walked away.

Hishn nudged Dion in the thigh. *The raider's fang was slow; yours was sharp in his hip. He will nurse his wound for a long time.*

Dion didn't smile. "He might," she agreed softly. "But I think it will not keep him away from here for long. That look he had . . ."

His eyes are far away by now. And his blood feeds the largons now. You were fast enough to chase him off. He will not return for you.

But Dion shook her head slowly. "I wasn't fast enough, Gray One." She stared down at her hands. The tremble was no longer visible, but she could feel it in her bones. "I was so distant from everything I saw," she murmured. "I didn't even notice him until he was upon me. If I had been with my children, they would be dead by now."

You need to run more in the forest, away from your towns and cities. You are distracted with your humanness, when you should be like the wolf.

"No." Dion shook her head. She gripped the thick fur in her fingers, letting the greasy feel of it stick on her skin. "I think it's more than that." She rubbed her fingers together as if the touch of the fur would clean the blood from her hands. "Tule is right, Hishn. I'm getting lost in you. And I think I'm getting tired. I don't want to fight anymore. Every day seems filled with violence, and the times between the battles now are just dreams that confuse my life."

There are dreams and there are memories, corrected the gray wolf. *Which predator do you flee?*

Dion stared at the wolf. "Sometimes I think you're too much in my mind."

It is part of the gift of your Ancients. Do you want distance now or more dreams?

"I don't know." Dion looked back down at her hands. "All I know is that I don't want my boys growing up knowing only steel. I want them to understand compassion, not just justice—to hear music, not just sound. I want them to learn the forest as I did. I want to see the joy in their eyes when they play with your pups and hear the packsong in your mind."

They are ours, as you are, Hishn returned. *I teach them the packsong with my own cubs.*

Dion nodded at her image. "They're like when I was younger—when I was first learning your voice. They're like a bridge to me, between the gray and human worlds. Sometimes . . ." Her voice trailed off. "Sometimes I think they are the only thing that holds me to my humans."

You are wolfwalker. Neither human nor wolf. There is no need to be only one.

There was a faint taint of an alien image to Hishn's thoughts, and Dion gave the wolf a twisted smile. "Like Aiueven—neither familiar nor foreign?"

The bright ones who flew in our minds long ago—they are still among us. Your strength makes you close to them.

It wasn't what Dion expected as a response, and she eyed the wolf, suddenly curious. "What do you mean?"

The bright ones. They taught the wolfwalkers to speak, and you are a wolfwalker now. Your voice, their voices can sing together.

She bit her lip. She had heard the alien voices in the echoes of the packsong memories, but she had never thought beyond that. That the alien birdmen had taught the colonists to manipulate energy—that was legend. That wolfwalkers still developed themselves in those alien Ancient patterns, that she had not known. "Do you realize what you're saying?"

The wolf seemed to shrug. *You wanted dreams. I sing an old memory.*

Slowly, she rubbed her temple. Aliens and wolves. Too close, still, after all this time. And Aranur wanting to circumvent the one while she wanted to keep to the other.

*You dream of distance, Wolfwalker, yet you cling to the hunt.
You long for the pack, yet you hold your own cubs away from us.*
The image of her two younger sons was clear, and Hishn's
mental link to them, a thin gray thread, was twined deeply with
the thick bond to Dion. *What wolfsong do you teach them,
Wolfwalker? What dreams do you want for your cubs?*

Dion stared deeply into the yellow eyes. Her answer was
simple but full of longing, and the howl in her mind was her
own. "I want my sons to dream of the stars, Hishn—as the
Ancients did. Not lust after steel as we must."

The wolf didn't blink. *The steel of your fang is your heartbeat. Without it, you would be worlag pickings.*

"Only if the raids continue."

Hishn whuffed against her thigh. *Raiders can be hunted.*

"Yes," Dion returned. "But I don't want the blood on my
hands anymore."

Hishn gripped her hand in white, gleaming teeth, and though
the pain of that grip made her shiver, Dion didn't move. Instead,
she reveled in the bright pain as if it were the path to her release.
No healing, no fighting—nothing but existence in fundamental
simplicity. That was what she wanted. Too much weight in the
steel she carried, was that what Tule had said? She touched the
healer's circlet. He had it only half right: Of steel and silver,
silver was the heavier.

Wolfwalker, Hishn growled. The image that Hishn projected
was instantaneous. Freedom, bursting green growth, and speed.
The feel of wrestling with half-grown cubs. The packsong that
swelled deafened Dion so that her fists shot up to cover her ears.
And then the packsong faded, and Dion was staring again at the
burial pyre. "And now the steel is fed again," she whispered to
herself. "But when shall the silver shine?" She began to tremble.

Wolfwalker.

Dion looked down. "Gray One," she whispered. She knelt and
buried her face in the wolf's fur as if she could shut out the
vision of her own memories. Fear of the raiders, of herself, even
of the wolves who seemed more and more in her mind, warred
with anger that she should be sent out so often to face herself and
that which would destroy her. But what frightened her most was
that the anger burned more fiercely than that frigid touch of fear.

IV

What dreams die that cannot be recovered?
What wolf howls that cannot be heard?
What weight shifts and does not break its bearer?
  How long can you live?

—Fourth Riddle of the Ages

It took the rest of the day to reach Dion's home, what with stopping in almost every village between Red Wolf Road and her own hometown to drop off rider after rider. Only Tule and Royce went back south to Kitman; the other riders continued north.

North . . . Dion scowled as they came in sight of Tetgore. She felt as if she were always riding north. Northeast from the Black Gullies to Ontai, north by northeast to Kitman, north from Kitman to the cliffs, and north again to home.

Hishn didn't wait for Dion along the way. Instead, the Gray One loped on ahead, eager to reach her own wolf pack where her own mate, Gray Yoshi, ran the hills. Dion watched the wolf go with a faint smile.

Aranur caught her expression. "She's escaped again, huh?"

"No meetings for her," Dion agreed. "She's more interested in wrestling with her own kind than in waiting with me while you analyze this venge."

"As are you," Aranur said shrewdly.

She shrugged.

"You no longer want to be here," he stated more than questioned.

She was silent for a moment. Finally, she said, "I need to get back to Kitman within the next couple of days or that ringrunner will lose the sight of both eyes, not just the sight of one. I need to check in with Jobe at the labs to find out about his new cultures. If they are viable, we'll have enough medicine for all of

74

northern Ariye for three months. And I need to start the nerve repair on little Wentcscho's leg."

"All that piled up during a single scouting mission?"

"All that. There is no break, Aranur. There's just another 'and.' "

"You don't have to be a part of every 'and' there is."

"There are things that need to be done, Aranur. You know that as well as anyone else. Problems to solve. Damage to fix. It's just that . . ."

"You're tired of being part of the solution. You want someone to care for you instead of you always caring for others."

"Yes." Her voice was low as she admitted it. Her dnu snorted as they came abreast of one of the outer hub stables, and it automatically slowed. She urged it on. They would not dismount till they reached the central hub in this town, where they would have to speak with the Lloroi, who was one of Aranur's uncles. Suddenly depressed, Dion stared at the two- and three-story houses they passed. In their clusters of six and eight, the homes looked comfortable and safe. Aranur had helped build some of those structures last fall, when one of these hubs collapsed. Some of those lintels had been grown by her own son Tomi, who was now one of the top door-men in Ariye. These people were friends with whom she had ridden and fought, lived and killed, sung and worshipped and danced. And she wanted to escape them. To run from them as if they, themselves, were raiders after her soul.

"It sounds terrible, doesn't it?" she said, her voice low. "Selfish and ungrateful."

"Yes," he agreed simply.

"Am I wrong?"

"To feel as you do? Or to act as you want to?"

She didn't answer. Under the rootroad arbor, she could see the Lloroi's home in the distance. Aranur's family crest came from that house; his blood was in that line of leadership. It was one of the oldest, tallest houses in the county. Over centuries, new growth had been grafted onto old so that alcoves and window arches rose up like hope out of history.

Dion raised her eyes toward the peaks she could just glimpse through the trees. Her own family came from another county, across the desert, across the kilometers, in the mountains of Randonnen. The villages there were smaller, the people seemed closer. The goal of recovering the Ancients' ways was blended into each person's life so that no one family, no single elder or Lloroi, carried the burden of the future. Her people were not her children to be cared for, but friends with whom she simply shared part of herself.

How could he understand that, she thought, when he was raised to lead, not live with, this county? He looked at these people as his children. Like a brood hen, he was responsible for them all, yet the weight of that didn't bother him. And since she had Promised with Aranur, they looked at her the same way. Like a prize they had acquired when Aranur mated. She had never been prepared to carry the weight of so many lives. She had never studied the history they expected her to know; she didn't speak like an elder; she couldn't meet their demands. She didn't have the vision for the future that Aranur did—that everyone in his family did—and that his county expected of him. She looked down at her hands. They were trembling again, and she clenched them tight.

"Dion?" Aranur's voice was soft, almost lost in the rhythm of the hooves.

She looked up. His strong face seemed unwearied, as if the ride had been ten minutes, not ten hours long. She felt like a weed beside him—like strength without substance. Push too hard and the strength is gone, and all that is left is hollow.

"I . . . I can't do this anymore," she said to him at last.

"So stop being available," he said abruptly, harshly.

She stared at him. His outburst had been like an attack. But his steely gray eyes did not look away. "What did you say?" she faltered.

His face didn't change expression. "Stop letting people put their troubles on your shoulders. If you don't want the burden, don't accept it as readily as you always do." He almost glared at her. "I can't keep you from your job—moons above know that I've tried it. There's only one person who can relieve you from your burdens, who can give you a vision of something other than the weight of the work you do each day. That person is yourself."

Dion's cheeks paled. He was furious—as furious as she had ever seen him. His voice had bitten out the words as if he were biting at her. "This has been ... building up in you for a long time," she said finally.

He nodded curtly as they reined in at the elders' hall. "It has been building up since I met you."

"I'm sorry," she whispered.

"Sorry doesn't change your habits, Dion. You have to do more than apologize if you want anything more out of life."

She stared down at her hands and fingered the leather of the reins.

He dismounted, then looked at her, his voice quiet. "You get so caught up in the here and now—in what you think needs fixing this minute. But the world can't be fixed in a single life-time. Or by any single person. You have to look ahead, to choose what you fix today so that you build tomorrow stronger."

"I know that," she said sharply as she slid from her dnu.

"But you don't live that," he cut back in. "Moonworms, Dion. You always have a choice: You can spend your life all at once, or you can spread yourself out over time. Sometimes I think the wolves fill your mind with history more than vision—you don't even see the future, just a past so long that you feel you don't want it to go on any longer."

She touched her sternum, where two gemstones had been studded into her bone. Aranur stepped forward and covered her hand with his, his long fingers touching the bumps made by the gems. "We're bonded, Dion, as tightly as stone to the mountain. That's what these studs represent. One for the Waiting Year we lived with each other, and one for the Promise itself. You try to shoulder your burdens alone, but we are two together." His gray eyes were intense as a wolf's, and she stared deeply into his expression. His voice was soft. "No matter what you see through the eyes of the wolves, you have your own eyes too. Your future is with me, not just them. In the present, not just the past." He pulled her hand to his own sternum so she could feel the two matching studs there. "Remember me, Dion, not just the packsong you hear through the minds of the wolves. You can seek the future through the past, but you can live only in the present. Choose that present—choose your direction—well. There are futures you can barely even imagine just waiting to be discovered." He looked at her for a moment more, then went into the council chambers.

Dion remained silent while Aranur gave his report to the elders. The circle of faces listened intently, asked their questions, listened to Aranur's answers, then went into their usual argument. Dion and Aranur escaped. They were met outside by a gray-haired man and a lanky, hard-faced woman.

The older man, his grizzled beard trimmed short as a fingernail, studied Dion as she moved to her dnu. "It was bad?" he asked.

"Bad enough, Gamon," she returned.

Aranur met his uncle's gaze. "Mjau took a deep cut in the gut, but Dion got to her in time. Mjau will live, though she won't be up to riding or walking anytime soon. NeHendar was killed."

"Moonwormed raiders," the older man muttered.

Absently, Dion rubbed her elbow before mounting, as though the joint still rang with the force of the raider's blows. Aranur caught the movement and frowned at her. "There was something else," he said to Gamon and the lanky woman. "One of the raiders cut Dion off from the venge."

"Cut her off?" Tehena's voice was sharp.

"It was deliberate," Aranur said, answering the unspoken question. "And the raider trying to take her knew her name."

The grizzled man eyed Dion thoughtfully. "You said 'take her,' not 'kill her.' "

Aranur nodded.

Dion met the older man's frown with a steady gaze. "He was stronger than I, more skilled, and more focused." She shrugged at Aranur's suddenly hard look. "He . . . startled me enough that I made mistakes. He had two chances to kill me because of it, but his blows were disabling, not mortal. Even when he had me against the ground, he tried to hit me with the hilt of his sword, not the blade. When he couldn't completely disarm me, and when Hishn went after him, he dropped me like a hot coal. By then our venge was getting the upper hand of the raiders, and he fled. He blocked the pass route behind him."

"But he didn't try to kill you on his way out?"

"Didn't throw a blow."

Gamon touched her shoulder, rubbing it absently, and Dion looked from the gray-haired man to her mate, caught by their similarities. Both were tall, lean, straight-haired, and strong-boned. Aranur was simply a taller, younger copy of Gamon. They had the same exacting eyes, which could turn to ice in a second, but Gamon's were more often filled with wisdom where Aranur's gaze was driving. She loved the older man deeply, not just because he was Aranur's uncle but because he listened more than anyone else to what she couldn't say.

Now Gamon ran his hand through his hair. "So did he want you as a slave or hostage?"

She shook her head. "The raiders tried before to use wolf-walkers against the counties, and that mobilized us like the threat of plague. They wouldn't try that again. It would have to be as a slave or healer that they wanted me—but I'm not sure that really makes sense either. I'm not so valuable that a raider would risk what this one did simply to take a slave. And there are dozens of healers that would be easier to get at."

Thoughtfully, Tehena fingered her stringy hair, twisting it one way, then the other. "You've made a lot of enemies, Dion. Maybe it's simple revenge."

Aranur shook his head. "I can't see that. Most of Dion's enemies are dead."

"We've been rather . . . thorough," the lean woman agreed.

He scowled at her. "No simple raider would want revenge against Dion so badly that he would plan a series of raids into Ariye on the chance that he might catch her up in them."

"What about revenge against you?"

"We're talking about Dion."

"Aye," Tehena said meaningfully. He gave her a sharp look, and the woman shrugged. "Using her to get to you is not an original idea," Tehena added. "The question is whether they have a goal in mind, or are just working the spur of the moment."

Dion eyed first one, then the other. "Raiders are hardly more than cutthroats and slavers. They've not got the organization to plan so far ahead or the cohesiveness to stick together on a long-term plan."

"They've had charismatic leaders before," the other woman returned flatly.

"Aye," Gamon put in. "But in every case, they were political leaders who used the raiders as a disorganized army. They weren't raiders themselves. And there hasn't even been anyone trying that since Longear died." He paused. "Well," he amended, "that's not quite true. But the two who did try that were dead the day they made their bid for power. The raiders themselves saw to that."

Tehena shook her head. "I wasn't thinking of a political leader from the outside using the raiders, but one from within the raider ranks themselves. They've got their own hierarchy. Who's to say that they can't grow their own leaders in time?"

The four looked at each other soberly. Gamon cleared his throat and indicated with his chin the Lloroi's house, in which the elders still met. "Did you tell them about Dion?"

"No." Aranur ran his hand through his own black hair in a gesture identical to Gamon's. "I don't want them to know."

"If Dion's in danger . . ."

He sighed. "The raiders have made two attempts to take me also, Gamon."

Dion stared at her mate. Gamon's eyes narrowed. "You never said anything about that to us," the older man said sharply.

Tehena shrugged. "We didn't know it was anything more than a fluke. Not, at least, until this happened to Dion."

Dion rounded on the other woman. "You knew about them and Aranur? And you never told me?"

Aranur caught her arm. He nodded at the Lloroi's house. "Keep it down, Dion. This isn't something my uncle—my other uncle—should know."

"Why not?" she demanded hotly.

"What do you think the elders would do to you if they thought you were raider bait? Neither they nor the Lloroi would allow you to take such risks, whether or not you would take them yourself. I have to live with the fact that the one thing in your life that gives you a break from everything else is running with the wolves. But I know you like myself. They think of you differently. You're the Gray Wolf of Randonnen to them. The Heart of Ariye. Their own wolfwalker and scout and healer. You think they would give you any more scouting assignments if they knew about today? Let you run around in the wilderness as you're used to doing now?"

Her eyes sparked with violet fire. "Your uncle may be Lloroi, but he has no right to keep me away from Hishn—"

"No," he agreed. "But he can make sure that you have so much to do here that you cannot get away. The elders could easily find some reason to require you to stay."

Tehena nodded. "Mjau and her gut wound. That blind ring-runner in Kitman. Whoever else they dig up for you to tend. We have enough moonwormed raids to deal with that I'm sure they can keep you busy."

Dion stared at them mutely.

"You're off duty for the half month?" Gamon asked her finally.

"For four ninans," she answered. "Until the boys go back to school."

He raised his gray eyebrows. "I thought you were being reassigned in two ninans."

"Two ninans?"

"They've got a tricky scouting job coming up in the northwest. If you can't go, neFored will have to take neCeltir, and he's not half as good at leading that cliff trail as you are. But, if you're off duty . . ." Gamon shrugged.

Dion's jaw tightened almost imperceptibly. "Aranur asked for the time so that I could stay home with the boys while they were out of school."

Gamon touched her arm. "I'm not complaining, Dion. I'm just surprised. You don't usually get so much time off when the raiders are getting active." He glanced meaningfully at his nephew. "Let me know if you want to come over for a game of stars and moons then," he said. "I'm getting tired of beating Tehena."

The other woman snorted. "I only let him win because he outranks me."

Gamon shrugged. "A win by the moons is as sweet." The two strode off.

Dion was left to stare after them. Aranur looked at her soberly. "You earned the break, Dion. Gamon knows that."

"I earned it," she agreed slowly, "but I can't have it, can I? Knowing that the elders are already wanting me to go out again even when they give me time off—that puts the pressure there already. How can I enjoy these ninans when I know that, as I take time with my boys—and with you—someone else is at risk by my absence?"

"You think you're the only one who should take risks?"

"You know I don't think that," she retorted.

"Do you want to quit?"

"No," she returned sharply. Too sharply, she realized. Her voice already betrayed her. She took a breath. "I want our sons to learn duty and discipline, and the only way I know to teach them that is by example. But how can I teach them if I'm not where they can see me?"

"They understand your duties, Dion."

"Do they? You see them more than I do. You're their father; I barely feel like an aunt. What kind of example do I set?" She looked up then, meeting his gray gaze with eyes filled with self-loathing. "I don't know how to nurture them. I never had a mother from whom to learn mothering. I had a father and a twin brother and a roughhouse life in the mountains. I wasn't prepared for motherhood, but to run and explore like a wilding. I'm the perfect wolfwalker, but even with Hishn's four litters of pups I haven't learned how to nurture my own except as a distant healer. I am a mother, yet I have no mothering to give to my sons. What do they get from me?"

"It's the way you were raised, Dion—"

"Aye," she threw it back. "I was raised to act and yet think, to fight and to heal, to run trail yet need my home, to want nurturing but be too independent to accept it. Everything I do—everything I am is dichotomy. What balance can my boys get from me when I cannot balance myself?"

He pulled her close. She resisted for an instant, then went almost hungrily, violently into his arms. He crushed her to him. Then, lightly, he stroked her hair. "You are yourself, Dion. That's all they need from you."

Dion shook her head, but Aranur pressed her closer. The strength of his arms sunk like teeth into her body, and she pressed herself against him as if he were all that she sought. Deep in her mind, Hishn howled. In her head, Dion snarled with the Gray One until her mind was blank and echoing with the packsong.

Her need built like waves, smothering Aranur's words until all she could feel were his arms like steel bands.

They didn't speak as they rode out of town, though Aranur frowned as he studied her. She was changing, he realized—her joy was being squeezed away. Some of it was disappointment in herself; but some of it was from him. She was trying to please him, to be what the county expected her to be as a weapons master's mate. And she was taking risks with the raiders because she saw it as her duty. He wondered if what she needed wasn't to mother the boys, but a mother to nurture herself.

The twisted roads skirted the fields of grains and new tubers. In the flatter part of the county the towns were built in hubs, with the houses around the commons for livestock. Here, where the rising mountains folded the earth into ridges, the layout of the towns seemed haphazard. Contour farming gave the county the look of an Ancient painting: Lush lines of rootroad trees shifted the flat, striped texture of the fields to a doubly arching canopy, and the dirty white lines of the roads themselves brought stark delineation.

Their own home was in a small cluster of four houses, halfway up the hill that overlooked the town. The wild growth that reached almost to the sides of their home hid the excavations of Gray Hishn and her packmates so that the ground appeared smooth, not pitted and sunken as it really was. By the time Dion and Aranur rode up the narrow track that led to the stable, their two boys had climbed down from the watch point and were running across the commons. Suddenly, Dion found her eyes blurring. She had to turn away from Aranur to get a grip on her emotions.

But he caught her arm. "Dion?"

She took a breath and shook him off. "It's nothing. I'm fine."

"Are you?" he asked steadily.

She took another breath. He was right. Tule was right. She needed to back away. She watched him almost blankly as she realized that even she herself believed it. "I'd like . . ." She paused. "I'd like to take the boys with me back to Kitman tomorrow—if the skies are clear of lepa."

Aranur studied the way she stood, still half poised as if ready to leap back on her dnu—or as if she had not even stopped running trail. "What about Still Meadow? The boys have been on Gamon's case daily for a hint that he would take them out there."

Her smile was crooked, twisted by bitterness at the thought that her boys would beg Aranur's uncle for the trip she should have been there to give them. "I'll take them across the grassland on the way back—as long as it's not still too boggy. Still Meadow is a stone's throw from Kitman."

His lips firmed as he read the set of her expression. "You're going to finish up with that ringrunner yourself, aren't you?"

She nodded, watching the boys scramble through the gates. "Her eyesight depends on it. I told her I'd come back."

He studied her. "Dion, the raiders . . . I won't be able to come along this time."

"You know they never strike on the main roads. And even if they came back for a second attack, they couldn't reach as far as Kitman with all the crews on the roads."

He watched the boys race toward the commons fence. "And the boys?"

"Do you really think there is danger?"

"No. But it still bothers me."

She touched his arm. "It's the thought of the raiders' intent that bothers you, not the reality of their position."

He sighed. "I think you know me too well. Still Meadow is as safe as anywhere else," he agreed.

"The boys could use the time in the woods. They've almost forgotten what it's like to simply run trail for the fun of it."

"Like you?"

She looked up. A faint smile touched her face. "Like me."

"Momma!" Olarun cried as he vaulted the commons fence. "Look at me!" He sprinted toward his parents.

"Look at me, Momma!" Danton echoed. The smaller boy dove between the rails, scraping one shoulder and half twisting as his forward motion was arrested. He ended up in a tumbled pile of lemon grass. He sat up, his lower lip trembling, and Dion thrust the reins in Aranur's hands and sprinted to his side. But by the time she got there, he was standing, shoulders back, pretending not to feel it, and she was left to hug Olarun awkwardly while respecting Danton's control.

Aranur watched them drag Dion off to show her their textile patterns. He wondered later, as he sat at the kitchen table and watched her with the boys, if she knew how much they needed her. Just as she pushed herself to please him, they vied for her approval: the fabric patterns both boys shoved in her hands for her perusal; the look on Olarun's face when she praised the bandaging he had done on the barn cat's open puncture; the way Danton tried to string his own bow to show Dion that he could . . . Aranur found himself wondering if Dion was right— if she had done enough for the elders. The more she did for them, the more ingrained her duty to them became, until it over-shadowed everything else. Even now, as she showed their freckled younger son how to feather an arrow, her eyes were half focused. He knew that Hishn was in her mind, and that she automatically read the patterns of human movement across the hills near their home. But if she simply ran trail without purpose, without scout-ing, just to enjoy the forest, would that be enough?

Then he looked past his mate and his children to the weapons on his wall. His jaw tightened again, and he had to force himself to relax and smile as Danton aimed an imaginary arrow. If raiders were watching his mate—and him again—there could be no complacency between them. This county was wide open, and the raiders were too widespread. As long as Dion ran trail alone, she had to protect herself. He didn't worry about the boys. A mother was the fiercest predator a man could ever face—and Dion had the strength of the wolves in her arms. No one would hurt their boys. As for Dion . . . He knew, watching her, that no matter how long she lived within his boundaries, he couldn't keep her from the forests, from the Gray Ones who had locked themselves into her mind, or from the mountains that were part of her soul. Yet if the mountains, the forests, the wolves were not enough for her, what could give her the strength she needed to face the burdens she bore?

He glanced involuntarily toward the door, where he could hear the faint scuffling on the porch. Hishn had returned and was finding a place to nap. He glanced around his home, with its arched windows and smooth, polished root floor. It had been graciously grown, with large, open rooms and mountain views from the windows, but few visitors stayed here who weren't family. It wasn't Dion who drove them away, he knew, but Hishn who made people nervous. The wolf had fought for Dion before, when Dion's bond was new, and Dion had not understood how it would affect the wolf. Because of that, Hishn had lost some of her instinctive wariness of men. More than once the creature had turned against those with whom Dion simply argued. Aranur's lips twisted in an ironic smile: His mate was opinionated enough that when she argued, she did it passionately, and the wolves responded to nothing if not to strong emotions. Had the Gray One been male, it would have been the same, but in a different way—the protectiveness and jealousy would have turned to territoriality. As it was, no matter how large their home, there was room only for Hishn, her cubs and mate, and Dion's family with them.

Dion turned then and smiled at him, and automatically, his expression lightened. She raised her eyebrows, and he shrugged. They would talk later. They always did, when the moons were riding the sky. But the sound of the wolf on his porch made him wonder, with the elders prodding and duty pulling, how long he could keep Dion there.

* * *

Aranur had already left for town by the time both boys were ready to ride, so after saying good-bye to her older, adopted son, Tomi, and the young woman to whom he had Promised, Dion had the two younger boys to herself.

Once the three had skirted the town and made it to the southern track, Danton, irrepressible as a pup, began egging his dnu to jump this little bump or race ahead when Dion wasn't looking. Hishn, trotting just ahead of the boy's dnu, took it upon herself to discipline the youngest boy, and Dion had to hide her smile as Danton received his third warning. Hishn had the patience of a worlag, but her teeth were also just as sharp. Danton had not yet learned not to push the Gray One's tolerance, but he was growing older, and Hishn was ready to wean the boy of his antics.

Olarun, however, was a different matter. Dion smiled at her older son with pride. He was already skilled enough in the woods to have been allowed to run trail by himself, and he was eager to learn, asking question after question. If she hadn't been so amused by Danton's antics, she could have showed Olarun twice as much, but as it was the boys competed with each other as if they were in a fighting ring. By the time they reached the intermediate town of Sharbrere, they were picking at each other mercilessly.

"You have your choice," Dion told them firmly. "Either settle down and behave, or I'll leave you here in Sharbrere till tomorrow morning. I can't have you acting this way in the clinic." Olarun flushed, and Dion turned to her saddlebag to dig out their lunch while they decided.

Danton poked his brother in the side. "It's all your fault," he whispered.

"Is not," Olarun hissed. He shoved Danton away.

But the younger boy tripped over a stone, falling on his rump. He was up again in an instant—not to pretend nothing happened, but to hit Olarun in the stomach. Dion whirled.

"Danton! Olarun!" she snapped.

Hishn had moved away to lie down in the shade of the fence around the commons where they had stopped, and now she flicked her ears. *They have your temper, Wolfwalker.*

"Don't I know it," Dion muttered. She looked from one to the other. Both boys were tousled, their clothes rumpled and dirty. She had a sudden vision of herself and her brother in front of her father's smithy. She and Rhom had fought like this—when they wanted their father's attention.

"It's another hour to Kitman," she said quietly. "I must do some healing there, and I don't think either of you is really interested in waiting for me at the clinic." Olarun shot Danton a venomous look, and Dion sighed. "Perhaps you two should stay here tonight, with Nior. Then we'll have the next three days all to ourselves. You won't have to worry about getting lost among the patients or—" She shot them a stern look. "—getting into trouble while I'm working. When I'm done there, I'll come right back, and we can be together."

"Just you and us?" Olarun ventured. "No escorts or scouting? No ringrunners or messengers who will take you away?"

There had been an unconscious longing in Olarun's voice,

and Dion forced her voice to be steady. "Not this time. It's just you and I, boys."

Danton eyed her from beneath long lashes. "Promise?"

"Promise," she assured them. Pray the moons there would be no emergencies, she added, and that the ringrunners could not find them. She shook herself. There were other healers; other scouts. Her boys had to come first sometime.

She left Olarun and Danton in Sharbrere with some friends the boys had known since birth. When she rode out again, promising to meet them at the crossroads to Still Meadow, they were happily arguing over who would be the leader in the game of wolves and raiders.

Dion made it to Kitman with plenty of time to tend the ringrunner's eye. It had been kept raw as she had ordered, and within an hour, she was able to repair the wound enough so that it would heal the rest of the way on its own with standard treatment from the local healer.

Dion felt a strange pang as she left the young ringrunner's room. The loss, she knew, was artificial. She didn't really know Merai. But part of her rebelled at that thought. It didn't matter that she would not see the runner again; Merai was now part of her life. She could feel Merai's will as if it were tangible, and the young woman's determination was strong as a wolf—like Aranur when he was focused, or Gamon when he worked toward a goal.

"Why did you choose to ride the black road?" she had asked the ringrunner as she worked.

"I was fast," Merai had answered. "And I ride well."

But Dion had caught her hesitation. "And something else?" she prompted.

The ringrunner shrugged. "And . . ." She seemed reluctant, but her voice was steady as she said, "And I wanted to be like you."

Something clenched Dion's gut. Was she also to blame for this ringrunner's blindness? "Like me?" she managed to ask.

"You're the Heart of Ariye," Merai answered.

"That's just a story, Merai."

"They say you Called the wolves once, back before the Dog-

Pocket War, and that the Gray Ones Answered. They say it's why there are so many wolves now in Ariye."

"I suppose that's true enough." Dion's memory flashed back to an image of a tall, thin man who clutched her arms as she gripped his, while their minds paired in the Call. Sobovi, who died later on the Slot, a hundred meters from safety . . .

"And they say you can trail like a ghost . . ."

Dion shook herself out of her memories. "That," she smiled faintly, "is exaggeration. I slip up as often as anyone else. The storytellers just don't like to admit it—makes the stories seem mundane."

Merai thought about that for a moment. "I heard neRittol telling some boys about Pacceli's and my ride, and he never mentioned that the whole way back I was so scared that every breath I took felt like a scream."

Dion began rebandaging her eye. "That sounds about right. A good storyteller lets you feel as if you could do everything the hero did and still feel everything you would normally feel. Which means, of course, that they always tell the story right, but they never quite tell the truth."

Merai gave Dion a twisted smile. With her lips only half healed, the scabs stretched in a macabre expression. "It was a story neRittol told that made me want to be like you, Wolfwalker. I remember it from when I started training to ride the black road, and I had to choose to work the town towers or learn the longer night-relay shifts. I was scared of the night sounds at first, and neRittol found out about it. So he told me how you came to Ariye."

Dion raised her eyebrows. "And what are they saying about that now?"

Merai grinned wider, then winced as her lip split. "They say that Aranur stole you from Randonnen because he realized you were a moonmaid. And that you brought the wolves to Ariye to keep you company, and that they howl at night because you are lonely to return to the moons. I was never afraid of the wolf sounds again," she added. " 'The moons are Dione's home,' neRittol told me. 'As they will again be ours. She is our guide to the stars.' And I've wanted to be like you ever since."

Dion had no answer for that.

She didn't linger once she had healed the girl's eye. Merai's words disturbed her as much as the ringrunner's blind faith that she could heal that damaged eye. And, difficult as it was to hide the internal healing from the eyes of nurses and others, it was even more difficult to answer a patient's questions without revealing more of what she had done. The healing art of the Ancients, taught to them by Aiueven, was considered something lost with the domes. The few times wolfwalkers had tried Ovousibas since the plague, their wolves had died in fevers. Whatever trick the Ancients had used to keep their wolves alive was thought to have died with them in the plague.

When, thirteen years ago, Dion had tried the healing technique, Hishn should also have died. But the wolves Dion had Called to show her how to use Ovousibas also showed her a different way of using the bond—an Ancient way, not the way of healing described by the stories that had resulted in so many wolf deaths. So when Dion healed others, the focusing of internal energy burned only against her mind—like light through a lens— leaving the Gray Ones untouched by death. And the wolves acted as a buffer for her—against the patient's pain—so that Dion could aim the energy where it needed to go, healing the body instead of burning her mind.

She put her thoughts aside when she stopped by to see Merai's healer before she rode back out of Kitman. He was in the clinic still, laid up with spring fever.

Brye frowned when she entered his quarantine room, but she simply shrugged. "Wolfwalkers don't get sick," she returned in answer to his unspoken question.

He scowled at her, but she knew it was more because she was able to get around than because he didn't want company. "Merai?" he asked without preamble.

"As well as can be expected. She'll lose the one eye, but the other should heal."

"Pacceli?"

"Recovering." Dion smiled faintly. "But you knew that already."

"You blame me for asking?"

"Not with you stuck in this bed."

He harrumphed. "I heard you brought your boys with you. Planning on sticking around this time?"

"Uh-uh," she shook her head. "And I left them in Sharbrere for the night. They'd have done nothing but fight if they'd come here with me, and they can stay with friends there. Besides, I'm heading back tonight, so you can't stick me with any more healing."

He ignored the jibe, frowning at her other words. "It's still spring, Dion. Riding the black road isn't the safest way to travel. I'm sure you heard what happened to Merai and Pacceli." He gave her a deliberate look.

She made a face at him. "I'm going only halfway, and I have a bit of an advantage over ringrunners, Brye. There's a wolf pack gathering in Moshok Valley. I'll spend the night with them. I'll meet my boys at the crossroads to Still Meadow well into the daylight."

He picked irritably at the covers of his bed. "Checking the wild plantings?"

She nodded, hiding her smile. "I have four ninans, and I'm making the most of them. I'm taking the boys back through the woods with me so that they can brush up on some plant identification. Tomi—my other son—is great at teaching the boys textiles—and I think he will start them on lintel design soon—but he was never much interested in wilderness skills." She smiled faintly. "I had originally hoped you'd be up and around by now so that you could come with us—you always had more patience in teaching than I—but I promised the boys it would be just me."

Brye flopped back on his pillows. "Hells, Dion. I'd drink worlag piss if I thought it would get me out of this place sooner. Don't know how the patients stand it."

"Because you'd kill them if they didn't," Dion returned easily.

The brown-haired man grinned. "True. True. But then, that's the privilege of a healer—to control life and death. Speaking of privileges, and of your impending flight to the forest, how do the skies look? Still clear enough to spit in?"

"Uh-huh."

He studied her face. "What's the matter? You don't like the lack of menace in our fair Ariyen skies? I've always thought of you Randonnens as daredevils—and you especially, Dion—but I never figured you for being one to seek out danger and embrace it."

In spite of herself, Dion laughed. "I'm not—and I'm just as glad as you are to see the skies still clear. I just don't like the fact that the lepa haven't flocked yet. It's getting late for their migration hordes."

"Sure," Brye shrugged. "But you know as well as I do that every four or five years they don't flock at all; they migrate in small groups instead."

She agreed reluctantly.

"Ah, don't look a gift horse in the mouth, Dion. Maybe the moons are shining on you."

"On me? Hah."

"And you with those violet eyes. It's rumored you're a moon-warrior, Dion—you can't deny that, at least. The moons look after their own."

Dion gave him a sober look. The moons were no patrons of hers, she knew. She had stolen the secret of Ovousibas from them through the memories of the wolves, and they were punishing her for her crime. Like Prometheus chained to his rock in the sea for stealing fire from the gods, she, who had stolen life itself, was chained to the burden of healing.

She smiled and said the proper things and left Healer Brye to his bed. Then she sought through the packsong for Hishn's voice. The lupine song that washed through her mind released her from her duties. Yellow eyes, gleaming into her thoughts, urged her from walk to jog to run to sprint until she tore through the forest like a flash of thought. Even when the moons took over the sky and darkened the shadows by contrast, Dion forced herself on. The fierce joy that replaced the dread in her guts was the gift of the Ancients, the gift of release, the gift of Hishn's wolf pack.

V

Where one lepa circles,
A hundred eyes watch.

At dawn, the gray shadows scattered among the trees. The wolf pack surrounded Dion like a tide as she threw herself up the trail. She didn't care that her thighs had long since numbed or that the pain that stabbed at her ankle was like a dozen needles. She had slept heavily, but not deeply enough to rid herself of a vague sense of disquiet. She was running now to kill her thoughts, to deaden her burden and drown herself in the packsong. She had hours, she sang out into the wolf pack. Hours of freedom. And then her boys would run with her, free with her in the forest, stretching their young muscles like the yearlings beside her and learning to leap with the wolves.

Up. Up to the ridge, sang the wolves in her head. Their voices were shadows of her own thoughts—snatches of lupine songs filtering through her mind. *The hunt!* they howled. *The hunt is on the heights.*

Farther now, beyond the first ridge, the wolves passed Dion, streaming around the short cliff. She sucked air as she forced her feet after the flood of gray shadows. Up the short cliff, then up again, across the slope of a slick morning meadow. As they had called out to the Ancients so many centuries ago, they now urged Dion with them. *Run with us, Wolfwalker!* they howled. *Run with the pack.*

She paused and spun dizzyingly at the top of a ledge where it fell into a ravine, caught herself, and laughed at the thrill of fear that clenched her stomach. She sang her voice into their minds, her mental howl filled with the joy of her sons, her mate, her life. They washed her howl back into their memories. It blended with the thin threads of other human voices, shifting the tapestry until it became rich and thick with the numbers of Ancient wolfwalkers. Wolf eyes, the images frayed with time, were overlaid with slitted yellow eyes. Voices were accented. Power surged. Through the oldest memories the rhythm rang of cold and piercing power. It was all-encompassing, engulfing. It was both light and dark cracked open; it was shards of energy melting. It was a rhythm that shifted and transferred itself from alien to wolf to human. It was the rhythm of Ovousibas.

It struck a chord in Dion, resonating in her mind. Instantly, the wolves caught the resonance. *Run with us!* they cried out. But the thread of their song was now twisted with the thread of the ancient, internal healing. It coiled more tightly around their voices so that the death that had come to the wolves through the ages—the slow decimation of their numbers—became an underlying whine. *Run with us,* they cried out. But what they sang in their memories was, *Find our death. Find our grief. Run with us, Wolfwalker!*

The wolfsong radiated out from the first places, the truncated mountains of the Ancients. It flowed across rivers and valleys, and climbed back into the mountains of Ariye. Forward through the ages it moved, until it curled again around Dion's legs and clutched at her hands. She threw her head back and stared at the sky where once humans and aliens had flown. Her hands, smudged with dirt, reached up to the moons that floated so far away.

The wolves paused, caught on the edge of the ridge. Their throats loosened, their voices rose, and the wail of their ancient grief was thrown with Dion's gaze into the sky. Their longing was Dion's, their grief in her mind. And when she began to run again, to drive that from her mind, the wolves became a wash of gray that raced after her on the sun-dried ridge below the ancient moons.

Run! they howled into her head. *Hunt with the pack, Wolfwalker!*

The old female sang out, *The high trail!*

Cross the heights, the others returned. *The trail of sky and stone!*

Like shadow water, they flowed up the trail toward her, then beside her till they reached the rise of broken stone where the rocks jutted out like knuckles. The Gray Ones had to leap and pace, turn and jump to make their way up again. Beside Dion, the yearling in the lead lost his balance as he tried for a higher rock. *Wolfwalker!* he cried out.

Dion reached like a flash, snagging her hand in his scruff. She jammed her other fist between two boulders and hauled on the yearling's fur, straining to hold him until his front paws reached over the edge. Thrusting hard with his hind legs, he kicked off pebbles. One hind leg caught her roughly in the chest. He yelped his apology. She squeezed her eyes shut against the dust he threw back and ducked her face into her elbow, then pushed hard, shoving him up. An instant later, his weight was gone, and he bellied over the edge. Dion and the other seven wolves jumped up after him.

At the top, ahead of Dion, the old gray female hesitated. Yellow eyes bored through Dion's violet gaze, neither one challenging, but neither giving ground. Then the yellow gleam faded into deep, aged tones. *Wolfwalker,* the female sent.

Slowly, Dion reached out. This wolf had never run with a human—had never bonded as Hishn had—and although the female accepted Dion into the pack, the wolf was wary as a predator. She barely stood for Dion to touch her shoulder, but her mental voice reveled in the touch.

Wolfwalker, she sang softly again.

Dion's voice was a whisper. "You honor me."

You carry the weight of the pack. Your love binds you to Gray Hishn. Your promise binds you to us. Run with the pack, Wolfwalker!

Dion ducked her head, unable to hide her sudden rush of feeling. The old one almost touched Dion's thigh with her nose, then was gone along the trail.

The wolves had already run around the next set of cliffs by the time Dion reached them. It was a quick climb to the top, and halfway up she grinned at the gray wolf who waited impatiently above her at the rim, where the cliff had eroded into scattered dirt paths.

Hishn eyed the wolfwalker, then turned and snapped at Gray Yoshi when he urged her away. *Wait,* Hishn told him flatly.

Dion, one hand on the top rock, paused at the sharpness in Hishn's tones. She could see Gray Yoshi with her own eyes, but that was only visual. The image of the male in Hishn's mind was harsh and unforgiving, and Dion could not move closer.

If the pack leader picked up Dion's hesitation, he gave no indication. Instead, he snarled. *The human can catch up later,* he sent.

Hishn bared a mouthful of teeth. *She is my wolfwalker.*

Dion's hands began to ache from their hold. She steadied herself, waited another minute, then determinedly hauled herself up and rolled over the edge of the boulders. For an instant her eyes met Yoshi's hostile yellow gaze, and she halted on her hands and knees. The gleaming eyes seared her mind with accusation. Then the Gray One turned away. He did not look back as he loped after the rest of the pack. Hishn snarled at his backside, then ducked her head and sniffed at Dion's cheek.

Dion got to her feet only slowly. She said nothing as she gazed after Yoshi, but Hishn felt the hurt in her mind. The massive female nudged Dion in the thigh, then butted her head under Dion's hand until the wolfwalker gripped the thick fur. "Hishn," Dion said softly.

He sings his loneliness.

"I feel it—like a knife in my mind."

My mate does not speak for the rest of the pack.

But Dion couldn't hide what crossed her thoughts. Yoshi had not and would never forget what had happened to his wolfwalker. Where Dion had survived, the man had died; and the gray wolf, alone and abandoned, blamed Dion for his grief. It didn't matter that it had been a raider bolt, not a blade of hers, that had speared the man in the chest. Sobovi had given his life so that Dion could escape from the raiders with others up a cliff. Raiders who had been after Dion and other wolfwalkers like her . . . Raiders who were after her and Aranur again . . . Hishn had kept her safe back then, but at what cost? And Gray Yoshi, waiting at the top of the cliff for his own wolfwalker, had found that death climbed with Dion instead.

Hishn gazed at her unblinkingly. *Sobovi lives on in the song of the pack.*

Dion, looking after Hishn's mate, tugged at the fur beneath her hand. Memories passed on from wolf to wolf. Hishn's new pups, if Hishn mated again this summer, would know Dion not only through Hishn, but also through Yoshi's eyes. She looked down at her hands. The taint of blood—of Sobovi, of the others who had died from raider wounds she could not close, from raider swords they could not dodge . . . All that clung to her thoughts. Raiders . . . And her duty forced her to face them. She wanted protection, she realized. She wanted a place that was safe. A goal that was not built on violence, but on the hope of some other future. Her fingers trembled, and she thrust herself away from the wolf and clenched her hands like fists.

"Come," she said. Her voice was flat and sober. "The pack runs far ahead."

Hishn eyed her, then turned back toward the path.

When they reached the top of the ridge, Dion halted to catch her breath. Hishn snarled at Yoshi, but the gray male looked once, deliberately, to the west, then turned his shoulder to Hishn's snapping teeth and loped after the others down the slope.

Dion followed Yoshi's gaze. There was only one thing to the west: the split, truncated mountain on which his wolfwalker had died. Like a dream, the mountain remained, unnaturally shaped, and forbidden to humans. Sobovi's death was only one attributed to that mountain; raiders, too, had died there. And Aranur's sister, and Aranur's men, and the hundreds of Ancients who had been struck with plague . . . Eight hundred years ago, that mountain had been a tall, rounded, lumpy peak. Then the Ancients had landed, cut off the top, hollowed it out, and carved the deep slot through its center. The tethers that had linked this world to the stars had once run through that slotted mountain. Now only wind whistled there.

Dion gazed at the mountain with loathing and longing, unable to separate being drawn to the sky from being linked to the death on the planet. Hishn growled low in her throat, and Dion touched the wolf's fur. The freedom she felt with the wolves was only a whisper of what the Ancients had had. The symbols left over from the time of the Ancients—their slotted peaks and stone-round domes—represented both death and freedom. It was as if, on this world, the two were inextricably entwined. The gift of one was the other, and the price of the other was the one.

Hishn caught Dion's hand in her teeth. *Blood flows because it feeds us. So the hunt returns, like the moons to night—it is the pattern that must be. Death is life, and life is death. Only the packsong lives on.* The gray wolf bit down so hard that Dion jerked her hand free and swatted at Hishn's ears. The Gray One laughed in her mind. *Sing with the pack, Wolfwalker. Our blood is yours. We own each other here.*

As if called by Hishn's images, from below, the wolf pack seemed to coalesce into a single driving need. Hishn's ears flicked toward them. Dion caught the echo of Gray Yoshi in his mate's mind: His urgent tones pulled Hishn like a leash.

Dion's voice was soft. "We are bonded, Hishn, you and I. But we each must have our own goals." She looked after the male. "Go," she urged. "Go seek your mate. Your heart belongs to him, not me."

Hishn hesitated, but Yoshi's call was strong. Yellow eyes gleamed. Then the massive wolf bared her teeth and raced away on the trail.

Dion cut east over Dry Ridge. She could already hear her sons on the trail through the ears of other wolves. The voices of those wolves—a small family group—echoed from pack to pack until they reached her mind through Hishn. The other wolves didn't run right beside her sons, but they could tell, through the noise of the riders, where the boys and their escorts were. It would be an hour before the small group reached the crossroads; they were moving swiftly, but they were late. Dion smiled faintly. Danton had probably run off to play when they were supposed to get started. It would have taken Olarun some time to find and haul his brother back.

Dion climbed Lookout Rock before she passed it—there was a lookout stone on each ridge—to check the skies again, but there was only a single dark shape soaring to the east. Deliberately, she let her gaze roam the ridges on all sides of the message tower before she allowed herself to read the flags. When she did finally read the patterns strung up against the sky, she felt her jawline tense.

"Someday you'll damn them to the seventh hell," she said to herself about the elders. Her words held no anger, but her very quietness was a curse. The council . . . They knew she had left to be with her boys, yet they still called her to work. To the council she was a healer, not a mother. In their minds she had only a wolf family, not a human one. She felt her fingers clench and unclench, then wiped the dirt from her scarred hand onto her leggings. Finally, she turned and made her way down the ridge.

She found the ringrunner on the road near the stone corral. He had been waiting long enough that his dnu and the relay beast he had brought for her were staked out and lazily poking around in the ferns. Vlado himself was relaxing, though his eyes were alert enough to catch her movements the moment she came down the trail. She greeted him reluctantly.

The lean man studied the wolfwalker as she read the message ring—Dion had never been good at hiding her feelings. Right now, she was grim—almost guilty—and her hand, which had strayed to the hilt of her sword, rose unconsciously to tuck a wisp of hair under her silver healer's circlet. Her eyes were shadowed; there was no mistaking the strain in the lines of her face. "Dion?" he asked quietly.

She looked up.

"Are you all right?"

She shrugged. She'd known him long enough that she could answer truthfully.

The man frowned and touched her arm. "If you need to talk . . ." His voice trailed off, but the invitation to Kum-jan was clear.

Dion looked back down at the message. She didn't trust herself to answer. There was an anger growing in her—an anger that the elders would call her even as they promised her a short release. If she opened her mouth, she would lash out at Vlado; and he stood there with his proposition held out like a compliment, well-meant as his friendship, as if sex was the release she needed. Even as she stared at the message ring, she felt that anger harden even toward him. How many such offers would have come her way were she not a wolfwalker? And how many would have been advanced had she not been a master healer, the one who was Aranur's mate? Scouts had their own etiquette for sleeping on the trail, and some were as open with their bedrolls as they were with their information, but Dion wasn't one of those. Her Promise with Aranur was like her bond with Hishn—complete, engulfing, exclusive. To dilute either bond would trivialize the strength of her love and leave her unfocused and lost.

A tiny twig snapped behind them in the woods. Dion's slender body tightened, then relaxed almost as quickly when she recognized the woods' sounds that followed the twig snap. Vlado found his own body relaxing, as if his senses had taken their reassurance from Dion's wary acceptance. He eyed her thoughtfully. The wolfwalker was not just strained, he realized, but dangerously so. He almost reached out to touch her again— to massage some of that strain out of her muscles—but her body shifted almost imperceptibly away. He shrugged to himself. It wasn't a rejection of him, he knew, but a reflection of her bond with the wolves. Where one was wary, the other was remote. But both were instinctively aware of every motion around them. She had told him once it had come from being raised in Randonnen, where she had run trail since she was old enough to stand and where the wolfsong was strong as a storm, but Vlado was not so sure. He'd seen her after she'd fought on a venge, and he'd been with her after she'd hunted with the wolf pack. Both times her eyes had been wild and not quite human: hungry, predatory—almost feral. He didn't care what the others said—it was no set of moons that claimed this woman. The wolves had a hold on Ember Dione, and he didn't think even Aranur knew how deeply their teeth had sunk in.

Dion stared at the message stick, letting her fingers register the haste in the crudely carved slashes and the tight but uncured knots. When she glanced up at the man, Vlado nodded.

"It came through the watchtower on Restless Ridge," he said in answer to her unspoken question. "They need a healer within three hours. They requested that it be you."

Dion stared down at the message. She was silent for a long time. Then, finally, she said, "Send Khast."

"Healer?"

She held the message ring out to the runner, but he hesitated for the briefest moment before taking it. Dion looked up. Her face was tight, but her voice was steady. "Send Khast," she repeated. Then she turned away.

Like a wolf, she faded into the forest. There was a moment when the sunlight shattered the ferns that shifted in Dion's wake; then the shadows swallowed her as if she was one of their own.

Vlado stared after her. He could swear he had seen a shadow of gray deep in her violet eyes. It had had no gleam, no spark, as when the wolfwalker was angry; instead it had been a guilt, a bitterness—a clouding of her mind. Slowly, he strapped the message ring back on his belt. He looked once more toward the forest. Then he mounted his dnu and, catching up the other creature's reins, started the beasts up the road.

From the shelter of the forest, Dion watched him go. Her fists were clenched at her sides; her lips tight with the words she wanted to shout. Wait! I'll go— But her jaw was locked, and her feet didn't move. She forced herself to breathe, and the sound that sucked between her lips was harsh. I should have gone, the thought pounded in her head. It should be me, not Khast. She had seen the uncertainty in the messenger's eyes—in all the years he'd run with her, he'd never heard her turn down a call.

The gray fog in her head swamped her suddenly, and she swayed against a tree. Rough bark caught on her fingers; her forehead pressed the cool wood. But it was not guilt that forced her fingers into the bark; it was a growing ice in her gut. She pushed herself away from the tree and stared once more down at the trail below. Then she began to run.

By the time Dion reached the crossroads, the stone in her belly had loosened and her body had tired itself into the trail lope that covered the four kays like the wolves. She paused when she saw the boys below. The chest-high ferns hid her from their eyes, and she took the moment to revel in their youth. They were intent on building a message cairn, and their young voices filled her ears like a packsong as they ordered each other to do this and that, teased each other, then agreed excitedly on the next idea. So straight, so eager they were. So many dreams . . . Pride and love warred in her so that her eyes blurred, and for a moment their figures wavered. Irritably, she brushed at the tears. If Aranur thought she was overworked now, what would he do if he knew she'd been crying?

She was within meters of the boys before they saw her. Olarun felt her presence first, and he looked up sharply, his young ears already distinguishing sounds. It took him a moment to pick her out from the ferns. Then he poked Danton roughly. "There she is! I saw her first!"

The younger boy scrambled to his feet. "You did not!"

"I did too," Olarun retorted.

"You always see her first," Danton muttered sullenly. Dion nodded to the three rider escorts, and they smiled acknowledgment and began to gather their things. They didn't bother to grasp arms with her before they returned to the village; she was already being pulled away on each side by her boys.

"Momma," Olarun said eagerly. "Come see what we made. It's a message cairn. Look!"

Obediently, Dion bent to examine the cairn. "Oh, this is nicely done," she told them. Their faces flushed with pride, and she looked closer at their work. "I like the way you've built the opening," she said. "A ringrunner will be able to pull a message out without the rain dripping inside while he does it."

"That was my idea," Olarun said proudly.

Danton pushed him aside and pulled Dion down to look through the opening. "But I'm the one who made the message platform inside. See?"

"To keep the messages off the dirt? I had no idea you knew how important it was to keep messages from being blurred," she told him. "You've built an excellent structure. Any scout would be proud to use this cairn."

"Do you want to use it?" Olarun asked eagerly.

"Can you make a message right now?" Danton put in.

Dion looked down into his face. "We'll leave a message ring for your father," she agreed. "But you have to help me make it."

The boys almost fell over themselves to shove into her hands the pile of sticks they had already gathered. By the time they had chosen a single stick to use, then slashed and dyed and knotted their message in the wood, it was late morning, and the sun had risen enough to begin warming the shadows. Dion gathered her sons, checked their small packs, and led them off into the forest.

Danton immediately stirred up a largon nest that Dion pointed out, and they had to run for their skins while the large-jawed crawlers flooded out in search of the intruders. Then the two boys dared each other to taste the yucky leaves Dion found. She laughed at their expressions as they spat and coughed over the flavor. Finally, she led them to a bramble patch growing over a tiny plot of extractor plants. She pulled a new root from the soil, cleaned it off, cut from it two slivers, and wrapped each in a sweet bramble leaf so the boys could get the taste of the other plant out of their mouths. Olarun carefully took the rest of the root and put it in one of his belt pouches.

Dion smiled her approval. "How much are you carrying now?"

"I have one dried root, and this fresh one."

"And if we were to be out for a ninan, and you were going to eat only wild plants, how many roots would you need to carry?"

"Two if they were from the garden," he returned proudly. "Just one, if it was wild."

Danton scowled. "It'd be bitter if it was wild."

"Wild or not, extractors are lifesavers," his brother quoted importantly.

Dion half smiled at her younger son. "Life is an acquired taste, little wolf. You'll understand that more when you're older."

The younger boy scowled at his brother. "If I was as old as you, I'd eat meat all the time when I went out by myself."

This time Dion smiled without reservation. "You'd certainly try to do that, I'm sure. But it's more difficult to make a good snare than it is to pull a tuber from the ground. You're more likely to find roots than rabbits laying around for your supper."

"Besides, meat has more toxins than plants," Olarun admonished.

"Meat is different than plants," Dion corrected. "Most meats do have more toxins than plants, but some meats have less. It takes a while to learn how much of the extractors to use with each type. Until you know exactly which animals contain how much toxin, the best rule to follow is to use twice as much extractor as you would if the quantity of meat was a plant."

"How come we have to use extractors anyway?" Danton asked. "Why can't you just heal the plants so they don't make us sick when we eat them?"

This time Dion laughed outright. "It is we, not the plants, that are the problem, little wolf. This world wasn't made for humans, and the food that grows here naturally is poison to us even now. The extractor plants, when cooked with the native food, strip the poison from what we eat. Without extractors, there would be almost nothing safe to put in your mouth. After a while you would be very, very hungry."

"I'm hungry now," he returned.

Dion mussed his hair. "Then let's eat when we get to Still Meadow."

As she brought the boys to the edge of the meadow, she let her mind range across the hills to Hishn. The ridge between them barely dulled the persistent thread of Hishn's voice, and the Gray One sent back a shaft of lupine joy. Dion let it curl her lip as she told the boys to pull out their packed lunches. For claiming to be as hungry as they were, they ate slowly, constantly stopping to pick at this leaf or that, to bother this bug, to see which of them could dig their feet deepest into the dirt.

Dion wondered, as she watched them, whether either of them would bond with the wolves. They could hear Hishn clearly, but neither had taken one of the gray wolf's pups. Hishn said it was the strength of Dion's own bond that allowed them to hear the packsong, and their love for Hishn that prevented them from separating the wolf cubs from their wolf mother. But the boys were growing fast. Soon they would be independent enough to seek out their own gray packsong, to hear the wolves for themselves.

Danton, having finished his meatroll, shifted his gaze to the meadow. "Why can't we ever ride dnu up here?" he asked.

"Because dnu get bogged down in the marshy parts of the meadow," Dion answered automatically. "And dnu don't like wild wolves."

"There aren't wild wolves here now."

"No," Dion agreed.

"Were there wild wolves on OldEarth?" Olarun asked.

"And on the moons?" Danton added.

Dion smiled. "OldEarth had only one moon."

"I bet there were hundreds of wolfwalkers on OldEarth," Olarun said to his brother.

"I bet there were thousands," Danton retorted.

"I bet I could have been a better wolfwalker there than you," the older boy shot back.

Dion watched them with a half-sober smile. Her sons would never see OldEarth—not if the aliens kept humans earthbound instead of allowing them once again to reach for the stars. She sighed, then studied the skies and the angle of the sun before risking a more open position in the meadow. But there were no lepa in sight. Whatever lone beast she had sighted earlier from Dry Ridge had either gone down on its prey or flown farther away. Tenantler Ridge, to the west, looked clear; and the wolves would have noticed if anything had flown over Moshok Valley to the east. "Ready to go?" she interrupted the I-bet game of the boys. They nodded emphatically, and she adjusted the packs on their shoulders.

Her eyes scanned the meadow, searching for movement and color that would indicate predator or prey: the shrubs that sprouted branches a hair too thick, the lumps in the grass that weren't rocks . . . But the meadow movements were normal, quiet. There were no warning calls from the grazing creatures, except those that reacted to the boys.

"Predator check," she told them, pointing to a small stand of silverheart trees. Obediently, they moved into the stand and squatted down into the ferns so that they could see her from between the thin trunks. From the edge of the meadow, she glanced at them, gave Olarun a stern look when he punched Danton on the shoulder for poking him, and then stepped out into the grass. She moved slowly, cautiously, then ran a hundred meters into the meadow in a serpentine pattern. With Hishn's senses in her nose, she had to narrow their bond so that the odors in her own nose were stronger than the ones the gray wolf sent. But the only creatures she scared up were a flock of pelan, and the birds settled down again within seconds, telling her that there were no predators visible from the air.

She turned, grinned, and waved for the boys to join her. They barely waited for her gesture before they raced each other from the forest. Danton tripped, and Olarun shouted gleefully at him; the younger boy was up in an instant, trying to catch up to his brother.

For an hour, they raced through the meadow, running, teasing each other, playing tag. Dion showed them the shallow ground caves made of old, crumbling lava rock that, over time, had humped up into mounds of soil and brush. They had a moment's excitement when one of the entrances collapsed beneath Danton's weight, but Dion yanked him clear before his legs were caught in the rubble. They were more wary of the caves after that.

Danton peered carefully into another shallow cave. "Momma, how come there aren't any worlags here?"

"Because, little wolf, this meadow is half swamp, especially in spring and fall. It's too wet for worlags," she returned absently. "They'll take to snow, but not water."

"I told you so," Olarun hissed to Danton.

"I bet a lepa would live here if it wanted to," the younger boy retorted.

Dion half smiled. "Lepa are cave-dwelling birds, that's true, but they wouldn't climb down into a lava tube—ground caves are where the worlags live, and worlags kill lepa as easily as lepa kill wolves. Only if a lepa is desperate to chase its prey will it ever try to get inside a ground cave."

"What if one did? What if one chased you down a cave?" Danton persisted.

"Then I'd light a fire to keep it off. Smoke disorients lepa the same way it disorients a dnu. And no lepa will attack you through fire."

"I could build a fire in a cave," Olarun declared.

"So could I," Danton put in quickly.

"You both know how to build fires," she agreed. "But it's different when you build a fire in a cave. You don't want to smoke yourself out of the cave and right back into the lepa's claws. So you have to build the fire downwind as always, but close enough to the front to protect you and not so far outside the cave that the lepa can get between you and the fire. Of course, you could always choose a cave with a built-in chimney—one that has a nice living room, with plenty of windows . . ."

Olarun rolled his eyes. "Oh, sure, Momma."

She just smiled.

She took them along channels of sluggish spring water that hid between the low grasses. There were striped eels in the mud, and curled balls of worms; there were spray beetles on the rocks. Dion let a handful of beetles crawl around on her hands and nibble lightly at her skin. She looked at her boys, at the expressions on their faces as they felt with awe the tiny mouths of the insects. There was excitement in their voices. There was a lightness in her sight. She set the beetles back on the rocks and sat back on her heels. For the first time in ninans she felt free. Slowly, she got to her feet. Then she threw out her arms and twirled, letting her voice howl with Hishn's mental cry. Olarun leaped up and began to spin with her. His young voice tried to imitate the terraced tones of the wolves, and Danton started laughing. The three collapsed in a heap of rough-housing play.

Finally, Dion tossed the boys away. "Enough," she said, breathless. "You won't have enough energy left to make camp."

"Yes we will," Danton protested, throwing himself back on her.

She took his weight easily and swung him in a circle, dropping him gently on a mat of grass. Then there was nothing for it but to do the same again with Olarun. "Ah—" She stopped them with a gesture from leaping back up. "No more. We have to choose our campsite."

"Parcit Pond," Danton said without hesitation.

"Moshok Valley," Olarun said as quickly.

Dion smiled at her youngest. "Parcit Pond is a swamp right now. Do you really want to sleep in the middle of a swarm of biting, stinging, creeping, slithering crawlers, bugs, and eels?"

"Yes," Danton said firmly.

Dion grinned at his stubborn expression. "Then I'll make sure we find you some. But both the pond and the valley are kays away."

"The valley is closer," Olarun said confidently.

"Yes, but the state you two are in, it would take six hours to get over the ridge and down to the flatlands to camp."

"The wolves are in the valley," Olarun urged.

Dion gave him a careful casual look. "How do you know that? Can you hear Hishn?"

"He's just saying that," Danton cut in, the jealousy on his face as clear as water. "He can't hear anything."

"I can too hear her." Olarun puffed up his chest. "She's like a creepy little fog in the back of my mind."

Dion got caught between a laugh and a choke. "I'm sure Hishn will appreciate the compliment," she managed finally. She opened her mind to the gray wolf and sent on to Hishn an image of the creepy fog. Hishn's response was immediate and sharp.

Dion glanced at the sky. "You want a swamp, Danton; and Olarun, you want the wolves?" Both boys nodded. "Then how about Jama Creek? It's just this side of Moshok Valley; it's swamp on one side and rock on the other. The lava tubes, rotten as they are down there, lead back along the cliffs. And," she added, "there's a wolf pack denning there." Her eyes became unfocused for a moment. "In fact," her voice grew soft, "if you look very carefully—" She pointed toward the distant edge of the meadow. "—you can see three of the wolves there now."

Eagerly, the boys turned. The tiny dots at the edge of the grasses were almost invisible. Not until one of the yearlings moved did Danton see where they were. Olarun mistook a rock pile for the Gray Ones, and it was minutes before he recognized the real lupine shadows.

By the time Dion began to lead her boys east, the wolves had disappeared. The sun was afternoon-bright and hot as an insult. The meadow became humid, the muddy grass sticky, and Dion moved them along more quickly. Once they started across the expanse, there would be no turning back, and she had no desire to be in the meadow after dark. The spring gatherers would be out in force by the end of the ninan, judging by the circles that marked their digging-test patches, but there was no one else in the meadow as yet to keep them company. And she could not have led her sons along the perimeter—the creeks and bogs that lined the meadow were treacherous in spring.

She scanned the skies, then listened for the noises of the other creatures in the meadow. There was no nervousness, no wariness except in the animals that watched her own steps. Still, she kept her bow strung and her sword loose in its scabbard.

Three times, she did a predator check, leaving the boys simply lying in the grass rather than crouched in fern stands or near old, burned-out logs. Predators tended to find shade themselves when they weren't doing serious hunting. Several times she ran on ahead, then stopped and climbed on a log or hump of rock to watch the wind-movements of the grass behind her sons. She had done this so many times for herself; now she was doing it for them. The pattern of life seemed to connect past and future, and Dion found herself smiling. She studied the grasses and let herself stretch to see back along their trail. But the early afternoon was quiet, and the meadow was well named. Nothing haunted their footsteps.

Each time she checked their backtrail, she let her mind expand with the senses of the wolves. She couldn't tell if it was her imagination or not that there was a hint of her older son in that bond, but Olarun assured her that he could tell when she opened her mind to Hishn.

Do you hear him? she asked the gray wolf on the other side of the ridge.

He is faint, like a wisp of smoke, Hishn sent back. *I hear the echo of his voice in yours.*

Dion couldn't help her rush of pride. She couldn't articulate what she felt, even to the wolf, but it swamped her like a wave. *Someday,* she told Hishn, *he'll run with Aranur and me. And the packsong between us will be full and rich with the depth of family, not just with you and me.*

Hishn snarled. *Young. Strong—he is one of us already. Young wolf! Wolfwalker cub! Wolfwalker!*

Dion raised her wolf-clouded eyes to the skies. The east was clear, and in the south only a line of pelan crossed the afternoon blue. Hishn's wolf pack, kays away, brought down an old, sick eerin, and the sense of that kill made Dion pause until her eyesight cleared. When she could focus again, there was a single blot, heavy and dark in the west, where the sun angled down over Tenantler Ridge. Warily, she eyed that shape. "Come," she said. "It's getting late."

She hurried them now, as if the angle of the sun were a lance pointing to her sons, but the single lepa in the distance circled only that ridge, eyeing something else. Dion tried to shake her chill, but she couldn't help remembering Gamon's stories of other late migrations. Where one lepa circles, a hundred eyes watch . . . She studied the birdbeast for a long moment, then eyed her boys critically. Then she took their packs, lashed the small bundles to her own, and made a game of racing to each water channel that cut across the grass.

They made good speed, but Dion's shoulders were beginning to twitch. She knew that feeling, and it made her hurry the boys more. But although there was no place here to hide, they were close to the caves and the end of the meadow, and no lepa could hunt them from the sky once they were back among the trees.

Wolfwalker? Hishn's voice cut through her unease.

Dion shook her head, forgetting that the boys could see her. They stopped, watching, and she eyed the clear sky as if it were a liar. *I'll feel more comfortable when we get near the caves,* she told the wolf. *I don't like this openness.*

You are close. I can feel your nearness to the pack, and they can smell the mold of the caves from their dust wallows. The caves you seek are between you.

Dion glanced at her boys' faces. *What about the other end of the meadow? There's a lepa circling over the ridge, and it's been in the sky too long. What are the other lepa doing back there? Are they shifting, moving, getting ready to migrate?*

Hishn's voice seemed to split into a dozen images as she sent out the call to the wolves. The flood of voices that returned filtered out in the gray wolf's mind so that what she returned to Dion was a tapestry of lupine threads. There were wolves near the meadow, but only to the east, by the deeper lava tubes. The west was lepa country, and even with new pups to feed and hunger ripe in their bellies, the Gray Ones avoided those ridges.

Ten minutes later, a second lepa joined the first one in the sky. Dion saw it rise from the same ridge as the first had appeared. She pushed the boys harder now, but they didn't complain. There was something in her voice that alerted them. "This way," she said, a bit too sharply, when Danton veered to the left. "Around these rocks, not over them," she told Olarun when he automatically started up. "The caves are just up ahead." They ran now in earnest, not with eagerness, and Dion ran half backward, one sharp eye on her flagging sons; one wary eye on the sky.

The grass whipped at their leggings, slapping them with green, husk-heavy heads. The suddenly soft patches of ground tripped up their feet. "This way," Dion urged them. "Watch that patch of fireweed."

Grazing creatures leaped up from grassy hiding places and bolted away from Dion's haste. The wolfwalker kept up the pace. A small group of herd beasts spooked at the other end of the meadow, and Dion caught their distant panic out of the corner of her eye. She looked back. For an instant, her own breath choked her. There were no longer only two lepa in the sky. What had been only two pairs of wings had turned into a hundred. The blackness that was spewing into the sky was like a fountain of ink.

"Run now, boys," she said sharply. "The caves. You can see them there on the right."

"Momma—" Danton started.

"Don't talk—*run*," she snapped.

Olarun looked over his shoulder. He faltered.

Dion slapped his shoulder forward. "Don't look back. I'm here. I'll be with you. Faster now, Olarun."

The boy jumped a water channel and slipped in the mud on the other side, but Dion hauled him up before his feet were wet. They lost seconds. Danton was silent, scared, straining to keep the pace, crowded by his mother as she urged him on. He tripped and fell in another water channel, and Dion paused to jerk him to his feet. Olarun ran ahead. She could hear the meadow rustling now as other creatures fled, and she shot her warning to the wolves that echoed in her mind.

Wolfwalker! they returned. *The dens in the east. The safety of the darkness.* They shot back an image of the lava tubes, narrow and crumbling and damp in the ground. Gray Hishn, in the valley, had already passed on Dion's warning, and the Gray Ones who had hunted earlier now fled their open kill like mice from a growing storm. They reached the shelter of the trees and dispersed like dust in the wind. *Wolfwalker!* they howled.

Dion didn't answer them. Her emotions were broadcast through Hishn, even if she were silent. She had no breath to concentrate thought, except to push her boys. Once they were in the caves, they'd be safe. The caves were rotten, but they were deep, and no lepa would follow them in.

But Hishn read Dion's fear and the distance from the lava tubes, and the bond between them shocked tight. *Wolfwalker,* the Gray One howled. Dion felt the wolf's strength lift her legs. Her eyes unfocused, the grass blurred, and then she went flat, face-first in the grass as her foot collapsed a digger's hole. Danton heard her fall and half stopped. Instantly, she was up. She leaped toward him, snapping at him to keep going. The boy fled.

But even while her legs pounded and her hand half drew her sword, Dion's blood froze in her veins. The meadow went dark behind her. She looked back. The shadow sweeping across the sun was a horde of black lepa. They had risen like an oil fire, blocking the sky with darkness. Seconds, seconds, and the bird-beasts would reach her, and her sons were not yet safe.

Hishn! she cried out.

The gray wolf howled. Yellow eyes gleamed. Energy, heat, power was thrust into her mind as if the wolves had channeled their own speed to her legs. Dion's body jerked ahead. She chanced another look over her shoulder. Then, with lupine power filling her, she grabbed Danton and slung him up. He wrapped his arms around her neck, his legs around her waist. She didn't feel his weight. But she could almost feel the wind from the wings that gathered overhead, and the furious silence of the racing flock was a nightmare running them down.

Olarun, ahead of her, faltered. "Get inside," Dion shouted at him. "You're safe. Don't stop now."

But the boy caught a glimpse over his shoulder of the sky as black as coal. The lepa had flocked into a massive fist, and as he watched, they seemed to hammer down from the sky. A rain of black predator bullets began to pierce the meadow, spearing the eerin that didn't make the safety of the forest. Other lepa kept on, sweeping across the meadow. Olarun could see their wings.

He could see their faces. He could see their slitted eyes. He froze, tripped, and fell backward mere meters from the cave.

"Get up," Dion screamed, sprinting toward him. Olarun, his eyes wide and staring, didn't move. She reached him, reached down, grabbed his arm and, spinning, slung him into the cave. Instantly, hot air thick with stench engulfed her. Danton screamed. Olarun cried out. The wolves howled in her head. Her feet, light with the Gray Ones' speed, left the ground, but her leap toward the cave went on forever. The rock entrance filled her sight like an earthen maw, then shrank and fell away.

Talons dug into her backpack and hauled her into the air. Massive wings beat the air by her head. Her stomach dropped sickeningly as she soared up. She screamed and clutched at Danton, but other talons raked her arms. A blinding fury of greasy feathers and stabbing claws whirled and beat at her eyes. Abruptly, she was half dropped as three birdbeasts tore at each other for possession of her body. Another birdbeast dug its talons into the backpack and jerked her airborne again. The pack straps cut into her shoulders. Danton's weight yanked her sideways. Something tore into her legs. Danton screamed. Olarun and Aranur were suddenly in her mind, and the gray wolves were thick behind those voices. She felt herself drop, was jerked sideways, and was hauled up again as a talon sank deep in her shoulder. She couldn't help her scream. Vicious claws caught her right leg and shredded the boot from her calf. Fire lanced through her body. Danton's arms loosened, and she screamed at him, clutching her son more tightly.

Your fangs—
Your steel—
Your sword—
The voices shouted.

With her left hand clutching Danton, her sword seemed to leap into her right. Her head jerked back as her warcap was torn away. One of the claws struck Danton's cheek. He shrieked. She cut, wildly, one-armed, enraged. A spray of blood flashed out from a birdbeast who dove at Danton's back.

Abruptly, she was snatched like bread from one beak by another, her body slung sideways as the talons dug into her hip. Another lepa clawed at her arm. She screamed again. And then, suddenly, like a vision, she felt the rhythm of their attack. She kicked off a lepa that screamed in for a killing blow and slashed another, using the first birdbeast for sloppy leverage. Desperately, she twisted to keep Danton from the claws. The reek of blood splashed across her chin. She elbow-locked her sword arm on a wing that came too close to the boy and felt the wingbone snap. Screaming, she twirled her blade. The steel cut beneath her, then across the neck of lepa who came in over the beast she had grabbed. She could feel the wolves gather, goaded by Hishn, as if to race to protect her. *Hishn!* she screamed. *Stay back! Stay away!*

Their instinct and fury sprang into her hands. She became an airborne demon, striking the beaks away. Thin bones snapped. Muscles tore. The lepa became a frenzied pack. The wingslapped thunder blinded her; their grunting deafened her ears. A birdbeast grabbed at her calves, and she kicked, then clutched it with her ankles. Suddenly panicked, it beat against her with its wings, tangling another beast. She didn't feel the jerk of a leg in her armpit as a limb caught for an instant there. But she felt the savage wrench as the pack straps cut again across her shoulders before they broke themselves. The pack was jerked away. She almost fell, but the talons in her hip held just before more sank into her sides and shoulders. She swung wildly, half upside down. Like a newborn babe, her back was bared to the lepa.

The sudden ripping, viciously deep, shocked her. Her hand spasmed; her sword flashed away, spinning down through the air. Curled around her, Danton jerked. Then the two of them twisted and rose sickeningly as one lepa tore her free from the rest. For an instant they rose above the horde. Danton was weak around her waist. She clutched him, feeling the slap of his legs, limp against her own. She screamed at him to hold on, and grabbed at her long knife with her other hand. There was a din in her mind that was not from herself, but from wolves and human voices. Aranur, Hishn, Yoshi, Olarun . . . They screamed terror into her fury.

The other lepa followed her up like a column of dirty black. Then they were on her again. A beak tore flesh from her thigh. A talon pierced her calf. Like a feather twisting in a vicious wind, she was jerked, pecked this way and that. They beat at Danton like chickens on corn. She tried to curl around his body, but her hands were slick with gore. Theirs, hers, his . . . Her elbow was ripped, and the boy was half torn from her grasp.

Enraged, she shrieked. Her knife flashed out; the steel fed. The air itself drank blood. Midair, legs flailing, she clawed her son's weight back to her. She broke him free of the lepa's grip, but the birdbeast who had her lost its hold. Both humans plummeted sickeningly. For a moment, she held her boy, face to face. Black hair, slick with blood; eyes torn; cheeks slashed. His mouth hung open, loose and slack, his soundless scream too late to reach her ears.

Then he was torn away.

The lepa screamed their triumph. Twisting, shrieking, Dion fell like a stone as her son's body soared away. There were only talons and beaks in her face; only blackness in her sight. And then she struck the ground and felt it give way, burying her in stone.

There was pain and blackness and blood behind her eyelids, but some instinct moved her, made her fight toward a pocket of air. She left flesh on the rocks, and blood in the dirt. Her arm, broken and caught, made her shriek. The lepa tore at the ground, but her tomb was of rock and the blackness that swept into her mind. Danton, she whispered, but her lips didn't move. Olarun . . . Aranur . . .

Stones crushed against her ribs. The dust clogged her mouth. The rocks drank her blood. Her hand twitched once. Two fingers clutched air.

In the silence, a wolf mother howled.

VI

What is Will?
And where do you find it?

—Questions of the elders at the Test of Abis

They half pulled, half dug her body from the narrow cave. Aranur had broken the rotten rocks that bound the entrance, throwing the lightweight stones to the side until he could see her torso. She was facedown, half twisted in the tiny tunnel down which she had crawled. Mud had caked raw muscle and leather together in ragged masses of filth. One arm was twisted, as broken as her body. In the dark, he couldn't see her breathe.

He didn't remember dragging and lifting her free of the tunnel. He didn't know that he struck out at the men who tried to help him staunch those sluggishly bleeding wounds, or that he snarled back at Hishn as the gray wolf bit at him when he moved Dion from the earth. He had had to wait as darkness fell and drove the lepa away. Had had to wait, shooting the few beasts that warily worried the smoking entrance to Olarun's cave and those that pecked at the broken ground where Dion had been crushed within. Had had to wait two agonizing hours until he could get to his son and convince himself that the boy really was alive. The fire Olarun had set had discouraged the lepa from following him into the cave, but not before the boy had been slashed in the shoulder. Olarun was cold with shock as much as with dread—the same dread that tore at his father.

With the gray wolf snarling into Aranur's eyes and the sun closing down on the horizon, Aranur had felt every second of his son's terror, every slash in Dion's life. He had run out toward the caves even before the last lepa rose into dusk, throwing off

116

the hands that tried to hold him back. And like an arrow, he had gone straight for his son.

Now Olarun, his arm and shoulder bound with thick bandages, watched his father without speaking. The boy's face was white; he didn't seem able to move. He whispered once, when he saw his mother's body, but Aranur didn't hear.

Aranur turned then, with Dion in his arms, and shouted for someone to put the boy on a dnu. The gray-eyed man looked once, long and hard, at the dusk meadow strewn with shards of lepa bodies torn apart by their own kind, then up at the moon-bright sky. The only sign of his youngest son was a single strap from the boy's tiny pack, caught in the thorns near the cave. Aranur's square features were masklike. Then he mounted, with Dion in his arms, and from the grass and open graves of lepa, they raced as if devil-drawn.

The wolves surrounded them like a sea of gray. Not just Hishn's pack, but another had joined them at the meadow. The eighteen shadows that paced the dnu compounded the beasts' nervousness. Already skittish from the blood scent and lepa, the dnu grunted and half reared on the road, but the wolves refused to shift away. As though they herded the riders, the wolves kept close, snarling and snapping at the riding beasts' heels. Aranur tried twice to rein away from Hishn, but the massive wolf turned and growled with menace, and the gray wolf's mate snapped at his calf. With a chill, Aranur cursed Gray Yoshi, but the gray male glared back and snarled.

They were barely onto the main rootroad when a third wolf pack swept out of the forest and merged with Gray Hishn's pack. The riders with Aranur paled. Thirty-two wolves now ran before and behind them.

They rode in a thunder, fast—like a storm. They reached the turnoff for the small town nearest the meadow, and Aranur tried to rein in, but the wolves snarled at his dnu. He tried again to turn, and the wolves bit at his beast. He cursed. Jerking on the reins, he forced the dnu's head to the left, but the wolves threw themselves at the riding beast, and the dnu squealed. Instinctively, Aranur drew up his legs, and the teeth missed his calves, skidding instead along the side of his riding beast.

"Hishn," Aranur screamed, "let us turn."

But the Gray One didn't slow. The den, the home, her sons, and the darkness of shelter she knew . . . The urgent need for safety burned in the remnants of Dion's mind, and it drove the wolves like fire. Three more wolves joined the sea of gray, and then another small pack of four. Aranur raced through a town and could not stop. The villagers leaped from the way of the wolf-human horde, stunned into silence as the gray sea flooded past.

Another town, and the wolf pack swelled. Thirty-nine became close to fifty. Hishn beat at them with need. The smell of blood, of earth, of sweat, of fear, of wolves beat at Aranur until he felt his own nostrils clog with urgency.

The wolf pack grew again, and the dnu began to sweat heavily with fear and exertion. The double weight of himself and Dion was beginning to tell on his mount. He tried to pace the dnu, so that the wolf pack slowed, but the Gray Ones bit at his heels. He tried to open his mind to Hishn, but the wolf refused to meet his eyes. He could only clutch Dion and strain to hear her in the packsong in his mind.

More wolves—too many wolves—surrounded the riders now. The weight of them filled Aranur's sight so that the forest began to seem fogged. He could feel their gray mental threads; hear their packsong, thick and driven and dark. Dark? Darkening. Fogging more: Dion's voice, so deeply woven into the song of the wolves, weakened, faded. Went still.

Aranur felt it and screamed, a hoarse, strange cry. Half-human, half-wolf, his voice shocked through the forest. Hishn howled. The wolves surged. Like a single wave, the packsong crushed through the stillness to the last whisper of Dion's mind. They found her lungs and forced them to move. They found her heart and bit at it with their minds, driving it to beat. Seventy wolves sank their mental teeth into her soul and yanked it back from the path to the moons.

A heartbeat pinched through Aranur's mind. Then a second tiny pound. Dion's chest didn't rise, but a shadow of breath seemed to whisper. Gray wolves, close and raging, refused to let her go. And finally her heart beat again and pushed what was left of her blood through her veins.

Aranur screamed again—a desperate sound, and again the wolf pack surged. This time it was physical. And, as if his own need had added to Hishn's, the wolf pack picked up their pace. Urgency bit at his thoughts, as though it were he, not Dion, caught up in that bond. His eyes, which once had been a solid gray, seemed tinged with a glint of yellow.

One woman's dnu began to falter, and the wolves bit at its heels. The riding beast, exhausted from the sprint to the meadow and the race that it could not now escape, squealed and jerked ahead. Olarun, clutching the saddle horn, felt his own blood chill. He had seen the eyes of the wolves who snapped at that dnu, and there was something there that he had not seen before. It had none of the gleam of the eager hunt or the steady gaze of the pack mother. Those eyes were not as he had ever seen them, and it terrified him like the eyes of the lepa.

He tried to stretch as his mother had described, letting himself hear the packsong. But what he realized was a roaring din, like a fire in the tops of the trees. Hishn was no longer a creeping fog—a light touch in the back of his mind. He had found the wolf's voice, and it was not gentle or firm, but vicious and driving and wild. The boy tried to call out to his father, but he couldn't seem to speak. He could only sit, with the burn of the gashes in his shoulder, while the wolves forced them toward home.

An hour passed, and the wolves refused to slacken their pace. Two more towns flashed by. The message relays had caught up with them, and the villagers emptied the streets, standing on porches and peering from behind their windows at the flood of lupine gray. A group of relay riders tried to join up from one town, but the wolves repulsed them viciously. Aranur shouted to the riders to get a relay of dnu waiting ahead in the villages, and the riders fell back while the wolves raced on.

They didn't ride the main roads home—the wolves chose the shortest routes, the routes that Hishn knew. There were places where the dnu were forced at a run up steep, slick hills or through the rocky streams. Aranur could feel the trembling in the muscles of his own beast—the dnu ran more from terror than strength, but the wolves would not let it slow.

They came to another village, and there was a set of relay dnu waiting. The relay men, unmounted, started the dnu running free by whipping them with rope until the beasts scuttled ahead of the wolves. When the pack swallowed up the riderless beasts, some of Aranur's men and women were able to transfer over. Olarun was half lifted, half thrown from one onto another saddle, but the man with whom the boy had ridden was not able to switch with him. The boy found himself, his mind dull with pain and exhaustion, clinging one-handed to the saddle horn. The stirrups, set for an adult, were too long for his skinny legs. He couldn't hold his seat. A shaft of fear hit him as he felt his body slip.

Hishn, he cried out unconsciously.

The wolf howled back in his mind. The gray sea seemed to shift. A dnu was forced close, its eyes wild and rolling. Then someone's hand crushed his on the horn. The boy jerked, but the weight was gone as quickly as it had appeared, and Tehena slid into place behind him. Her hard, lean arm caught him around the waist before he could slide off beneath the trampling hooves.

Hishn, he cried out again, unconsciously trying to reach his mother.

Only a snarling returned.

They rode.

Three villages and another hour passed, and the pack still swelled as if the night called them like darkness. The wolves now numbered eighty. The villages through which they flashed were blurs in their exhausted sight. The moons fled overhead, leaving a patch of sky dark as death in which the eyes of the stars stared down. And Aranur clung to his mate as though she could feel his strength around her. Only the sense he had of the gray wolves within her gave him hope that she still lived.

When they reached the outskirts of the Lloroi's town, the wolves did not run around it. They drove straight through as though they could see the house that overlooked the town. Gray Hishn didn't lead, but she snarled into the packsong, and Yoshi pushed his way forward. As though the other males had given way to Yoshi, they followed the gray male's direction. Through empty streets, past knots of people standing in the dark. Through the outer hubs, then the center one, while the dnu hooves clattered on. Onto old stone roads from the Ancient times. And out again to darkness. Twenty minutes, Aranur told himself. Twenty minutes to their home.

When the riders fell in behind the pack, Aranur didn't look back. He knew who they were: the healers, summoned by message rings that had been run through the darkness. They rode well back from the tide of gray, and the wolves, linked to Dion, ignored them. And then they were into the rising hills that led to Dion's home.

The dnu, pushed to shreds of endurance, gasped as they leaped up the roads. Aranur held his knees firm, guiding his dnu over rough spots as it began to stumble. He could see the lights from their house, and he felt a wash of relief weaken his grip. Gamon, he thought, and Tomi—both were there. He didn't even notice, as they swept toward the lights, that the sea of gray had lessened. Gray shadows, filtered out by the trees, disappeared into the rocks near his home. When he reached the yard and swept past the gate, there were only eight still with them.

Hishn growled in his mind, and his dnu, as if suddenly released, collapsed. He barely kicked free, leaping away from the saddle and the weight of the dying beast. As his boots struck earth, he stumbled with Dion's weight but somehow kept his feet. The riding beast, limp as a carcass, sprawled on the courtyard stone.

Aranur ran for the house with Dion in his arms. He shouldered aside the white-faced women who waited anxiously on the porch. Hishn flashed through the crowd at his heels, somehow shifting ahead of him so that the wolf's fangs, even more than Aranur's haste, moved the healers aside. "Hurry," he snarled. "They're holding her."

"This way—" And, "Who's holding her? What do you mean?"

"The wolves," he snapped, not knowing how it sounded. "They've got their teeth in her heart."

His uncle Gamon appeared and pulled him toward the bed that had been covered with sheets and bandage pads. As Aranur laid Dion down and staggered back, suddenly relieved of her weight, he realized that the darkness of his clothes was not the night, but her blood. He started to reach for her again, but was shoved unceremoniously aside.

Suddenly there were too many people, too many bodies in the room. People reached for the same bandages; washes of cleansing fluids splashed together. Someone stepped on Hishn, and the wolf bit a woman's knee. The woman screamed shortly, terrified, and Gamon jumped between them.

"It bit me," the woman sobbed.

"Get it out of here," one of the healers snapped, not even bothering to look.

"Gamon—" another healer started.

Aranur's hard voice cut through the din. "The wolf stays—unless you want Dion to die."

The room went silent. Then it burst again into action. This time, Gray Hishn was not bothered.

Aranur was pushed back to the wall. He found Olarun beside him and pulled him to his side. The boy stared at the healers, at his mother, at the wolf. When one of the healers herded Gamon out the door, the boy almost fled before them. He hesitated in the hall, looking back at the room that seemed to seethe with healers. Gamon said something to him and touched his arm, but he didn't hear. The boy's lips moved, then he turned and bolted toward the front door. He was running by the time he hit the porch.

"Olarun," Aranur shouted.

Gamon caught the other man's arm. "Let him go. His shoulder wound is stitched and sealed against jellbugs. It's his heart that needs to bleed now."

Aranur stared into the dark. His son. His only son. Because Danton now was dead. It hit him then that his youngest boy was gone. His knees weakened. A void swept in. "Danton," he whispered. He swore, long and low-voiced, in the night. The darkness cursed him back.

Gamon tried to pull him back in the house, but he resisted. With the light from the house behind him, the forest was black to his eyes. He could not see Olarun. "Dear moons," he whispered. "Oh, gods . . ."

"He'll be all right." Gamon pulled on his arm. "He'll come back."

Aranur couldn't take his eyes from the forest, the courtyard, the night. There were still wolves there—he could feel them. Like a sea of gray, they seethed at the edge of his mind. And they were with Olarun, he realized, following the boy in the darkness. Something tried to scream free inside Aranur's chest, but the steel of decades hardened his face. Slowly, he turned back to the house.

Gamon looked as if he wanted to ask a question, but Aranur shook his head. He went back and, from the doorway, watched the healers work.

It was time that killed his hope more than anything. They worked over her far too long, cleaning wounds so deep that Dion's soul should have escaped long before the dawn. Time, which should have given her life, ate at his mind like worms. He fixed an image of his mate in his head and held it there as they worked.

And later, when dawn blinked at the sky and silhouetted the mountains, the healers dispersed. The night nurse checked Dion, then stepped away, and Aranur was left alone.

He sank down into the nurse's chair. Dion's form was swathed in bandages, some of which were already spotted with blood. Only one hand was without coverings. He touched those fingers, cold and still on the sheets. Then he gripped her hand hard. His head sank onto her forearm.

"Live," he whispered.

"Live."

VII

What do you have but yourself?
Whom do you face but yourself?
What do you hear but your voice in the night?
Whom do you know but yourself?

—*Answer to the* Second Riddle of the Ages

Aranur awoke when the dawn healer did the final check for her shift, and he eyed her blearily.

"You should get some sleep," she advised gently. "You'll be no good to her, getting sick yourself."

Aranur shrugged. But he stood and tried to stretch cramped limbs. Between the wolf-driven ride and sitting all night, his legs had stiffened to logs. He looked for Hishn, but the gray wolf wasn't there. He chilled.

"It's all right," the healer assured him. "Dion is all right. The wolf just went out to relieve itself, I think."

Aranur paced the room. "Did Olarun come back?"

"He's asleep. Downstairs."

Aranur raised his eyebrows.

"He didn't want to sleep in his room, or in the one you share with Dion. He's over by Gamon and Tehena, camped out on the living-room floor."

"I'll be back in a minute," he told her.

"Better to be back in a few hours," she returned gently. "After you've had some sleep."

He ignored her.

When he returned, he found the day healer had taken over and was sitting in his chair. He looked at the man, looked at Dion, then looked back at the healer until the man glanced up and caught the expression on his face. The healer eyed him for a moment, then stood, saying quietly, "I'll take this chair," and moved to the other side of the bed.

Aranur sat down heavily. When he took Dion's hand, he squeezed it as if to tell her he was back. Then he put his head down again on her arm, as though he would be able to feel her pulse through her skin.

Five days passed. Five nights dragged on. Tehena settled in to one of the guest rooms and refused to leave. The hard-faced woman wasn't cook or hostess, nurse or nanny or helper, and she pestered the healers with hovering and constant criticism. Her words, acidic as worlag piss, irritated even Gamon. But somehow having Tehena there made Dion rest more easily, and it was Aranur who forced the healers to let her stay.

Tomi, Aranur's eldest, adopted son, and Gamon finally took over the nursing so that the healers could go home. The healers didn't argue: inside, there was Tehena; outside, eight wolves had refused to leave, and they surrounded the house like a gauntlet. The yard, pitted with sleeping holes and wallows, was an obstacle course of gray bodies and bones through which the healers had to tiptoe.

A ninan went by like a trial in which voices drone on without pause. There were words in Aranur's head that circled like a lepa flock. Danton was dead. Dion was not living. Olarun was no longer there. Olarun, his own son . . . And Danton—Danton was gone. The boys' room was shut, and no one—not even Olarun—opened the door. Aranur tried to bring some of Olarun's things from the room the two boys had shared, but his son put them back in the hallway outside the room as soon as Aranur turned his back.

It was guilt, not his shoulder, that bothered the boy. Olarun refused even to enter his mother's room. Each morning, he would go to the doorway to see if Dion had opened her eyes before he would turn away in silence. Aranur couldn't get him to speak of what had happened. In the boy's eyes, it was his fault that Danton had died, that his mother lay like a statue. Aranur could almost see the logic in Olarun's eyes: If he blamed himself, surely his father blamed him too?

And Dion—she lay still as death. It was weakness, said the healers, from the loss of blood, but Aranur wasn't so sure. There was a quietness about her that disturbed him—a quietness that echoed in his mind where, before, the gray swell of the wolves had rung with the tang of her voice. He found no solace in the assurance that she needed sleep to heal. She was conscious, he knew; he could feel it in the way Hishn looked at her. But he could not reach her. He stared down at her body. His son, his mate . . . He stalked from the room like death.

As though Dion's growing strength was reflected within the wolf pack, the wolves grew surly, then vicious. Twice they erupted into violence, fighting among themselves. The second time, Aranur and Gamon were standing on the porch eating some of the soup brought over by Tomi's Promised. One of the younger males slowly trotted too close to one of Gray Yoshi's bones, and the pack leader snarled. The young male didn't move fast enough out of the way. Instantly, the wolf pack was a frenzied mass of fur and snarls and slashing, ripping teeth. A moment later, it was over. The young male yearling was dead.

Aranur and Gamon stared at the wolf body. "Moons above us," the older man murmured, his soup bowl forgotten in his hands.

"They killed one of their own." Aranur's voice had a stunned quality.

Gamon tried to shrug, but his eyes were caught by the limpness of the wolf. "Males always challenge males."

"Not that young. That male was a yearling—he wasn't old enough to challenge Yoshi or any other adult." Aranur started to step down from the porch. "He had to be sick for them to kill him. I want to take a look at the body."

Gamon caught his arm. "Might not be a good idea to walk into that right now."

Aranur hesitated. Gray Yoshi looked up and caught his gaze. There was an impact of anger and grief that hit him like a punch. He staggered. His soup splashed out. Gamon cursed.

Aranur caught his balance against the porch post. He glanced down at the soup bowl he had emptied over his and Gamon's boots. "Sorry," he said belatedly.

"They got to you, didn't they?"

Aranur looked out at the wolves. "That they did," he agreed softly.

"They're getting to Dion, too."

"I know it."

The older man ran his hand through his gray hair. "Something has to break her out, Aranur. Something or someone."

Aranur's voice was instantly sharp. "I am trying, Gamon."

"Yes, you're trying," his uncle agreed. "But it might not be you who can reach her right now. She needs something else that's stronger. She's alert enough to hear the wolves—we know that. But she doesn't seem to care."

"What do you want me to do? I've talked to her. I've urged her. I've begged and pleaded with her to live. By the gods, I've cursed her. I've even had Tehena curse her—and you know the kind of vitriol that scrawny woman can spout. I've brought nearly every friend Dion has to the house to try to force her to wake. By all the moons that ride the sky, I can barely stand to see her as she is." He gestured impotently at the house. "That . . . apathetic body in there—that's not my mate. That's not the Dion who climbs and runs and breathes the wilderness. That's not the woman who stood with me before the council, who Called the wolves, who fought with me to protect her right to run her own trails. That body in there—that's not the Gray Wolf of Randonnen. Dion—my Dion—is the one who conned me into camping out in a stinkweed patch—remember that? She's the one who put fireweed in my extractor bag. Who danced with me on Dawnbreak Cliffs. That in there—that's not my mate. That's what's left of someone when the person is gone. It's nothing more than a shell."

"She'll heal, Aranur—"

Aranur cut his uncle off with a gesture. "It's not just her body, Gamon. It's her center—her heart. Can't you see it? It's no longer the heart of a wolf. It's broken—shattered like glass. And I'm not enough to mend it. Me, Olarun, Tomi, the wolves—we're not enough to help her."

Now Gamon sounded angry. "So when Danton died, so did she? She's gone, and you're just going to accept that?"

"Dammit, that's not what I'm saying. It's just . . . She's just . . ." He half raised his fists to pound on the porch, then let them fall helplessly. For a moment that seemed to hang between them forever, he stared into Gray Yoshi's eyes. Something old flickered deep in the yellow gaze; some gray-bound grief released. Aranur's breath caught like ice in his throat. When he could finally breathe again, when he turned back to the house, Gamon followed in silence.

The eyes of the wolves turned after them. Deep in the pack-song, a thread of gray shifted, twisted, curled around another thought. An older grief, brought by slitted eyes, washed through the memories. Longing swept back and forth in the packsong while the fire of the fevers burned away at their griefs, leaving only graves behind. The wolves howled, and Gray Yoshi stirred. He gathered those threads together. His yellow eyes gleamed as he blended the song and sent it to Hishn's mind.

At Dion's bedside, the gray wolf rose and placed her head on the bed next to the wolfwalker's arm. Softly, Hishn whuffed. Her whine was so low that it was more mental than physical, and somehow it reached the wolfwalker.

Dion didn't stir, didn't open her eyes, but a single tear formed at the edge of her eyelashes. It hung for a moment, like hope before it falls. Then it slid down her face to her hair.

VIII

Demon within
Doesn't hide in your heart—
He is meshed with your Self
From which you can't part.
When you feel Demon's touch
He is goading you on;
When you feel Demon move
He is guarding his own;
When you hear Demon shriek
He has taken his hold—
Not of your heart—
But your soul.

—The Tiwar, in Wrestling the Moons

Dion stuffed an extra tunic into her saddlebag, then strapped the bag closed. Her other saddlebag was packed; her weapons were oiled and sharpened; her herb pouches were full; her dnu was eager to go. Gray Hishn waited for her at the edge of the forest, where the narrow road led from their clump of houses down toward the town. There were wolves in the mountains—she could hear them like a thunder in her head. As though her illness had made her more sensitive, their voices called her strongly.

She looked at her hands on the leather. She was thin, she realized. Her fingers had been scarred before with living, but now they were gaunt—more bone than flesh. She ought to eat more, she told herself absently, knowing even as she did so that she had no taste for food. The healing the wolves had promoted in her for the past three months had sapped her as much as it had made her whole. Her lips twisted bitterly. Whole . . . If she hadn't been a wolfwalker, she'd still be tender from the wounds she'd sustained. As it was, with the ridges of flesh missing along her shoulders and back, with the muscles of her legs as seamed as a patchwork quilt, she was as whole as she was ever going to be. As whole as one could be when one had a void in one's heart. As whole as one was who was no longer a mother. As whole as one who was lost. She wondered what that ringrunner's storyteller would call it, then lost her expression completely. No good, no lesson, no truth could come of this. No storyteller could put a better face on what she felt right now.

Aranur covered her hand with his. His grip was not gentle, and she looked up. "Don't start," she said softly, looking up.

"You can't run away."

"And you can't protect me from my memories."

His gray eyes were like flint. "When I told you to make yourself less available to everyone, I didn't mean this."

Dion stared at him. Her expression was suddenly stricken, and Aranur's grip tightened. "Dion?"

She tried to speak.

"Dion?" he asked more sharply

"If I . . . What you said, Aranur. Don't you realize? If I had answered the healing summons, we would not have gone to Still Meadow. The boys would have stayed in Sharbrere. We would never have been caught by the lepa."

He crushed her hand in his. "Don't do this, Dion."

"How can I help it? That message ring Vlado brought from the elders . . . If I had agreed to do my job, our son—my little wolf—would still be alive."

"You can't know that—"

She cut him off, her voice harsh. "I know that the one time I reject my responsibility, I lose the life of our son."

"You didn't reject your responsibility; you were supposed to be off duty. And the boys had been promised a trip to Still Meadow. Their escorts could still have taken them out—everyone does it. Then both of them—and their escorts—would be dead. At least you saved Olarun."

"Did I? I was uneasy about the lepa from the start, but I didn't listen to myself. I was so determined to be with the boys . . . Oh, moons, Aranur, but what if I was so desperate for this break from work that I sacrificed our son?"

Aranur was shocked at how haggard she looked. He didn't remember grabbing her, but he was suddenly shaking her, shortly, viciously. He couldn't help it, even when she cried out at his grip. "Don't say that," he snarled. "Don't think it. Don't let a single word of that cross your lips again. I'll be damned if I let guilt kill you after all that you've survived."

She stared back at him. "And what have I survived?" she repeated harshly, finally. "My son—your son—is dead because I took him to Still Meadow when the lepa were flocking. My other son won't speak to me because I killed his brother and left him to face the lepa alone. Even the wolves reject me because of Sobovi's death on my hands."

"Everyone goes to Still Meadow this time of year. And the lepa were late in migration. You had no way to know they would flock. The spring diggers had gone there at dawn that day, and they saw no sign of flocking." His grip was hard enough to bruise her, but neither one of them noticed. "And Gray Yoshi may resent you, Dion, but he doesn't reject you, and you know it. It was he, not Hishn, who led the pack to bring you home. Even I felt it. He is as much a part of you through Gray Hishn as you are part of the pack."

"You speak of meadows and lepa and diggers and wolves, but do not speak of our sons."

His expression grew bleak. "Damn you," he whispered. He dropped his grip, and she closed her eyes. Finally, she turned away.

"Damn you," he snarled louder. He grabbed her arm, forcing her to face him again. "Don't you dare run away from me now. You've survived worlags and plague and raiders and wolves. You've survived me, for moons' sake. Even if you can't look at me now, I'm still here. You still have me. You have Tomi. You have Gamon and Rhom and the rest of your family. You have friends, Dion, who care about you—"

"Words. Words." She shook him off.

"What you need is here, Dion, not out in the wilderness."

"What I need is here? By the light of the moons, have you no sense? All that I have here are ghosts, Aranur. Every time I turn around, I see my son." She grabbed the fence post beside her. "This is the post he used to climb. That is the tree he fell out of last fall. Over there is the hole he buried his boots in to keep me from seeing the way he'd cut them up—"

"Don't you think it's the same for me?" Aranur's voice was quiet as stone.

Her tone matched his. "Yes, I believe it is the same for you. And I wish I could ache for the way you feel, for your grief, for the emptiness in your eyes when you look for him in the morning. But I can't. I can't feel anything but that which now consumes me."

"We feel the same thing, Dion—"

"No," she cut in sharply. "We don't. It is not you who carries the blame for Danton's death. It is I."

Aranur didn't answer.

"My love," she said, "I can't see myself anymore."

"I can see you. Why isn't that enough?"

She shook her head. "You—your choices are so simple, Aranur. Raiders ride, and you draw your sword and cut them down if you can. I must choose to lift my hands to the blade, or lift my hands to heal. I hold the decision of life and death, not in clear defense as you do, but in cold rationality. I cut off one side of myself in order to loose the other. So I am a healer, but I killed my own son. I am a swordswoman, but I heal my victims. Look at me, Aranur. Tomi isn't mine—he still dreams of his real mother. And Olarun rejects me for Danton's death. I am a mother without children—and a child without a mother. My world is life and death without balance, and it's tearing me apart."

"And if you ride away, what do you think to find? Danton's soul? A mother for yourself? A sword that magically doesn't kill, or a healing technique that does? Why not just ask the Aiueven for a stepping stone to the stars? Even that's more likely than balancing the things you've lost."

"It's not just that." She clenched her fists. "Don't you see? I've lost more than my sons and myself. I'm too close to the wolves and too far from all of you. I've lost my own humanity. Staying here won't give me back that."

"Balance, wisdom, humanity . . ." He gestured sharply, angrily. "They're not out there, Dion. If you find them at all, they'll come out of yourself."

"And in my heart, I know that's true," she agreed.

"But you're still going to go."

Dion's voice trembled. "Dammit, Aranur, I don't want to breathe here. I don't want to see or hear the ghosts. I don't want to eat. I don't want to live."

"And out there, you will."

"I don't know," she almost cried out. "But I do know that here, I cannot survive Olarun's blame, nor yours, nor my own."

"Then take someone with you."

She almost laughed, but the sound was harsh and without humor. "A bodyguard? A nanny?"

"Me."

"It's your blame I'm trying to escape."

"I don't blame you—"

"Don't you? Isn't there some tiny, hidden part of you that says, 'If Dion hadn't taken them out in the meadow, Danton wouldn't have died'? We don't touch anymore—our hugs are perfunctory, not desired. We barely speak or eat together. By the moons, we don't even sleep together anymore. I'm like an alien in my own home. And why is that? Can you honestly say that there is not some part of you hating and blaming me even now?"

His voice was harsh. "You confuse what I feel with what you think you deserve."

"But you don't really deny it, do you?"

Aranur couldn't answer.

"I'll ride with the wolves," she told him quietly. "They've always been company enough."

"They're the past and the present, Dion, not the future. You need something more than that to become yourself again." He paused. "Your future is here, with me, with your family. You'll not find it by running away."

But from the forest Hishn's ears flicked as the wolf read Dion's resolve. The Gray One howled deep into Dion's mind, and the sound echoed into the void of her emotions. For a moment Dion almost believed that the packsong could fill that void. Then the mental howl faded, and what it left was emptiness.

Aranur watched her eyes unfocus and focus, and he knew that Hishn was with her. His voice was almost desperate when he spoke. "Have you forgotten the raiders? They're active as worlags in fall right now, and even the wolves can't protect you from them. You can't expect to outrun them—you still limp like a lame worlag. You've got a sword, a bow, that blade hidden in your healer's circlet, the knives in your boots . . . But none of that can stand against a single surprise attack."

She couldn't meet his gray gaze.

"Don't even think it, Dion," he snarled. "Letting yourself be taken or killed will not absolve you of the guilt you think you deserve, nor will it bring Danton back. It would merely strip Olarun's mother from him more permanently than your running away does now."

"That isn't fair," she whispered.

"But it's what you were thinking, wasn't it?"

She looked down.

"Take someone with you. Take Gamon or maJenia or ma-Trawek."

She shook her head.

"Take Ruttern, then. He's good. Or neBraye."

"No."

"At least take Tehena. The way she's been hovering over you the last three months, I can't believe she would let you ride out alone anyway."

"I sent her to get some things from town."

His face hardened. "So she doesn't even know that you're going."

Dion shrugged.

This time when Aranur grabbed her, she didn't flinch. He dug his fingers into her arms as if to force her to feel him. "You'll take someone with you. Promise me, Dion. If you love yourself at all—if you love me even a fraction anymore—take at least one rider with you."

She stared at him for a long time. His face was gaunt like hers, she realized. There was no shadow of stubble along his chin, and she found herself wishing he had one to soften the hard line of his jaw. Without it, he looked bleak. Lost. She reached up and touched his cheek, then dropped her hand to his arm. His lean muscles bunched beneath her touch.

"Take Kiyun," he said desperately.

When she finally spoke, her voice was soft. "I will wait while you get him."

Something in Aranur's eyes seemed to die, but he nodded, a short, sharp movement. Then he took the reins from the post and mounted her dnu. He wheeled and gave the dnu its head, letting it thunder out of the courtyard.

Dion looked across to the forest that hid Gray Hishn. "Kiyun,

Tehena . . ." she said softly. "It doesn't matter who it is, or how many there are. It will not make a difference."

* * *

Aranur rode hard, by instinct more than by sight. His urgency drove him to drive the dnu, as much to tire it so that Dion could not ride far on its back as to dull his own thoughts. He didn't wave at those he saw on the road. He didn't pause at his uncle's house even though his aunt was on the porch, looking up as he rode by. Instead, he pushed the dnu's pace through the first city hub, then the next, until he reached a long, vaulted structure.

When he dismounted, he stood for a long moment before entering the building. The wide, arched porch was more like what one would see on a library than on a house, and the doorway, arched and pillared with intricate growths of aircoral, belonged at a museum, not a home. He couldn't help noticing, as he paused in the entryway, the two sculptures that decorated the entrance.

"Kiyun," he called out. His voice was harsh, and he felt his lips tighten automatically.

"Back here," a voice echoed distantly from within.

Aranur stepped through into the main hall of the home. It was a vaulted room lined with paintings. They were not of recognizable shapes and figures, but were rather splotches of color, shades that shifted from one monochromatic palette to another. Dion had bought them one by one but had never brought even one of them home. Instead, she had asked this man here to hold them for her, building this collection. Did she think this swordsman's hands could appreciate the delicate touch of the brushes that had applied the colors here? Did she think this man's blood-weary eyes could find philosophy in the aggressive bursts of paint? The sculptures that stood between the paintings or in clusters of two and three were twisted figures, human and otherwise. Kneeling together, clinging or struggling, the figures echoed pure emotion. And Dion had asked Kiyun to hold them.

Aranur stared at the man who was sitting, sipping a mug of steaming rou, but as he entered, Kiyun got swiftly to his feet, setting down the mug. The two men eyed each other for a long moment.

Kiyun was as tall as Aranur, but his hair was brown where Aranur's was black, and his shoulders heavier with muscle. His hands were thick where Aranur's were lean; but his face, though strong, appeared almost soft compared to Aranur's hard expression.

"How is Dion?" Kiyun asked finally.

Aranur's voice was flat. "She's running away."

"You want me to . . ." Kiyun's voice trailed off. Want me to talk to her, he wanted to say, but the look on Aranur's face killed the thought.

Aranur made a show of looking around the hall. "You keep, what, twelve of her sculptures now?" he asked instead.

Kiyun did not nod. "Twenty-two paintings, twelve sculptures, three art-message rings."

"She's never brought any art home."

The other man shifted uncomfortably.

"You are special to her," Aranur said.

The man shrugged.

"She has always cared for you."

"She doesn't love me like that," Kiyun returned.

Aranur gave the other man a hard look.

Deliberately, Kiyun took up his mug of rou.

Aranur's voice was cold, unforgiving. "You offered her Kum-jan."

"She asked me to," the other man said calmly. He nodded at the cold fury that glinted in Aranur's gray eyes. "She asked me to do so as a friend, so that her rejection was public. Only a woman who wants an exclusive bond with her mate will publicly reject Kum-jan from an intimate friend."

"She didn't tell me that."

"No." Kiyun paused. "I've never hidden what I feel, Aranur."

"I know it too well." Aranur bit the words out.

"And you think someday I'll try to take her from you," the other man returned, his voice hard. "You're dead wrong, Aranur. Of all the things I feel for Dion, one of them is respect. Even if she were to offer Kum-jan now, I would refuse her that. She will never want me except as a way to reach toward what she thinks she has lost with you. It is you she chose as her mate, not me. I would never be enough."

And I am not enough now: She seeks what she has never had, and I cannot give that to her. Aranur's thought was written on his face. Kiyun said nothing. Aranur stared around the hall, one part of his brain automatically cataloguing the number of paintings against the years he had been with Dion. "She is riding out tonight," he said finally. "I can't stop her."

The other man put down his mug and waited.

Aranur had to force the words out. "She said she would ride with you."

"All right."

Aranur glared at the other man.

"Say it," Kiyun said. "You might as well."

"You . . . She . . ."

"She is yours, Aranur. I'll not touch her."

Aranur didn't trust himself to speak, but his eyes were cold and icy.

"I'll swear it, if you need the words," offered the other man.

Aranur turned abruptly away. "Don't let her get too close to the wolves. She's lost right now. She could . . . She . . ."

"She will be all right," Kiyun returned. "Whatever else she is, she is still Dion. She's strong, and she knows, deep down, that you love her. She won't abandon you and Olarun, even for the wolves."

It wasn't the wolves that scared him. Aranur didn't know why he thought that, but he knew suddenly that it was true. He stared down at his hands. Long-fingered, lean, strong hands they were, skilled at pulling and holding together men and women in a common cause. But strong as they were, desperate as they were, they could not hold on to Dion. "Those who have strong passions, create strong self-destructions," he said finally, flatly. He looked up. "Make sure that she seeks healing, not death."

The other man nodded.

Brown eyes bored into gray. Neither man moved. Finally, Kiyun held out his arm. Aranur stared at him. He turned on his heel and strode from the room. Kiyun was left standing, arm out, as if the emptiness of the room would shake Aranur's words from the air.

"He doesn't know," he told the paintings finally. "He'll never understand her. The world is black and white to him, but she lives in shades of gray."

* * *

It was dusk when Dion rode out, and there were three riders with her, not one. Gamon, Tehena, Kiyun—when they showed up together, Dion merely looked at them, then turned her dnu toward the darkening forest cliffs.

Aranur, alone in the courtyard, watched her go in silence. Olarun refused to see his mother off; he had disappeared instead. And the others had sensed the chill of Aranur's fury. They left quickly, so that only the twilight, which gathered around Aranur as the wolves gathered to Dion, stayed to keep him company.

Aranur's voice was cold and hard as he watched the riders reach the upper ridge trail. "Damn you, Dion," he breathed. "But you've made me love you more than life. You've made yourself a part of me until I can't turn around without looking for your touch, listening for your voice. Now you think you have to leave me to become whole again by yourself." He stretched his own mind to hear the faint echo of wolves, but all he found was a wisp of fog that shredded beneath the moons. A lone wolf howled up on a ridge, and the sound hung over his ears. His jaw muscles jumped, his gray eyes narrowed. "You are torn, Dion, and so you tear me. You need balance, but you won't find it without me." His fist pressed against his sternum. The two gems of their mating, which studded his bone, were hard nodules under his fingers.

His voice grew intent, and only the night saw the steel that glinted in his eyes. "I am yours, Dion, and you are mine. You can't lose me by leaving me, no matter what you think you deserve." He watched a shadow flit across the ridge, and he knew that it was she. "You'll face yourself—and me—again, or you'll find no future you can live with. You can't hide in the packsong forever, Dion. You can't hide in whatever you seek. If you don't come back to me on your own, I'll track you down like a wolf does a deer, to the ends of this world and beyond. Through the mountains, through the wolves, through alien peaks or the depths of the sea—on the very path to the moons, if I must." The gemstones ground into his bones. He didn't notice. "By the Gray Ones," he breathed. "By Ovousibas, by all nine moons, by all the Ancient curses, I swear this, Ember Dione maMarin: By all the gods of past and present, I'll find for us a future. I'll bring you back to me."

IX

South and down along river mountains. South, where trails were hard and dry above brutal, white-watered rocks. South, away from the mountains, away from Ariye, Dion kept their dnu turned. Two days on the trail turned into three, then five, then eight. And all the while, the ground lowered itself from the mountains to the border hills that ringed the coastal valleys. The trails, which had been half rock, became softer soil and dirt. The summer air, which had been clear and cold at night, grew humid and warm with moisture. And the sea began to flavor the wind.

From the hilltops, the summer fields stretched out like swatches of rolling green caught between taller, darker forests. Thick lines of barrier bushes gave way to stone or wood-weathered fences. It was easy to tell where the plants of the Ancients were grown. Within the fields of indigenous vegetables and grains, as if guarded by their contoured rows, the irregular patches of darker and lighter shades made a poxlike pattern of color. Seeds of the Ancients, Dion thought, carried across the stars. Like the seeds of their past, carefully guarded and protected by legend and books. Or the germs of new science, grown up behind walls and sheltered from alien eyes . . . She couldn't help the look she gave the moons. If the moons could give the Ancients a world, why couldn't they give her peace? But the white orbs floated silently in their distant, blue-humid sky.

Four times they crossed raider sign on the roads. The first time it was old sign, the deep hoofprints and shards of wagons locked into hardened mud where the traders had driven their

139

caravans. The other two signs were more recent. At the fourth place they passed where raiders had fought, the stone cairns on the side of the road marked funeral pyres. The cairns still shifted and swirled with ash that had not yet been blown off by the wind.

They passed villages and small towns, skirted caravans, and watched the young men and women who traveled on their Internships and Journeys. Small groups, large groups, and once or twice, single riders . . . The days blended from one to the next.

Early into the second ninan, Dion eyed yet another pair of riders as she waited with Gamon and the wolf near one of the roadside message cairns. Kiyun and Tehena were checking the snares they had set out the previous night, while Dion and Gamon broke camp.

One of the young riders on the road raised his hand in greeting as he passed. Gamon waved slightly in return. His gray eyes followed the riders. "Young," he murmured.

Dion nodded.

Gamon glanced at her, then motioned with his chin at the riders. "You were young like that when I met you. You and your brother—new as spring grass."

Her eyes unfocused, as though she could feel her twin even at this distance.

Gamon caught her expression. "We could ride back east into Randonnen. You could see him and your father."

Abruptly, her eyes focused. "No," she said flatly.

"Dion, you need your family right now. If not Aranur and Tomi and Olarun, then why not your twin and his mate? You need someone to talk to—and you've always been able to talk to your twin."

"He already knows. There is no need to tell him."

He eyed her steadily. "He might be able to feel your pain at this distance, but don't you think you owe him more than that? At the least, you should give him the reassurance of seeing you—of seeing that you're okay."

She couldn't meet his eyes. "I sent a message ring," she said, her voice low.

"It's not the same." He studied her. "Ah, Dion," he sighed finally. "You haven't even seen your father in two years."

She looked up then and met his gray, faded eyes. "What would

I say if I saw them, Gamon? 'Greetings, Father. I've killed your grandson?' Or, 'Say, Rhom, did you notice that really dark period when I let your nephew die?' I look back, Gamon, and wonder how much danger my father really let Rhom and me get into when we were growing up. Then I look at my life and the life I've led my boys into, and I know what he and Rhom think of my taking my sons out on the trail. Their blame is deserved, Gamon. And that's something I'm not ready to face."

"They would never blame you. Only you do that. And your brother has taken his own children out on the trail."

"But never far from home. And Randonnen is safer than Ariye. The lepa don't breed in our mountains, so there is never danger from a flocking. The worlags are smaller, and we don't even have barrier bushes. There's no brown fungi or fruga bushes or eyemites or spiela. But here in Ariye, all those things fill your forests, and they are dangers every day. By the moons, Gamon, I've taken my boys out where even adults are wary."

"Aranur learned to run trail that way. I learned that way when I was a boy. Even the Lloroi grew up that way. How else would your sons grow up?" he demanded.

"Inside the barrier bushes," she retorted.

"You'd rather have them ignorant?" Gamon shot back.

"I'd rather have them alive."

Gamon was silent for a moment. "You can't change the past, Dion, and you can't bring Danton out of the grave, but you still have two sons. Tomi may not be your blood son, but he loves you like a mother. And Olarun will eventually return to you in his heart. He just needs time and comfort."

"It's comfort I can't give him, Gamon."

"Aye. He and you—you're the same. You need someone to comfort you, Dion, so that you can again comfort your sons."

Her lips twisted. "You think I need some kind of a mother?"

"If you do, that's one thing I can't get for you. You'll have to settle for your father and brother."

"I've said no, Gamon."

"And you mean it," he added, so flatly that the words meant the opposite of what he said.

She closed her eyes for a moment. "I don't want to ride those trails again. There are graves in Randonnen, too."

"You were not so uneager when I met you."

"That was a long time ago," she retorted.

"Not to me. I remember it clearly. You and your twin—you were so alike, so different back then. So protective of each other, and yet so independent. And that damned wolf, hovering and snarling like a mother guarding her pup after Aranur knocked you out. I had known it would have to be a different kind of woman who hooked my nephew's heart, but I'd never thought he'd be so anxious for a mate that he'd tackle a woman from her dnu."

A ghost of a smile touched Dion's lips, though the expression did not reach her eyes. "My jaw hurt for a ninan afterwards."

"What did you expect—fists of feather? He was a weapons master, even then."

"Even then," she agreed.

Gamon studied her face. "He needs you, Dion. Both he and Olarun. You know that just as you know your wolf. It's been a ninan. You've run far enough. If you won't go to your own family, go back to your mate and your sons."

"I can't—"

"Why not?" Gamon cut her off sharply. "You need Aranur and Tomi and Olarun as much as they need you. That, you can't deny."

But Dion was already shaking her head. "I can't go back," she repeated.

"What holds you to this trail?" he demanded. "Your search to find yourself again, as you so quaintly put it to Aranur? Your need to escape the blame you heap upon yourself? You can't tell me it's Hishn—the only reason that mutt is dogging your heels out here is that you're pulling her as surely as if you put a rope on her neck and tied her to your dnu. She'd be back with her own pack now, running with her own mate, if you were at home. You may have brought the wolves back to Ariye, but it's not as though there are so many anywhere that you can sacrifice any wolf's litters. And Hishn—she's one of the few wolves who gives birth to more than one pup at a time. Compared to Ancient years, most Gray Ones' litters are barely token births. Hishn is the rare wolf who gives forth live—not dead—wolf cubs. Are you going to sacrifice your own Gray One's children because you can't face your mate?"

Dion couldn't answer him.

"And how long, Dion, before the raiders find out that you're riding these trails without Aranur? We crossed raider tracks this morning. If they find out you're here, they could try again, here, to kill you."

Slowly, Dion looked up. "You and Tehena and Kiyun—you've been talking about this behind my back?"

"You've seen the signs as clearly as we have."

"I won't go back."

"Yet," Gamon added almost grimly.

Dion's violet eyes glinted. "I'm no pawn of yours, Gamon, to be pushed here and there by mere words."

But the older man's gray eyes had their own steely tone. His voice did not back down. "I can push harder, Dion, if you need such motivation."

Something in her cracked. "Why do this to me?" she cried out. "Why say these things when you know I can't hear them yet?"

"You've had enough time, Wolfwalker." He used the title deliberately. "You need to start facing yourself again."

"And you've appointed yourself my spirit guide?"

"Someone's got to, and it might as well be me. I'm not just a friend, Dion, I'm family. I'm your uncle—through love if not blood—so I can say these things—and more, if necessary—to get you back where you belong." He caught the twist of her lips. "You think that's humorous?"

She shook her head. "It's not that. It's that yesterday Kiyun went on about the same thing. 'I'm not family,' he told me, 'I'm a friend, so I can say these things to you.' "

Gamon grinned sourly. "And Tehena, how did she put it?"

"She didn't put anything. She just asked where I wanted to go."

"Moonwormed woman. She'd follow you though all nine hells and back if you asked it of her."

Dion fingered a twig beside her, snapping it off absently. When she realized what she was doing, she threw the stick on the ground. Hishn stretched out and took the twig in her teeth, shredding it into fragments. Dion watched the wolf, letting Hishn's sense of taste bring the bitter flavor of bark and sap to her own tongue. Her voice was quiet when she finally said, "I need more time, Gamon. I want to see land other than that in

Ariye. I want to see rivers and valleys where the fog isn't heavy with pain and death and loss. I want to see the ocean again. I want, Gamon, to go someplace where there aren't so many ghosts."

The older man didn't speak for a moment. Then he touched her arm.

"Please," she whispered, not even knowing what she was asking.

He pulled her to him, hugging her roughly. The hilt of his sword caught on her hip, and the archer's patch on her forearm snagged on his tunic. Gamon shook his head as they untangled each other. Dion looked up into his grizzled face. "You Ariyen men—you never can learn to hug."

"And you Randonnen women are always too stubborn to reason with."

"It's a gift," she told him wryly.

"It's a pain in the neck, Dion."

"Gamon—"

"I know, I know. I'm just along for the ride, after all, seeing as how you aren't much for conversation these days." He glanced up the trail to see Kiyun and Tehena riding down.

Feeling Dion's frustration, Hishn growled beside him.

He ignored the wolf. Deliberately, he said, "Remember Red Harbor, thirteen years ago?"

Dion's face shadowed. "How could I not?"

"Do you also remember what Aranur told Tyrel after the boy's sister died?"

"I do."

"Say it, Dion. Say the words."

Her violet eyes glinted dangerously, and Hishn rose slowly to her feet. The hackles on the wolf's neck rose into a bristly mass. Dion didn't notice. "I'm tired of hearing the words, Gamon," she said, her voice hard. "And don't give me that 'you have to go on' line again. If you haven't lost a son, you can't understand what I feel. If you haven't caused the death of your own child, you'll never understand what I live with."

"You're wallowing in guilt."

"Why shouldn't I?"

"Because you'll kill yourself if you keep on."

Her voice was suddenly quiet. "And why shouldn't I do that, Gamon?"

The older man stared at her. He realized suddenly that the strain that pulled at the wolfwalker's face was so much a part of her body that it could break her very bones. And that Hishn didn't hover around Dion because the wolfwalker called the wolf, but because Hishn was herself afraid of losing her wolfwalker.

Dion's eyes were dark. "Why should I go on?" she repeated. "Why should I let myself live? Just because I have a skill that the county needs? Because there are people who want to use my body, my skills?" Her fist clenched. "Am I nothing more than a tool to the people I've counted as friends?" Her knuckles, white before, began to shake. "What part of me is allowed to be human? What part of me may grieve?"

Gamon's face hardened slowly. "You think you're the only one to lose a child?"

"Yes." Hishn's snarl was in Dion's throat, and the wolfwalker's voice was harsh. "At this moment, right now, I am the only one who has lost a child. I don't care who else feels grief right now. I don't care how many ghosts you've hung on your sword. And for once, I don't give a damn about another person's loss. Don't talk to me about others' deaths, about going on, about being strong. I *can't* feel anything but myself right now—don't you at least see that?"

He nodded slowly. He glanced at Hishn, then back at the wolfwalker, noting the almost yellow glint to her shadowed eyes. "I can see that," he said quietly.

"Then why can't you leave me alone?"

"I'm not doing this for me, Dion, but for you and Aranur. My nephew never was one to run away from his problems, and he won't let you do that either. Take too long to heal out here, and he'll come after you and force you to face yourself. You'll hate him for that, Dion. It will be a knife between you."

Her face tightened. "I understand knives."

"Yes," he agreed, "more than most, you do. But do you need to wound your own mate as you wound yourself?"

"Gamon—"

"Whether you face yourself now or later, the circumstance

doesn't change, Dion: Danton died. You didn't." His voice was suddenly hard. "Deal with it."

"I need time."

"You have the rest of your life to grieve, Dion. How much time do you have to love those who are still near you?"

"I don't have any more love to give," she cried out.

"You do, Wolfwalker. You wouldn't feel this strongly about Danton if you didn't have more than enough love in you for the rest of your life."

"You haven't a clue how I feel, Gamon. Don't speak to me of love."

Like a wolf himself, the lean older man rounded on her. His gray eyes were suddenly as steely as Aranur's, his hands like vises on her arms. Hishn was up and beside Dion in a flash. Gamon ignored the wolf, but the Gray One's teeth were bared. "I lost my mother, my father," he breathed in Dion's face. "I lost all my brothers but one because of raiders. I lost two nieces who were like daughters to me, and you and I both know I could have stopped their deaths if my sword had been a little faster. There was a woman I would have Promised with who died in my arms before I could tell her what I felt." His voice tightened to a snarl. "There was another woman I lost to my own reluctance to Promise. Don't tell me I don't know what you feel, Wolfwalker. I've lived long enough to lose a dozen lifetimes."

Dion eyed the older man warily. Gamon's calm wisdom had ripped away, leaving only the steel behind, and it was a hard, bright, bitter knot. She knew suddenly where Aranur got his iron will—it had been forged here, in his uncle Gamon. She tried to speak, but her lips were curled back with Hishn's, and her throat tightened as if to tear out the gray-haired man's words. She sucked in a breath. Nothing loosened in her chest, but suddenly, Hishn backed down.

Gamon studied Dion's face as if to find a hint of anything insincere. Then he nodded, shortly.

Kiyun gave Dion a sharp look when he and Tehena rejoined her and Gamon. But she shook her head at him, and the burly man said nothing. He just reined in by the wolfwalker and led the way out onto the road.

It was midmorning by the time they reached the turnoff for

one of the farming villages. But as they came around the hill, Kiyun, in the lead, signaled for them to pull up rather than ride on. "Smoke," he said quietly, pointing through the trees. The bare wisp of gray was battered apart by the slight wind, but not before it made a faint, but distinctive streak.

Automatically, Dion sent Hishn into the woods. The gray wolf snarled at her, and Dion felt the pull of the pack as Hishn tried to get her to fade back in the forest with the wolf. Dion resisted. Her toes clenched in her boots as Hishn's mind sucked at hers.

Enough, Gray One, Dion sent sharply.

Come with me, sent the wolf. *Come home to the pack. You have no need to hunt here.*

If the hunt finds me, who am I to fight it?

Hishn glared at her balefully, then faded back so that she disappeared.

Beside Dion, Gamon squinted at the dull morning sky. For the last day and a half, the clouds had gathered into a gray pallor relieved only by the near-hidden passage of the moons. "That's Prandton," he said softly. "We're close enough to the last raider strike that this town could have been hit on the same run."

Automatically, Dion touched her healer's circlet, then pulled her warcap down to make sure it covered the silver. Her finger caught for a moment on the seam that was concealed in the design of the silver. The hidden blade was like a needle in her mind, reminding her that even the silver symbol of healing she wore hid unbalanced death within it. Abruptly, she dropped her hand. She didn't notice that it fell to the hilt of her sword as she closed up in a knot with the others.

The riders slowed as they rounded the last bend before entering the village hub. It was summer, but instead of being filled with activity, the clumps of houses were shuttered against the gray, humid daylight. Two homes and their shared stable were gutted and smoking, and a third home around one of the commons was still smoldering with glowing coals. Tools were discarded, and woodpiles scattered between the clustered homes. And there were two bodies in the street, surrounded by rocks and chunks of wood.

In the distance, a woman stepped out, caught sight of them, and ducked hastily back into her house. A flash of paleness from another structure showed where someone had peeked from a window.

As if their moves were choreographed, Kiyun and Tehena spurred their dnu ahead of Dion so that she fell behind with Gamon. A moment later, they skirted the bodies in the street. Both dead men had been brutally beaten. Soberly, Kiyun dismounted. The others remained warily on their dnu, their weapons resting but ready on their saddles and thighs.

Kiyun looked up. "Raiders," he called softly. He stood and studied the town, absently kicking aside one of the clubs.

"Looks like a trial block got out of hand," Gamon murmured to Dion.

Soberly, she nodded. They dismounted. Dion knelt by the two bodies, studying them. Then she sat back on her heels.

Wolfwalker? Hishn called. *The smoke you smell is harsh and old. Leave this place with me.*

I need to stay. Don't worry. There is no danger here.

But the gray wolf snarled. *There is death in your nose.*

And in my eyes. Dion couldn't help her answer, and she almost flinched with the strength of the howl that Hishn sent up from the forest. The massive wolf moved then, back to the street, following Dion's voice.

Gamon caught a flash of face at another window as the gray wolf loped into town. He started toward the house but had barely put his hand on the gate when the door opened. A stocky man stepped out. Behind him, a woman and two youths peered out from the doorway. The farmer had a sword in one hand, the steel newly cleaned and oiled but the blade itself too small for his grip. He held it firmly, but as if it were a tool, not an extension of his arm. "And who will you be?" he asked finally.

"Gamon Aikekkraya neBentar," the older man answered first.

"I've heard of you," the other man returned. "A weapons master, you are."

"Ah, Moriko, I told you someone would come." The woman's voice, low as it was, sounded hard to Dion's ears. "I told you we couldn't hide. And one of the weapons masters here. We'll all be blamed, for sure—"

"Quiet," the man said harshly over his shoulder.

"What happened?" Gamon asked soberly.

"Raiders," he said shortly, "as any fool can see."

Gamon ignored the bitterness in the farmer's terse words. "When did they strike?" he asked instead.

The farmer regarded him for a long moment. "Near dawn," he said finally. "They were waiting in the hills for first light when we went to the fields for the second planting."

"How many?"

"Fourteen, fifteen. Maybe more." Moriko glared at one of the gutted houses. "I wasn't exactly counting their pretty faces."

"You drove them off?"

The farmer eyed the older man. Finally, he said, "They caught us off guard. Killed two; wounded nine or ten of us. Might as well have killed Lege, too, for all that they've left him a vegetable."

"Do you have a healer?"

"Not anymore." Moriko's voice was flat and hard as Gamon's. "Yrobbi was grabbed by a raider. Had a heart attack and died on the spot. Raiders would have killed the old man anyway—they went for his circlet as if it was gold till they realized he was a man, not a woman." The farmer shrugged. "They were looking for someone specific, I guess; he just happened to get in the way."

Dion tensed, and Kiyun, beside her, laid his hand on her arm. She didn't seem to notice, but Hishn's snarl turned toward the big man. Slowly, Kiyun removed his hand.

"We sent word to every village months ago," Gamon told the stocky man sharply. "You were to keep a watch posted at the relay stations and a few archers on duty at all times. Where were your archers? Why didn't the watch stations warn you?"

The farmer's eyes narrowed. "We've always been ignored by the raiders before this, so our archers were in the fields, planting, with the rest of us. They have families to feed too, you know."

"They had families to guard—"

"Our crops," the other man cut in, "had to go in before the rains came so that the soil didn't clot up. Roots can't grow through clotted soil; they grow around the clods instead, and that kills the roots later—dries them out like bread when they're exposed to the summer heat. Our archers know that as well as any of us." His eyes darkened. "And it was just for half a ninan while the weather held. Four or five days—anyone would have taken that chance if their livelihood depended on it."

"Even if their lives depended on doing something else?"

The man's lips tightened, but he didn't answer.

"So you figured the raiders wouldn't know that you had dropped your guard for the planting," Gamon said, disgusted. He pointed to the bodies. "What about those two?"

The other man shrugged, suddenly uncomfortable.

Gamon just looked at him. "They lie here, in front of your house. Are you willing to take the responsibility for that yourself?" From the doorway, the woman listening wailed softly.

Gamon brushed Moriko's sword aside and took his arm, pushing the farmer to look toward the bodies that lay in the street. The farmer jerked free. His wife almost flew from the doorway, but Tehena moved like a flash between Gamon and the house, giving the other woman a look that stopped her in her tracks.

"These weren't trial-block deaths," Gamon said flatly.

The other man swallowed. "Lon— Some of the men got angry. Things just got out of hand."

"You mean you had a lynching, not a trial. Why?" Gamon demanded harshly. "Where was your village Voice? Where were your elders?"

"Elder neBalrot was sick," Moriko retorted. "Two of our women and three of our men were taken or killed. We've got four farmers out of action for at least a month, and plantings on which we depend for survival. Yrobbi would have been killed if he hadn't died on his own. And the only reason his intern wasn't killed, too—they were looking for anyone with a silver band— was that Asuli isn't one to help with the plantings. She hid beneath one of the porch stones when the raiders hit us in the fields. And it's lucky for us that she did, because without her there would have been no one to tend to our wounded."

Tehena snorted. "So you made the raiders pay for your hurts by beating these two to death? Now that's a civilized response."

"Lon neHansin started it," the man snarled back. "He threw the first rock."

"The first rock? How many did you throw after that? And how many did your mate throw?" Gamon cursed under his breath. "You're no better than the raiders themselves. Go on, hide in your house. Pretend you didn't have anything to do with it. It won't help you. This lynching will crawl around in your heart and fester till it rots your insides out. It'll eat at you until you look over your shoulder every time you turn around. Every time you swallow, the rot will grow in your throat till it chokes you as dead as you beat these two men. They may have been raiders, but they were still human beings." He kicked a stone toward the man. It rolled to a stop at Moriko's feet, and the farmer jerked back from it.

"No one," Gamon added forcefully, "deserves to die this way. And no one with a soul should ever have a hand in killing another man this way." He gave the villager a hard look. "Where are your wounded?"

Moriko struggled with his own anger, holding his voice.

Gamon cursed again under his breath and turned away.

The other man let out an oath. "You," he snarled at Gamon. "You turn back to me now."

Gamon half paused and looked over his shoulder. His expression was not warm.

But the farmer wasn't daunted. Moriko took a step toward Gamon. "You're a fine one to talk, neBentar. Oh, it's easy for you, isn't it, to come in here and judge our lives. You think you can tell us what's right or wrong, what we should or shouldn't have done. But you're not the one who had to make the decisions. You're not the one who has to live with what happened. We made our decisions based on things that you, in your distant town, with your high-and-mighty training, don't have to consider—like how we'll feed our families, come winter, if the crops don't go in the ground now." He spat to the side. "You, with your fancy sword and bow—where were you when we needed another archer? Where were you when the raiders came? We've lost brothers and sisters and sons. You've lost nothing here. But you stand there with the . . . the gall to tell us we were a little bit rough on the raiders who killed our daughters and sons? Who the hell do you think you are to judge us when you don't live here?"

Gamon's voice was dangerously calm. "You think we have to live here to understand what you did? You think proximity defines what is right and wrong?"

"It sure as hell defines who gets to make the judgment of it."

"I disagree." Gamon turned away again.

The villager grabbed the older man's arm. Like a gray wolf himself, Gamon whipped his arm in a tight circle, catching the farmer's wrist in a flash and twisting so that the stocky man went down hard to his knees. The man's mate cried out, but Tehena grabbed her arm. For a moment, Dion's vision flickered: It was Aranur who held the man, not Gamon. It was Aranur's voice that rang in her ears. The link between Hishn and Dion was thick with both their mates, and the wolf's longing swamped her. She sucked in a breath, but Aranur's icy gray eyes hung in her sight. Then his straight black hair faded to gray; his lean, strong hands became gnarled with age. And Gamon stared down into the villager's face until the other man went pale from the pain.

"Do you feel this?" Gamon said softly. "This is proximity. What does it mean?"

"I don't know," Moriko gasped.

"It means pain, man. It means that I take advantage of you and cause you this pain—or more. I could push a little and break your wrist. I could push a lot and break your wrist, elbow, and shoulder all at the same time." He stared down into the farmer's eyes. "If I do break your bones, for no reason other than that I want to do so, is this act right or wrong?"

"It's wrong, damn you."

"Whether I do this to you or your mate, or to the farmer in the next town, does it change the rightness or wrongness of what I do?"

"No," the farmer gasped. "For moons' sake, let go—"

"So proximity to the act has nothing to do with the act itself."

"All right, all right, I get your point. Please—"

Gamon released him. Abruptly, the man fell to his hands and knees. When he looked up, his dark eyes were raging with suppressed fury. "You son of a worlag."

"Yes," Gamon agreed.

The farmer got slowly to his feet, his wrist cradled in his other hand. "Now what?"

"Now we tend to your wounded."

"Just like that? You come in here, spout your truths, berate our actions, bully us, then say you'll tend to our wounded?"

"What else? You expect us to set up your trial block for you? Put you before your own elders for the lynching with which they probably helped?"

Moriko's face tightened.

"Your wounded?" Gamon prodded.

"You're fighters, archers." The farmer almost made the words a curse. "You have nothing to offer our wounded."

"We're fighters, archers, swordsmen—yes. But—" Gamon indicated Dion with his chin. "—she is also a healer."

The man looked at Dion, then at the wolf. "Healer Hashiacci?"

"Healer Dione," Gamon corrected flatly.

"Dione? I thought ... We heard ..." Moriko struggled to contain the anger that still colored his voice. "I didn't know," he said finally, to Dion. "But with Yrobbi dead, we ... need you. We'd be honored by your presence."

She nodded, not trusting her voice.

"Jorg neSecton was hurt badly—that's his house there." He pointed shortly. "You can see the corner of the roof sticking out from behind the bakery. And Lege—he took a bad blow to the head. He's in the next hub over, second house around the commons. Asuli's with him, I think. There are others, but they're not so badly off."

Dion nodded again, then went to her dnu and pulled her healer's pack from her saddlebags. Moriko watched her move, noting the limp that still clung to her walk. Gamon gestured back at the street. "Get some people together. Bury or burn your dead."

The other man eyed Gamon stonily. "I'll do it," he said, "because it has to be done, but I'd keep quiet with the others if I were you. You weren't here, and you don't have to stay to deal with what happened. We don't need your words rubbed into our ears like salt in a wound."

Gamon's expression didn't soften. "Truth in willing ears is sugar on the peach. It is the unwilling ear that needs honesty." He met the farmer's eyes steadily, as if to reinforce his message, then finally turned away. Dion went with him, her healer's pack slung over her shoulder. Tehena and Kiyun, ignoring the farmer, led the four dnu to the central commons, then made their way to the commons house, where they would wait till Dion was done.

Left behind, Moriko watched them for a long moment before turning to his mate. She eyed him warily. She could see the fury that laced his clenched fists. When he gestured for her to go down the street and help get some others together to build the funeral pyre, she moved with alacrity to do it.

When Gamon and Dion reached the first wounded man's house, Gamon knocked on the door. They could hear a child crying inside, then quick footsteps, and the door opened. The woman who answered looked pale and worn. "Yes? What do you want?"

"There's a healer here," Gamon said shortly. "She'll see to your mate if you wish it."

Dion pushed back her warcap so that her healer's band was visible. There was no mistaking the intricate silver patterns and blue-stone inlay of its simple circlet, and when the woman saw it, her face cleared. "Oh, may the moons bless you," she cried in relief. "It was too much to hope that a healer would come in time. Asuli—our intern—has done what she can, of course, but Jorg was hurt badly—very badly this time. This way, Healer. Come in. I'm Cheria. Jorg, that's my mate, he took a cut on his thigh, and one on his ribs—I don't think that's too serious—and he's had a knock on the head, but it's the cut in his thigh that worries me. I nearly fainted when I saw all that blood—" She stopped abruptly as Hishn padded inside. She caught the violet of Dion's eyes. "Healer . . . Dione?" she asked. "The wolfwalker?"

Dion nodded briefly.

The taller woman made the sign of the moonsblessing, then moved quickly to a curtained doorway. She pulled the fabric aside. "Our intern, Asuli, stitched him up and put the salves on, but we didn't know what else to do. I'm just trying to keep clean bandages on him. I'm afraid—" Her voice broke off as she caught sight of her daughter's face peeking around the corner of the hall. She lowered her voice. "He's so pale, Wolfwalker. And the swelling—his skin is so tight on his legs . . ."

Dion moved to the bedside and sat by the man who lay against the dark blanket. She felt his head and checked his eyes, then took a pulse. As she ran her hands over the man's body, lightly feeling the wounds within, Hishn came and sat beside her. The gray wolf sniffed the unconscious man, then looked at Dion. *His blood is slow in his veins,* the wolf sent.

Dion nodded absently. "His blood leaks from inside."

"Wait in the next room," Gamon said to Cheria.

The woman hesitated, then ducked through the blanket as if afraid to watch Dion work. "Lori," they heard her say to her child. "Go on down to Perix's house for me. I need that basket of thread she keeps upstairs."

"Can you do it?" Gamon asked quietly.

"It's not as bad as she thinks."

"But?"

"He is bleeding to death, slowly, from the inside. He'll be dead by dusk if we don't do something now."

"Dion, you are strong enough to do this now?"

Dion's face shuttered like the houses outside.

"Doesn't matter if you are, eh? You'll do it anyway."

"It's my stubborn streak," she told him.

"I hadn't noticed," he said sourly. "Do you need anything?"

"Just silence." She sighed at his expression. "I can do this, Gamon. It will be a simple healing, and I've done almost nothing for ninans except treat some of the wolves for fever."

"I thought you usually only treated parasites and gashes in the Gray Ones."

"It hasn't been a good year for them either."

The older man frowned slowly. "Dion, while you were still . . . recovering, Gray Yoshi killed one of his own yearlings. Did it right in front of Aranur and me. Aranur said the yearling had to be sick. Was there fever in Hishn's pack?"

His voice broke off as Cheria moved in the next room, and Dion shook her head, nodding meaningfully at the curtained doorway.

Gamon nodded, but his eyes were watchful as she began to work.

She fell silent then. As if in a trance, she and the wolf sat unmoving, unblinking, almost as if they no longer breathed. Dion's hands hovered over the man's leg, not quite touching the stitched gash. Minutes passed. A shadow crept into Dion's blank face like a slow change of seasons, and Gamon could see where her hands were no longer steady as she held them out. "Get out of there, Dion," he breathed, watching the pull of physical weariness fight the needs of the mental healing. "Gray One," he said sharply. "Pull her out!"

As though Hishn heard him, she growled sharply. Dion started, blinked, and focused again. Gamon helped her to stand, and Hishn gave him a baleful look, but he nudged the wolf back with his boot. "Go on, you gray-eared mutt," he said. "The day your wolf-walker can't heal a simple gash is the day I hang up my own sword and retire." He ran his hand through his graying hair. "And all nine moons know I'm too young to retire, council seat or not."

Dion snorted. "If that's what it will take to get you off the council, I should fumble a healing deliberately. All nine moons know that the other elders would appreciate it."

Gamon grinned without humor. "Ah, yes, but guess who I'd recommend for my replacement?"

"Don't even thing about it," she warned sourly. "There's not a chance in all nine hells that I'd bind myself to a council even more than I already am."

"Kiyun served his term. Tehena served hers, though she fought it like the plague. I've served two terms already to make up for the decades I avoided it. What makes you think you can escape your fate for so long?"

"The wolves, Gamon. They'd never let me step into such danger."

"Hah. I think they thrive on it."

But she didn't smile, and Gamon studied her for a moment before handing her her cloak. "You want to look at the others now?" he said finally.

She nodded. She pushed the blanket aside and ducked through. Instantly, Cheria got to her feet. "How is he? Will he be all right? Asuli said—"

"He will be all right," Dion told her. "Your intern did a good job with the stitching and herbs. She should be able to do the rest from here on out."

The woman's worn shoulders hunched slightly, but she forced herself to ask, "Will he . . . walk again?"

"It will be a while, but yes, he will walk again."

The woman sank down on the chair. For a moment she

merely sat, looking blankly at the rug. Then she sprang to her feet and hugged Dion fiercely. Hishn, beside Dion, snarled, and Cheria didn't notice, but she did feel the ridges of scar and gouged flesh on Dion's shoulders. Abruptly, she stiffened. "Healer, you— I'm so sorry—I forgot. We'd heard . . ." She stepped back abruptly. "You're so thin," she said finally, briskly. "You need food." She bustled to the kitchen.

Gamon watched the woman with a grin. "The ubiquitous stew, I imagine."

Dion shrugged.

"Better watch out," he warned. "You might start to like it."

Dion raised her eyebrow, but Gamon's sharp eyes noted the almost imperceptible stretch of her lips. It was not a smile, but it was a lighter seriousness. He felt a tension release from his own shoulders. "Come," he said. "You have another house call to make."

Cheria hurried out of her kitchen then. "Where are you going? Healer, I'll just be a moment. It's small enough thanks to feed you supper for what you've done for my Jorg."

"Later," Gamon called back.

Outside, the village felt hostile and closed. The gray sky seemed to press down on the summer heat so that thought itself was stifled. A small party of men and women were building a funeral pyre off to the side of one hub of houses, and Dion and Gamon heard the curses clearly as they dragged the raider bodies up. The two crossed the streets in silence, as if their own voices were themselves oppressed.

The door to the other wounded man's home opened before they reached the porch, and a slender young woman stepped out, eyeing them, but letting them come up on the porch before she spoke. "You're here to see Lege," she stated more than questioned. Gamon frowned, but the young woman ignored him, meeting Dion's level gaze with her own. The plain, uncarved silver band of an intern circled her brow, and her dark blond hair swung freely as she gestured with bare courtesy for them to enter. "I'm Asuli maLian, intern to the late Healer Yrobbiquipel."

The young woman's voice was almost haughty, and Dion studied her for a long moment. "Healer Dione," she replied finally.

At her side, Hishn snarled so low in her throat that Asuli didn't hear. *She challenges you,* the gray wolf growled.

She is young, Dion returned.

But Hishn gave the intern a baleful look. Dion's own lips began to curl, and she had to force her expression to steady. "I am here to see Lege," she reminded the intern softly.

The other woman barely nodded. "His concussion is critical," Asuli returned. "He is declining. There is nothing more to be done except wait for him to die." She gestured for them to enter, but as Dion neared her, the younger woman drew herself up almost imperceptibly and tried to look down her nose. Dion, slightly taller, narrowed her eyes but said nothing. When Asuli turned her expression on Gamon, the lean old man quelled her with a look so cold the young woman took an involuntary step back.

"Where is the patient?" Dion asked shortly.

"Through here," Asuli returned, striding past Dion to lead the wolfwalker through the house. "But you won't be able to do any more than I. I followed Yrobbi's directions to the letter."

Dion stared at the intern's back. A spark of ire roused in her gut while beside her, Gray Hishn's bristle was up. When Dion passed the intern to enter the room, she stifled an impulse to snap at the other woman's expression.

She is the thorn in the paw, Hishn sent. *She is the bitter scent of the lepa. Slap her down now, or she will challenge you again.*

"No," Dion said sharply. Asuli and Gamon looked at her. She shrugged, and Gamon, with a glance at the wolf, nodded. The intern watched Dion with narrowed eyes.

When Dion saw the still, gray form on the bed, she hesitated. She sat beside the man's body and took his pulse. But when she looked at the man's eyes, she had little hope. One pupil was blown—dilated twice as large as the other. There was no response to the light. She glanced down at the wolf and met the yellow gaze.

He is dead already, the wolf told her.

There is death, and then there is final death, Dion returned. *Ovousibas has made the difference between life and death before. Perhaps it can do so again.*

Gamon saw the expression on her face. He turned to motion

or Asuli to leave the room, but the intern was standing with her
hands on her hips.

"I'll stay," she said flatly, before he could open his mouth.
"The man's my patient, and I treated him carefully—there's
nothing more to be done. If you think to do something different,
I will judge that treatment."

Slowly, Dion turned her head. But the other woman didn't
move.

Dion stared at Asuli for a long moment. Then, even more
slowly, she stood. The master healer's band she wore was
worked with the ancient lapis lazuli, not the flashier holspet, but
the intricate carvings on the simple circlet made her rank plain.
At Asuli's words, Gamon could almost swear that the silver of
Dion's circlet itself glinted with the same anger that flashed in
the wolfwalker's eyes.

Dion's voice was deceptively quiet. "Asuli," she said, "I recognize you as an intern. But as a master healer of Ramaj Ariye
and Ramaj Randonnen and the outlying districts of both counties, I will judge the condition of this patient. And it is I, not you,
who will judge your skills in handling this patient properly."

The young woman didn't back down. "If you think you can
do something more, I have the right to stay and see what you
claim I've done wrong."

Gamon eyed the stiffening of both women's jaws. Dion's
temper had been nearly dormant since Danton's death, but he'd
bet on the speed of the sixth moon before he'd bet that her flash-
fire rage had died with her son. If it was this intern who could
break the emotion free from the wolfwalker's heart, Gamon
would not interfere.

Dion's gaze was steady, but a tiny muscle jumped in her jaw.
"I haven't said you did anything wrong, Asuli. I merely want to
see if I can do something more. I ask you again, leave this room
while I work. It's hard enough to do certain healing techniques
without someone's hostile breath going down my neck."

Asuli was already shaking her head. "I have the right to see
anything you do to my patient."

Hishn growled.

"You do have the right." Dion's voice didn't quite mask the
steel behind her words. "But if you stay, you will be silent; you

will not move no matter what happens; you will not disturb me in any way."

The younger woman opened her mouth in automatic protest, but Dion cut her off. "If you disturb me during this time—" The steel of her voice was obvious. "—you risk *my* life and the life of this man. And, as a master healer, if I deem your actions improper, or worse, deliberate, your rank will be stripped from you, and you will be exiled from ever joining the healers' ranks or ever again abusing whatever skills you think you now have. Trial blocks are not just for raiders."

Asuli stared at her for a long moment, then finally nodded shortly.

Dion turned away from the other woman, sitting again beside the wounded man. She barely had to touch him through the internal healing to feel the cold, clutching gray that had grown over his mind. Nerves hung lifelessly; blood flowed sluggishly where it flowed at all; pink coils of brain were compressed and crushed from swellings along the skull. The wolfwalker shivered when she opened her eyes to Gamon's empathetic face. "He is already dead," she said flatly. "He will never regain consciousness."

"I told you that already," Asuli said flatly. "I've already done everything for him that could be done."

Gamon watched Dion bite back her temper. Thoughtfully, he eyed the intern.

"If there are others waiting to be seen, I will see them now," Dion said curtly.

The few others who had serious injuries did not need Ovousibas to get them on the road to healing, though they might be ninans getting back to their work. Dion noted with wary surprise that Asuli, obviously seeing where the wolfwalker's concerns lay, was screening the patients, admitting only those whose injuries might cause permanent damage. It was quietly done, and Dion would not have noticed it except that Hishn, outside, saw those who were turned from the door.

"How is it going?" Gamon asked in a low voice, passing Dion a bowl of stew.

Dion followed his glance toward the intern. "She is compe-

ent, but that doesn't make up for lack of courtesy. I'm beginning to feel like throttling her myself."

Gamon grinned without humor and cracked his knuckles.
"Let me know if you need any help."

Dion pushed away her empty bowl, and Asuli moved quickly
to Dion's side.

"Is there anyone else to see?" Dion asked flatly.

"Just one man." The intern gathered Dion's tools and herbs
automatically and led them out toward another hub. As they
climbed the steps to the front door, the woman paused. "My
la—the man's elbow was cut so that the tissues and nerves were
separated. He'll probably lose the arm."

Dion studied the other woman's face without speaking.

Slowly, Asuli stiffened. "I don't see what else you'll be able
to do for him that I haven't already done."

Dion had to tighten her lips to hold back her words. But Gray
Hishn, following at a distance, snarled loudly enough that Gamon
looked warily over his own shoulder.

Easy, Hishn, Dion sent.

She walks as if she bites at your heels.

I cannot strike her simply because of what she says.

I can, the Gray One sent.

The rush of lupine heat that flashed in Dion's mind almost
made her stumble. *No!* she snapped back. *This is a human thing,
Gray One. Do not interfere.*

The snarl that returned made Dion's own hackles rise.

The door to Asuli's home opened before they reached the
porch, and the blond woman who gestured them inside was
already talking. "Asuli," she rounded on the intern, "we needed
you back hours ago. Wains is in a great deal of pain—"

"I've brought the healer," the younger woman cut in abruptly.
She brushed by her mother. "He's in here," she said over her
shoulder to Dion.

Inside, the man at the table looked up. His right arm was in a
sling, and his fingers were curled in a frozen fist. He started to
get to his feet, but Dion motioned for him to stay seated.

"Healer Dione," he greeted her. He looked down at his hand.
"We're honored to have you."

"The honor is mine," she returned automatically. She nodded

and gestured for him to take his arm out of the sling. "Was it a clean blow or a crushing blow?"

"Clean, Healer—like a sickle through wheat." His face was stolid. "Don't know that you can do much at this point. I can't feel a thing below the elbow." He nodded with his chin at his daughter. "Asuli said the nerves were cut, and I'd never use the arm again—a pretty present for the moons to give a farmer."

Dion's voice remained steady, but there was a hint of steely gray in her violet eyes. "The moons sometimes give back what they take away." She began to examine his arm.

"Not this time," he grunted. "Asuli said the use of it was gone for sure."

The intern patted his shoulder. "She just wants to look, Wains. She can't do anything I haven't already done."

Dion stilled. Gamon looked from the wolfwalker to the intern. In the heavy silence, he instinctively edged toward the door. For a moment, no one moved. Then Dion seemed to explode.

"How dare you—" she snarled, her fury cracking like a whip across the room. "How dare you presume to know my skills!"

Asuli took a step back, but Dion was incensed, rousing the wolf's ire to sizzle with her own in the dim room. Gray Hishn was on her feet, teeth bared and bristle up.

"You have barely begun your internship, but you presume to judge my skills? You, who can't recognize potential, but see only despair—even in the health of your own father?" Dion followed Asuli back. Her finger was like a sword stabbing toward the younger woman. "You are not even halfway through your twenties; there are two hundred years ahead of you in which you could learn if you wanted. Your menial learning now is nothing compared to what you could know later. Right now you haven't even the experience to see beyond what is to what can be. A cut can't be healed—that's your attitude. A crushed joint cannot recover. Yet those healings occur more often than an intern like yourself would know. You're blind as a nightbird and twice as shallow as its cry. If you don't change to add some compassion to your skills, you will be forever in the dark." She barely took a breath to keep going. "Keep your ignorant tongue in your head where it belongs," she snapped, "lest you wag it where it will get cut off."

She turned back to the man who gaped at her from the table, ignoring the open-mouthed intern. "Sit still. Be quiet," she commanded sharply to Wains. She straddled the bench so that she sat beside Asuli's father. *Take me in, Gray One,* she commanded shortly.

Then walk with me, Healer, Gray Hishn returned. But Dion's fury was like a creature in its own right. It grabbed the gray wolf's focus like a mudsucker so that the link between the two snapped shockingly taut. Their minds slammed together. Something ripped apart and merged instantly back together. It was not Hishn who led Dion this time, but Dion who led the wolf. Down, left, farther, *in*. Energy snapped and sparked between them. The power of each one's body merged into a single resonant chord. Somewhere in the backs of their minds, yellow, slitted eyes blinked, but in the seething mass of gray-fed fury, neither Dion nor Hishn noticed.

Abruptly, Dion's consciousness drove into the wounded man's body. She barely pulled the gray, pain-killing fog around her mind as she shifted with the internal healing. Like a spear, she plunged into the wound. Tendons, ligaments, nerves—all had been neatly severed by the raider's blade. Firmly, she pulled the tissues together, welding them with her will till they held. Her fury held her where her will would otherwise have weakened, and she stayed, blending and weaving the tissues until the gray fog became a biting chill. She struck back at the fog, anger fueling her strength, but the gray wolf snarled and, like a fish on a line, she was hauled back, hauled out of the healing.

She opened her eyes, blinked once, shuddered like a ghost, and fainted.

"Healer?" Asuli jumped forward.

Hishn whirled, her teeth bared. Gamon barely caught Dion before she fell forward; then he lifted her slender form away from the bench. He glanced at the man she had treated, but Wains wasn't watching the wolfwalker. The other man was staring at his hand.

"By the blood of a hundred worlags," the other man said softly. "I can feel my fingers." He moved them fractionally, watching them clench almost imperceptibly, then relax. Finally, he looked up. He saw Dion's figure in Gamon's arms and half rose. "What happened to her?" He looked at his daughter. "Is that it?" he asked. "That's all?" He stood up. "Why did she faint?" he demanded. "I felt . . . things moving. I felt . . . But she didn't do anything—" His voice broke off at Gamon's hard expression. "No offense, weapons master," he said hurriedly, "but she barely even touched me—"

"Aye," Gamon returned shortly, motioning with his chin for Asuli's mother to open the door. Hurriedly, the woman obeyed, then stepped back as the gray wolf snarled, slinking out the door before Gamon could step forward. Asuli was still staring at Dion.

"Asuli—look!" Wains caught the young woman's arm. "By the light of the seventh moon, I can feel my arm." He grasped the wounded limb with his other hand. "Look, I can move it, wave it, close my fist—ah, hell, that hurts—"

"Don't move it," Gamon said sharply. "Let it heal first. Get that . . . daughter of yours to bind it up. Give it some time, or you'll tear out what the wolfwalker did for you."

Asuli gave Gamon a look as hard as his own. "And just what, by the second hell, did she really do? I watched her. Wains was right. She didn't touch him. She didn't do anything but close her eyes for a while, then faint."

Gamon shouldered coldly past the young woman, ignoring her questions. Hishn was already down on the street, her fur stiff across her lupine shoulders.

Asuli shook Wains off and tried to catch Gamon's arm. "Wait— What happened? What did she do?"

Gamon merely strode down the steps and didn't answer.

He barely reached the street before Dion blinked blearily and struggled against his strength. He set her on her feet only at her insistence, but backed off as he saw the anger that still flashed in her eyes. He glanced only once at the intern who stood on the porch and stared after them. The young woman had an odd expression on her face, but she said nothing more. When her father called to her again, she turned and stepped back inside.

X

Release your heart
  And let it race away—
Like the pounding of your pulse
  When you are breathless;
Like a drum
  Beaten with urgency or hate;
Like time
  Twisting out beyond the stars;
Like love
  That has no boundaries.

A few hours on the road, and the dull rhythm of the hooves of the dnu had beaten conversation to silence. Dion's fury had left her as suddenly as it had arisen, leaving her drained and dry as a dusty sinkhole, and Gamon, watching her out of the corner of his eye, pushed ahead to ride beside Tehena. "We should stop soon," he murmured to the lanky woman. "She's pushing it to stay in the saddle."

Tehena shrugged. "She wants distance."

"Five kays ought to be enough."

"You're thinking about raiders, or the intern back in that town?"

"Both, although I couldn't tell you which one I'd rather not face."

Tehena grinned, but the expression didn't lighten her hard-lined face. "From what I saw of that intern, Dion deserves all the distance she can handle, raider threat or no. She can make it to Caeton. She won't be able to see the ocean from there, but she'll be able to smell it."

Gamon's shoulders twitched. "Holguin is closer," he said flatly.

"Dion never liked Holguin."

"She doesn't like raiders either."

The lanky woman shrugged. "They attacked three towns in two days. That's a lot, even for a bold raider band. You can bet they're long gone by now. They could be as many as twenty kays from here—they could be halfway to the coast."

"Could be," he agreed deliberately.

Tehena gave him a sharp look. "Even if they were actively hunting Dion, it's not likely they could guess exactly where we'd be at any particular time. They can't afford to hang around searching for her in this area now that they've made a few strikes. It's more likely that they've made their bid for her for the month, and now they'll crawl back under their rocks."

"There are other towns through which we must ride."

"Sure, there are a dozen to choose from, this close to Sidisport. But you think any of them would welcome a raider gang? This isn't raider country here. Sidisport is. Dion should be safe till we reach the coast."

"It's a risk, Tehena."

"Not much of one."

"You heard what that farmer said as clearly as I did."

"Aye," she acknowledged. "But they are not actively hunting Dion," she insisted, "or they'd be on our heels, not striking randomly around us. What happened in Prandton—and the other towns—was simple vindictiveness."

"Vindictiveness?"

She shrugged. "Find a group of dim-witted risk takers like those villagers back there, and hit them hard. You're guaranteed some fun, and raiders aren't known to pass that up when they're handed that on a platter."

"Moonworms, woman. Don't you have any feeling for the healer and villagers who died in that town?"

"As much feeling for them as they had respect for you, Gamon."

The older man snorted.

"Look, Gamon, if the raiders were hunting Dion with any kind of intent, she'd hear it through the wolves."

"You have a hell of a lot of faith in her."

"She's a wolfwalker."

"She's also vulnerable right now," he retorted in a low voice. "It was no secret that she was badly injured in that lepa attack. If some raider wants her—alive or dead—then he also knows that now, when she is weak, when she is far from Ariye, is the time to try to take her."

Tehena gave him a thoughtful look. "She might be vulnerable, Gamon, but she isn't weak."

"She sure as hell isn't back to normal, either."

"That's what you expect? For her to be normal again after she killed her own son?"

"She didn't kill her son," he snapped.

"Tell her that."

For a moment, the two glared at each other.

It was Gamon who broke the silence. "The last few days, we've been moving too directly toward the coast. If the raiders are looking for healers, they're just too close around us. I want Dion in the bigger towns."

"She doesn't want to be in the larger towns."

"What's your point?"

Tehena stared at the older man. Then she actually laughed. The sound was harsh, but for all that, it was a laugh.

"That's six," Gamon said.

Tehena raised her thin eyebrows. "Six what?"

"Six times you've laughed since I met you. You're making a habit of that, you know—laughing once every two years, whether you need it or not."

Slowly, the lanky woman lost her smile. Her voice was flat again when she said, "Maybe I don't have much to laugh about."

Gamon couldn't help the glance he shot over his shoulder. "We'll have less to laugh about if we let her walk into a raider trap."

"We all have eyes, Gamon."

"Aye."

He said nothing more.

Tehena studied him for a moment, then dropped back to ride silently beside Dion. But as the afternoon turned into dusk, Dion's own shoulders began to twitch. Unconsciously, she projected her concern to the wolf who loped steadily ahead of them in the dusty road.

Wolfwalker, Hishn returned. *You feel predator eyes?*

I feel as if we're being followed, she returned.

Leader? the gray wolf sent. Hishn's image of Aranur was clear in Dion's mind.

I hear his voice, Dion acknowledged, *but this is something else.* Instantly, the gray wolf turned back, but Dion stopped her. "No, Gray One. I'd rather you stayed with us."

"Dion?" Kiyun asked.

She motioned with her chin. "Something or someone's following us."

"Raiders?"

"I don't know. It's familiar, and yet not familiar. Like hearing Aranur's voice at a distance."

Kiyun nodded. "The trees are thick along this stretch, and there's a hillock up ahead. We can pull off and wait there to see who it is."

She nodded in turn. The prickling along her shoulders did not dissipate, and Gray Hishn warily snarled at the trees into which they took their dnu. Tehena and Dion dismounted, drawing and stringing their bows. Then, with the dusky sun already down among the coastal hills, they climbed the hillock and lay down in the brush to watch the road. Kiyun and Gamon waited below. Gray Hishn started up the hill with Dion, and the wolfwalker caught the gray wolf's scruff for a moment. The dusk eyesight of the wolf was sharper than hers would ever be, and she let herself fall into Hishn's mind.

Warm dust, the gray wolf sent. *Movement on the road.* The pound of the dnu's hooves were faint in Dion's ears, but loud in the ears of the wolf. Dion found herself relaxing, letting Hishn's eyes and ears work for her.

It was not long before the rider approached. It was a single figure, riding fast. "Woman rider," Dion murmured to Tehena.

Tehena's pale eyes narrowed. "Quirt musk in a worlag's den," she swore softly.

Dion glanced at the lanky woman, then back at the rider. Suddenly, she understood. "Even the moons wouldn't be that cruel," she muttered.

"Want to bet?" Tehena wormed back from the hillock but didn't unstring her bow. Dion gave her a sober look. She followed Tehena more slowly.

Kiyun, noting their actions, peered around the hill. Then he jammed the arrow back in his quiver and slung his bow over his shoulder. A moment later, he spurred his dnu out onto the road.

He came out of the hill-hidden forest like a heavy worlag.

Asuli screamed. The intern's dnu reared its two front legs uncertainly, nearly dumping her in the road. Kiyun, leaning out of the saddle, grabbed the reins from Asuli's hand. He hauled the six-legged beast around, his face cold. "Just where, by all nine moons, do you think you're going?"

The young woman stared at him, recognizing him finally as he spoke.

Kiyun bit the words out. "You'd better have a damn good reason, woman, for risking raiders to ride alone on this road."

Asuli tried to jerk away, and her dnu half reared again. Her curse this time, as she fell out of the saddle, was vicious. She hit the road like a sack of coal, hard on her buttocks and back. She gasped. It was a full second before she scrambled back to her feet. Automatically, she reached for her dnu, but the riding beast skittered away from her flapping cloak. She chased Kiyun back, grabbing unsuccessfully at the saddle horn, then at the reins he held. "Let go of my dnu, you worm-boned, lepa-faced dung beetle," she snarled. "I have the same rights to this road that you do."

Kiyun again backed her dnu out of reach. "Where's your escort? If you're so incompetent as to fall out of the saddle at the first start of your dnu, what makes you think you can use the road to which you claim to have travel rights?"

"You mock-eared bat. Give me back my dnu!"

She made another grab for the beast, but Kiyun danced the two dnu out of reach of her hands again. He realized suddenly that she was wearing a traveling cloak, not a lightweight, summer work cloak. Startled, he glanced at her saddle. The bags lashed to the saddle were full and heavy, judging by the way they barely shifted with the beast's movements. "Just what are you up to, Asuli?"

She made a lunge and caught the reins. Angrily, she held on until the beast, frightened, chittered and threatened to stomp on her feet. "Damn you," she snarled. "Let go of my mount. I'm a licensed intern. I have the right to study with whomever I wish."

"The right to study . . ." Kiyun stared at her.

She took the opportunity to rip the reins from his hand and jerk her dnu away. She was mounted in an instant. "The Healer Dione is obligated to teach me," she spat at the burly man. "Get out of my way. You've no right to stop me from riding to find her."

From the trees, Dion sucked in a breath. Tehena took one look at her face and found her own hand on her knife.

"No right, perhaps," Kiyun said flatly to the intern, "but plenty of rationality. From what I saw of you back in your village, you couldn't make good with the wolfwalker even if you were dying. Turn around and go back before you run into real trouble."

Asuli merely looked at him.

"Go back," he repeated.

Abruptly, she spurred her dnu straight at him. Kiyun's dnu, off-guard, skittered sideways.

"You daughter of a lepa—" he cursed.

But she was past him. She ran her dnu straight around the hillock and right into Gamon's beast. The older man's beast, startled, shouldered hers, and the two dnu slammed together. The intern went flying. For the second time, Asuli landed in the dust, her too-large cloak tangled in both brush and limbs. This time she lay still several seconds.

Hishn eyed the woman as she would an eel, and Dion found her own lips curling. "Easy," she murmured, though she didn't know if she calmed the wolf more for herself or for Hishn.

Asuli got slowly to her feet. She refused to rub her ribs or buttocks, but she bit out her words as if they hurt as much as her bruises. "So. You were all just sitting here, watching that man harass me."

Kiyun looked down at her from his saddle. "You'd have preferred an arrow to an insult? No one has business traveling alone—not with raiders about."

"I have the right to ride however and wherever I wish."

Dion asked quietly, "Why?"

Asuli didn't pretend to misunderstand. "I have the right to apply for internship, Dione. I choose to do so with you."

Tehena and Hishn moved forward as if one. "Excuse me?" said the lanky woman. "What idiot's babble is this?"

Asuli ignored Tehena and addressed herself only to the wolfwalker. "You have no intern with you, so I have the right to apply to study with you. You are obligated to give me a trial period before you can say no to me—"

Gamon stared at her. "The Healer Dione has over a dozen interns," he corrected. "All of whom work hard and treat their patients—and their teachers—with respect. She has no need of someone like you."

"She wears the healer's band. She is bound by the healer laws. One of those laws says that she must take on any student that asks to study with her if she has no students with her. She is obligated to me—"

"Not true."

"Ask her." Asuli's voice was flat. "Ask her if she is or not."

Gamon gave her a long look. "Is this true?" He turned to Dion. "Can you be obligated to take this . . . this . . . on when you already have so many back home?"

"Those rules were set to make sure that healers trained interns," Dion said flatly. "They were meant for those few healers who didn't want to be bothered with sharing their knowledge, not for those of us who have a dozen in training already."

"You have no such interns with you," Asuli shot back.

"I do not work right now as a healer," Dion returned forcefully.

"Oh no? What about Prandton?"

Dion looked mutely at the intern. Finally, she said, "I would only be cheating you if I took you on now. You'd learn little in a ninan before you returned home, and I plan no research, no in-depth work. You'd get as much from any healer as you would from me. There's no reason for you to travel with us when you could stay safely in a town."

The intern eyed Dion knowingly. "You're as selfish as you say I am," the other woman said slowly. "The only way you could cheat me is if you don't take me on. After what you did in Prandton, you owe me explanations." She gestured at her saddlebags. "I don't request pay, and I've brought my own gear and supplies. I add no burden to your party."

Gamon looked at Dion. The question in his eyes was clear.

Asuli caught his glance. "She has to take me on."

"The weapons master," Kiyun said quietly, dangerously, "is speaking to the wolfwalker, not you."

"You could dispute this," Tehena said in a low voice.

"I could," Dion agreed, "but it wouldn't matter. I took her patients away from her. I healed them, thereby challenging her treatments of them. She has the right to request training with me so that she can learn what I felt she was lacking. And according to the old laws, unless I already have students with me, I must accept any intern who wishes to train with me."

"For how long?"

"The old laws may put us in untenable situations sometimes, but they don't lock us into them forever. I must accept her for a period of one ninan—"

Asuli had been listening, and she cut in then. "At the very least, you have to accept me for one ninan."

Dion merely looked at her. "There is not enough weight on my shoulders, but I must carry you as well?"

The intern did not flinch. Instead, her lips firmed, and she set her jaw.

Tehena scowled. "Dion, you don't have to let her back you into a corner like this. Those laws were intended to protect, not punish, people like you."

Dion didn't take her eyes from the intern. "Yes," she admitted, "but the intern is right. I am obligated."

Tehena spat to the side. Her voice was cold and hard, and the look she gave the young woman was as venomous as a mud-sucker. "We're stuck with her?"

Dion shrugged.

"I'd as soon sleep with a lepa," Tehena muttered.

Two bright red spots burned in Asuli's cheeks.

Gamon eyed her as he would a roofbleeder. "You, Asuli, claim to take internship rights with Dion?"

She nodded.

"Then you obey Dion in all matters of healing. You obey me in matters of everything else."

"Gamon—"

"Weapons Master," the older man snapped. "You will address me with the respect of which you are so obviously ignorant, or you will not travel with us, internship rights or not."

"The old laws—"

"Older laws than the ones you claim state that your rights do not usurp the rights of others. You put Dion in a hint of danger, and I'll boot you back on the road. The old laws bind you as well as Dione."

Asuli regarded him for a long moment. Finally, she nodded.

Hishn eyed the intern with baleful yellow eyes, and Dion followed the gray wolf's gaze. *A ninan only, Hishn. Then she will be gone.*

Nine days can be nine centuries in the memories of the wolves.

Dion didn't answer. But the low howl that she projected was caught up by the wolf in her lupine mind. Hishn rubbed her head against the wolfwalker, then disappeared into the forest.

The ride was silent after that. Asuli did not bother to make conversation; she merely eyed Dion now and then as if studying her.

They barely made it to Caeton before night was full upon them. It was a dark night, with the moons still hidden behind the overcast sky. There was no sense of impending rain; rather, the heat was heavy with humidity, and the salt air, so close now, was sticky on their skins.

Dion's shoulders still twitched, but she said nothing to the others as they stopped at one of the inns. Instead, she hung back in the stable as the others trooped toward the main house.

Wolfwalker? Hishn asked, standing at her side.

"It's nothing," she said softly.

It is Leader, Hishn returned. *Gray Yoshi runs with him on the road.*

"I know."

Hishn growled, deep in her throat, and the soft sound grated on Dion's ears. The gray wolf's longing for Yoshi was strong, and it pulled Dion to the door of the barn so that she too stared down the dark road. Her hand automatically dug itself into the thick scruff.

Hishn strained beneath her grip. *Come with me, Wolfwalker! Your need to run is as strong as the pull of the packsong.*

Dion felt the softness of the hair beneath the gray wolf's greasy overcoat. She felt the sticky warmth of the lupine pelt on her summer-hot hand. The wolf's breath whuffed against her legs as Hishn nipped at her thigh, and Dion let herself revel in the discomfort. Her own legs tensed to leap forward; her chest expanded as if to take a breath to run. Her eyesight shifted subtly so that she saw clearly through both the gray wolf's yellow gaze and her own, and the night was alive with contrast.

The howl that hit Dion's ears was not from Hishn, but from the wolves who had gathered outside the small town. Like a ghost, the howl rose, floating beneath the clouds. It hung over the inns and houses till Hishn lifted her head and howled back. The gray wolf's long, lean body trembled.

Abruptly, Dion released her. The wolf almost leaped into the courtyard. "Go, Hishn," Dion whispered. She sucked in the hot air until it felt as if it scorched her lungs. "Gamon is right," she breathed. "You would be with your own mate right now if it wasn't for me. And you are one of the only wolves who has litters of more than one."

Hishn half turned at the end of the stone expanse. *Wolf-walker, come!*

Dion's jaw tightened. "Go, Gray One. I cannot. Go get yourself another den of pups. Gray Yoshi is waiting for you out on the plains. You cannot stay with me."

But the gray wolf didn't move. *Your voice is alone, but twisted with mine. Your heart is still caught in the grave. You think of death, cold and old, and look toward life, but you move toward neither. Release yourself, Wolfwalker!*

Dion stepped back toward the stable. The darkness of the doorway seemed to swallow her. "Go." She forced the words out. "Run free, Hishn."

Run with me! Run with the pack!

Dion's fists clenched. "No!"

Then I will not go. Yoshi will greet me here.

Hishn did not move, and Dion snarled. "Go, Gray One, or I shall drive you away. This is no home for you. The worlags would tear your pups from the earth and kill them within days of birthing. The scrub birds would pester you like fleas. You were born to run in snowy peaks, not humid, sandy heat."

Wolfwalker!

"Go! I can't bear the guilt of your losing this year's pups just because I am running away."

Hishn's yellow eyes gleamed, and the moons, half obscured by the overcast gray, seemed caught in that lupine gaze. *Yoshi found me,* the massive beast sent. *Your mate will find you, as well.*

Dion's voice was a whisper. "I know."

Hishn snarled. The gray wolf stared at her through the night.

"Go," Dion breathed.

The shadows were suddenly empty.

Dion felt her throat muscles tighten. Her eyesight blurred, but it was not the wolves. *Hishn!* she cried out.

The packsong burst up into her mind. Yellow, slitted eyes gleamed, and images twisted. Dion's need was like a hand tangling in wet yarn, catching in every voice. Wolf howls flowed back over her, driving into the corners of her skull and filling the cracks in her thoughts. Hishn snarled across them all, drawing them around Dion like a blanket. And she ran. Dion threw back her own head and howled. The sound hung, long and lonely, in the night.

XI

To wash myself in your waters,
To cleanse my soul in the sea.

Tehena found Dion in the courtyard. "Asuli bunked down?" Dion asked as the other woman approached.

"Uh-huh." Almost unwillingly, Tehena added, "She had some stamina to stay in the saddle as long as she did, judging by the way she walked up to the bunkroom."

"Does she need a riding salve?"

Tehena snorted. "If she does, I'd not be the one to give it to her. Let her feel for herself what she's gotten into. She's the one who was so eager to join us. Maybe she'll leave us alone that much sooner when she finds out what it's like riding with a wolfwalker."

"Thanks," drawled Dion.

"You've never ridden an easy trail, Dion."

"If I could find one to run, I'd take it as fast as the second moon."

"Hishn wouldn't let you."

Dion hesitated. Her voice, when she spoke, was quiet. "I sent Hishn away."

"Away." Tehena's eyes narrowed as she took in Dion's tone. "You mean away as in farther than a scouting?"

"Back to Ariye. To mate. To have her pups."

"What were you thinking?" the other woman said sharply. "That with Asuli here, you had enough fangs out for one group of riders?"

"She's not that bad to ride with."

"I'd rather teach a worlag manners."

176

"You might get your chance," Dion returned dryly. "There was worlag sign in the forest near where we picked her up."

"That only makes sense," Tehena retorted. "That intern is a worlag's spawn." The lanky woman gave Dion a cold look. "We don't need her with us, Dion. You don't need her at all."

"I haven't the option of turning her away. Not yet, at least."

Light spilled out of the inn as a couple of villagers left, calling their good-byes over their shoulders. Tehena and Dion, cast suddenly into shadow, were nearly invisible. Neither villager noticed them, but Gamon, who followed the others out, caught their still figures with his sharp eyes. He nodded to them unobtrusively, then moved on to the stable to put the dnu out to graze in the inn's commons.

Tehena watched him go. "Hells. Maybe if Gamon and I put our brains together, we could get rid of her in just a few days. I've seen that old man play some mean jokes on his students."

Dion's gaze followed the older man. "He's proud of you, you know."

The sidelight from the stable threw Tehena's too-sharp face into strong relief. "He should be," she retorted. "It's his own teaching he's proud of."

Dion gave her a sharp look. "He respects you more than you do yourself."

The other woman snorted again.

"He's your friend, Tehena."

"He's your friend, Dion, not mine. To me, he's just a grizzled, gray-haired pain in a poolah's rear."

"Look who's talking about gray."

Tehena grinned slowly and fingered her stringy hair. "Yes, but I've had this since I turned thirteen. Back then, I was more concerned about keeping my head than with keeping my hair color brown. As for Gamon, he only claims friendship because he has no sense of my age—or lack of it, as you would say."

Dion's voice was quiet. "I wish I could have given you back some of that—the youth you lost."

"It wasn't yours to return."

Dion shrugged. "Ovousibas . . ."

Tehena's voice was suddenly sharp. "Ovousibas is an alien soul-sucker sunk deep in your human brain. You'd better watch the way you use it, Dion, or it will steal what's left of you from yourself."

"I don't see you complaining about what it gave you."

"It wasn't Ovousibas that gave me anything. It was you." The woman raised her thin hand, cutting off Dion's automatic rejoinder. "I'm not ashamed of what you've done for me, Wolfwalker. When you met me, I thought I was going to die. Hells, I deserved to die, and you know it. But you gave me hope. You gave me a weapon—your own weapon when you left me. Then, later, when I found you again, you gave me a chance to be a person again. It wasn't Ovousibas that gave me a reason to live—it was you. It wasn't Ovousibas that took away my addiction to dator—that was you, too. And it wasn't your moonwormed internal healing that removed the drug tattoos—even that was you. You gave everything to me as if you expected nothing in return, and I took it all, without questioning what you offered. Thirteen years, Wolfwalker, and still you don't ask for payment."

"The healer's gift is freely given."

"Hah."

"There is no debt between us," Dion said more sharply.

"There is, Wolfwalker." Tehena stared into Dion's violet eyes. "And if there's anything you know about me, it's that I always pay my debts."

"And when," Dion said softly, "will you finish paying this debt off?"

"The day you stop feeling guilt for your son." The lanky woman's voice was as flat as her chest, and she nodded at Dion's expression. "The day you stop paying everyone else's price and start living your own life. The day you run free with the Gray Ones and break your leash to the council."

"My guilt—my debts are not yours, Tehena. You have no right to judge them."

"No? You chained me to you with your moonwormed generosity, Dion. You might as well have leashed me to your county with steel cable. You think I can break free of you now?"

Dion's face shuttered. "I refuse that weight. I refuse to be responsible for you."

"You made yourself responsible for me the day you took my bread and slop and made me beg for my food."

"That was a long time ago."

The other woman nodded. "Yes. I hated you, then, you know. I hated your strength, your determination. I hated your hope. You made me feel small and mean and dirty. And you terrified me."

"Then why did you follow me? Why come with me to Ariye?"

"Because you were a focus for me—you were the direction I lacked."

"And you still try to make me that now."

Tehena tilted her head in acknowledgment.

Dion's face tightened. "You can't live your life through mine, Tehena. You have to find your own way. Of all the things you have learned in Ariye, surely you know now that you can do that here."

The lanky woman shrugged. "Some people weren't meant for freedom."

"Worlag piss," Dion snarled. "If you're afraid of freedom, say it. Don't hide behind false obligation."

"Speak for yourself, Wolfwalker."

Dion stared at her. The shadows seemed suddenly brittle. A light went on in the inn as another pair of riders opened the door and went in. Tehena's gaunt face was suddenly cast into light and dark planes. Her eyes, dark and embittered by day, were unfathomable by night.

Then Tehena shook her head. "Ah, moonworms, Dion. Freedom's something tangible to you, but it's just a word to me. Bottom line is, I wouldn't know what to do with myself if I was on my own."

For a moment, the wolfwalker didn't move. Then she laid her hand on the other woman's arm. They were silent for a long time in the shadows.

When Dion returned to the inn, Tehena remained behind. The lanky woman's gaze followed Gamon as he closed the common's gate behind the dnu and started back across the courtyard. But he hesitated when he saw her alone. "Tasting the last of the land air?" he asked as he joined her. "We'll reach the coast road tomorrow, you know."

She shrugged. Absently, her fingers stroked her forearm.

Gamon let his gaze seek the inn. "How is she?"

"She sent the wolf away."

"Sent the—sent Hishn away? Why?"

"Didn't say. But I'd say that Aranur's getting close, and she doesn't want him to find her just yet."

Gamon's eyes narrowed. "He might have let her go when he had to face her need so squarely, but he'd not have been able to live with that for long. I figured him for her trail within three or four days."

"It wouldn't have been an easy trail to follow."

"No," he agreed. "Unless he had a Gray One to help."

"What do you mean?"

"Hishn's mate—Gray Yoshi."

Tehena shook her head. "Aranur's never run with a wolf. What makes you think he could do so now?"

"Aranur and Dion have been mated a long time. He can hear Hishn as well now as a first-year wolfwalker, and if he wanted to Call a wolf to help him, it's likely that one would Answer."

"All right, I'll buy that. But Yoshi? That's the one wolf who shouldn't help."

"Have you ever seen a mated male wolf separated from his female? They mate for life, you know. There's a longing in each one that pulls it to the other, no matter how far away they are. Hishn's a strong-willed female, and she's got some hold on that gray-eared male. Yoshi might allow Hishn to run with Dion a few months, but not for much longer than that. And it's growing late into summer. He'll lose the chance to mate before long. I figure, right now, Yoshi's urge for Hishn is so strong that he'd run the nine counties to reach that gray mutt." Gamon eyed the dark road as though expecting the wolf to appear any moment. "And with Aranur to push him," he added, more to himself, "who knows when they'll arrive."

Tehena chewed irritably at her thin lip. "You think the raiders know that Aranur is out after Dion? Dion may be worth taking alive, but Aranur—he is worth killing."

The older man shrugged. "Aranur is careful. He knows how to keep out of sight—how not to be himself if he needs to."

"Dion doesn't."

"Aye." He glanced at the inn. "That's part of the problem, isn't it?"

* * *

Dawn was overcast again, but the heat was already gathering. By the time they reached the coastal road, the thin clouds had burned off, and they were sticky and hot. Asuli kept her mouth shut so that Kiyun gave her wary glances more than once, but the young woman remained silent.

The valley fields had given way to the low hills of the coast, and the villages were built more on clay and glass industries than on farming. The plains had given way almost abruptly into forest again. Mosses seemed scraggly, but the undergrowth grew more thickly where the thinner canopy let in the light. The stone road felt pressed in by the seaside.

Dion, riding up front beside Kiyun, watched the forest with wary eyes. Even without Hishn, she felt the predators more than saw them. The senses of the other Gray Ones were thick in the back of her mind. She stretched across the distance to feel the gray wolf she knew.

Wolfwalker! the faint voice echoed back. *Release yourself! Come with us.*

Dion looked down at her hands. They were already clenched on the saddle horn. She forced her fingers to relax. Then she shoved her mind away from Hishn's and focused on the wolves nearby. It was their senses, not Hishn's, that expanded her sense of smell and broadened her eyesight to catch each motion that occurred around them. Within half an hour she could taste the acrid scent in her nostrils as she found the predators' trail. As the wind stiffened into midmorning, the odor didn't dissipate, but strengthened instead. Dion knew the scent well. "Worlags," she breathed.

Kiyun caught her sudden tension. "Dion?"

"Worlags," she repeated. "They're close."

Kiyun signaled Gamon, and instantly the grizzled man reached down and loosened the arrows in his quiver. Tehena followed suit. Within seconds, their bows were strung and their arrows ready.

"How many?" Kiyun asked quietly.

Dion shook her head slightly. "Can't tell." But she stretched her senses into the pack, and the Gray Ones in the east Answered.

Wolfwalker!

Gray Ones, she returned.

We hear your voice. We see through your eyes. You are part of the pack, Wolfwalker.

She sent them the impression she had of the beetle-beasts, and the wolves shot back a jumble of scents and sights. They had crossed the beetle-beasts' trail the day before. Some of the acrid scents had been strong, but some had been weak as rabbit piss. Dion relaxed imperceptibly. A family pack, she told herself. There would be only a few adults.

But back beside Tehena, Asuli watched their automatic preparations with a strange expression on her face. The intern swallowed visibly. "I don't know how to use a weapon," she told Tehena, keeping her voice carefully steady.

The lanky woman barely spared her a glance. "Then keep out of my way."

"Couldn't you give me a sword at least?"

"You can use one?"

"No," Asuli retorted. "But I could try. It would be better than having nothing to fight with."

"You've got your tongue to protect you, girl. Compared to you, the rest of us are defenseless."

The intern's lips tightened. Tehena turned away, her faded eyes watching the forest intently while Gamon closed up from behind.

"Stay in the middle," he ordered sharply. "Stay with Tehena."

"Thanks a lot, Gamon," Tehena muttered.

He didn't bother to respond.

The forest was close enough to the road that they could glimpse four of the beetle-beasts in the shadows, but the worlags didn't move closer. Dion counted the two adults and two yearlings. Their purple-black carapaces almost shone when the sun hit them, and their beetlelike jaws clacked together. Their feet made no sound as they ran, first on four legs, with their middle, almost vestigial arms folded against their bodies, then on six with their middle arms lightly touching the ground. And like a wind in brittle branches, they chittered constantly.

Dion let her ears catalog their sounds. They were pacing the riders, but there was no overt threat as yet in their noise.

"Can't we outrun them?" she heard Asuli ask faintly.

"They will not attack," Dion returned.

"How do you know?"

Tehena snorted. Dion, her senses scanning the forest for a change in the worlags' manner, didn't answer. If this family group met up with more worlags, the riders might have to run or fight; but as it was, there were too many of them for the beetle-beasts. Worlags weren't sentient—not as Dion would define it—but they were clever enough at that. They were as likely to set a trap as a poolah who buried itself in soil, waiting for its prey.

For an hour, they rode with the worlags pacing them while their shoulders prickled with the soft chittering. Then the riders crossed into the swampy lowlands, leaving all but scrub forest behind.

Asuli watched Tehena unstring her bow. "Why don't they follow us?" she asked Gamon.

"Too wet for worlags."

"And we're safe now?"

"From worlags," he returned.

Kiyun and Dion exchanged glances. They were close enough to the coast that the danger here would be from two-legged, not six-legged, beasts, and Dion shrugged at Kiyun's unspoken question. Asuli knew the dangers from raiders; if she chose to ride where raiders struck, it was her risk to take. But Dion glanced back at the intern. The younger woman wasn't as non-chalant as she appeared; her knuckles were white on the reins, and her back just a bit too straight.

Kiyun followed her gaze. "If she had half a brain, she'd have stayed behind, at the inn. We were clear about the dangers."

"I don't think that's the issue with her."

"Then what is? Pride? Sure, by the second moon, she's got a sackful of that."

"Perhaps. And perhaps she really is dedicated to healing."

He snorted rudely.

"Don't you think that what she saw me do—or not do," she corrected, "might have sparked her curiosity enough to risk this ride? She's smart. She didn't mistake what I did for what I told her."

"She's in rebellion, Wolfwalker. She's just stubborn enough to refuse to back down when told she should go home. It's not an eagerness to learn that drives her to follow you. It's willfulness and selfishness and ignorance of the road."

"That too," Dion agreed.

Kiyun grinned without humor.

Dion let herself sink into the packsong that surrounded this part of the scrub. Even without Hishn strongly in her mind, she could hear the wolves clearly. It was a large wolf pack—their voices were thick in the meadows that hid between the low hills—and the sense of them was like a dull roar, where Hishn's voice was now dim. There was no sense of fever within them as there had been with the wolves near her home. Whatever disease had struck in Ariye, it was contained in those mountain peaks. She knew she had healed the sickness from the Gray Ones that ran with Hishn, but she still tested each new lupine bond with which she came in contact.

Hishn . . . The ache in her chest cramped down, and Dion caught her breath. Death, longing, loss . . . There were old tones, not just her own grief, in that mental song. Stretching, deliberately torturing herself with longing for her own gray bond, Dion felt Gray Yoshi's tones mix with those of Hishn's. They had met then, up the valley. They were running the distance home. And with summer's heat filling their urges, they would mate soon in the woods while Dion kept running, even though she was now alone . . .

"Tell me I did the right thing," she whispered.

Wolfwalker! Hishn cried out faintly. Even at that distance, the fierce joy in the gray wolf's tones answered more clearly than any image could.

Gray One, Dion returned. Then she shut her mind to the wolf. But as the sound of Hishn's voice faded, Aranur's eyes hung before her. "You can't hide in the packsong forever . . ."

She shuddered. "One day," she whispered. "One day to the coast. Then I'll return to you."

But she felt him behind her, hunting, like a wolf on her trail.

When Kiyun murmured her name, asking if she felt all right, she could only shake her head and spur her dnu to move faster.

Dion's first glimpse of the sea was from the top of a low hill. She thought at first that the sky had changed back to a cloudy color, but as she paused on the rise, she realized that she was seeing the waves. She caught her breath. So many years since she had seen the ocean . . .

Low dunes, half forested and half grass, stretched south shortly to the sea. A herd of coastal eerin, small and sandy-colored, moved into the shelter of a stand of trees as the riders appeared on the open stretch. Several flocks of seadarts combined, their shapes at first a gnats' nest, then a concerted flow of purple-white movement in the sky. Dion saw them and breathed deeply the salt tang. The white that frosted the tops of the waves shifted and rolled as the waters washed in, and she could taste the ocean now, not just see it.

" 'To wash myself in your waters,' " she quoted softly. " 'To cleanse my soul in the sea.' "

"Dion?" It was Gamon.

She kept her eyes on the ocean. "I need to run for a while, Gamon."

"Here?"

"I'll be all right. There are wolves nearby; no worlags." She glanced behind her at the other three riders who straggled up the low hill, then she dismounted smoothly.

The older man took her reins. "We'll wait here, then."

She nodded, but her eyes were still on the sea. She took only one small pack from the saddle, then jogged off into the brush.

When Asuli and the others arrived, the intern's sharp gaze caught the missing pack almost immediately. It was a healer's pack, not a running pack, and Asuli looked around. "Where is she?" she asked.

Tehena glanced at Kiyun, who was already unsaddling his dnu. "Where she needs to be," the lanky woman answered shortly.

Asuli's brown eyes narrowed. "If she's working, I have a right to be with her."

Gamon looked up slowly. "All this talk of your rights, Asuli, and none of the rights of Dion?"

"She's accepted me as intern. She must teach me."

He straightened. "Teach you what, woman?"

"Whatever there is to learn."

Gamon looked her up and down. "And that is what you want? To learn?"

"That's what I'm here for," she returned tersely.

"No." He shook his head. "You want to do. You don't really care to 'learn' at all."

Asuli's voice was strangely low when she answered. "And so what if that's true? If I'm smart—if I can do what others can't, who's to complain?"

Gamon studied her for a long moment. "You must hate your patients like the second hell," he murmured. "You must hate us even more."

Her voice was flat. "Don't you feel the same about me?"

"You've left room for little else."

Abruptly, Asuli turned and stared out at the marshy scrub. "She's out there, isn't she?"

"No one crosses the marshes," Tehena said shortly, shouldering past the younger woman.

Asuli snorted. "Not even the great Wolfwalker Dione?"

The lean, hard-faced woman bit back her words, but the look in her eyes was lethal. Asuli stayed her ground only out of a sudden fear to move.

"Get your saddle off your dnu," Gamon told the intern flatly. "You might as well let your mount wait in the shade. We could be here for a few hours."

Already a kay away, Dion jogged steadily across the mossy ground, letting her leg muscles get the hang of running again after riding for so many hours. The insects were as loud as an orchestra, and they clouded her hearing so that she was startled when the Gray Ones suddenly surrounded her. Abruptly, she halted.

Wolfwalker, they sent.

Wild as hawks, they sniffed her warily. The threads of their mental packsong were suddenly loud in her mind. Like a weaver, she pulled those threads around her until they blended into a cloak of gray. Somewhere behind that shroud of gray, a pair of yellow, slitted eyes watched. Dion shivered. There was something in that gaze that did not belong in the packsong, yet the Gray Ones did not seem disturbed. Instead, two of the yearlings mock-growled at her, and the older wolves trotted back to the shade. The gray cloak in her mind seemed to loosen; the image disappeared, but the sense of urgency stayed with her.

It was two hours before she returned to the group, and when she did she was sweating like a rast in an oven. The cool breeze blowing off the coast did nothing to dissipate the humidity that clung to the marsh, and Dion's clothes were gritty with sweat and salt. She dropped back to a walk as she approached the rise, but Gamon still heard her coming.

He got to his feet. "Ready to ride?"

She wiped her forehead on her shoulder. "I'd rather swim, if I could find some cold water."

"East or west—it's your choice to the rivers."

"West," she returned.

"The Phye?" Tehena frowned. "You sure you want to go to Sidisport?"

Dion dropped her healer's pack on her saddle. "I want to see the ocean where it hits the rocks."

"And then?" Gamon said softly.

The wolfwalker stared down at her hands. They were stronger than they had been a ninan ago—her fingers no longer trembled. She looked up into Gamon's gray eyes. "And then," she said, "we go home."

XII

*There is no difference between need and love
when they meet beneath the moons.*

—Yegros Chu, Randonnen philosopher

When they started along the marsh road, Asuli trotted her dnu until she reined in beside Dion. "What were you doing out there?"

Dion glanced at the other woman's face. "I'm a wolfwalker, not just a healer, Asuli."

"And I'm not to be part of that."

"No."

"Wolfwalker or not, I need to know what you did before—in Prandton."

Dion shrugged.

"You know what I mean, Healer Dione. My fa—Wains's nerves were severed; yet after you were with him, he could feel and move his fingers again. And Jorg had been bleeding internally—there was nothing I could do to stop it. He would have been dead by nightfall. After you saw him, he stabilized."

Dion didn't answer.

"You aren't one of those faith healers, are you?"

Dion gave her a sharp look. "Of all things that I am, that is the one thing I am not."

"I found no marks on Jorg's body that the raiders had not made for him or that I had not made in crimping his wounds together. But he stabilized only after you were with him, doing nothing, according to Cheria, but sitting by his side. Sounds like faith healing to me."

Dion snorted. "Faith healing is nothing more than a stealing of life for adulation or power or gold."

188

"And you get none of those things—not even adulation," the intern retorted.

Dion's eyes narrowed. "If you think so little of me, why are you here?"

"You did something to Jorg, to my father. I want to know what that something was. I pick things up quickly. Show me once, and I'll be able to practice whatever it is on my own. But if the great Healer Dione is nothing more than a faith healer, I'll expose you to the very moons."

Dion stared at her. Suddenly, she laughed. It was a choked sound, but it was a laugh.

Asuli eyed her warily. "Why are you laughing? Why aren't you angry?"

"Why should I be angry?" Dion asked the sky. "Because you have the tongue of a bilgebeast and the temperament of a shrew, and you force both of them on me? Because you're as arrogant as a raider with twenty men on his side? Because you play with people's lives as if they have no value? Because you add to the weight on my shoulders as if it is a game to you—to stack the blocks as high as you can to see when they will crush me?" She looked at Asuli, and the intern realized suddenly that the wolfwalker was not at all calm.

"Why," Dion asked softly, "do you think I should be angry with you?"

This time, it was Asuli who was silent.

They reached an inn on the banks of the River Phye by early evening, before the sixth moon had risen. The sky was still heavy with heat. They didn't ride into the courtyard at the inn; they dragged themselves and their dnu. The heat had sapped both riders and beasts so that the commons, with its cool, green, ground cover, invited them to bed down there rather than in the house. It was with difficulty that Dion turned her dnu loose in the commons and went to the sweltering inn. Inside, the evening was long as a sermon and stifling as anger. By the time they bedded down, even Kiyun was irritable.

Dion came awake suddenly. The moons hung at an angle, shining almost blindingly into the room, and there was nothing moving. She slid out of bed, her hand on her sword. In the upper bunk, Tehena snapped into alertness at the change in Dion's breathing. The lean woman didn't speak, but she shifted to grasp her own sword, which lay beside her. Dion had already moved to her overtunic at the foot of the bed.

"Dion?" Tehena breathed.

It is nothing," the wolfwalker returned.

Dion threw on her clothes, shifting her sword from one hand to the other. Then she glided across the floor and was out the door. Tehena was left to stare at the moonlight and listen in the silence.

The hallway was dark; the only light was that cast by the three moons that rode low in the sky. Dion could hear the man now—outside the inn. His breath was controlled, but loud to her sensitive ears, and the dnu from which he slid panted heavily. She waited till his sounds faded, as though he walked the beast toward the stable, then she slipped outside. Her bare feet were silent on the porch.

Like a wolf, she followed the man toward the stable. The stones, set into hard-packed dirt, were cool beneath her feet. She hesitated at the door to the barn, her sword held tightly—ready—but down at her side. She found him waiting for her like a raider.

He eyed her for a long moment. Then quietly, he said, "Dion."

"You could have waited for me."

"I never had much patience."

She studied him. He was leaner, she thought, than when she had left him—his face was harder somehow. There were shadows under his eyes that even the dim stable light couldn't hide. But she couldn't move toward him, and he didn't shift to touch her.

"Will you come back to me?" His voice was hard.

She couldn't answer.

"I need you."

"I love you," she whispered.

"Then come home."

She didn't remember either one moving, but suddenly, she was in his arms. His strength engulfed her; his arms crushed her to him. She pounded on his chest, hitting him over and over, crying out, "Damn you, damn you."

Finally, she collapsed against him, half sobbing against his chest. She looked up finally, and their lips met with bruising force.

"Damn you," she whispered.

"I know."

She kissed him urgently, deeply. He lifted her from the floor so that she was pulled completely against him. Their urgency grew into a violence. She snarled low in her throat, and he answered the sound. His gray eyes glinted; her violet eyes flashed with an almost yellow light. He started to lift her into his arms, but she wrenched free.

"No," she half snarled. "Not here."

She backed from the stable, then turned and half ran toward the road—toward the forest. Halfway there, she stopped and looked back.

He didn't hesitate. He reached her in a second. This time when he touched her, she didn't fight him. Instead, she drew him with her.

In the inn, in the darkness, Tehena watched them meet. Then she turned and gathered her things. When she moved quietly to the floor in Gamon and Kiyun's room, it was Kiyun who asked softly, "Dion?"

"Aranur," she returned. She rolled to her side and stared at the wall. Sleep was a long time coming.

XIII

She swallowed pride,
Held out her hands and begged:
  "I cannot be what you want me to be;
  I cannot do what you want."

"I know," said the Tiwar.
"That's what makes this so delightful."

—*From* Wrestling the Moons

Dion rose at dawn. She dressed in silence while the gray voices called in the back of her head and the moonlight gave way to the sun. The warmth of the summer was still caught in the soil, which steamed lightly at the edges of the courtyard. Dion felt as if she saw the wolves in that fog.

Behind her, Aranur murmured, and she turned to watch him sprawled on the bed, one sheet tangled around his leg, his face gaunt in the early light. He looked frighteningly worn. He murmured again, restlessly, and softly, Dion answered. Her voice, woven into the packsong that touched the back of his mind, calmed him in sleep so that he breathed more easily. Absently, she rubbed her forehead where the circlet pressed on her bones. Then her gaze sharpened.

Below, on the road, two riders raced into the courtyard. Their dnu, sweating, drummed to a halt, and one of the riders leaped down. "I'll see if she's here," the youth called over his shoulder, already sprinting to the inn door. "You ride to the next inn. NeHaber's fever's too high to waste time. He'll die if we can't find the healer."

Dion cast a glance at Aranur, then took up her pack, slid her sword belt over her shoulder, and quietly slipped out the door. She met the innkeeper on the stairs.

"Healer Dione," the man said in relief as she handed him her healer's pack while she jammed her warcap on her head. "There's been an accident," he continued. "Two days ago, a worker was

burned when one of the glass furnaces blew. Last night his fever
shot up. They can't bring it down."

Dion nodded, buckling on her sword belt. She was already
moving with him to the door. "Is my dnu ready to ride?"

"I took the liberty of ordering it to be saddled," he said hurriedly, handing her pack back. "The messenger is outside. He'll
take you there. It's the west side of town, on the waterfront. The
Raven district."

She nodded again. "Tell Ar— Tell my friends, when they
wake, where I've gone. I'll send a ringrunner back telling them
how long I'll be, or if I want them to join me."

The messenger, a well-built youth, was waiting impatiently
on his dnu. Dion barely had time to toss her healer's pack on the
back of the saddle before the young man spurred his riding
beast out of the courtyard. She mounted as her own dnu began
to run. She cast a single glance back at the inn, but there were no
faces in the window. Then she looked ahead to the road.

The morning air was warm. In her head, Dion could hear the
wolves nearby. They had been drawn by her presence last night.
She let their senses fill her nose as she urged her dnu up even
with the youth's.

"How far?" she called across.

"Thirty minutes. Over the River Phye."

"In Sidisport?"

He nodded.

"What happened?"

"They were working with a steel alloy when one of the glass
furnaces blew. NeHaber was right in front of it."

She studied the rider surreptitiously. He was older than she
had at first thought in the shadows of the inn, slender and clean-
shaven, brown-haired, brown-eyed—almost boyish. But he rode
as if he was born to the dnu. "How did you know where I was?"
she called.

He gave her a wry look from across the saddle. "You really
want to know? As I heard it, a cousin of the man who is courting
the mother of the healer's intern was at your inn—he thought—
last night. He'd had a bit too much grog to remember exactly
which inns he'd been visiting. But he told his cousin, who told

the intern's mother. The intern told his healer. It's the healer who is tending neHaber who requested that you help."

Dion grinned. "I'm sorry I asked. Which healer?"

"Urth neVonner. He's new here, out of Ramaj Eilif."

"I don't know him."

The other rider shrugged. "He knows of you—but then, who doesn't?"

It took only a few minutes to get within sight of the bridge over the river. In Ramaj Ariye, the River Phye was white with standing waves and rapids that smashed against black rocks. Here near the sea, it was wide and slow, sated with brine, and sluggish. She glanced down at the water and then back at the road. The slick, gray river was heavy with silt washed from the soils of Ramaj Ariye.

There were few people on the bridge, and the two riders crossed the spans at speed. From the bridge, Sidisport looked like any normal town. It had seawalls to protect it from tsunami and the storms that broached the outer reefs; it had wide, arched gates at the main roads. The city was almost eight hundred years old—one of the oldest on this planet. It had been started as a colony by the Ancients, then filled with refugees from the domes. Now it was one of the largest cities in the nine counties—and a home to many raiders. Dion checked the holding thong on her sword, making sure it was easily loosened. As they reached the other side of the bridge, she removed the thong completely.

The city gates were as wide as a dozen carts, the outer areas full of quiet activity as the people began to go about their business. As she rode past, she couldn't help eyeing the businesses. The workshops and textile sellers, groceries and guard houses . . . A painting in a gallery window caught her eye, and she made a note of the street so that she could return to check the price. It was a painting that Kiyun would like. She took a deep breath and let it out with the rhythm of her dnu. These structures looked so innocuous, as though blood had never touched them. Dion touched the hilt of her sword again. She, for one, knew better.

Most of the houses they passed were built of stone, not of coralline or the shaped trees that the Ariyens used. The structure of the city was also not one of circular hubs, but of houses built around private courtyards and squares of private commons. The two times Dion had been here before had both been at night, and she had seen little pattern in the buildings. Now, with the morning sun shining blindingly across the white stones, the city seemed light, not dark.

The messenger cut through to another main street, keeping their dnu to a canter. The inner areas were busy already. The streets, while wide enough to keep from being choked, were crowded. They had to push past two morning markets where wagons were parked on the sides of the road, piled precariously high with produce, dried meats, and pastas, while their vendors stood next to the display boards and discussed the merits of this planting or that crop with their customers. Dion had to dodge a child with a partitioned basket of boiled and raw eggs, while another with a load of extractor roots ducked under her dnu's neck as she hauled the beast up short.

Between the buildings, Dion felt almost lost. Her sense of direction was fouled by the constant walls and movement of too many people. Only the sunlight, as it broke between roofs, showed her east from north or west. "How much farther?" she called to the messenger as they broke free of another bustle and headed south toward the seawall.

"Not far. We'll have to circle and come back in from the west."

"Isn't it faster to ride through?"

He shook his head. "It's not safe down there, Wolfwalker. Sometimes the merchants go at each other like six-legged rasts in a cage, and when they do, it almost always involves the waterfront. Better to ride around it, even if it costs a few minutes."

"But people live along the seawall."

"Aye, but if you're not in the housing areas or markets, it's better to stay off the streets until later in the day."

She nodded. In her head, the wolfsong began to stir as if the wolves were rousing, and Aranur, not the Gray Ones, was wanting to hunt her trail. Dion's lip curled back from her teeth, her nostrils flaring and her nose wrinkling. He'd be angry, she knew, when she returned. He would have ridden with her.

They zigzagged into a side street where the buildings were

more utilitarian and the facades spoke of productivity, not produce. There was little traffic; the workers here did not start their jobs till later, and the streets, though close to the waterfront, were almost clear. They passed a lab, a glassworks, and a foundry before they turned into another main street where the apartments stretched in a row toward the seawall. Dion rubbed her sword hand on her thigh. The warm salt air seemed gritty here, as if it could not be cleaned by wind when it was within the walls of the city.

"To your left, by the stable," the messenger called to her. "The apartment is two blocks down."

She nodded.

When they turned the corner at the old stables, the sun hit Dion straight on. For an instant she couldn't see. Then her dnu half reared in panic.

Instinctively, Dion yanked her sword from its sheath. Figures rushed at her from the sides. The gray fog in her head was suddenly thick. She swung her blade down, her eyes unable to see. Metal clanged; her swing was parried. Hard hands grabbed her legs. She jerked back and kicked at the hands, but they hung on. Her blade was caught in a sword breaker, then wrenched from her hands. Her dnu seemed to stumble. Abruptly, she was unseated.

She went down, striking out as she fell. Someone cursed under his breath as she kicked out viciously, and she realized that the entire fight was near silent. She opened her mouth to scream, but was struck in the gut. Her lungs and stomach recoiled. One of her knees hit the street with jarring force. She lunged back up. Almost, she broke free, jerking, striking, staggering to her feet, her mind filled with gray rage. Then one of them hit her on the back of the head hard enough to make her vision split. Her knees buckled like paper.

Instantly, her arms were trussed behind her with cutting force even as she was half dragged beneath the stable eaves and into the harnessing area. Her hands went numb within seconds.

Inside the raiders paused, stripping her weapons from her belt and boots. They did not touch her circlet. Then they hauled her around to face another man even as others took her riding beast and rode it out of the building. She tasted blood under her tongue and swallowed thickly. Her eyes were dark and flat. "Where's the ringrunner?" she said harshly.

"Where's your wolf?" the burly man returned. His black hair, half-curly, was rumpled as if he was not used to rising so early. His face was weathered and almost swarthy in the shadows. They stared at each other silently. "NeLosto?" the man asked over his shoulder.

"On his way," one of the others returned.

He nodded. "We'll take a short walk, Wolfwalker," he said to Dion. "But a word of warning: No screaming. No calling out."

She stared at him almost bitterly. "You think to threaten me? What have I to lose?"

"Other lives depend on yours. Think on that, Dione."

He backed away, took the light cloak he was handed and flung it over his shoulders without taking his eyes off her. One of the raiders called him by name, and she tasted the syllables of it: neVenklan, like violence. She eyed him, memorizing his features. A moment later a thin line was noosed around her neck. Automatically, she pulled against it, but the noose instantly tightened. She froze before she choked. NeVenklan, behind her, breathed in her ear, "Not a good idea, Dione. I suggest you stay close to me."

She didn't fight them when they slipped a summer cloak around her and jammed a hat on her head, tying it on under her chin so that the noose on her neck appeared to be no more than a ribbon from the hat. The raider behind her put his own hat on, then put his arm around her as though he were her lover. She jerked away, choking as the line tightened again. There was a sudden surge in her mind as the wolves seemed to gather with her lack of breath.

The raider watched her eyes as she fought for breath, refusing to panic before him. Finally, he loosened the cord across her trachea. "I said, 'close,' Dione," neVenklan said mildly. He tugged her back into position.

They walked like that—next to each other like lovers—down the street from the stable. Squinting, Dion could see the whole waterfront. There were wagons parked along the street, blocking its length with the bundles and boxes stacked around them. But there was no one working to load or unload them to whom she could call out. There were almost no dnu in the tether squares by each rowhouse's set of stairs—even the dnu seemed to be roused late, for safety.

The houses in the first street were only two stories tall, as if they had been deliberately shortened to leave the second street's views intact. Dion looked to her right. At this end of town the seawall was high off the bay—at least a dozen meters from the water. Beyond it the bay stretched out like a small, sparkling ocean. The sidewalks were wide with tree-shaped benches. The apartments that lined the street were tall and narrow, each one with its stairs and picture windows; each one with its tiny window boxes for herbs and vegetables. It looked picturesque, not dangerous. Dion bit her lip. When an older couple came out of one of the rowhouses, she automatically tensed.

"Uh-uh," neVenklan said softly. He tugged on the noose so that she coughed. "You'll lose your hand if you do."

He shifted slightly, and she could feel the cold steel against her forearm above the ropes. She pressed her lips together. But in her mind, the wolves had gathered. Yellow eyes seemed to see past her thoughts. Lean muscles bunched with speed. It wasn't Hishn—the thread of that Gray One was too far away already. But yellow, slitted eyes still stared back at her, and there was a gray din in her skull. The eyes confused her, but the din was the weight of the wolves nearby. They were hunting field rats in the scrub grass, and she could feel their hunger. *Gray Ones,* she called.

Wolfwalker! they sang back.

Help me.

You run with the pack. We run at your side.

Carefully, she built an image of Aranur and projected that, but the wolves snarled in her mind when she sent it. The image and scent of the inn bothered them. These were not wolves who had ever bonded; they were wild and skittish near humans. They wanted to hunt with her, to run with her, not to move into human towns. She built the image again, sending it this time with all the urgency she could muster.

There was a hesitation in the pack. Then they began to gather. As if their acquiescence had changed their openness to her mind, she could feel each one more clearly. Gray fur seemed to lift with the morning breeze. Wolf feet seemed to drum the ground. She breathed in, sharply, deeply, and didn't notice the raider's sudden pressure against her back.

Wolfwalker! they howled.

NeVenklan took her boldly down the long block on the waterfront. Sidisport followed the curve of the shore—half the town was protected, on the inner curve of the bay, while the other half of the city sprawled here, up along the bluffs, exposed to wind and weather.

Dion eyed the seawall that separated her from the water. NeVenklan caught her doing it and chuckled. "It's fifteen meters down, Dione. There's only rocks to greet you when you land, and the current is like a shark. Even if you survived the fall, you'd drown before you could scream."

She didn't bother to answer.

There were six Ancient schooners moored in the bay: one large three-masted ship, and several smaller two-masted vessels. Along the docks there were dozens of fishing boats—at least ten of which had been built by the Ancients—and dozens of ketches, sloops, and yawls. It was easy to tell the Ancient-built vessels from the others. The newer boats were built of wood or the fiber-and-glue layers that gleamed purple-white in the sun. They required constant painting and coating to keep them from breaking down. The Ancient ships and older boats were built of green-brown seafiber that seemed dull and lifeless, yet was made of living organisms—technology of the old ones still viable today. All that those hulls and decks required was enough seawater and sunlight to keep growing and enough sanding to keep them smooth. A new coat of seafiber every eight decades, to replace any wearing patches, and the hulls would stand up to the worst of storms, with the decks strong, and the masts unbroken.

Dion stared at the ships. She had promised herself a view of the sea, and she had it now, she acknowledged. And with the raider noose so snug on her neck, the Ancient science mocked her. With all their technology, the Ancients could not have foreseen how they would leave this world. Their dream of living with, not on, the planet was reality; but their other dream—of touching the stars, of soaring between sky and earth—had been turned to dust by disease and time, by the bloodlust of raiders and venges.

It wasn't far to the raider's nest. NeVenklan stopped at a set of rowhouses one block down, one block away from the sea-wall. They had taken no chances of her running away on her own dnu. Her riding beast was tied with two others to the hitch-ing rail in the front of the house, and she had to walk to the building. Her healer's pack had already been removed from the saddle, and neVenklan didn't hesitate as he prodded her up the steps to the door.

Inside, she was thrust down the hallway and into a half-furnished room. In spite of herself she tensed when neVenklan passed the tail of the noose to another. He was close enough to kick. Her back muscles tightened as her body almost blindly started its move. Then, abruptly, he struck her cheek.

Her head snapped back. Her mind went blank. Then the red, wolf rage hit hard. Half dazed, she jerked free of the raider, rip-ping the noose cord from his hands. NeVenklan reacted instantly, grabbing at her shoulder. Hands caught her from behind, snag-ging the noose line, and the thin cord choked her suddenly like wire. Her eyes went wild. She couldn't scream—the rope cut off her breath. Her lungs heaved instantly. Terror howled into her mind—her throat was being crushed. Wildly, she fought the bonds, kicking at the raiders so that two of them went down with her in a pile. Brutal hands grabbed her again. Her flesh tore beneath the ropes. She jerked free for half an instant and lashed out, catching someone in the groin.

The man bent slowly over, but another grabbed the ropes around her wrists and threw her brutally against the wall of the room. She thought her chest, her throat would burst as the air tried to explode from her lungs. Then neVenklan grabbed the line on her neck and loosened the noose. She slid to her knees, choking.

"Alive," neVenklan said coldly to the man by the wall.

The other raider shrugged. "Alive enough."

They eyed her. Slowly, she looked up at them. Her throat still felt crushed, and there was a burning on her neck. Something slid down her chest, and she knew it was blood. Her lip curled back, her nose wrinkled. Unconsciously, she bared her teeth.

NeVenklan nodded slowly, noting her unfocused eyes. "Enough," he agreed.

He hauled her roughly to her feet, then prodded her up the stairs to an empty room. There was a heavy-duty hook in one of the walls, near the ceiling, and it was over that which he tossed the line. He brought the rope down at an angle across the wall and secured it to a cleat near the door. She was left there, tethered by her neck, with one raider at the doorway.

NeVenklan paused by the guard. "If you see her do anything odd, come down and get maLien or neProtel to stand with you. Do not get close to her. And don't yell. Just come down to the landing and signal."

"Aye," the raider acknowledged.

Dion stared after neVenklan as he left the room, then eyed her captive space. Besides the guard and the shutters that blocked the window, there was nothing else to see. The room was dusty and dim. There was no furniture, no paintings on the wall. Even the one slight crack in the ceiling seemed a solitary statement.

Gingerly, she tested the noose, but it was chokingly tight. She tried jerking her head to snap the line out of the hook, but it was snug enough that the motion itself half strangled her. The man at the door simply watched. Finally, she stood, head down, her shoulder against the wall, trying to focus on the gray rage that had filled the back of her skull. Slowly, ignoring the swelling of her lips and the looseness of the tooth the raider had struck, she brought her thoughts back to herself.

"Gray Ones," she whispered.

Wolfwalker, they returned.

How long till you reach Aranur?

They were uneasy in her mind. *The roads are crowded with human smells. This is no place for us.*

They won't hurt you, she sent back with a snarl. *You run with the moons at your back.*

Wolfwalker!

"Hurry," she breathed.

They growled in return, low in their throats, and the mental sound was unwilling, but she could feel them move, their bodies warming as they left the shade of the scrub for the open heat of the roads. It was already an hour and a half past dawn, and they had kays to go to reach the inn, but they moved like fire. Soon they would reach Aranur.

Slowly, Dion raised her head. She tried to ease the ropes on her arms, but they were tight as a miser. All she could do was lean on the wall and listen to the raiders in the room below. Their voices, muffled by the wooden floors, were still loud enough for her sensitive ears that she could make out what they said.

"It's her, all right," one of the raiders spoke.

"Aye. Did you see her eyes?" the other answered. "There's not many who could lay claim to that color . . ."

"Bandrovic's been waiting a long time for this."

"Long enough," another man agreed. "He could have grabbed the Ariyen months ago, if he wanted."

"Like worlag sweetmeat," the first one retorted sarcastically. "He wasn't ready before. The venges showed him that."

"You think he's ready now? The Ariyen will put up a hell of a fight—he, of all people, should know that . . ."

NeVenklan's voice cut into theirs, silencing the group. The voices, when they spoke again, were too soft for her to hear.

She bit her lip, as if that tiny pain would bring more focus to her mind. But the voices of the wild wolves, once they were called, seemed to hold on to her thoughts. She bit her lip harder. There was a snarled response in the packsong. Then the gray wolves curled like snakes around her thoughts, pressing in from all sides. "Aranur . . ." she whispered.

She didn't know how long she stood there, her mind clouded with fog. It wasn't until she heard neVenklan's voice and the door opening in the room below that she was able to focus again.

Dion couldn't help the sudden jump in her heartbeat. But the footsteps, though light, were not Aranur's—he would not have walked so easily past a roomful of raiders. She waited, and the man below crossed to the stairs. But when the raider came in sight, the wolfwalker's eyes widened.

"Aye, Dione," he said. "It is I."

Those dark blue-gray eyes, the shallow seams in his face. Wide shoulders; heavy, gnarled hands; and gray-peppered hair . . . It

was the raider who had tried to take her before out on Red Wolf
Road. The one who had herded her away from the venge, then
said her name like a promise. His eyes had been in her nightmares; his face, hanging over hers, while he powered her back . . .
She took a half step toward him, her face tightening into a snarl
as the noose brought her up short. In her head, the gray voices
gathered.

The tall man untethered the noose from the wall, flipped it
out of the roof hook, and let the line fall slack on the floor. Then
he waited.

"What do you want?" She forced the words out.

"Where is your wolf?" he asked.

"How's your hip?"

Slowly, he smiled and stepped forward. "The wolf, Dione.
Where is it?"

Her weight shifted fractionally.

Bandrovic kicked her almost negligently, anticipating her
attack. The blow, flickeringly fast, caught her on the thigh, smashing her like a mallet. She staggered back, her face blanched, her
teeth clenched to keep from gasping. Only the wall kept her from
falling. She stared at him, then slid to a half-crouched position
as her right knee slowly gave way.

Bandrovic studied her. "That's all the fight that's in you?" He
glanced at the guard, who shrugged. Bandrovic took Dion's
shoulders and stood her up again, balancing her firmly as her
scarred leg refused to hold her weight. He pulled her to him and
grabbed her chin, tilting her face up. When he kissed her, his
lips were dry and hard against hers.

She shook back, instinctively revulsed, and Bandrovic stared
deeply into her eyes. Then he kissed her again, deeply. She
made a choked sound and struggled, but it was Bandrovic who
pushed her away.

He stared at her with narrowed eyes. "This is it? This is the
great Healer Dione? The ghost of the forest? The Gray Wolf of
Randonnen? The Heart of Ariye? Where is your fight, woman?
Where is your fire?"

He hit her then, hard, on the cheek. Her head rocked back,
but there was no sound except the smack of his hand on her
face. It was calm, calculating, and the raider's expression was

intent, as if he judged her will by her lack of reaction. He hit her again. The third time, she raised her head from his blows and spat blood on his boots.

He eyed her almost curiously. "No cursing, no crying. No fury of the Gray Ones . . . Where is the fighter who refused to die? Where is the legend I've followed? Or do you simply face your path to hell with the stoicism of a stone?"

She forced her words out between clenched teeth. "There's no fear of hell in me. I've already faced the moons."

"So I heard. You died in Still Meadow, and the wolves pulled you back. That, Dione, must have been interesting." He studied her intently. "It touched you, didn't it—your death?"

She couldn't answer.

"Your eyes—they're almost dark now. There's little life left in them. Your face is drawn. Your expression set, not fierce . . . Whatever you found on the path to the moons has painted your soul with blackness." His voice trailed off, as if he spoke more to himself than to her. "You'll be no figurehead like this. You'll be no use to me."

He raised his hand as if to strike her again, but she didn't blink. Slowly, instead, he ran his hand through his hair. The gesture was somehow so like that of Gamon that Dion's eyesight blurred. Bandrovic saw it and nodded. "That's it, Dione," he said softly. "Call your wolf. Call her and your mate to help you."

Abruptly, she focused.

He pulled a knife from his belt and held it to her throat. She didn't flinch. Abruptly, he jammed the point of the blade under the noose. The rope tightened, and Dion choked horribly. Then the rope slit and fell away. The ring of reddened, half-torn flesh that was left behind burned in Dion's mind. Blood dripped down her throat. Her eyes shifted with the sudden wash of gray feet that padded through her skull.

Bandrovic, without taking his gaze off her, said to the other man, "Go up and check the flags. They'll be coming soon."

Dion tried to speak and choked. She pushed herself away from the wall. Swaying, she had to force the hoarse words out. "What do you want? What are you after?"

He ignored her words, and the guard spoke first. "MaKathru's already up on the roof."

Bandrovic shook his head. "Send her out on the steps with Rossotti. The two of them are clean enough to pass muster. And send neBugeya to check the seawall. I want the dinghy ready to sail as soon as we descend."

"What about her?" The raider indicated Dion.

The tall man shrugged. "She's nothing now. I'll use her as bait."

Dion's voice was hoarse. "Bait for whom?" she asked. "For the wolves? Gray Hishn isn't coming. I sent her away days ago. You're a fool if you think I'd call her back just to set her up in your trap."

He didn't smile. "I saw your eyes, Dione. You Called the wolves—you couldn't help it. And they can't help their Answer. You Called them years ago, and they Answered. You did it again this spring—the counties were full of the stories. Time and again, you Call your wolf and others to your side. You're careless, Dione. You're predictable as night after day. When you're in danger, the Gray Ones gather like winter worlags. And Aranur comes running with them."

Dion felt a chill slide down her neck with her blood. "It's not me you want at all," she breathed. "It's Aranur you're after."

"I'd have taken you too, if I could. But there is no heart left in you."

"I'll do what you want." Her voice was almost desperate.

"I know," he said. Deliberately, he turned his back on her and strode to the shuttered window. He opened the shutters and stared out at the bay where the tall ships rocked at moorage.

She took a half step forward. The raider at the doorway shifted with warning, but she ignored him. "Why Aranur?" she demanded. "Why like this? You could kill him more simply a dozen different ways."

Bandrovic shrugged. "Death is so final, Wolfwalker. There are other, more useful conditions."

"He'd rather die than be used against his family, his county. He'll be no hostage for you."

Bandrovic closed the shutters. "He'll have no choice," he said.

XIV

One breath
From life to death;
One glimpse of fate;
One instant that hangs
  Forever
Before the ax
        Falls.

Bandrovic left her alone in the room; the guard had gone upstairs. Dion sat on the floor, her shoulder against the wall. Her cheek throbbed where Bandrovic had hit her; she could no longer feel her hands. She let her eyes close as she sought the mindless distance of the packsong. Aranur . . . He had been a presence in her thoughts for so long that she still felt as if he hunted her. Even knowing that her mental plea couldn't reach him, she still built a picture of him in her mind and set it in the packsong.

Her forehead rubbed against the wall, and her circlet shifted. Deliberately, she rubbed her head against the wall again so that it loosened around her skull. She reached deeply into her mind. Yellow, slitted eyes blinked back, swamped with the sense of the wolves. Her voice was barely a whisper in the empty, shuttered room. "You took my sword, you took my knives. But you left me my healer's band. You thought like I did—that smooth silver was life, not a knife of death. But the silver and steel are meshed in me. I am both, not one or the other. And I might not escape myself, but sure as the moons can cross the sky, I can and will escape you."

Carefully, she worked against the wall until the circlet was skewed on her head and she could push it off to fall into her lap. Then, gingerly, she worked it until she had it between her knees. It was easy to bend down and use her teeth to rotate the band until the seam was up. Even easier to release the hidden catch.

The tiny blade Aranur had insisted be concealed in the circlet was free.

She grasped the headband in her teeth and dropped it against the wall, where her thigh pressed against the wood. Then she tried to allow it to slide slowly to the floor, but she didn't have the right angle. The circlet dropped with a thunk. The small sound made her freeze. But there was no cessation of low voices from below, and she cursed quietly, more in relief than anger. The gray shadows gathered in her mind. "Hurry," she told them. "Find Aranur." They were running now along the side of the road, and their snarls when they passed a short caravan were almost audible to her.

It took minutes to get the headband up far enough between her body and the wall that she could hold it there with her hip. She couldn't reach the exposed blade with the ropes between her wrists, but as she strained to stretch far enough, she realized that she didn't have to cut the line there. All she had to do was cut the ropes around the outer part of her forearms—that should loosen the rest enough for her to work herself free. And she could just get her forearms to the wall where her hip braced the circlet's blade.

Five minutes? Ten? She didn't know. Tension made time drag with the effort and race with the fear of discovery. She could feel something start to give. It wasn't a sensation in her hands so much as in her shoulders as her arms parted a fingerwidth.

Noises wafted into the room as people moved along the street. Below her the raiders became quiet. She almost had her arms free when there was a sudden noise overhead, then the sounds of someone descending the steps. She froze. With her arms still behind her, and her body leaned up against the wall as if for support, she looked as though she had hardly moved from when Bandrovic had left her. The raider didn't even bother to give her a second glance before hurrying down the stairs. Dion rubbed harder on the rope.

One of the ropes separated, but the others remained tight. Doggedly, she kept on working. She crushed her impulse to hurry. Her shoulders were beginning to ache from the tension of moving up and down at that angle. Another strand separated. She wriggled her wrists and felt the bonds loosen—enough to allow her shoulders to roll. She wrenched them again and felt her flesh tear.

Below, the voices raised briefly. A door opened and shut. Dion felt the loop on one wrist slacken again. She rubbed again on the tiny blade until she felt her arms begin to pull apart. Viciously, she strained at the rope. One of her wrists wriggled free. Her arms, still bound, began to tingle, and she bit her lip against what was coming. When the burning hit, it was all she could do to keep her hiss from becoming a scream. The circulation that returned to her flesh was worse than a raider beating.

Slowly, she twisted until the ropes loosened further and she could pull her whole arm free. She gasped silently in relief as she brought both hands in front of her. Her wrists were a bloody mess. She tried to extend and clench her fingers, but they were purplish blobs. Deliberately, she kept at it, shaking free of the loops and chunks of rope. Some part of her mind automatically stretched to the wolves as though Hishn could take some of the burning in her hands, but it was the other wolves who answered. Suddenly alone in the wolf pack, she was swamped by their intensity. She had to bite back the sound that rose in her tightened throat.

Wolfwalker, they howled back into her head.

Hurry, she thought, clenching her teeth, but she didn't project the word.

We hunt your mate, they sang, still caught by the message she had sent before. *We run with the wind, Wolfwalker!*

She shook her hands, then worked them for several minutes, stretching and clenching her fingers and fists until she could feel enough to take her headband from the floor and close the hidden clasp. Finally, she did it, then jammed it back on her head.

She took what was left of the rope and slunk to the door. There, she stopped and listened. The raiders were still downstairs, speaking in low tones. Carefully, she eased up the steps. She almost held her breath on the way up, but nothing creaked.

It was two flights up to the door that led to the captain's walk. There were no sounds at the door other than those of the bay birds and breeze. Carefully, she eased the door open. There was no one on the small walk. The only movement, other than herself, was the light rippling of the two signal flags that flew at the top of the flagpole. A small red standard fluttered on top, and underneath it, a plain yellow one with a large green circle lifted and flapped desultorily. She was tempted to change the flags, picking colors at random from the box against the balustrade, but the urgency that filled her made her feet itch for the ground.

The rowhouse, one of five in the block, was situated parallel to the waterfront. The front of it faced west; the back faced east. This captain's walk was slightly higher than the two rowhouses to the south, and the walks to the north were slightly higher than the captain's walk. It gave the shared roofs a staggered appearance, as if some lost, nostalgic farmer had tried to terrace the town.

Dion studied the bay. The sparkling water lay like a bed of diamonds, and the wind was blowing crossways to the tide. The bay was cut with white lines where the tide and surface current conflicted. Moving carefully to the edge of the walk, she studied the street below. Even with the rope, she couldn't go down the front of the house—there were two raiders on the steps: a woman shelling beans as if she lived in the house, and the messenger who had lured Dion there. The few people moving along the block would be no help to her. If raiders could come and go at will, the neighbors must not care.

The captain's walk extended halfway back along the roof. There, the surface became peaked, with the northernmost rowhouses sharing a roof and the other three rowhouses sharing another sloping surface. Dion eyed the slick tiles warily. Then she sat down and removed her boots. She tied her footgear together with one of the chunks of rope and slung the boots over her shoulder. Her feet would give her better purchase than any leather soles.

Carefully, she eased out into the vee where the two roofs met. It took only a moment to reach the other end of the house. There, she squatted and studied the street again. This street looked like the other one except that there were no raiders on the back steps. There were also no railings to which to attach her rope.

She chewed her lip. She could feel the wolves still gathering, hunting Aranur's trail like a pack of worlags, just as the raiders would hunt her should she jump for the street. Her landing would attract attention, and without some way to get away quickly from the house, she would be run down within seconds. Five minutes, ten ... She didn't know how long she squatted there thinking, waiting for something to change. Then, several blocks away, a rider caught her eye. It was a man moving swiftly, but she knew his seat. Gamon ... He disappeared behind another row of houses. Dion bit her lip so hard she drew blood. A moment later, another rider came into view, one block closer than Gamon. Aranur ... They were searching the blocks, riding them one by one to find her.

She stood and waved. Aranur didn't see her. He was almost out of the intersection. Deliberately, Dion whistled. It was a short, sharp blast, followed by a quick trill and a higher note—a sequence easily mistaken for birdsong. The tones carried clearly. Instantly, Aranur halted. He didn't look around, but he cocked his head. Dion repeated the final tone. This time he looked up. Urgently, she waved again. He turned his dnu and spurred the beast down the street.

Inside, on the first floor of the house, Bandrovic held up his hand for silence. The other raiders stilled. "Check the wolf-walker," he said to neVenklan. The burly man took the stairs two at a time.

"What is it?" one of the others asked.

"Aranur—or Gamon. They're here."

"How do you know?"

"That whistle—it's an Ariyen communication used in the Lloroi's family."

NeVenklan leaned half down the stairs. "She's gone," he reported. He started to run back up, to follow Dion to the roof.

"No," Bandrovic said sharply. "Let her go. She can't go down over the front—maLien is out there with Rossotti. She'll try to go down the back, and that will take her a few minutes. We can use that to our advantage. You two, get to the seawall. Pull the moving wagons the rest of the way into the street. Make sure it's blocked completely. You and you, cross Bicheppe Street—not so fast, dammit—and do it as if you belong there. You don't want to alert the Ariyens, and they don't want to attract attention, so they'll assume you're out going to work, and you will ignore them completely. Once across Bicheppe

Street, you can block them from turning east. That will herd them toward the seawall." He turned to the others. "NeVenklan, take your three and circle the block to the west. Come up on them from behind. I want them bolting for the seawall with no thought but speed. NeCrischyk, you're with me. We'll go straight to the waterfront and wait by the western wagon." He was already heading for the door. "Go," he said sharply. As one, they moved.

On the roof, Dion lay down and leaned out, her head upside down as she looked under the eaves for something to which to tie the rope. Aranur didn't call out a greeting. Instead, he eyed the street warily in both directions while she worked. She had to knock an eaver's nest from the bore hole in which it was built, but it took only a second to do so—the dry mud crumbled easily. Quickly, she passed the end of the line through the hole and knotted it. It wasn't long enough to reach more than halfway down the house, but that was enough to get her feet to the outer beams on the walls. She glanced down. Two riders started to cross the street a block away, and she ducked quickly back on the roof. When she peered back out, both riders were gone, and Aranur waved for her to hurry. Quickly, she pulled her sleeves down over her hands, then grabbed the line and let her weight swing off the roof until she hung on the rope by her hands.

She didn't try to climb down; her hands were still clumsy. Instead, she let the rope slide along her palm, heating her sleeve until it burned through just as she reached the second-story beams. She swung herself lightly to the new footing. Below, Aranur looked down the street and waved vigorously at Tehena as she came into view six blocks away where she crossed another intersection.

Dion eased herself sideways until she was over the back door frame, then she let go of the rope. She slid down the side of the house, hit the top of the frame, and stalled in place for just a second. Her body began to fall out. Deliberately, she shoved away. She landed with a heavy thud, falling half backward onto the steps as her right leg collapsed beneath her. Twisting like a wolf, she regained her feet. She sprinted down the back door flight and jumped the gate without wasting time to open it.

Aranur caught her arm before she left the ground, lifting her up behind him on the dnu.

Someone shouted, and Dion looked at Tehena. But it wasn't the other woman. Three raiders had rounded the corner of the street behind Aranur and ahead of Tehena, and they were charging Aranur even now. The tall man didn't wait. He kicked his beast into a gallop.

He would have turned into the side street, but there were two riders there just waiting for them to bolt into their arms. To the east, the two who had crossed a moment before already had their swords out. Aranur saw this at a glance and bolted ahead toward the seawall. Dion clung to his waist with one hand and drew her long knife with her other. Aranur didn't object. The raiders behind them were coming on like a horde of flocking lepa. And behind them, like a forgotten guest, Tehena came at a gallop.

Aranur didn't waste breath talking, and neither did Dion, but both cursed when they hit the waterfront. The road left and right was blocked by moving wagons. Aranur twisted his riding beast in a tight circle, cut off from the other roads. The dnu half reared, and he forced it to face the rushing figures. "It's the seawall or nothing," he shouted over his shoulder.

But Dion caught his arm. "No! Aranur, that's what they want."

"No choice—"

"It's you they're after. Give me the reins. I'll charge them. They don't care about me. You can get away on foot between the wagons."

"No," he snarled, twisting the dnu again, trapped between blockades. The small knot of raiders thundered straight at them. "Together or not at all."

"Aranur—"

He spurred the riding beast viciously. Dion felt the dnu's muscles gather. In her head, the wolfpack howled. Then the dnu leaped toward the raiders' swords. Aranur hacked and met the first attack on the right, but the raider on the left struck him on the shoulder. The reins went slack as he lost them. The dnu bolted wildly.

Another raider slammed into them from the left, and Dion sliced at the man's arm. The raider cried out as her steel sliced his sleeve. They broke free for an instant only, but one of the raiders hit his target dead-on. It wasn't Aranur, but the dnu, that he struck, and the riding beast screamed and reared fully. For a moment, Aranur and Dion clung to the beast as its middle legs pawed air. Then Aranur yelled, "Jump free."

She hit the road with jarring force, rolling and then tucking into a ball. A dnu leaped her cringing figure. Aranur landed meters away. A sword flashed near her, and she ducked under it and scrambled to her feet. Aranur took another flat blow to his shoulder. He staggered with the force of it. "Back," he snarled at her. "To the wall—"

His voice cut off as two of the raiders charged. Dion jumped for Aranur's side. She lashed out at the raider on the left, and the man danced back. She tripped on the curb behind her. The seawall—it was bare meters away. She lunged up on the sidewalk, twisted as a blade flashed at her, and grabbed the sword hilt of another lunging raider. Viciously, she twisted the blade free.

Aranur was already backed to the wall, but meters away from her. He slammed a raider with a brutal righthand blow as their swords jammed hilt-to-hilt. The raider aimed a kick, but Aranur shifted and took it on his hip instead. Another raider beat at Aranur's arms and head while the first man kept their blades locked. Dion lunged at one of the raiders and was brought up short as Rossotti was suddenly before her. His clean-cut face was so incongruous that she almost pulled her blow. Brutally, the man slammed her back.

Aranur heard her cry. He was suddenly like fire, flickering here then there with speed. As though he had not even been challenged before, he became a blinding weapon. He jerked his blade free and stabbed one raider in the side of the gut. The man screamed hoarsely and had hardly dropped when Aranur dodged around his body, kicking the man as he went.

Dion took a blow on her stolen blade and turned it aside. Took another beat-attack, and felt her rope-torn hands start to weaken. "Damn you," she cursed herself. Then Aranur was beside her. The messenger pulled back. For an instant, the raiders paused. Five of them circled Aranur and Dion. Behind them, the others guarded the group against Tehena, who slid off her dnu and ran at them. Blocks away, Kiyun and Gamon thundered down the street.

Aranur was half on his knees, his hands streaked with blood. "Dion," he gasped. "Let the wolves in."

She stood poised, waiting for the next, inevitable blade to stab in. She couldn't catch her breath. She couldn't answer him. It was all she could do to hold the wild wolves back from enveloping her mind.

"Do it, Dion! Now!"

His voice was filled with urgency. As though his words released her control, she abruptly opened her mind. The packsong flooded in, and the gray rage that had banked inside her skull flamed suddenly into fire. She didn't know that her eyes flickered yellow or that her stance and posture changed. She didn't know that her lips curled back and her throat tightened into a howl. With the flood of gray that filled her mind, all she could see was movement and contrast; the flash of sunlight on steel.

She lunged with blinding speed.

NeVenklan cut decisively. Dion sidestepped, keeping herself between Aranur and the raiders. Behind her, Aranur grasped the wall and dragged himself up. There was blood seeping through his jerkin, but Dion didn't see it. Her feet were padded, her hands like claws; in her mind, she smelled the raiders' moves before they made them, saw their muscles tighten before they lunged. Some sixth sense read their energies, their attention, the way they focused before they moved. Yellow eyes flickered in her sight. And her mind swam with a gray sea of rage and hunt lust, fired hotter with her need. There was no familiarity between her and these wolves—no sense of restraint, no separation of one from the other. They were wild and raw to her, not smooth as Hishn was. And opened to them like a bowl to the air, Dion's heart became solid gray.

She slashed inside a raider's reach and cut jerkin, but no skin. She lunged and beat aside the messenger's blade, then dropped the point of her blade suddenly and stabbed the man in the thigh. He screamed and cursed her but still managed to cut back. Bandrovic appeared beside neVenklan and lunged suddenly across toward Dion. But his blow wasn't aimed at her. It was aimed at Aranur. Dion howled. Lupine speed fed her arms;

gray power filled her legs. The steel slid by her ribs toward her mate, and her arm flashed in movement. She parried the blow and it struck stone. Bandrovic's lips stretched—into a smile.

Instinctively, she realized what had happened. Bandrovic had caught her attack, and neVenklan was already past her, parrying Aranur's blow. "Rast!" she screamed, trying to turn. This time Bandrovic's strike was for her.

The force of his blow spun her back against the wall. She hit the stone with brutal force. Grimly, she lunged toward her mate. Aranur was struggling with neVenklan, and the two wrestled desperately along the top of the seawall as another raider rushed in and beat at Aranur's head. Below, the tide cut across the rocks with single-minded intent, and the waves chopped up by the crosswind sucked at the sharp, black boulders.

Bandrovic danced out of Dion's reach and glanced over his shoulder. What he saw made him grim. Gamon and Kiyun were almost at the seawall. Tehena was staggering back, running to keep one raider between her and another. Then Gamon charged past the woman and slammed into one of the raiders. Kiyun slid from his dnu in a single smooth motion, landing half on a raider as he parried the man's blow while catching the man's shoulder with his other hand. The change in the fighting style was almost palpable. Instead of twelve trapping two, it was suddenly five against eight.

Aranur and neVenklan were still pressed against the seawall, but Aranur was using the raider as a shield from the others' blows. Bandrovic took one look at them, then struck hard at Dion, flinging her to the side and lunging past her. He was over the seawall and onto one of the built-in ladders before she could jump back to her feet.

She had barely leaped for the wall when someone grabbed her jerkin, slinging her around. She twisted, knifed the man, then went down with him as his hand stayed locked on the leather. Heavy as lead, the raider's body crushed her to the stone, trapping her leg and hip. She was frantic to wriggle free. Boots lunged by her head, and suddenly there was a flash of steel. A raider woman crouched beside her. Dion snarled viciously and cut awkwardly up from the ground. The woman blocked the blow, then jerked back and fell to her side. Gamon hauled the wolfwalker up.

On the seawall, Aranur heaved neVenklan over to let the man fall to the rocks, but neVenklan wasn't finished. His hand caught in Aranur's belt, half dragging the Ariyen with him. Aranur staggered, off balance. From the side, the others closed in. The first stunning blow caught Aranur on the arm; the second on the temple. His knees buckled.

Dion screamed inarticulately and lashed out without control. The fury of her attack was almost frightening. But there were four raiders now between her and the seawall, and two were putting a rope around her mate while the others tried to haul up neVenklan. Kiyun smashed into the group, and one of the raiders barely beat the burly man off. The other man holding Aranur's arms was caught by Dion's thrown knife. The raider arched awkwardly, then toppled toward the rocks below. That man broke the hold of the others on neVenklan, and neVenklan grabbed again at Aranur. This time the Ariyen was dragged over the wall.

Like lightning, the other raiders lunged. One of them grabbed the rope around Aranur's chest; the other grabbed his arm. Dion somehow melted through the fighting. She ripped a knife from someone's belt and slashed the hands that grabbed at her. Someone jostled the raider with the rope, and the man cursed as he lost his grip. He barely blocked the blow aimed at his heart. He wasn't so lucky with the other strike.

The other raider still clutched Aranur's arm, holding the Ariyen from falling. For a moment, Dion and he were side by side, reaching down to the gray-eyed man. Aranur hung with neVenklan's weight on his belt, dangling against the seawall. Together, raider and wolfwalker half pulled them up until they got one of Aranur's arms over the stone wall. Then another man, dodging Kiyun's blade, slammed into the man beside Dion. The raider lost his grip on Aranur's shoulder. Some instinct warned the raider, and he half twisted to see steel cutting for his back. He jerked, jarring Dion and shoving her aside. She lost her hold on her mate. Someone grabbed at her arms as she fell back. Aranur's grip, weak on the stone, slipped. Dion cursed wildly and fought against the hands. And as she struggled, with a short, strangled cry, Aranur let go.

XV

Where is hope,
When you can no longer hold it?

Dion ripped free and lunged forward, catching Aranur's hand. His weight swung him in a short, sharp arc, slamming him into the wall. His eyes flickered as he struck. Blood seeped from his jerkin. Dion half screamed her rage at his weight, at neVenklan's weight with his. Cold stone ground into her hips, her ribs. Her arm was tearing out of its socket. Then, suddenly, neVenklan's hand seemed to lose its strength. With an inaudible sigh, the raider let go.

NeVenklan's body struck hard. There was a sickening crack as his head hit the rocks: There was no doubt about his death. Below, Bandrovic barely glanced at neVenklan as he jumped awkwardly for the skiff that bobbed just off the rocks, laid out in the race of the tide. Three other raiders were already in it, letting down the sail.

Above, Aranur dangled like a doll.

Dion dug her fingers into his arm, drawing blood. She couldn't hold on. *Gray Ones,* she screamed in her mind. The strength that surged back crushed Aranur's wrist. She didn't notice the sounds of the raiders, Gamon's hoarse shout, the bay boats putting out with the tide. She didn't see the blinding sun or the flash of steel or the water that glistened like alien eyes. She didn't notice the tiny red stream that fell from Aranur's body. But the long, wind-pushed drips arced down to the jagged boulders that lay at the edge of the bay. And when they hit, the waves rushed past and sucked his blood from the rocks.

Dion dug her fingernails into his wrist. Her free hand clawed for a hold on the too-smooth stone. A sword clattered against the wall beside her, but she ignored its cold steel. She strained, and lifted her mate by a hand span. "Damn you," she screamed at the moons. And lifted again.

For a moment, Aranur's eyes focused. "Dion," he gasped. "The wolves . . ."

Someone fell against her, and her grip, jostled, slipped.

Aranur looked at her as if he were drowning. "Wolfwal—" he gasped.

Below, the tide water foamed over the rocks, and the rocks bared their teeth in the surf. A blade glanced off Dion's arm, cutting leather and flesh. She couldn't help her spasm. Her grip loosened.

"Aranur!" she screamed.

The wind stripped him away.

XVI

We die as we've always done—
  Leaving the living behind.

—From Journey's End, *by Sarro Duerr, 2212 A.D.*

Someone yanked Dion roughly from the wall. The hands caught in her jerkin, on her arms, and blindly, she fought like a wild wolf to stay on the stones. The howling in her head deafened her; the gray tide raced like the sea. She couldn't see beyond Aranur's eyes. Aranur's voice. Aranur's body falling, dropping to the rocks and the surge of the tide below. She caught one glimpse of his body, half on neVenklan's, half on the rocks in the water. Then the racing waves sucked him away.

She screamed his name, but Kiyun yanked her from the wall and leaped out of the way of the blade that smashed down where he had been. She beat hysterically at his arms. The man ignored her and slammed the raider against the stone. The raider staggered back. "He's gone," Kiyun shouted, dragging at her. "Come on! We have to go—"

Gamon pulled at her from the other side. Tehena took a cut on her arm and staggered back, but the raider who fought the lean-faced woman did not press the attack. Instead, he leaped for the seawall ladders and slid out of sight. Gamon yanked Dion through the opening the raider left while Tehena cursed at them to move.

In a loose knot, they backed away from the wall while half the raiders went down the seawall and the other half guarded the first group's escape. Gamon and Kiyun forced Dion away, and the raiders didn't follow them. Instead, Bandrovic's men melted away along the waterfront. Within minutes, the raiders were gone. The street was empty except for three bodies that lay sprawled and silent—half in the sun, half in the shade of the seawall—and the carcass of one of the dnu.

Dion wrenched violently free of Kiyun's grip and flung herself back at the seawall, but there was no one below. Even neVenklan's body was gone, sucked away by the tide. And out on the bay, where the brine waters clashed, the skiff raced southeast, angling across the tide. She stared at the boat, and in the bow, one of the raiders turned. They stared at each other across the bay—Bandrovic and her. Their faces were blank with the distance, and only their thoughts continued the fight while the sailing skiff shrank toward the ships.

Gamon followed her gaze, then urged her away from the wall, pulling remorselessly on her elbow until she stumbled away. There were no dnu on which to ride away; the beasts, riderless, had fled. They found only one of the beasts nearby, and that one was lame; both hind legs had been slashed, and it limped heavily. Gamon glanced back, where a ship followed the tide and the skiff toward the sea, then back at the faces that peered from the windows. "Let's get out of here," he said in a low voice. "Before someone gets too curious."

Swiftly, they walked through the streets. Asuli met them a few blocks away, hovering nervously in the shadows of a restaurant awning. No one spoke to her, but the intern slid from her dnu and offered it silently to Dion. The wolfwalker didn't notice. Asuli hesitated, then simply fell into step behind them. Gamon looked at Dion several times as they hurried, but the wolfwalker made no sound. Her face seemed blanched, and her lips were tightly shut; her neck muscles were taut as wires.

There was already more traffic on the streets, but few eyebrows raised at their appearance. In the one small market they pushed through, the vendors, noting the blood on their sleeves, left them alone. In fact, it took Gamon ten minutes to find someone who would give him directions to one of the city dnumarkets.

While Gamon talked to the vendor for directions, Tehena leaned close to Kiyun. "Aranur?" she asked, her voice low.

"Dead," he returned. "He fell on the rocks."

The hard-faced woman glanced at Dion. "Sure?"

"His body was twisted. He didn't move when the tide sucked him down."

Dion made a strangled sound—half sob, half snarl—and Kiyun grabbed her chin, pulling her to face him. She suffered his touch for a moment, then jerked free, her lips curled back. "She's deep in the Gray Ones." Kiyun's voice was soft.

"Best if she is," Gamon said flatly, turning to join them. Kiyun raised his eyebrows, and the older man nodded. "Better for her not to think. You need a healer?" he asked Tehena belatedly as the woman wrapped a rag around her arm.

The woman shrugged. "Time enough for that." She nodded at the wolfwalker's wrists. "What about Dion?"

"She'll heal herself. She always does, when she's with the wolves." Behind them Asuli made an odd sound, and Gamon glanced over his shoulder. "You might as well go home now, woman. By the time Dion works again, your ninan will be over. She's no use to you right now."

"Perhaps then, I can be of use to her."

The older man just eyed her. His voice was cold. "You'll do what you want anyway, I imagine, and to hell with everyone else."

Asuli said nothing, but stayed with them like a leech.

They bought dnu at one of the city markets and began to ride to the inn, but Dion turned her dnu back to the seawall instead.

"Dion," Gamon said sharply.

She looked at him. Her violet eyes seemed drowned in darkness. The yellow glint was dull.

"North and east, Dion. Not south."

"Gamon," she whispered. "Is he really dead?"

Something blurred the older man's vision. Slowly, he rubbed his forehead. His lips moved, but no sound came out, and he realized that he hadn't spoken. He cleared his throat. "Aye," he said finally.

She didn't nod. Her eyes, unfocused, seemed to see through him. In his head there was an echo of something dark. The echo swelled, rose and fell, and he knew it for the howl of the wolves. With the sun striking his shoulders, a chill hit his blood. He didn't speak, but he took Dion's reins and forced her dnu with his, east, back to the inn.

She rode with them, but there was an emptiness in her that blinded her to what the others did. She had thought she was already empty—naught but a void when Danton died. But there must have been some corner of her self that still held emotion because now that too had drained away. The void within her cried out for sound, for something to fill it. And there was no answer at all.

She barely noticed that Tehena packed her things on her dnu, or that Aranur's things were packed with them. But when Gamon gestured for them to ride out again, north, back to Ariye, she turned her dnu south and west instead.

With a glance at her face, Kiyun shrugged at the others and let his dnu fall in with hers. Gamon hesitated, then did the same. A few minutes later, with the wolves filling her head, Dion rode back toward the sea.

She rode without stopping, and the others followed. Back through the markets, the stone streets, the sun-filtered shadows. Unerringly, she headed for the seawall. The city bustled as if it had not noticed the bodies in its streets, the wagons that had blocked the waterfront. The bloodstains had already been sanded on the stones, and the raider bodies were gone. The noon markets were busy, the sidewalks full. The city turned blind eyes to death.

Dion saw the seawall. Her eyes, she knew, saw the fitted stones, but her mind saw the raiders upon them. Her ears heard the clatter of dnu hooves on rock, but her mind heard the clang of metal. She didn't remember dismounting or climbing over the seawall. She didn't remember the cold steel of the access ladders in her grip. But she felt the rocks when she stumbled across them. She felt her knees press into their rough texture, her hands rub across their edges. With her eyes unfocused, she simply knelt at the water's edge, ignoring the rough touch of the waves as they sucked at the rocks before her.

The sun burned at her from both sky and water, and brine spray showered her lightly. Her mind relived the fight. She could have seen it from her own eyes, but she had the memories of the wolves to double her vision. As she had let them into her mind in the fight, the violence was now in the packsong. She stretched, and the wild wolves howled with her. Their drive to hunt Aranur . . . Their urgency . . . The bloodlust they thrust into her mind. Over and over, the scene replayed. Aranur hanging on to her arm. His eyes, his voice. Her arm—jostled. Her hand—slipping. And his body, falling away.

She started when Kiyun touched her arm.

"Dion," he said softly. "It's time to go."

She shook her head. The sun was still low.

"We can't stay here at night," he said.

She frowned and looked vaguely at the sky. The sun was low, but it struck her eyes from the right, not the left. It had crossed both water and sky and was sinking back to the hills that ringed the bay. She shivered as if the brine spray had stripped away the sun's heat. Slowly, Kiyun helped her stand. She swayed, then stumbled to the access ladders. She didn't remember how she got up, but somehow she was astride her dnu again, staring out at the bay. Her skin burned from the sun, but she felt cold as ice, and she shivered as though it were winter.

Kiyun leaned back to her saddlebags. He pulled her cloak from the bundle and started to put it around her shoulders, but she choked out a sound and spurred her dnu forward. Startled and chittering like a stickbeast, it bolted down the road.

Blindly, Dion let the dnu have its head as she fled from the Sidisport sun. The others simply followed. She didn't know how long she rode or where the dnu took her. But it was dark when it stopped, and the eastern road was empty of city buildings and homes. The dark pressed in with mugginess, and it seemed to resist her as she slid from the saddle. The night was thick with wolves.

Unconsciously, lupine memories filled her skull so that she knew the land over which they rode. She didn't glance at the others as she dismounted and unerringly led her dnu from the road toward a short-grass clearing. When she reached the meadow, she unsaddled the beast, placed the gear by a log, and led the dnu to the stream that wound through the trees nearby. When it had drunk its fill, she lay down and let the cold water shock her face. Then she tethered the dnu to the log, walked into the grass, and lay down. She didn't speak as the others followed suit. Asuli said something to Tehena, but no one answered the intern. Within minutes, the clearing was quiet as a grave, the night as thick as a shroud.

Dion lay with her eyes open. The grass was half stiff with the dryness of summer, and the ground was warm and humid at her back. Four of the moons hung heavily in the sky, and they looked like pairs of eyes. Eyes that searched for her. Eyes that stared ... Yellow eyes, gray eyes ... A fist caught suddenly in her throat, and it choked her breath so that for a moment she thought she would suffocate. Then a body rustled in the grass. Another slunk by a moment later.

The wolves found her beneath the moons and curled up beside her. Their hot breaths whuffed the summer pollens, and their musk scent filled her nose. The packsong swelled in her head. Overhead, the stars shifted, the moons swam in the blue-black sea. Dion, surrounded by the wolf pack, slept.

* * *

They camped without fire. They rode with mindless urgency. They sped through villages and didn't stop, and camped only when Dion dropped from the saddle in exhaustion. For four days, they didn't even speak.

There was something wild yet fragile about the wolfwalker, as if she would somehow break were she disturbed by human speech. And there were wolves around her like clouds of gnats. They weren't seen so much as felt, so that a solid screen of predators surrounded the wolfwalker's group.

By the end of the fourth day, they had crossed into the eastern hills and out of Wyrenia Valley. They bought supplies at two of the villages through which they rode, but Dion barely waited for them to complete their purchases before spurring her dnu farther east. By the sixth evening they were deep in the forest, where roads as ancient as the wolves appeared, ran for kays, and sank again beneath the soil.

Asuli tried twice to get Dion to talk with her, but the wolfwalker said little, and Tehena watched her carefully. "There's a storm there," the lanky woman muttered to Gamon one dawn. "It's brewing as surely as if it were winter."

He followed her gaze. For a moment, he chewed on his lip. "Might be a good thing for that storm to break. There's something in her that's losing its hold."

"You mean the wolves?"

"Aye. They're holding her—like they did before. I think without them she would throw herself away."

"She's not that weak."

"Maybe not. Maybe so. But with Aranur . . . gone—" He forced himself to say the words. "—the weight of her decisions rests on her shoulders alone. I don't think she can bear it."

"She's always made her own decisions."

"No . . ." His voice trailed off. "She has an independent mind, but she's never really been on her own. She's always had someone to rely on—her father, her brother, Aranur, Hishn. Now there's no one but herself. Now she is truly alone."

"She has us," Tehena said sharply.

"Aye. Us."

But he said nothing else, and Tehena was left to study him as she studied Dion: in silence, with a wariness that was growing into fear.

That noon, when Asuli deliberately accosted Dion, Tehena merely watched, the thoughts turning over and over in her hard-faced head. Dion was watering her dnu at the river at which they had stopped, and the intern led her own dnu up beside Dion's. The bank of the river was soft with silt, and the current swift but quiet. The sound of their words carried easily.

"Healer Dione," Asuli said. "It's been days since I interned with you. When will you begin to teach me?"

Kiyun looked up as he heard Asuli's voice and started down toward the bank, but Tehena put her hand on his arm. Gamon gave her a sharp look, but held his peace. Kiyun, looking from the one to the other, subsided uneasily.

At the river, Asuli pressed Dion. "You owe me a ninan, Healer Dione. You've done no work since I joined you, and by the old laws, my ninan starts with your teaching. You'll not get rid of me by ignoring me, no matter how long you do it."

Dion did not look up. Her voice was flat. "There are no patients here, Asuli. There is no work for me or you."

"You're a master healer. You can teach theory if nothing else."

Dion's voice grew sharp. "I have no skills to give you."

"No skills?" The intern's voice was dry. "All those years of wearing that circlet and there's nothing you can pass on?"

"No. Not now." *Not ever,* her mental voice snarled.

"So you're giving up."

"I'm giving nothing. Leave me alone, Asuli."

The intern didn't back down. She set her jaw instead. "And what will you do if you don't work—if you don't teach me? Sit here alone and savor your pain? Chew on the grief each day till you choke?"

Dion raised her head. She said nothing for a moment, but her lips were curled back, her eyes flared and glinting violet and yellow together. Asuli took an involuntary step back. The fury that had filled Dion's chest seemed to burst suddenly out her throat, tightening her muscles so that the sound she made was pure wolf. Asuli began to back away.

Dion wasn't aware of moving, but her legs tensed so that she stalked the intern up the bank. "What do you think to take from me?" she demanded in a low voice. "The 'secret' of healing? My knowledge? My blood?"

"I want to know what you did to my father—how you healed his arm. I deserve that, at least."

"And you offer—what? Anything?"

"It's your duty to teach me."

"So you offer nothing. No thanks. No gratitude. No easing of my workload in exchange for taking you on. You simply want to take what you think the world owes you, draining what is left of me like a mudsucker emptying a corpse." Dion's eyes glinted violently. "You leech of a lepa," she breathed. She followed Asuli back. "All of you—you're like bloodworms. Haven't you taken enough from me? The endless scoutings. The constant studies in everything a weapons master's mate should know— every history of the Ancients, every text of settlement, every science they think to recover. Even in the clinics you haunt me with every disease and condition and injury and death. 'Healer Dione, we've done all we can. Please, just see one more child.' One more fever-burned woman. One more worlag-scarred man. Every time I turn around, someone has sucked another ninan away. And now there's you. Teach me this. Give me that. Fourteen interns are not enough duty—you call the old laws to cut out another piece of me and assign it to yourself. When do you stop?" She grabbed dirt from the ground and shook it at Asuli. "When I'm sucked dry as this dust?" She flung the dirt away.

Asuli opened her mouth, but the wolfwalker snarled inhumanly. The intern gasped. Eyes wide, Asuli stumbled in a swift turn and hurried up the bank, her back twitching as though Dion would spring and tear at her flesh in a rage.

Under the trees in the shade, Kiyun and Tehena stood stiffly, eyeing Dion with wary expressions. Gamon started down the bank toward her, but the wolfwalker didn't look at him. Instead, she stared down at her hands. They were trembling again. She felt the flood of gray sweep her mind, knew her arms were beginning to shake. She turned back to the water. She must have made some sort of sound because the two dnu spooked at her footsteps and bolted back up the slope. Gamon barely caught the reins of one of them as it thundered past through their camp, scattering packs and gear.

On the dusty bank, Dion stared at the river. The water was clear and cold, and the standing waves were touched with both white river froth and sunlight. Heat burned its way into her hair, her shoulders, her face. Overhead, the sky was almost clear, with only a few streaks of high, gray clouds. The moons hung like eyes in that vastness.

"The moons mock me," she whispered. "And the sun burns away at my grief."

The water glistened and slicked its waves. The long clouds reflected along its length so that a dozen gray wolf packs streaked through the stream: blue on gray, gray on black. The water seemed to swell against the riverbank. Suddenly, Dion threw back her head and howled. It was a harsh scream—a sound not meant for human throats.

"Damn you," she raged at the moons. "You've taken everything from me: my mother, my son, my mate. Tomi was never mine to begin with, and Olarun—you've turned him so he won't even look at my face. What have you left me? The silver and steel? You think to bind me to this life with that?" She tore the healer's circlet from her forehead and hurled it out into the water. It struck the opposite bank and clattered into the rocks, dropping into water that stole its silver gleam. "Take it," she raged. "Take them both. I'll be no slave to either one." She fumbled with her sword belt, jerking it off almost frantically. "Take them," she screamed. She spun the weight of the blade over her head, then loosed it at the river. It hit with a flat, slapping sound, and sank out of sight in the waves.

Dion sank to her knees. The silt depressed slightly, curving around her knees, and some part of her brain noted that her weight crushed the soil even as the weight of the moons crushed her. The weight of the moons ... The weight of her future. Aranur's goal to touch the stars, and hers simply to survive. And it was she again who walked away, while her future died with him. She closed her eyes. Memories raged in her head like the nightmares that clung to her sleeping hours. The howl of her voice crying out for her mate was a sound that didn't stop.

"Dion." It was Gamon's voice, quiet but somehow cutting through the swirling blindness. He didn't touch her, but she knew he squatted beside her in the sun.

Her voice was quiet. "I'm no use to anyone now. I'm not a healer. I'm not a scout. There's nothing left in me to use."

"Don't do this, Dion."

She looked up then, but her eyes were unfocused—not with the sense of the wolves, but with some inner pain so dark that it blinded her to him. "Don't do what, Gamon? Don't scream? Don't cry? I knew you for a year with Aranur, and you never warned me even once: When I Promised with him, I mated with death. Your county is steeped in blood."

"My blood and yours, Dion. Aranur was a son to me—as you are a daughter."

"Then the weight of this should be on your back, not mine. I'm breaking now with grief."

"Aye." His voice was quiet.

"How could they do this?" she cried out. "How could they take everyone—everything—from me? Is there no mercy in the moons?"

"Mercy's a human concept, Dion. It doesn't belong to the moons or skies."

"The Ancients owned the sky, the stars. But what do we own now? Look at us. We struggle to recover the barest of the old technologies, and what we do recover, we must hide from alien eyes. The Aiueven are legend not just for their plague, but for the death they bring to us each time we advance our sciences. By the moons, Gamon, we live like near-animals. We die in our forties from swords and disease when we should be living three centuries. I can't protect my sons from this world, Gamon. Survival here is a matter of hours, not days or months or years." She thrust out her fists. "Look at my hands. They're not strong enough for what they have to do. I couldn't keep the lepa from my son. I couldn't hold on to Aranur when the raiders decided to kill him. I could watch them die, but I couldn't save them. I can't change death to life, no more than I can halt the tides or touch an alien star." She clenched her fists. "You fight for a future that won't exist. It's worthless, Gamon—every goal your county has. We'll never recover what the Ancients had. All we'll do is sacrifice our families to the god of the endless future."

Gamon's jaw tightened. "The future is all that holds us together, and deep inside you know that. It's what makes us human—the vision to see what we can become, not simply what we are at this moment. You know what I'm talking about, Dion. It's not just blind hope. If our ancestors hadn't bred and set out the mining worms, we'd have no metals today. If we didn't breed and set out the worms in our own lifetimes, our descendants would be as metal-poor as the first of the Ancients themselves. What we do now depends on what our ancestors did before us; and the things we do now define what our descendants can accomplish. And we're almost there, Dion. A few more decades, and we can begin the real work in the county. Aranur knew that; that's why he pushed so hard for you to learn everything with him. He wanted you to live the vision with him. To someday touch the stars and watch your children fly like Aiueven in the sailplanes of the Ancients. The vision is true, Dion. You can't abandon it now."

She didn't move. "I can, Gamon, and I have."

"No," he said sharply. "Without the vision to see forward, we don't just live like near-animals, we become them. Is that what you'd prefer? Would you condemn your own bloodline to poverty and ignorance? Give up your dreams, your hopes, your ethics? The raiders, the venges—they're just what we face this moment. There will be better years ahead."

"But I can't live with this existence."

"You don't believe in existence, Dion. You believe in life."

She made an inarticulate sound. Gamon covered her fist, and she stared at his hand. The gnarled skin was weathered from decades of trail work and fighting, but the aged fingers were lean and strong, and the pressure of his hand on hers was firm.

"Aranur believed in life, Dion. He knew he might not be able to reach his goal in his own lifetime, but that didn't mean that he denied that the goal was worthwhile. You know that, too, deep inside. He might be gone, but his dreams live on. You'll have to face those, Dion—his memories and his dreams, not just his death. You must see that."

Gray, grayer, darker, black; the flood of death swept her mind like a badgerbear rushing through night. She heard the river and knew it was before her, but she could no longer see it. Frigid water flashed beneath the summer sun. Clear depths fractured against the black rock on the other bank. She blinked, and realized with vague surprise that it was her mind which was black as night. "I'm blind," she said quietly. "I cannot see."

Gamon looked at her. He opened his mouth, but no sound came out. It was not until Tehena finally moved beside Dion and took her hand that Dion got to her feet. The wolfwalker stood uncertainly, as if she had no balance, and Tehena touched her arm. Then, as if the wolfwalker were a child, Tehena led her away to her dnu.

Kiyun watched them as the lean woman mounted and took up the reins for Dion's beast. Tehena looked back and gestured toward the trail; Kiyun nodded silently. Tehena and Dion rode out, leaving the others behind.

For some time no one spoke. Then Kiyun took a collapsed grappling hook and the rope from his saddle bundle and moved down to the riverbank. Asuli frowned as she watched him, then went after him to the bank.

Slowly, Gamon got to his feet. He ran his hand through his hair and stared at the gray-slick water. "We're losing her," he said.

Kiyun stood beside him. "Aye," the man said simply.

"We have to do something." Gamon's voice was hard.

"Something," Kiyun agreed. "But what do you think to do? She's gone too far," he said, more to himself. "She's on the blood side of the moons."

Gamon had no answer for that.

Steadily, Kiyun uncoiled the rope and knotted one end to the hook. Then he spun the hook across the water. It was not a wide river; the hook landed well back in the trees. A few minutes, and the hook was set, and the tall man knotted the other end to a thick trunk on the bank.

Asuli watched his preparations. When he started stripping down to his shorts, she asked sharply, "What are you doing?"

He peeled off his shirt and dropped it onto his boots. "Diving."

"For what?"

"For what Dion thinks to throw away."

"Kiyun, this river comes straight off an ice pack. That water's freezing."

"Aye," he agreed.

"The current could have carried those things half a kay already."

"Maybe. The circlet fell near the other bank in that eddy, out of the main current. And the sword is heavy. It sank where the water's deep."

"And you can dive that deep?"

He shrugged.

"You're a fool," Asuli told him sharply. She turned on her heel and went back to her dnu. She looked down the trail, but Tehena and Dion were out of sight; so she sat on a log and stared instead at the ground.

In the river, Kiyun knotted a safety line around his waist, looped it over the grappling line, and waded into the current. Briefly, he cursed under his breath at the frigid chill. Then he began to dive.

XVII

"I wanted to save the world,"
  said the wolfwalker.
The eighth moon smiled faintly.
  "It's enough to save yourself," she said.

—From **Night Mares and Wolfwalkers,**
     Tales to Tell Children

There were days that passed, but Dion didn't know them: she had turned inward and was deafened by wolves. Twice she disappeared, turning off the trail and riding alone, only to appear again hours later with a wolf pack fading back into the brush behind her. She pushed herself during the day then collapsed, exhausted, at night. She accepted staying in villages only because Gamon insisted. When she did sleep, she cried for Aranur at night, and woke with the names of her sons on her lips. And between the towns, where the forests were thick with wolf packs, she flickered in and out of their campsites like candlelight in the wind.

Halfway through the second ninan, she returned to camp without her dnu. It was Kiyun who saw her first, standing uncertainly in the dusk shadows at the edge of the small clearing. Quietly, he said her name. She looked at him blankly. He said it again, and this time she shivered. Then she moved into the firelight. She left again the next morning and ran with the wolves on foot.

They zigzagged through the hills, moving without direction—even backtracking—until they turned vaguely north. By the end of the third ninan they were well into Ramaj Randonnen. The thin line of the river they followed began to grow as more mountain streams enjoined it. The air grew colder with the altitude, and they began to face ice in the mornings, but the sun was still hot at midday, and the air was dry as dust. Only night itself was cold.

One day, Dion left them when a wolf pack loped past the riders. One moment, she was walking with Kiyun; the next minute, she was gone. Kiyun mounted the dnu he had been leading, and they rode on, following the thin road that occasionally appeared.

It was barely dusk when Gamon and the others found a clearing in a stand of randerwood trees. They made camp efficiently, dug out a fire pit, and lined it with rocks. One moment, they were snapping the fallen branches for a fire pit; the next, she was at the edge of the clearing, watching them from the trees. It was Kiyun who saw her first again, and he stiffened in spite of himself. Gamon and Tehena looked up sharply. Like a wolf, Dion eyed them warily, and behind her, two of the Gray Ones melted back into the brush.

"Dion," Gamon said softly. "Come."

She hesitated, but Tehena gestured calmly. Finally, the wolf-walker stepped out of the dusty shadow. They could see her sleeve now, where it was gashed, and the stain of blood along it. Gamon motioned for her to come closer. She shrugged away, half shifting toward the forest. Only when Gamon stopped moving did she halt. Then, gingerly, he motioned instead toward her bedroll, which Kiyun had already spread. She hesitated, then moved to sit on the blankets. She curled up like a wolf beneath them, closed her eyes, and slept.

"Her arm is gashed," Asuli said, her voice low.

"We noticed," Kiyun said flatly, going back to snapping wood and stacking it in the fire pit.

"It should be treated. She'll get jellbugs if she runs around with an open wound like that."

The tall man fed the fire. "Dion won't get jellbugs."

Asuli stared at him. "Are you that stupid? It's summertime—the jellbugs are breeding like flies."

"Watch your tongue, Asuli."

"Just because she's a healer doesn't mean she's suddenly immune to the dangers to her own body."

Kiyun gave her a grimly amused look. "You want to treat her? Go ahead and try."

"You'd let her die just because she doesn't want to be touched right now? What kind of Kum-jan friend are you?"

Kiyun's voice was suddenly hard, his face shuttered. "There is no Kum-jan between us. We're friends, not lovers, Asuli."

"You look at her—"

He cut her off. "No," he said flatly.

"Fine," she retorted. She stalked to her saddle and pulled her own healing kit from it. But when she squatted down beside Dion, the wolfwalker's eyes opened, and the snarl that came to Dion's lips was audible. Deliberately, Asuli reached for Dion's arm. Then she froze. The blade of a knife lay against her wrist.

Asuli didn't move, but her voice had the barest tremor. "It needs the sealing salve. There are jellbugs out here, and parasites that can clog your blood like hair in a water pipe. You, of all people, know that."

Dion's lips moved, but the words were mangled by the packsong that flooded her thoughts.

Asuli reached for Dion's arm again. "You've got to put the salve on—" The knife pressed into her skin. She gasped and jerked back. Eyes wide, she stared at the wolfwalker. "You would cut me?"

"Don't touch me." This time Dion's words were clear.

"You've got to fix that open wound. You'll die if you don't close it off."

"The wound is closed. There are no jellbugs in it."

"I don't believe you."

"That's your prerogative." Dion slipped the knife back in its sheath, but Asuli had no doubt that the steel would flash out again should she try to touch the wolfwalker.

The intern's lips compressed. "You don't want me to see the wound because it's already infected, is that it?"

"Think what you want."

"I think you want to die, Healer, but you haven't the guts to kill yourself quickly; you'll let the jellbugs do it for you. It will just be a matter of time."

"It's always a matter of time, Asuli—time to live or die. Time is nothing more than a measure of moments between memories."

Asuli stared at her. There was something in Dion's eyes that caught her attention. "You're doing it, aren't you?" she said slowly. "What you did before—in Prandton? Only you're doing it to yourself now. That's why you think you can't get jellbugs."

"I'm no longer a healer for you to harass. Go find some other amusement."

"Teach me."

"You can't see through your own eyes, Asuli. How can you think to see through mine?"

"Or through the eyes of the wolves?"

"The Gray Ones require wolfwalkers with love and empathy, not hatred and aggression."

The intern's face shuttered. Abruptly, she stood up and walked back to her saddle, where she dropped to watch Dion from across the clearing. She could feel her frustration jelling into hard determination. She breathed the words almost silently as she spoke to the air between them. "You might not like me near you, Dione, but no one else ever has either. Your disdain will not be enough to get me off your back. I'll have my internship, Dione. I'll take it from you if I have to save you myself to get what I want."

As if she somehow heard the words, the wolfwalker eyed the other woman, then turned her back and slept.

The Gray Ones came for Dion at dawn, and she woke as they slunk up to the camp. Kiyun, on guard, watched them come. They edged around him warily but waited while he handed the wolfwalker one of the ash-baked tubers. Her hands trembled when she took the cooked root. Kiyun hesitated. He could feel the terrible rage that was consuming her from the inside out. "Dion," he breathed. He touched her hand. She suffered the touch, but barely. When he met her eyes, he felt a chill. Abruptly, he stepped back.

When Dion slipped silently out of camp, Asuli sat up. The intern eyed Kiyun thoughtfully. "Why don't you go with her?" she asked.

"She needs to be alone. I'll not take that last thing from her."

"She's alone whether she's with us or not."

Kiyun didn't answer.

Asuli got up irritably and put her gear together. "We're barely a day from the Colton villages. When will we buy her another dnu? Or will she simply walk all the way back to Ariye?"

Kiyun looked down at the fire and stirred the ashes to see if there was a spark. His voice was soft. "She may not go back to Ariye."

"She's Ariyen—at least ever since she mated with Aranur. Where else would she go?"

"She could stay here. Her heart is still Randonnen."

"She has obligations. She can't just quit her duties. The council wouldn't let her."

Tehena, awakened when Asuli spoke, got up and packed her bedroll. "When Dion speaks, the elders listen. When Dion doesn't speak, the elders still listen. She's not part of the council; she's the voice of the wolves and the wilderness. She's bound by her sense of duty, nothing else. She can walk away when she wants to."

"As she is doing now."

Tehena shrugged. "She has that right."

"She had no right to abandon the people who rely on her. That's selfishness, not self-preservation."

The other woman spat to the side.

Asuli eyed her, then packed her gear in silence.

They reached the Colton villages by late afternoon. It wasn't a large town, but rather a series of small hubs separated by fields and streams that cut through the small farming valley. There was a commons house, but half of it was a stable, and the other half was being used as storage for bales of fabrics that were being packed for transport to other towns.

NeCrihu, the stableman, was as tall as Kiyun and broader, if that was possible. Wiping his hands on a lice rag, he met them in the stable courtyard. He didn't offer to grip arms with them, but it was not an insult. Instead, he looked them over without speaking, his dark brown gaze lingering on Dion's face and the glint of yellow that clung to her eyes. His steady eyes noted the line of lesser tan on her forehead where she had worn the healer's circlet, then a warcap. He didn't smile at the way Tehena shifted almost protectively in front of the wolfwalker; instead, stuffing the lice rag in his pocket, he said calmly, "You're looking for dnu?"

"Two trail dnu with staying power," Tehena said tersely. "That one, there—" She indicated the beast hitched to the currying post. "—is fine. And one more for carrying supplies."

"You're taking the ridge route to Changsong? Or the north marsh route through the valley?"

Tehena glanced at Dion. "Ridge route," she said.

He followed her gaze, but he was already shaking his head. "I've no dnu to sell you."

"Why?" Tehena's eyes narrowed. "You think we're raiders?"

The dnuman shook his head. "You, perhaps. Not them."

Tehena didn't smile.

"I'll not sell to you," neCrihu repeated. "But I'll loan you the beasts till you get to Changsong." He walked to the barn. Taking a message ring from a bin, he wrapped a couple knots in the already prepared stick, cut it with the carving knife hanging by the door, and handed the stick to Gamon. "Give this to neCollen, in Changsong. He'll sell you something there to ride, and send these back to me."

"How much?" Tehena asked.

He shook his head. "I'll not take gold from you."

"You'd loan them to us, not rent them?"

NeCrihu glanced meaningfully at Dion. His voice was soft. "Ember Dione is one of ours."

"And that's enough?"

"Here, yes."

Tehena's lips tightened, but Kiyun touched her arm. Abruptly, she nodded.

Evening found them out of the valley and back into the mountains. There, the north forests were thick and the old roads rough as the back of a worlag. The next night found them up on a ridge. Clouds gathered one day, then burned away; gathered again the next. A single wagon caravan passed them on the road; the wagoneers stopped, and Gamon and Kiyun spoke with them at length. Then the forest was silent again.

In the morning, one day out of Changsong, Dion left at dawn when the wolf pack howled from the ridge. But the others had barely finished breakfast when she returned. She melted out of the forest like a ghost; Asuli jumped when the dnu beside her grunted its warning. Dion looked at the intern, then at Gamon and the others. She was breathing quickly, as if she had run, and her hands were stained with dark patches. But the marks weren't blood, Kiyun realized; they were sap stains and something else.

"Stay," Dion said tersely. She stooped and took his machete from his pack. Then she faded back into the ferns. She was out of sight within seconds.

Asuli stared after her. "Stay?" she asked Gamon. "What does that mean?"

The older man rolled his eyes.

"It means stay," Kiyun answered for him.

"Stay and do what?"

"Wait." Tehena uncinched the saddle she had just tightened onto her dnu.

"Wait?"

The lanky woman dropped the saddle over the log beside Asuli. "Wait patiently."

"That's it? No questions asked? No 'What will you be doing, Dione, while we sit here on our behinds?' "

Tehena shrugged.

Asuli seemed to explode. "You're a bunch of idiots," she snapped. "What do you think she is? A moonmaid? A god? The wonder healer, the great Dione—"

Tehena's open slap struck so blindingly fast that Asuli's whole body rocked back before she knew she had been hit. The hard-faced woman glared at her like a lepa.

Asuli pressed one hand hard to her cheek. "You can't silence the truth," she managed. "No matter how you strike at it." She checked her hand for blood. Gingerly, she touched her cheek again.

Tehena didn't move. "And what do you see as truth, Asuli?"

"Dione's just a woman," snapped the intern. "And a poor excuse for one, at that. She's no elder to command you here and there. No venge leader to demand your loyalty. She throws away what she is just because she's too lazy to look at herself. You ask what the truth is? It's that Dione is just another weak-willed person who can't handle life as it is." She sat down on a log and rubbed at her cheek.

Kiyun shook his head. "You know nothing, woman. If Dion has our loyalty, it's because she earned it."

Asuli snorted. "When?" she demanded. "How long ago? Five years? Ten years? Twenty?"

"Dion has been many things to many people—"

"Who cares what she was before? It's what she is now that's important. It's always what you are now—that's the only thing you have to work with to make things happen in your life."

"That's worlag piss. Dion is what her past has made her."

"Dion is selfish and useless," she shot back. "Is that what bought your loyalty?"

Gamon's voice was mild. Kiyun, having heard that tone before, eyed the older man warily. "So you think," Gamon said, "you should throw a person away if they become useless—or inconvenient."

"It's not a matter of inconvenience. Don't twist my words, old man."

Gamon's gray eyes glinted.

Asuli gestured sharply toward the forest. "You let her run around with the wolves like a wilding. You don't do anything to stop her, to make her face what she's feeling. This thing with the jellbugs—does she think she'll avoid death just because she's a master healer? Or avoid raiders if she stays out of Ariye? She can't run away from Aranur's death—or the death of her son or, hell, the death of anyone she's ever known. Death is her lifestyle. The woman's not just a wolfwalker—she's a moon-wormed scout. She's lifted her sword against raiders as often as she's used her scalpel—probably caused as much death as she's prevented." Asuli jabbed her finger at them. "And you, you're all as much to blame for the way she's acting now as she is herself. You're so caught up in her reputation, you don't care that you're simply making it easy for her to run away—to escape herself no matter how much it costs everyone else. You're like a bunch of disciples trailing some sort of messiah. Anything she needs, you get her; anything she does, you accept. But you're blind as she is if you follow her. She's hardly even human."

Kiyun's jaw tightened visibly. "What is human?" He threw the question at her. "Words? A speech pattern? Emotions? Thoughts? You think you are more human—somehow better than she? Dion is more human than either of us will ever be. She's seen eight centuries of birth and death. She's felt eight hundred years of grief. You have the option of forgetting, of letting memories fade. Dion doesn't have that luxury. Those wolves, who make her so 'blind' to you, accentuate every emotion. They carry every event in their memories and play them back, again and again. When her son was killed, the wolves were there in her mind, locking that memory into their packsong so that it haunts her, day and night. When Aranur died, the wolves were there— she let them into her mind to help her find the strength to hold him as long as she did. And now the image of his death is with her every moment, in the packsong of a dozen wolves. She can never escape it now." His jaw tightened. "You think we help Dion run away—for a few days or ninans or years if we have to? You're goddamn right, we do."

Asuli looked at Tehena. "What about you? You're going to let her run away too?"

The other woman's eyes narrowed.

"You think she can be responsible for you when she's escaping herself? You, who are so desperate for her to give you direction, to give you purpose? Don't you see? She can't give you a reason to live—not when she's lost herself. And if she's not willing to pull herself out of whatever hole she's in, what will you do for her? Help her dig it deeper? Or help to get her out?"

Tehena's light-colored eyes were intent as a wolf on its prey. She opened her mouth, but Gamon put his hand on her arm. The lanky woman stilled with difficulty.

Slowly, Asuli got to her feet. "She can't save you—not as she is," she said quietly. "She can't even save herself."

Tehena watched Asuli walk away. An odd expression crossed her face, but she said nothing. The long day passed in near silence.

Dion did not return that night, and Asuli was restless. She paced the camp at dawn and fidgeted with the fire until she drove Kiyun to cursing.

"By the moons, woman, can't you settle down?"

"Where is she?"

"Do you care?"

"Does it matter?" she shot back.

He cursed again. "I'm going to check the snares," he muttered. "If you see her, tell her I'm waiting here."

"I've already seen her, and she doesn't care where you wait as long as it's away from her."

Asuli merely nodded. But when Kiyun left camp, she watched with sharp eyes. And later, when Gamon was digging up tubers and Tehena was checking their fish traps, Asuli disappeared.

When Tehena returned from the stream, she had a fat fish in her hands. She prepared it, wrapped it in leaves, and set it in the hot ashes of the fire pit before she realized that the intern's absence was more than a momentary lapse. Slowly, she stood and glanced around the camp. When she moved east she located Gamon easily. She circled the camp, but although there were two peetrees within forty meters of their site, the intern was not at either one. Tehena chewed her thin lip.

Then she set off in the direction Dion had taken at dawn. There was a wide game trail—used by everything from herds of eerin to worlags and badgerbears—and it was that which Tehena followed.

She had gone only two kays when she heard human sounds: steel on wood, cursing, half sobs. Within twenty meters she spotted Asuli. The intern was crouched near the top of a rocky rise in a stand of koroli bushes, where the fat, waxy, summer leaves hid her shape. When Tehena climbed the rise silently and followed the intern's gaze, her thin lips tightened grimly.

The lanky woman was within meters before Asuli realized there was someone behind her. Abruptly, the intern turned, her belt knife half drawn before she realized that it was Tehena who stared at her.

The lean-boned woman looked at Asuli, then nodded meaningfully back at the trail. Asuli's face shuttered. For a moment, the younger woman looked as though she would resist Tehena, but there was a reason the hard-faced woman was rarely challenged. Tehena's eyes, flat and hard, were empty of empathy, and Asuli had no doubt that Tehena would kill her if she felt she would protect Dion by doing it.

Asuli rose as quietly as she could and followed Tehena back. When they were partway there, she cleared her throat and asked, "What was she doing back there?"

Tehena gave her a cold look. "Carving a message ring."

"On a fallen tree?"

"You can think of something else big enough to hold her grief?"

Asuli shook her head. "She wasn't carving—she was attacking that tree. Slashing it and spitting at it. I watched her rip branches apart with her bare hands and reach into the core where part of the trunk was hollow. She tore the sapwood out with her fingernails. She screamed at the wood and cursed it. Cut herself and bled all over the bark."

Tehena didn't answer.

"And those wolves . . . An entire wolf pack was there, digging at the trunk and watching from the bushes."

Tehena shrugged. "They seek Dion as she seeks them."

Asuli chewed on that for a moment. "Why?" she finally asked.

"Because she has nothing else, and they give to her instead of take from her. Because they speak to her where we can't reach her with our words."

"Any of us could speak to the wolves, couldn't we?"

It was more of a musing than a question, but Tehena answered sharply. "Not if you want to remain living or sane."

"What do you mean? They say that all you do is look in their eyes—"

The other woman cut her off. "You provoke a wolf that way, Asuli. Just like with any dog." The intern opened her mouth to protest, but Tehena cut her off again. "Just because some wolves do communicate with humans doesn't mean they all do—they're still wild animals protecting their packs and dens and food. You stare at one and you're challenging it. The Ancients engineered the wolves to communicate, but you learn to do that only by looking into a Gray One's eyes."

"If it's just a physical challenge, why doesn't the Gray One run away?"

"It would—it's naturally timid. But when you meet its gaze with your own, you lock it to you through the engineering of the Ancients. The wolf has to stay until you break the contact or it finds a way to break away. You challenge it physically by looking into its eyes, but you challenge it emotionally and psychologically by the human dominance of forcing it to communicate. If the wolf doesn't like it, if it feels trapped enough, it can attack you—with body or mind."

"What do you mean?"

"I mean, a cornered animal will lash out with whatever weapons it has. A wolf trapped in a mental link with a human will lash out against that, too. The human has only one brain to think with; the wolves can pull the weight of the entire pack-song. You challenge a wolf, you could lose your mind."

"That's not how the storytellers describe it."

Tehena snorted. "How many storytellers are wolfwalkers? I've been with Dion for thirteen years; I've talked to the wolves myself."

"*You* looked at a wolf—heard its voice in your head?"

"Once." Tehena motioned for Asuli to go on to the camp, and the intern passed her warily.

"What happened?" Asuli prodded.

"I tried to do what Dion does—look into one's eyes and communicate. I provoked it instead."

"It bit you?"

Tehena looked at her, then slowly rolled up her sleeves. The ragged scars stretched from elbow to wrist. She motioned for Asuli to stay in camp. Then she went back to tend the fish traps.

Thin ice formed overnight in their pans, and the cold dawn brought them from their sleeping bags quickly to build the campfire up. The evening chill sent them back to their bedrolls as soon as the wind cut through camp. Asuli spent the time cutting and gathering herbs while the others took turns hunting and gathering and building up the camp. Tehena spent long hours away; Dion was not often seen. By the end of the first ninan in the camp it had become a full resting place, with a rude corral, two lean-tos, and a firewood rack. Riders stopped by twice to see what they were setting up, and traded salt and sugar and flour for pelts and Asuli's herbs.

Halfway through the second ninan, they attracted a poolah with the scent of baking tubers. Their first warning was from Dion, who appeared in camp as suddenly as a sharp sound. "Poolah," she said shortly. Smoothly, the others took up their weapons. Asuli looked from one to the other, uncertain what to do. She had a knife, but nothing else, and she realized abruptly that she lived here at the grace of the others. She made a half sound, and Gamon gestured sharply for her to stand closer to the fire.

The sightless head of the low, slinking beast was visible within minutes. Swinging slowly from side to side, the brown-speckled head followed their scent toward the clearing. It seemed to flow forward over the ground, between trees. Then it went still for a moment as it touched its tongue to the trail to check the strength of the scents. Like a shadow, it flowed forward again. It stopped just outside of the camp. Asuli made another small sound, the fear tightening her throat, and the poolah shifted subtly. There was a moment in which nothing moved; the forest itself seemed to hang in anticipation. Then the beast sprang toward her.

The intern screamed. The arrows from all four archers struck solidly, midair, in the poolah's body. The beast shrieked with Asuli and fell, twisting and jerking, short by meters of the fire. It died hard, leaving the ground torn and the fire-pit rocks scattered. Asuli almost backed into the flames herself while the poolah before her died.

They had meat that night for dinner.

By late evening, the treespits clouded the chill air like day-bats, drawn to their camp by the scent of the poolah and the radiating warmth of the fire pit. Tehena's watch was filled with snaps and rustlings.

When Gamon rose to take over the watch, Dion rose with him. She squatted by the fire for a moment, her eyes up, away from the flames. She didn't speak as she let the heat of the ash pit reach her hands, toasting them with warmth. For an instant, a pair of yellow eyes caught light. The wolf blinked, then disappeared. Dion rubbed her temple, then stood, walked to the edge of the clearing, and melted into the night.

Gamon watched her go with a tightened jaw. "By the seventh moon," he muttered. "She's got to stop."

Tehena shook her head. "Who will make her? You? Me?"

"One of us has got to."

"If Aranur couldn't convince her to stay in Ariye for his sake—or for the sake of the sons she has left, what do you think we can do here? Not even Olarun stopped her from running."

Gamon pulled on his mustache. "Olarun's part of the problem," he said. "You saw him before—he wouldn't speak to her, wouldn't look at her. Aside from Tomi, who is growing his own home now, Dion doesn't think she has a son left."

"Olarun will get over it."

"Like you did?" The older man nodded at Tehena's forearm, where the woman unconsciously rubbed at her scarred skin. "That tattoo you wore chased your family away like the plague. Your family rejected you just as Olarun does Dion. You've never gone back to show them differently. You've never gotten over their blame of you for getting into drugs. With Dion, Olarun blames her for Danton's death, and he's chasing her away as surely as if he took a sword and stabbed her."

"He's burying his blame."

"Aye. And burying it so deep it would take the gods themselves to uproot it."

Tehena laughed without humor. "You want to buck the gods on this? I say, let Dion have her distance, Gamon. She's strong. She's a wolfwalker. She'll survive." Her voice grew quiet, more for her ears than his. "She has to," she breathed. "I need for her to live."

Gamon didn't answer.

In the faint light of the ash pit, Tehena gave him a sharp look. "What's the matter?"

His voice was quiet. "Sometimes strength is its own weakness, Tehena. Dion's problem is not that she's strong, but that she never learned to be weak."

"Old man, you talk like a fool. No one needs to learn to be weak."

"No?" He gave her an amused expression.

"Don't give me that look," she retorted.

"Why not? A bit of what you call weakness would do you a world of good. Put some softness in your voice once in a while. Strength shouldn't be a shield, woman, but a sword."

"And just what does that mean?"

He shrugged. "Dion may have run from Aranur, but you run from men in general."

Tehena actually laughed. "You're worried that I haven't been with a man?"

"That's seven," he returned. "And you've had the opportunities."

She scowled at him. "With drunks, braggarts, and sods."

"What do you expect? Hang out with the drunks, and they're the only ones who will proposition you. Get yourself into some decent society, and you'll meet someone better."

"Oh, sure, Gamon. I'll just take my past and tuck it in the closet while I go visiting."

"We don't judge you by your past, Tehena."

"There's a good one," she retorted. "Tell me another one, Gampa."

He ignored it. "We judge you," he continued, "by what you've done since you came to Ariye."

"And what have I done?"

He looked at her set face. "You've ridden on the venges with Aranur and Dion. You've helped train the strategists she recommended. You nursed Dion when she was hurt. You've been her friend. Moonworms, woman, you've helped her through more than her share of grief."

Tehena's voice was flat and hard. "It all comes down to Dion, doesn't it? There are plenty of swords and strategists in Ariye, but only one Ember Dione. As long as she needs me, as long as she protects me from my past, I'm accepted in your county. That stableman—he practically gave us these dnu simply because we ride with the wolfwalker. No one would do something like that for me. Face it, Gamon, I have no value by myself—I'm nothing without Dion."

Gamon's voice was hard. "No one but you defines your life that way."

"No?"

"You're . . . efficient on your own, woman. You're straightforward. You're loyal to Dion. You're—"

"A drug-addicted, prostituted, baby-murdering, jail rat?"

Gamon closed his mouth.

"Hard to hide the truth when I wore it on my arms."

"Most men don't even know where you came from."

"Enough of them do to see me as less than a raider."

"A man who wants intimacy won't see you that way."

"Right. And I have such a body to attract them, too."

"Make friends, Tehena. That's all it takes. You've never offered Kum-jan to anyone in Ariye."

"What about you?"

Gamon turned to look at her, thinking she was joking. But the grin died on his face; her expression was deadly serious.

"What about you," she repeated.

He stopped. He stared at her hard, lean face. He saw the way she rubbed her forearms, and for a moment his memory flashed back. A lone rider whose flesh was littered with the scars of drugs and violence . . . That bitter voice taunting him as she waited for Aranur's judgment while her past stared all of them in the face. Gamon shook his head. "No, Tehena," he said softly. "Not that between us."

She watched him as his body language visibly withdrew from her. Then she turned and walked to her bedroll, lay down, and closed her eyes.

She rose at dawn and took the water bags to the stream. She cracked the ice that had formed on the tops of the bags, rinsed them out, and filled them. Then she sat back on her heels and stared at the river. She was not surprised to turn her head and see a wolf eyeing her from the forest—the Gray Ones were always thick around Dion.

Tehena watched the wolf from the corner of her eyes. Then slowly, she straightened. The wolf didn't move. "Well, Gamon," she muttered under her breath. "Between you and Dion, I've nothing left to lose."

She turned slightly so that she faced the wolf. "Gray One," she said, her hard voice as soft as she could make it. "Hear me." The wolf shifted subtly. Deliberately, she turned the rest of the way around.

The wolf almost faded back into the brush, but Tehena looked straight into its eyes. There was a shock in her mind of another voice—of a ringing, echoing sound. The snarl that rose in her head made her shudder, and she had to fight to keep from clenching her forearms where old scars from wolf teeth had long since healed. There were suddenly two Gray Ones there.

"I Call you, wolf," she said hurriedly. "I Call you as the Ancients did."

The wolves snarled again.

Tehena's heart began to speed. She felt a chill on her fore-head and knew that she was suddenly sweating. Death from a blade was fast and clean; from the wolves . . .

The yellow eyes glinted; the white teeth gleamed. She could feel their wariness, their instinctive desire to run. She knew that there were others nearby. *Human,* a lupine voice returned.

"You honor me," she said automatically.

The wolf did not answer her greeting. Instead, it was sud-denly closer. The image-words were thick with emotion that choked Tehena's breath. *By what right do you Call us?*

The snarls that struck her from the side were in her ears, not her mind. The Gray Ones seemed to move forward, and Tehena felt her heart clutch her ribs. She stayed her ground, knowing that to move was to become a deer, an eerin, to be run down and slashed to death. "By the . . . Right of the Wolfwalkers," she managed. "For Ember Dione."

For the wolfwalker, he returned.

"I need her. I need her to be alive—to be . . . To be my . . ." She couldn't quite force the words.

She is your packleader, the wolf cut in.

It had been a statement, not a question, but Tehena nodded jerkily. "She is lost, and you have to bring her back. You must Call her and give her purpose. You have to make her want to live."

The gray voice was hard, and the wolf seemed suddenly closer. *Why do you not Call her yourself, human?*

"I cannot."

Cannot or will not? The yellow eyes gleamed, but they were neither friendly nor warm. Instead, that gaze pierced her chest.

Tehena's voice was ragged. Her words were dragged out by those eyes. "I've made too many . . . mistakes in my life. I can't . . . can't risk making another. You have to do this for me."

You wish for us to take responsibility for you, as your pack-leader did for you before. You wish for us to help her, so that she can lead you again.

She didn't answer. She knew they could see into her mind. "You can gather the packs," she said instead. "There's time enough. We could be here another ninan."

You ask this for your sake, not hers?

Tehena felt her heart shrink within her. "I might as well die without her. I'll die for her, if that's what you want."

So you Call us and offer us blood in return. But it is your blood you offer, not hunt blood or kill.

There were suddenly too many wolves, and Tehena felt the sweat drip down her cheeks. Her voice trembled. "By the Right of the Wolfwalkers," she repeated. "By the . . . light of the moons and the Laws of . . . of Landing, I ask you to reach Dione. You have to make her live."

The yellow eyes seemed to devour her soul. *You are no wolfwalker to Call to us.*

The gray tide swelled; the wolves leaped forward. Tehena threw her arms up, then bit her scream into her own flesh, stifling her terror, as the gleaming teeth slashed down.

XVIII

Who does not know death cannot understand it;
Who does not know grief cannot assuage it—
You cannot live until you die.

—*From* The End of the Wolves, II

Tehena returned to camp at dusk, while the others were at the river. She burned her clothes and salved and bandaged herself as best she could. She was weak, but the gashes, though ragged and long, were shallow. She eased a long-sleeved tunic on and drew on another pair of leggings. She could handle the bleeding, and the scars wouldn't matter. The stiffness she could pass off as a fall. But in the distance, a wolf howled, and she shuddered. She moved closer to the fire.

Two days later, the sky was covered with light, high clouds. It rained lightly at noon—a drizzle that barely touched the summer dust and left the ground stale, not clean. But after the rain, when the sun had crawled barely halfway up the trees, Dion returned to their camp. Exhausted, she dropped to the ground by the fire pit. Tehena rose and left, and Kiyun dug a leaf-wrapped meatroll from the ashes and handed it to the wolfwalker. But Dion stared at the meatroll as if she didn't know what it was. Silently, Kiyun took the bundle back and unwrapped the food. Dion passed her hand over her eyes, took the roll, and ate.

The wolfwalker chewed slowly, as if the motion of her own jaw was exhausting. And when she was finally done, she said simply, "Pack."

When Tehena returned, they followed the old road north again, still vaguely trailing the course of the river. The centuries had changed the water's run, while the stones of the Ancients had merely settled in place. Now, with the road still somewhat straight, the river curved in toward the road and away again in loops. Dion disappeared with the wolves almost as soon as they hit the trail, and Asuli scowled after her. She couldn't decide if it was her imagination or not that there were more wolf packs here.

When they reached the place where Asuli had watched the wolfwalker before, the intern halted abruptly, and the others stopped with her. As one, they eyed the trampled forest. A massive tree, felled years earlier by lightning, had crushed the undergrowth and laid its length along the ground. But where brush and ferns had once grown up around its length, now there stood only broken, twiggy shrubs, raw pits of soil torn from the ground, and grasses bruised by boots and paws. The shadows didn't hide the white slashes cut along the length of the tree. The charred lines and symbols patterned in the trunk were raw as a fresh grave; and the stains of sap and dye plants were side-by-side with the marks of blood. Old branches were freshly snapped close to the trunk, as if to punctuate the message ring. The new, wiry growths that cut through the bark were like pointers to the sky. No simple message had been savaged into the log—full forty meters were carved and charred and stained in waves of pattern and poem.

"Moons," Asuli breathed. She dismounted. The others watched her move forward, as if in a dream, toward the tree. She stepped over the scattered bones of a rabbit without noticing the remains. Heedless of the thorns, she pushed through what was left of the brush to the message ring. Each day and night was carved there, she thought. Every absence of Dion from their camp was represented in the slashings the wolfwalker had left in the trunk of this tree. "What does it mean?" she asked, without looking over her shoulder.

Kiyun's face looked suddenly tired. "It is Dion's grief," he said finally.

"Rain . . ." Asuli ran her hands over the trunk where Dion's sword had cut the symbols harshly. "And dirt—no, soil. Dry . . . ground. And birth?"

Tehena cursed. "You have no eyes," she snarled.

The intern looked back. "Read it."

"It's a story—or, more, a poem. It's not a simple message, Asuli."

"Then don't give me a simple reading."

The lanky woman eyed her for a moment. Then, surprising both Gamon and Kiyun, Tehena slid from her dnu and moved to the fallen tree. For a moment, she simply let her hands and eyes feel the harsh cuts and slashes of symbols, the mix of colors and stains that drew and connected across the trunk. Some were crude, brutal with emotion; others were tiny, detailed, and precise as a miniature portrait. Tehena walked along the tree, climbing at one point over the massive length to reach the slashes along the other side. Her hard-lined face flickered once, as though she were a shadow of someone else. Then she vaulted to the top of the tree again and squatted upon it, letting her hands feel the message while her flat, hard eyes traced the stains. "It would be easier than grief." Her voice halted. She closed her eyes for a moment, her hands resting on the tree. Asuli waited. Tehena took a breath and began.

> Rain would be easier than grief
> Because it's cast away to soils
> That want to dry and be reborn.
> My tears are so much part of me
> That my throat is a white-knuckled fist
> Clenched around a marbled breath
> That my lungs can no longer grip.
> The rock of my heart has no way to beat
> So that my temples ache from my chest.
> And my eyes burn with the coals of a life
> That used to flare like a sun.
>
> Snow would be easier than grief
> Because its touch, which chills, then burns the skin,
> Is ice on a pond: Superficial.
> Cracked by a word, broken by touch.
> The cold in my heart extends to my hands
> So that they are blind on the ground.
> It freezes my face
> So that my parted lips, which try to form words,
> Are caught as a gulf on a glacier.

Storms would be easier than grief
Because they rage in exultation.
They draw out the fierceness of the world
And fling it around like laundry.
My grief can't rage, can't fight, can't fierce
Its way out past the bones of my body.
No sound drowns out the ache in my head.
No dreams bring true sleep; no touch, relief.
Only the ache, ache in my throat and eyes,
Like a mountain slowly crushing down
On what's left of the heart beneath it.

Death would be easier than grief.
   They speak of doorways, of hidden gifts,
   They speak of lights and gods and heaven.
   And in their stupidity, they speak of time
   As if it flows like a thickening quilt
   To comfort a night of chill.
There is no time in grief.
There's no gap between then and now.
Only the touch of the wind
On my salt-tightened cheek
Reminding me again and again that
The moisture isn't rain.

The forest was silent. Tehena didn't move. A bird flashed between the trees. The blue-speckled creature cried out as it caught sight of the riders. Like a spark of sky, it darted back into the canopy. Asuli stirred.

Something touched her cheek, and she brushed irritably at the bug only to draw her hand away with moisture. She shook herself, swallowed, and pointed over Tehena's shoulder. "You didn't read that," she managed.

Tehena followed her gesture. The other woman had indicated the thin trunk of a dead tree still standing, which was also carved and stained, but only in a single ring, and with sharper, finer marks. Tehena's face shuttered. "That is not from Dion," she said flatly. She slid from the fallen tree and walked back to her dnu. She didn't wait for the others but spurred the riding beast down the road, leaving Asuli to stare after her.

Asuli looked at Kiyun. "What does it say?"

He hesitated. "It is the response to Dion's grief."

"Who carved it? You?"

He shook his head.

She jerked her chin at the road. "Her?"

The burly man shrugged.

"Read it—please," she added belatedly.

But it was Gamon who spoke the message ring carved and stained in the wood:

> Let your sorrow be my pain;
> Let your cry tear out my throat;
> Your tears will choke my breath, and
> Your rage burn my eyes—
> I will hold your grief for you
> > Until you heal.

This time, it was Asuli who was silent. She stood for a long time facing the two trees: the one, massive, broken trunk with the growth of new trees pushing out of its length; and the thin, dead, upright tree that stood like a guard beside it. When she mounted again, her face, for once, was thoughtful.

They had been one day out from Changsong when they had turned off for Dion and camped for half the ninan. Once back on the main trail, they reached Changsong by late afternoon. Since the inn was full of climbers, miners, and visitors to the town, they went to the commons house instead. Kiyun gathered their clothes and took them to the cleaning woman's house, while Asuli volunteered to arrange for their supplies so that she could sell some herbs. Tehena found herself sitting on the steps of the house, splicing two odd lengths of rope left over from the fish traps. Gamon came out and stood for a moment on the porch, then sat down beside her.

Tehena barely glanced at him.

"I was wrong, a few nights ago," he said finally.

Her voice was flat. "So was I."

"I mean, I was wrong to say what I did—to reject Kum-jan. To reject you."

"I don't need your pity, Gamon."

"That isn't what I'm offering."

"Then what? Your 'friendship'?"

"My apology."

"When even a man of eighty is horrified at the thought of touching me, that is a lesson, not an insult."

"Aye," he agreed. "But it was my lesson, not yours."

Tehena didn't answer. Irritably, she scratched at her arms.

He nodded at her forearms. "How is it today?"

"Itches like fireweed," she said, deliberately truthful. "But what do you expect when you rub up against a sap tree?"

Gamon shrugged with her. "Would have thought you'd know better."

"So would I," she said meaningfully.

He gave her a thoughtful look. When he spoke again, his voice was quiet. "I am sorry, Tehena. I said I didn't judge you on your past, but on what you were today." His gray gaze was steady. "I was wrong. I did judge you. All I could see was who you told us you were, not who you are."

"You have that right."

"I don't," he said sharply. "I've no right to forgive or judge anyone but myself."

"Nice statement. Too bad the logic isn't backed up with truth."

"Dammit, woman, I'm trying to apologize."

"Then do so and leave me alone."

"I'm sorry."

"Good."

Gamon pulled his salt-and-pepper mustache to his lips and chewed on it for a moment. "Still angry?"

She tightened the last part of the splice and began to coil the rope. "If you're worried that I'll cut your throat some night while you're sleeping, you can relax. I have better things to do."

"Like Kum-jan?"

"Go snort a worlag, Gamon."

The older man grinned slowly. "That's one I haven't tried. What about it, Tehena?"

"Personally, I'd rather bed a badgerbear."

"Good. I know just the man. Come with me."

She shook him off. "You're a mutt-faced hypocrite. Leave me alone."

"I'm serious."

"So was I."

"And I was a goddammed fool. Look," he said heavily. "We're friends—"

"*Were* friends," she corrected.

"*Are* friends," he retorted grimly. "Why did you ask me for Kum-jan?"

"Don't play games, Gamon."

"Can you, for once, just answer a moonwormed question without barricading yourself in that shell?"

"All right." She glared at him. "Why did I offer Kum-jan? Maybe it was to prove to myself just how worthless I really am. Maybe I was getting too comfortable in Ariye, and I needed to verify that you all still think of me as spit."

"Go snort a worlag," he retorted. "You just can't say it, can you?"

"I've not been humiliated enough? You want to humble me further?" Her voice was low and hard. "You know the mistakes I've made in my life. You know what I've done. I'd have died in that prison if it wasn't for Dion, and you and I both know I'd have deserved it. Now, I'm so afraid of being responsible for myself that I have to have Dion to be responsible for me. I can plan strategy, but I cannot give orders. I can follow Dion like a dog while she's hurting, but I don't dare try to help her myself. I know what she needs to face her future, but I'm so terrified of making a mistake that I can't even Call her to do that myself. I have to get the w—someone else to provoke her for me. She has to live, Gamon—for me, not for her. *I* need her." Her voice, low and hard already, sharpened as if she tried to cut herself. "Without her to be for me what I am not, I'm worse than nothing—I'm a murderer who should have been punished and wasn't. Prison doesn't compensate for the life of a child. But Dion gave me a chance to make it up. And I've tried. Moons know I've tried to make her proud of me."

"She is proud of you."

"She'd be proud of a rockworm that got itself to the surface. Maybe, just this once, I was hoping that someone else would see me differently, too. That what Dion believed about me was true—that I'm not just prison-fodder. Maybe I hoped that someone I've known for years—trusted, respected . . . and whom I thought might actually respect me a little by now—would think of me like any other person. Might sleep with me, as a friend."

He studied her. "Funny thing is, Tehena, it was me who was humbled, not you."

She stared at him. "You self-centered, egotistical, mud-brained, son of a worlag." Getting abruptly to her feet, she slapped the rope over her shoulders and started to walk away.

He caught her arm. "Tehena, I'm not mocking you. I've something to say—to a friend, as a friend."

They faced each other almost aggressively on the steps.

"I'm seventy-eight years old," he said. "I figured I'd seen it all, done it all, felt it all—life, living, dying, death. All I had left was a hundred and fifty years of passing on my wisdom. It hit me, this morning, that I've been almost arrogant in my perception of that—of my 'wisdom.' I may be nearing eighty, but I've still got a lot to learn, and I'm not half as wise as a worlag if I can't see you for what you've become. It . . . humbles me to apologize to you, a baby-murdering drug addict," he said deliberately, "for teaching me about learning to accept and forgive. I've been so short-sighted that I can't even recognize the only person—you—who understands Dion enough to keep her sane."

"So it's for Dion, not me, that you offer this apology—this Kum-jan."

"No. It's for me, and you."

She eyed him warily, as if he would bite, and the older man shrugged.

"I might be arrogant as an Ancient, Tehena, but I'm not too proud to apologize. And if, for once, you want to spend time with a man you know respects you, then take Kum-jan with me."

He waited. She didn't speak. He waited still. Finally, he

stepped forward and took her arm and led her to an empty room upstairs.

* * *

In the village, Asuli finished her trading and made a beeline for the local healer's house. It was an older woman with faded white hair and spidery arms who came to the door. The old woman's circlet was simple and old—made more than two centuries ago—and Asuli nodded at the healer in acknowledgment of her status.

"How can I help you?" the old woman asked.

Asuli stepped inside.

* * *

Dion could feel the wolves gathering outside the village. The packsong had grown since they had cut through the ridges and come down into the valley. Something had disturbed them and pulled them after her, and their voices were beginning to cloud her mind.

It had been hours since Dion and the others had arrived in the town, but for once she didn't want to move on. She knew almost no one here, and it was quiet except for the wolves. They were thick here—as though, she admitted, the closer to her childhood home she got, the stronger grew the graysong. Last night, the wolves had been in her mind, whispering and howling and curling around the slitted yellow eyes. This morning, they were a growing din that crashed against the insides of her skull. She clenched her fists to separate the sense of lupine pads on the palm of her hand from that of her own fingers.

Twenty years ago, Ramaj Randonnen had been one of the few counties that still bred a wolfwalker every decade or so. Twelve years ago, the wolves had come back to the county, spreading from across the River Phye into Ariye and Randonnen. If, in the years since then, the wolves had multiplied as they seemed to have, there should be wolfwalkers in every mountain village, wolfwalkers in every town. But Dion didn't stretch her mind to feel them. There were faces, old friends and teachers, in these villages who might recognize her still, and she had no wish to see anyone but strangers, who would not ask what had happened to make her eyes so dark.

The commons house had cooled quickly once the sun went

down, but the chill, like the wolves, seemed to draw Dion outside to the balcony between the rooms. Kiyun was already out there, watching the stars and the black silhouette of the mountains. For a while, they simply leaned on their elbows and watched the yellow lights in the homes and the people moving through the streets carrying late-night bundles and walking beneath the summer stars. Dion's voice was quiet when she finally spoke. "I hear his voice at night, sometimes," she said.

Kiyun glanced at her. "You hear the wolves—he's in their memories."

"I know." Yellow, slitted eyes flickered, and Dion shivered in the packsong. Hishn's voice, so distant, barely touched the back of her mind, as if the wolf howled her longing from a year away. Dion closed her eyes. She imagined she could see the massive wolf, but the eyes that looked back at her were foreign, not familiar.

Wolfwalker, the Gray Ones howled in her head. *Run with us tonight.*

"You have to let him go," Kiyun said. "You know that, Dion."

She blinked and rubbed her arms. "It's the dreams on which he has the strongest hold. At night, when the lights fade . . . The wolves howl inside my skull, and I see him when my eyes are closed as though my mind fights fever demons."

"He's dead, Dion. Let go of him, and you'll begin to sleep again. Hold on much longer, and you'll dig your own grave with him."

"It's not me holding him—it's his voice in the packsong. Danton died, and there was nothing left but emptiness. But with Aranur . . . I set the wolves to find him, and they hunted him even as he was dying. He could feel them, so he was in their packsong. And when he died, as he fell, he set his words in their memories, so that all I hear now behind the wolves is him calling, over and over and over again, 'Wolfwalker, wolfwalker, wolfwalker.' "

"He loved you, Dion."

She looked at him. "He was jealous of you, Kiyun. He was afraid you would take me away from him, just as the wolves sometimes did. He never understood that I could no more leave him than I could leave Hishn."

"I know."

Her voice trembled. "He thought I bought all that art for you because I took Kum-jan with you. He went to his grave thinking that I wanted more than him and took what I wanted from you. He never knew that I bought that art because you . . . you . . ."

"Because I was too embarrassed to buy it for myself." His thick, muscled hand covered hers. "And you were the only friend I could trust to buy it for me and not laugh at me." He squeezed her hand. "After all," he added wryly, "who would believe that a fighter like me was really a frustrated artist?"

That won a faint smile from her, but it faded almost as soon as it had touched her lips. The wolves howled, and her hands trembled, and she pulled away from him to clench her hands against her arms. "I loved my son, Kiyun."

"I know."

"I don't want to go on without him."

"I know," he repeated softly.

"And I hate *him*."

He glanced at her soberly.

"For leaving me." Her voice was low. "For racing away to the moons before I could explain the things I didn't say to him before. For abandoning me to deal with everything he planned and expected. For taking the path to the moons where he'll be up there with Danton, and leaving me a son who hates me. Moons, Kiyun. It isn't Danton who needs him in the heavens; it's Olarun who needs him here. But he's gone, and he's locked me into a life of nothing but duty. I blame him for dying—isn't that rich? And I blame the wolves for haunting me with his voice, his touch, his eyes, while they let my Danton's memory sit as still as stone." She rubbed at her temples.

"It's natural, Dion, to feel as you do."

"Is it? I wonder sometimes if this is some exclusive human thing—this blaming that we do. Is it the only way to balance the guilt in our lives—to blame others along with ourselves? Olarun blames me. I blame Aranur. Aranur blamed the raiders. The Ancients blamed the Aiueven." She stared out at the darkness where the stars hung like a swath of gems. "We're so far from the stars, Kiyun. We're so far from everything but ourselves. When we look here, at ourselves, what do we really see? The brightness of our future, or the blame we hold in our past?"

"The future is what you make it, Dion. If all you want to see is blame, then that is all you'll have."

Slowly, she turned her head. "Hard words, Kiyun."

"You need to hear them, Wolfwalker."

A woman and child walked on the street below them, and Kiyun eyed them absently before he recognized the intern beside some unknown boy. He pointed, and Dion followed his gaze. Her face stiffened slightly.

"Want me to stay?" he asked quietly.

She hesitated, then shook her head.

He shrugged and left. He passed Asuli on the steps. The intern had the boy in tow, and she barely nodded to him as she marched determinedly up the steps. Kiyun gave the boy a thoughtful look, paused, and after a moment went back upstairs. He stood in a shadow of the corridor and watched and listened.

Asuli barely knocked before entering the room. Dion didn't answer her, but simply eyed her steadily.

"Healer Dione—" Asuli reached behind her to push the boy forward. "This is Roethke."

The boy stopped hesitantly. "Please," he said. He faltered.

Asuli pushed him forward again, then stepped back into the hall, away from the doorway. She glanced at Kiyun, then pressed herself against the wall and like him, listened in silence.

Inside the room, Dion and Roethke looked at each other. Finally, Dion spoke. "I'm no longer a healer, boy."

"Yes you are."

"I'm not."

"You are. That woman said so."

"I have no circlet, no healer's pack."

"But my mother—she's sick, and you can help her. Asuli said you could."

"Asuli knows nothing, and you have a good healer in this village to see to your mother. Call on Elibi, not me."

"My mother has hairworms. They're in her blood. She didn't know, and they were there too long. Healer Elibi can't help her."

"Then I cannot help her either."

"But Asuli said—"

She cut him off. Her voice was harsh. "I'm nothing and no one."

"Please. Just look at her—"

Dion's palm hit the wall. The slam shocked the boy into silence. "I told you, I can't help her. I'm no longer a healer."

"You have a healer's band—that woman said you used to wear it all the time. That you took it off because you didn't want us to know you could help people like my mother. Why won't you do it? She's going to die. Why won't you help her?" he cried.

Something in Dion's chest broke. Rage blinded her, whirled through her brain with the wolves. "Damn you—" She struck out, snapping the bedpost with her hand. Roethke trembled but stood his ground. Dion no longer saw him. Too many Gray Ones flooded her thoughts, swamping her with heat and fire, hunger and hate, lust and eagerness and rage. Yellow eyes mixed with the graysong, and ancient voices screamed. She spun, smashing the nightstand, then striking it again as a drawer hung out, half broken. Wood shattered; splinters flew. Like a wire too tight, her body shook. The howl that tried to scream out from her lungs strangled instead in her throat.

"Please," Roethke begged in the abrupt and jagged silence. "She's my mother."

Dion's hands were paws; her skin was covered with a pelt of fur; her nose wrinkled back like a wolf. Her violet eyes were rimmed with yellow, as though a hundred wolves looked out her eyes.

"Please," Roethke said softly.

Somehow, the young voice filtered through. Slowly, Dion stilled. Her fists, clenched, pressed against her forehead; her ragged breathing smoothed. She looked at him for a long moment. He was not so young, she realized. He was as old as Olarun—as straight and tall. His young, thin face was pinched with fear, but he didn't back down—he didn't retreat in the face of her rage. Slowly, her nostrils flared, and she caught the scent of his stubbornness. The Gray Ones that coursed through her brain picked up the scent and echoed it back.

"Please," he said. "Don't let her die."

"Show me," Dion whispered.

XIX

It does no good to grasp what you can reach.
Stretch, because everything of value is beyond
what you can easily see and understand.
If you are afraid, if you have lost too much
and withdrawn from others, you must stretch
even further to touch what burns you and hold
what you fear. It's the only way you will ever
be alive again.

—Yegros Chu, Randonnen philosopher

The force of the Gray Ones hit her as she walked toward the boy's home, and she staggered with the weight of it. Roethke caught her arm to steady her, as though he had done it before, and Dion realized he must have nursed his mother as the woman had grown weaker. The pain caught her suddenly, like the stab of a knife, and she gasped. The gray wolves howled. The sound was in her ears, not just in her head, and the boy clenched her hand sharply.

"It's just the wolves," Dion tried to soothe, but her voice was half growl, half words. "They won't hurt you," she forced herself to say.

"Why are they here? What do they want?"

"Me." She could hear the wolves gathering, thickening, closing in on the village. They searched for her voice in the packsong and howled when they found the thread of it so close, so strong. Then, ahead of her, at the end of the road, one of the wolves gave voice.

Back at the commons house, Tehena, standing at the window, cocked her head as the howl rose. "So," she muttered. "They did come."

Gamon, standing beside her, didn't hear her. "That's close." He frowned. "They're practically in the village."

Absently, she rubbed one bare foot against the other. "They'll be closer, too, before long."

This time, he heard her. He glanced at her, and his gray gaze

263

caught her expression. "What do you know that I don't?" he asked. But there was a half knock at the door before she could answer, and Kiyun looked inside. "Asuli brought a boy to see Dion," he said quickly. "She's gone to do a healing."

Tehena turned swiftly. "A healing? Now?" She pushed away from Gamon and grabbed her socks and boots from the floor, hurriedly pulling them on. Gamon stared at her, and she stomped to set her feet in the boots, the left one only half on. "That wasn't part of the deal—" She cursed as she hopped on one foot. "Moonworms on every Ariyen bootmaker . . ."

"Part of the deal—what do you mean?" Gamon grabbed her arm, steadying her. Then he caught the look on her face. His gray gaze went cold. "What have you done, Tehena?"

The woman paused. She looked him straight in the eye. "I Called the wolves," she said.

He stared at her. "Have you lost your mind? They almost killed you before."

"Between Dion and what y—" Her voice broke off. She shrugged. "I didn't figure I had much to lose."

"And your arms and calves—those bandages? They don't hide sap marks or rashes at all," he stated more than questioned. "You're hiding slash marks from the Gray Ones."

"You talk to the wolves, you pay their price." She jerked free and jammed her boot on the rest of the way.

From the doorway, Kiyun looked at her oddly. "And the wolves," he said. "They listened to you?"

Her voice was hard. "Don't worry, it's not likely to happen again." She tossed her cloak around her shoulders.

He half shrugged in apology, but he didn't take his gaze from her face. "What . . . what did you say—to get them to come?"

She stared for a moment at her lean, hard hands. Then she looked up and met his eyes. "I told them that Dion was lost in grief and could no longer see the packsong. That she needs the wolves to help her find herself. To force her to live. I told them to find her a future."

"You Called them to . . . Call her?"

"Aye."

"But if she's doing a healing when they Call her . . ."

Tehena nodded. "She'll be drawing them like a magnet to

help her with the healing, and they'll be converging on her like a storm to Call her to heal them, too."

"She'll be too weak to resist them," Gamon put in. "She could be sucked into the wolfsong so far she can't come out again." He flung his own cloak around his shoulders and followed Kiyun into the hall.

Tehena's words, so quiet in the night, were lost as the two men strode out of the room. "And then where will I be?" she asked.

They asked directions to the boy's home from one of the men on the porch and strode quickly down the street. There were shadows of movement along the roads, flashes of light reflecting from eyes. Dogs barked constantly as the Gray Ones neared the town. Like Gamon and the others, the wolves followed Dion, gathering like a siege.

At the low, decorative gate to Roethke's home, Tehena eyed the two wolves she could see. Her arms and legs bothered her where the gashes were raw. She hadn't told Dion what she had done; she carried enough of a trail kit to treat her wounds alone. Now, facing the Gray Ones brought a shiver to her shoulders. She steeled herself to walk steadily past the gleaming yellow eyes.

It wasn't Asuli who opened the door, but a woman from the village. The woman nodded to them and motioned for them to step inside, but as Gamon tried to move past her, the woman stopped him. "I was told that they needed to be alone with Xiame," the woman said. But as Gamon heard Asuli's voice in the back room, he pushed firmly past.

"Wait." She pulled at his arm. "They said they need quiet—"

He shook her off. The woman looked at Tehena's face, then Kiyun's, and seeing their uncompromising hardness, hurried out the door.

In the back room, Dion and the intern stood beside a bed on which lay a woman. Roethke's mother, Xiame, was haggard, her face lined with pain even in unconsciousness; and the boy, between the two healers, clutched at his mother's hand. There was a cloudiness to the air, as if the song of the wolves had become tangible, and Dion's voice was hard as she answered the intern. "She's too far gone on the path to the moons; there can be no cure for her."

"I don't believe you," Asuli retorted.

Dion's shoulders tensed, but she forced her words to remain steady. "At this stage, there are too many worms clogging her veins. If I kill the worms, their decomposing bodies would fill her blood with clots and toxins. It would be like giving her a hundred tiny heart attacks with a heavy dose of deathbriar—she would die within a day."

"Imminent death hasn't stopped you before." The intern nodded at Dion's expression. "You know what I'm talking about." Dion shot her a warning look toward the boy, but the other woman ignored it. "I've seen you work. I know now what you do."

"I do nothing that others can't—"

"That's a pail of moonworms," the other woman retorted. "You can save her—if you want to."

"I can't," Dion snapped. "Even with . . . there's only so much I can do. This—it is beyond me."

"You don't know that until you try. What have you got to lose except a few minutes of your oh-so-precious time? It's not as if you have something better to do. You've given up everything useful."

"This isn't some sort of miracle, Asuli. It saps you like a mudsucker."

The intern didn't budge. "So you're not even going to try. The great Ovousibas Healer Dione won't lift a finger to help someone else—not when she can wallow in self-pity instead. Yes, I know," she added at Dion's wary expression. "I figured it out. I'm not called smart for nothing." Asuli failed to notice the way Dion's eyes began to burn. "I know what you're capable of, Dione. But you'd rather watch this woman die than soil your grief to save her. Look at her—" Asuli reached out to grab Dion's arm, then cried out in shock and jerked back, staggering against the bedpost. "Moons!" she gasped. Her arm tingled as if it had been struck with a sledge, and the pain radiated up.

Dion clenched her fists. Violet eyes and yellow, slitted eyes had merged into a single gaze, and the blast of energy had flowed through her body like rage. Her mind had spun left, focused her own self, and spun out again, loosing that fire at Asuli.

Caught in the sense of it, she Called to the wolves and felt them race to gather around her. In the village, in the ridges . . . The Gray Ones were close, as if they had felt her coming. They were eager, as though they had hunted her voice. Had she Called them or had they Called her? She swallowed hard and tried to separate herself. Her words were low and harsh. "The healing isn't to be spoken of. Do not mention it again."

Asuli, still backed against the bedpost, retorted, "You deny what you can do?"

"I sent Hishn away long ago. I have no wolf to help me."

"There are a dozen wolves around this town. Call one of them instead."

A shiver crossed Dion's face. They were too close, too thick in this village. If she opened to the Gray Ones here, they would Call her even more strongly.

Roethke looked up at her. "Please," he said. "You have to help her. She's my mother."

"Dione can't be convinced like that, boy," Asuli snapped at him. "She doesn't know what it's like to love someone else like a child does its mother."

Dion's lips tightened so far that skin around her mouth went white. A muscle jumped in her jaw. "I may not have grown up with a mother myself, but at least I know what it is to love like one."

Roethke touched her sleeve, snatching his hand back as he felt the fury within her. "If you don't have a mother, you can use mine," he said quickly. "She can be your mother, too. But please, don't let her die."

For a moment, Dion didn't move. Her violet eyes seemed to gleam. Then, as the boy got up quickly and moved almost hurriedly out of her way, she sat beside his mother. Blindly, she pulled back the sheets. Then she touched the woman's body, letting her fingers feel the sluggish pulse.

Gray Ones in the dozens seemed to shout inside her head. *Wolfwalkerwolfwalkerwolfwalker . . .*

Deliberately, she opened her mind to them. *Help me with this,* she sent.

Wolfwalker. Hear us. The pack Calls to you. By the Ancient Bond, you must Answer.

Help me, she whispered deep in her mind.

Answer! they howled back.

Her fists clenched against her temples. Her face went taut;

she made a strangled noise. From the doorway Gamon cursed. Tehena grabbed his arm, holding him back. "Not now," she said sharply. "Don't touch her. She's deep in the Call of the wolves."

Asuli eyed Dion intently. "Is she doing the healing?"

Tehena cursed the intern coldly. It was Kiyun who said, "Not yet."

Dion heard but didn't hear their words. The sense of the Gray Ones had swept in and filled her head like a maelstrom. Her consciousness was sucked down into the whirling gray. Images of dens, of night, of hot sunshine, of dusty trails clogged her mind. The hunt-lust of hot blood and tendon, the eagerness of the yearlings, the tumbling sprawl of pups, the snap of bones, the snap of teeth . . .

A howling rose outside the house, and inside, Tehena shivered. Dion didn't notice. "What do you want?" she whispered.

Your promise, Wolfwalker—of life, not death.

The images blurred and shifted. The voices of the wolves were suddenly overlaid with dimmer sounds, faded scents, and she knew they projected their memories. Back, back through time and distance . . . Back to trails she had almost forgotten. Back to Hishn, when the wolf was still young. Back to mountains, where snows fell like drifts of time, and the dome of the Ancients was a coffin of death filled with an alien plague.

There, deep in the packsong, the voices sharpened like teeth. Colors swirled and yellow eyes gleamed. White wings cut through the skies. Fire burned in Ancients' bodies, eight hundred years ago. Time jumped, and the fire jumped with it, searing her blood and burning her own body with the fire of a fever that would not cool. Her brother, Aranur, Gamon . . . Their bodies, wracked, convulsed in places of white light and flattened walls. A Call— hers, replayed in her head. Lupine voices drowned her in memory while flashes of healing swept forward. Ovousibas— she saw it again as the wolves remembered it through her. And her words cut over the healing, stubborn in her desperation, replayed over and over like a drummer layering beats on a song.

Take me back. Her own voice, spoken years ago, echoed in her skull. *Not just once, but back . . . Time . . .* She shuddered as the memories took hold. Her words rang in the packsong, and her own history struck her with the images of the wolves. *Show me how. The fever burns. Time . . . Time . . .*

And the shades of long-dead wolves, their voices raised in ancient howls: *The fire strikes. We die, Wolfwalker. We burn. The fire strikes . . . Death, Wolfwalker. Death, not life.*

Over the wolfsong, over the memories, Dion's voice rang out . . . *Teach me, Gray Ones. Ovousibas . . . I'll help you kill it . . . Kill it . . . I'll take it from your bodies . . .*

Death, our pups. The wolfsong howled. *Death, our births. The fire kills . . .*

I'll help you. Dion's voice layered over the packsong. *Show me how to keep my brother, the rest of us alive. Show me, and I'll help you.*

Live now. Live tomorrow. Live . . .

The packsong faded, and the eyes of the wolves stared into her mind. A single gray voice spoke then. *You hold life in your hands, yet you seek death. You forsake your promise, Wolfwalker.*

Plague. The image was clear. She could not help but recognize what she had felt before. "I've tried," she whispered. "But there is no cure. I cannot find one for you."

We bought your life with our deaths, the wolf voice answered. And time fled backward, but now the images were sharp and clear, and the death, she knew, was her own. She saw Aranur through the eyes of the wolves; saw Olarun standing near him in the dark. Saw the wolf pack gather at the meadow and race with her mate toward her home. Saw the Gray Ones force the dnu to run, and felt her death again. The darkness swirled. The ragged pain that throbbed through her heart—her old heart, her heart of months ago—weakened, dimmed, and stilled. And Aranur screamed her name.

Her nails cut through her skin. "No," she whispered.

We carried you. We held you—as you still hold our future. And we died for you because of it. Died with the fire in our wombs, in our blood, in our bodies.

The single voice withdrew. Dion sat, blinded by the images. In the room the boy stared at her. He started to speak, but Kiyun touched his shoulder to stay him. The boy swallowed and stepped back.

Dion let her own mind range free in the gathered packsong.

Each wolf passed her voice on, each pack picked it up and howled it to the moons. And far away, as if amplified by hundreds of wolves in between, she felt Hishn touch her thoughts.

Wolfwalker! the Gray One howled. The voice was faint.

Dion touched the wolf, reveling in the shocking joy she had almost forgotten. Then she went on beyond even Hishn. Back, she stretched, through the ninans. Back, to read the song of the wolves who had run with her to her home. The yearling that Yoshi had killed . . . The three wolves who had moved too slowly when worlags caught them against a cliff . . . The wolf packs that Dion had healed near her house, too blind in grief to notice what she did to cleanse them of the fever . . . And the slow deaths of wolves—thirty-two Gray Ones—who died at the hands of predators after they were sapped by the fire of the plague . . .

Her lips moved, but her voice had no strength. "Dear moons," she breathed.

Now you understand.

"Now? What do you mean?"

You have borne children, while our cubs die. You grieve with us now; we grieve with you. We are brothers in the pack.

"There was not enough death in my life already? My mate, my son—" Her voice broke. "—had to die that we could be bonded more tightly?"

Your promise was empty of urgency. The promise of life, to take the fire from our wombs. Our pups still die, Wolfwalker.

"I've kept my word," she whispered. "Every month I've worked to find the cure. I've gone back to the domes; I've searched your songs; I've learned every story of the Aiueven. But I can't find what I need to heal you."

Time moves on, Wolfwalker. We Call you now to help us.

She cried out almost silently. "But I can't see what I have to do anymore. I can't see beyond the blackness. Don't you understand? To me, death doesn't bind us together. It tears my promise apart. I can't work like this—even for you. I have no future without my family. I have only a past of blood."

Life, death—both live in us. They are the same, Wolfwalker.

Dion closed her eyes and rocked herself silently on the bed.

Time, Wolfwalker, lives in our minds as well as yours. Fight to live, not die.

"You ask much."

We ask for a future.

"And what if I have none to give?"

Then we will find one also for you.

Dion made a low, bitter sound.

Time, Wolfwalker, is life to us. We Call you now to run with the pack for the future of the pack.

"My promise . . ."

Life, not death. For you. For us.

The packsong raged suddenly, and Dion cried out. The harsh sound hung in the room like a ghost. Then it faded. Outside, the wolves began to howl. Dion's sight cleared slowly. The wolfsong was still there in her mind, thick as a winter pelt. The Gray Ones stilled, waiting. She swallowed, and her throat seemed to work. She felt something warm slide down her wrist; a trickle of blood spilled out from the cut of her own fingernails in her palms.

Wolfwalker, they howled. *Seek this life, as it is something you must do.* The image of Xiame was clear. *Seek life—your life so that you may seek ours. Your promise binds us as well as you. We will be here with you.*

She lowered her hands. Her fingers were stiff and white. She looked at Asuli. "You have your healing kit?"

The intern nodded.

"You will make incisions along the body—short and shallow where I indicate. Two incisions for each small area."

"You intend to bleed the worms out of her?" Asuli's voice was suddenly professional, matter-of-fact.

"Aye. You will swab the first incision with cytro to get it into the patient's bloodstream. When the worms appear at the second incision, you will wash that area with cytro again to kill any still-living worms. Remove all worm masses to a bowl—make sure none of them live."

The intern nodded.

"We'll do her feet first, then calves and legs, hands and arms. Torso and chest last. If we need to turn her, or do more than that, I will let you know."

"Should I close the incisions as you finish with one area?"

"Not till I'm done. Some of the worms will loosen and float

free in her bloodstream; those will have to be pushed out wherever I can find an open incision."

"She could bleed to death."

"I can control that." Dion glanced at the boy, who had made a strangled sound. "I will do my best, Roethke. I can promise no more than that."

Silently, he nodded.

Dion looked at Tehena, Kiyun, Gamon. "I will need help," she said flatly. All three moved forward, but it was Gamon who reached Dion first. He placed his hands on her shoulders and stiffened almost immediately. The wolfwalker's eyes were clear, but the sense of the wolves was strong in her, and he could feel the Gray Ones howling.

Slowly, she stretched her hands over the woman. *Take me in, Gray Ones.*

Then run with us, Wolfwalker.

Still caught in the senses of the wolves, her mind spun left and down. It was not a gentle thing, but a swell of power that sucked her along like a raging torrent. The body of Roethke's mother was suddenly owned by Dion. Her lungs barely lifted; her mind fought the sea of blackness that pushed in on herself. Her heartbeat slowed and pounded heavily as it was dragged down by the worms in her blood vessels. She almost choked with the sense of it.

Slowly, she dug herself out of the blackness and back into the gray of the wolves. Then she sank her mind into the walls of the blood vessels, where she could feel the worms. Entwining, burrowing into the walls of the blood vessels, the worms sought their natural symbiotic places but found human tissue instead. Where they would have strengthened a badgerbear's vessels, they clogged the human veins.

Dion felt this, saw this, sank her mind into the sense of it so that each tiny pain from the dying tissues became a pain of her own. Then she followed the first of the pains till she found the incision Asuli had made in one of the woman's feet. It was bleeding lightly, and from inside Xiame's body, the cold air hitting the blood was a tiny shock to Dion. Even as she located the site, she felt the cytro wash into the bloodstream. The toxin pulsed along the blood vessels, sweeping by the worms or paralyzing them in place. Dion's consciousness followed in that wake. Gently, she pulled a worm mass away from an artery wall. Carefully, she untangled the clot they formed and pushed it along the blood vessel. When she reached the area where the incision was, she opened the incision wider. Blood spilled out, pulling the worm clot with it.

In the room, Asuli couldn't help herself. "By the gods," she whispered. Even as she stared, the blood at the first incision point thickened into a tiny clot. It wasn't a scab; it was a subtly writhing, dying mass that was forced out onto the skin. Quickly, she doused it with more cytro and wiped it from the skin.

Dion swept on. Slowly, methodically, vein by vein, artery by artery, she followed the path of the cytro. Some of the walls of the blood vessels left behind when she removed the worm masses were patchy with near-dead cells. She had to stimulate those around them to heal even as she pushed the worms on. There were no clots in the smaller veins; hairworms needed space to breed. But there were hundreds of clots to find and untangle and push out of the rest of the body.

She didn't know how long she was there. The gray fog remained strong, thick with the presence of two dozen wolves, but she could feel the creep of exhaustion along her consciousness. Time . . . She had stayed in this body far longer than she had ever been in a patient before. Feet, legs, arms . . . Roethke's mother had been bled of most of the parasite masses, but there were still veins and arteries to clear near the woman's lungs and heart. If she left her patient now, the worms would replicate within hours and reseed the woman's body.

Dion tried to concentrate herself into the woman's chest, but her focus shivered. Like a thin leaf in a heavy wind, her mind suddenly shuddered. The gray sea swirled and sucked at her thoughts.

Wolfwalker, the Gray Ones howled.

Her thoughts set grimly. *Help me,* she sent.

But her body was drained. There was no more strength inside her.

In the room Tehena watched Dion carefully. She caught the drain of color from Dion's face, then the shiver that hit her arms. "She's fading," the woman told the others.

Gamon looked at Asuli; but the intern, still busy wiping up clots of worms that trickled out of the incisions, didn't notice.

Tehena followed the older man's glance. She stepped forward and took the wipes from the intern, then pushed Asuli toward Dion. "I'll do this. Help Dion now," she ordered.

Asuli jerked away. "I am helping. I'm doing my job."

Tehena pulled her back, and her lean hands were like claws on the intern's arm. "I can do this as well as you. We've all taken our turn with the wolfwalker. Now it's your turn to do it."

Asuli swallowed. "To do what? I don't know what she's doing."

"Ovousibas, just as you accused," Tehena said harshly. "Now help her survive what you pushed her into."

"I can't—" Her voice broke off at Tehena's expression.

"You want to be a healer," Tehena snarled. "Then start acting like one, for once. Dion can't do this alone. And we haven't the strength left to help her ourselves."

Asuli shuddered. She could still feel the burning shock all the way up her arms from when she'd grabbed the wolfwalker. "I can't," she repeated, shrinking back.

Tehena's fingers dug into the other woman's shoulders till Asuli gasped. "You're always telling us how much you know. How much better than everyone else you are. You've been bragging about your skills since you attached yourself to us like a leech. It's time you stopped talking and started doing." She gave a shove so that Asuli stumbled toward Dion.

The intern hesitated, but Tehena cursed her. Asuli moved as if in a dream. She dropped to sit on the bed beside Dion. This close, her skin prickled, and the hairs stood out from her arms. She could see the pulse in Xiame's veins, the subtle shift of clots. Gingerly, she touched Dion's shoulders.

The sting was mental, but it shocked her. She almost let go. But she set her jaw in stubborn lines and held on. Instantly, she swayed. The drain was like someone sucking the breath out of her body. Grimly, she held on. She had seen the others do this— hold on to the healer and stagger away, weakened by this thing Dion did. But to feel it herself . . . Gray voices echoed in her head. A wolf howl, lonely, was suddenly filled with other lupine tones. And the body before her opened up as if, through Dion's eyes, she saw not just the flesh and cuts she herself had made, but the inner vessels, the heart, the bones.

She felt the worms detach, paralyzed by the chemicals that had been washed into the blood. She felt the wolfwalker untangle the parasite clots and pull them from the body. And she felt the pulse of Xiame's body as if it were her own. Asuli's fingers dug into Dion's arms. She began to shake. She wondered vaguely, as she felt her knees wobble and her body weaken abruptly, if she would hit the floor hard or if one of the men would bother to catch her even though they hated her so.

Finally, Dion thrust her away. The wolfwalker opened her eyes; her own hands trembled like leaves. Her eyes were glinting. "It's not enough," she managed.

Roethke tried to take Asuli's place. "Use me," he said to her.

Automatically, almost repulsed, Dion warded off his hands. "You're just a child."

"I can do it."

"No," she said.

"I want her to live."

"You haven't the strength," Dion said sharply, but her voice was hoarse.

"She's my mother."

"You're too small, too young."

"Stand back, boy." Tehena pulled at his shoulder, her own voice flat and hard. But deep in her mind, an image flickered of a child of her own she had killed.

His young face set in stubborn lines. "I might not be as big or strong as you, but I have will," he said.

Dion turned unfocused eyes to him. Through wolf eyes, she saw his shoulders, straight; his face, set.

He stood his ground. "She has to live," he said. "Use me."

She stared at him for a long moment. Her voice was a murmur, more in the wolves than outside of them. "It is fitting, perhaps . . . that her life comes from you, since your life came from her." She hesitated, then stretched out her hand and touched him.

A minute only, and the boy was trembling. Tehena started to pull him away, but he cursed her with a childish word, and the lanky woman nodded grimly and let him stay with Dion. But another minute, and Roethke shook like a wire. Abruptly, Dion shoved him away. The wolfwalker trembled herself. She stared at his mother, unseeing. Her hand groped for something—anything, but what she found was the bedpost. Unconsciously, she clenched it. There was a sound without noise, as if the air compressed around her. Something seemed to explode. The wolf eyes glimmered; slitted eyes blinked. Energy flowed for a moment. The bedpost burned white-hot. And Dion pushed the last large mass of worms out of the woman's chest.

The spell was broken; the wolfsong dimmed and died. Dion slumped to the floor.

Kiyun leaped forward, his arms, weakened, were still strong enough to keep her from hitting the floor hard. Carefully, he lifted her and carried her out to the couch in the living room. Roethke was torn between following and staying with his mother, and he caught at Asuli's arms. "Is she healed? Is she all right? Will she be okay?"

Blankly, Asuli looked down. "She'll live," the intern said slowly. She got her healing kit again and began to close up the incisions.

Gamon and Tehena looked at each other. Kiyun rubbed his eyes. "Carry her back now, or wait?"

Tehena shook her head. "With the wolves outside? Who knows what they would do?"

"We'll wait," Gamon said flatly.

He nodded and sat heavily in one of the chairs near Dion. Ten minutes later they heard steps on the porch. Tehena stiffened and rose. It was the woman who had originally let them in, and she had a healer in tow. "Roethke?" the first woman called out.

The boy appeared. "It's okay," he told them. He half bowed to the old healer.

Elibi looked at him, then at the three who stood in the cramped living room, then caught a glimpse of Dion. The old woman stared. "But this is the Master Healer Dione." She moved to the wolfwalker's side, ignoring Tehena's automatically protective stance. Gently, she touched Dion's face. "Ah, Dione," she said softly. "It's been so long since you've come home to us."

"Who is she?" Roethke asked.

Elibi turned. "The wolfwalker, Roethke—you've heard of her. She was born just over those hills. Grew up climbing the same mountains that those in the inn are here to scale."

Gamon had gotten to his feet. "You knew her when she was young?"

"I trained her in Ethran medicine. She was barely a young woman then. So eager to learn—so eager to *do*. She looks . . ." Her voice trailed off. "She looks exhausted," she said flatly.

Roethke studied Dion. "She came to heal my mother."

"Aye, she would. She has that kind of stubbornness—never could accept the inevitable."

Gamon smiled without humor. "You know her, all right."

"Enough to be worried about her still."

"Worried?"

"That she still takes each patient on as part of her personal war against death. It always seemed to me as though since the moons had taken her mother from her, she would keep every one else from their path. I thought once that she'd try to depopulate the heavens one by one till she found her mother again."

Roethke's voice was low. "I told her I'd share Momma with her, if she could keep my momma from dying."

"Ah, child." Elibi's voice was gentle. "There's not much even Dione could do to help your mother now."

"But she did."

"Did what?"

"Healed Momma."

Elibi sighed. "Roethke . . ."

"I saw it," he insisted. "Her eyes turned gray, then yellow, and she melted the wood. And the worms came out of Momma's skin."

"Roethke," Gamon said quickly.

Elibi stared at him. "Dione has always tried her best, and she would have wanted to help your mother, but . . ."

Roethke shook his head. "She didn't want to do it."

"Dione would not have turned you down, Roethke."

"She cursed and broke the furniture. She snarled. Her eyes turned yellow then, too."

"And you stayed near her when she was like that?"

"Asuli said I had to be brave, no matter what she did, so that she would do the healing. Asuli said that lady would keep Momma from dying."

"Asuli said that, did she?" The healer's voice was mild, but there was a steely tone in it, and Gamon had a sudden vision of where Dion had learned some of her habits. The old healer put her hand on the boy's shoulder, then moved toward the back bedroom. She took in the worm bowl, full of bloodred, hairlike clots; took in Asuli, bandaging the last of the incisions. She eyed the intern for a long moment, then stepped in and checked Xiame's pulse.

Elibi frowned and checked Xiame's pulse again. She gave Asuli a sharp look. "When you came to see me, I thought you wanted experience seeing patients with parasites. You said nothing of this involving Dione—I'd have come with you if you had."

"Dione stopped wearing her healer's circlet. I thought this would snap her out of it."

Elibi's voice was hard. "At the cost of speeding Xiame toward death?"

"The patient isn't dying, Healer. Check her pulse again."

"Dione bled her—that's obvious—to get rid of some of the worms. But Dione would know that the cytro would leave too many dead worms in her bloodstream. There will be clots from Xiame's lungs to her brain. This woman will be dead in a day."

"You're wrong. The patient's pulse is stronger than before."

"I felt that, aye. But that could simply be a reaction to losing some of the worms."

"It's more than that. The woman is cured."

"Dione is no faith healer to play games with people's hope. She knows there's no cure for hairworms. She would never have bled a woman just because a boy asked."

Asuli shrugged and kept her eyes on the patient.

Elibi's lips tightened almost imperceptibly. "I may be old, but I've still the eyes to see what you're thinking. Just what did Dione do?"

Asuli finished her bandaging, then looked up. "I may be a temporary intern, but I don't dispute my healer's work, no matter how long I've been with her. That is for you and Dione to discuss."

"I don't doubt it." The old woman's gaze was sharp as she took in the alignment of the wounds.

Roethke watched her from the door. Finally, he asked, his voice small, "What does Ovousibas mean?"

Automatically, Elibi answered, "It's an Ancient art. One that the Ancients used with the wolves . . ." Her voice trailed off as she caught sight of the bedpost. She couldn't help her sharp intake of breath.

Almost involuntarily, the old healer reached out to finger the wood. The carved post seemed to have melted: part of it was detailed with designs of vines and flowers; part of it was shapeless and filled with finger depressions. She tested the bedpost for strength, pressing against it with one finger, then rubbing at the surface. Some of it came off like ash. The old woman found herself staring at Roethke's mother, at the pattern of the cuts, at the bowl that Asuli washed; when she looked up at the intern, whatever she saw made her blanch with a deep-seated terror. The healer closed her eyes for a moment as she sank heavily to the bed. "Moons above," she whispered.

"Healer," Asuli began.

The old woman raised a hand to halt the intern's words. Then she opened her eyes, set her wrinkled lips in a determined line, and called for Kiyun to come into the room. When he did, she pointed to the bedpost. "Can you break that off?" she asked.

He nodded.

"Then do so. Put it in the fireplace. Make sure it burns completely."

Elibi and Asuli covered Xiame with a sheet, and the burly man kicked the post. What was left of the wood broke off with a crack. He picked up the chunk with the melted end and rubbed his fingers over it. It felt odd—as if it was somehow lighter and drier than it had a right to be. The melted section almost crumbled in his fingers. Thoughtfully, he carried it out to the fireplace in the other room. When he started to build a fire, Gamon raised his eyebrows, but Kiyun gave him a meaningful glance toward the other woman who was there. Gamon joined him at the hearth.

"The healing—it was never like this," Kiyun said, his voice low.

The older man nodded. Neither said what they were thinking—that the currents that had crackled out of the wolfwalker's eyes were not of wolves or of humans.

Elibi returned to the living room and motioned for the other woman to leave. "I will send Roethke for you when we need you again."

The other woman nodded. She left quietly, but not before she took another glimpse of Dion's haggard face. Asuli, who had followed Elibi in, started to sit in one of the chairs, but Elibi shook her head. "You too," she said flatly. "You're staying at the commons house? Then go there and wait. I'll send for you when it's time to discuss what you've done."

Asuli's face shuttered, but she didn't argue. Instead, she turned sharply on her heel and strode from the house.

Elibi sat heavily in one of the living-room chairs. No one spoke, but the silence was not uncomfortable. It was merely one of waiting. After a few minutes, Tehena got up and went to the kitchen, foraging for something to eat. She came back with a loaf of bread, cold meatrolls, and tubers still warm from the ash pit. She offered some to Elibi, but the older healer shook her head, then went back to the bedroom to sit with Xiame.

It was an hour before Dion opened her eyes. Her breathing changed; then she looked at the room. It was still fogged, but the sense of the Gray Ones was fading. Slowly, she sat up. Her limbs no longer trembled—they felt rubbery and numb, as though they had passed through exhaustion into a state where they had no strength to shake.

Wordlessly, Tehena handed her a meatroll and a mug of rou. The wolfwalker tore into the meatroll, but waved away the mug as she let her gaze take in the others. "Asuli?" she asked. Her voice was still half a growl, but she didn't care.

"Outside," Tehena answered. "The healer sent her away."

"Elibi." It was more of a statement than a question, and Gamon nodded.

The other healer heard her voice and came into the living room. "Dione." She nodded.

Dion started to rise, felt her knees buckle, and sat again heavily on the couch. "Healer Elibi. It's been a long time."

"It has." Elibi looked at her soberly. "We need to talk, Dione."

* * *

Later, out in the front of the commons house on the cold wooden steps of the porch, Asuli stared at her hands. She had felt Dion's mind—had felt the wolfwalker's pulse as if it were her own. She had felt a power that reached past skin and bones into the very cells of another human being. She sucked in a long, slow breath. Everything she had done, everything she had learned in the last ten years was nothing. She put her head in her hands and cried.

XX

From the Blue Mountains north,
From the Night Islands east,
From the Red River west,
This land is Ilwaco,
Of suicide hills,
Of star-shattered skies.
Star-castles of ice,
And eyes made of stone:
Land of Aiueven
And alien death.

Elibi stood with Dion at the hitching post and watched the wolfwalker lash her gear to the dnu. "You could stay," the older healer said.

Dion paused and looked at her. "You know I can't, Elibi."

The old woman sighed. "Asuli will remain with me, then."

"I don't think you can do much with her in a ninan."

"I don't either. That's why I'm taking her on a full internship."

"You're not."

"I am."

Dion almost smiled. "I admire you, Elibi, but I don't envy you a bit."

"Nor I you, Dione. You've not chosen a simple road. What you seek . . ." The old woman shook her head.

"What I seek is a cure, Elibi. No more. No less."

"For the wolves or for yourself?"

Dion gave her a crooked smile. "I'm not sure there's a difference, but then, I'm not sure that matters."

"It matters to me."

"You always were a softie."

Elibi chuckled. "That's not what you said when you were my intern."

"And that's not what Asuli will say either, I wager. I think I'm going to enjoy thinking of her stuck here with you."

The old woman put her hand on Dion's arm. "I wish you

282

would stay, Dione. There is so much you could do here. So much you could teach the other wolfwalkers—so much you could teach me."

Dion shook her head. "I spent the last thirteen years of my life doing that in Ariye. They will send someone to help you. This, I do for myself, for the wolves."

But Elibi's searching gaze was shrewd. "It's not the wolves you'll be seeking, Dione. I see something else in your eyes."

The two women exchanged a long look. Dion touched her arm, and they hugged suddenly, almost fiercely. Elibi pushed her away. "Move, Dione. Don't stay put. Go run with your wolves in your mountains. You'll find no peace among the graves."

"I'll search where I must," she returned.

Elibi nodded slowly at the shadows in Dion's eyes. "When one has nothing left to lose, that is when one can do the greatest good."

"When you hear the wolves . . ."

"I'll listen for you."

Elibi watched as the wolfwalker mounted. Gamon, Kiyun, Tehena, Dione . . . The four figures rode slowly away, heading toward the mountains. Within minutes, they were barely distinguishable from the trees that lined the road. Elibi stared after them. Her voice was soft. "Ride safe, Dione—with all nine moons above you."

* * *

It took four days to follow the mountain roads to the fork that led to the home of Dion's twin brother. There Gamon paused and asked Dion to turn off toward the village with him. She shook her head.

He touched her arm. "They are family, Dion. You need to see him, and he needs to see you."

"He *knows* me, Gamon." The rush of emotion almost broke her, and for a moment she couldn't see. She swallowed and hid her shock that the waves of grief could still blind her. She forced her voice to steady. "He knows already what I feel," she said. "He lives with that, as I live with his emotions. As twins, we are too tightly bound for either to be unaware of the other."

"Awareness isn't the kind of comfort you need."

"It's enough for now."

"Is it? Or is it an excuse you use to keep from facing your family?"

"That isn't fair, Gamon."

"No," he agreed. "But it's true."

"I hate it when you're right." But she didn't smile.

"You're going to have to face them sometime, Wolfwalker. You're going to have to accept their comfort."

"It's not their comfort I'm avoiding." The older man started to interrupt her, but she cut him off. "Gamon, when I first bonded with Hishn, there was no one to guide me as a wolfwalker, to warn me about growing too close to the wolves. My father and brother—nearly everyone in my village—could see the changes I went through. But they assumed those changes were normal for being a wolfwalker. So I ran trail and learned to struggle and fight and survive. And then I came to Ariye, and kept doing those things because you had a need I could fill."

Gamon nodded. "You were so clear in what you did—so focused and confident. It was as if the Heart of Ariye had somehow become visible to us all, through you. All the centuries of working toward going back to the stars, and you made us believe it could happen."

She stared at him. "I never had anything to do with that part of the county. I never even thought about your goals until I mated with Aranur."

He shook his head. "It isn't that, Dion, but the other things you do that make you such a focus. You risked yourself, you sacrificed for us, and you didn't break, no matter what happened. You pushed yourself to do what was necessary, not just what you thought you could do. And simply by living, you showed us what a single scout could accomplish. Or a single healer. Or a single wolfwalker or woman." He let his gnarled hand cover hers. "It is never the big miracles that give simple folk heart: Hope is important, but it won't reach the stars like confidence will. You build that confidence. If something can be done, you do it. If it can't be done, you work around it. Aranur saw that in you long ago. It stunned him then—I remember it clearly—that you could do so much yet be so unassuming. It was as if, through your own simple focus, he suddenly saw the potential of every person he met. That is the Heart of Ariye, Dion. The potential.

The dream. The ability to harness and focus that potential, and the confidence to explore it. That heart is still in you, Dion. Randonnen, Ariye—they are the same. In you, they blend together."

She stared down the trail. "And yet I feel so empty."

Gamon rubbed her hand. "I won't lie to you and say that time will heal your wounds. But I do know it can give you other things to help fill in the void: Family. Your brother. Your father. Your other sons."

"Tomi nursed me long enough. He needs to go back to his own mate and finish building his own home. And Olarun . . ." Her voice trailed off.

"Olarun needs his family as much as you do."

"You are family, too, Gamon."

"I'm his grandfather," the older man agreed. "As much as I was a father to Aranur. But I cannot be his mother, Dion. Nor can I be the father he's just lost. Could you take someone else as your father or your twin?"

"No."

"And they would have it no other way, too. Come, Dion. Ride this trail with me."

"I cannot, Gamon."

"Why?"

"Because . . ." Her voice trailed off. "Because before I had children," she said softly, "it was all right to take risks, to explore. I put no one else in danger. I gambled with no other lives. My curiosity balanced the challenges. But then I had Tomi and Olarun and . . . Danton." She forced herself to say his name. "And suddenly I became torn between what I was used to doing and what I must not do in order to keep my children safe. I couldn't raise them the way my father raised me—to run wild in the forest with my twin. Randonnen is safer than Ariye. And as a child, I was drawn to the wilderness by my own curiosity and eagerness. I wasn't pulled to it or forced into danger with the wolves. But my children are surrounded by Gray Ones. They are affected by the wolves in ways that I never was. And every time I turn around, the Gray Ones pull my boys to the forest. I'm so used to running with the wolves that I did not see the difference between risking the forest for myself, and risking it with my family."

"Do you really think that a child of yours would have stayed out of the forest just because it was dangerous?" He shook his head. "If you think that, you don't know yourself very well."

"I know myself too well, Gamon. And that, I think, is the problem."

"You've done your best, Dion. None of the moons could ask for more."

"I tried to do my best," she agreed. "And with Tomi, it wasn't hard—he was already half grown when we adopted him. But with Olarun and Danton . . ." She looked up. "They were so little, Gamon—you remember that. One day, I just turned around, and they were old enough to start running trail, big enough to ride dnu. They had little-boy bows and little knives and survival kits. They had trail boots, not just home shoes. Like a night full of shadows, there was suddenly no clear-cut boundary. When were they too young to learn to swim or climb? When were they too small to stay out overnight? The dangers I take for granted— the worlags and poolahs and lepa—those should not have been part of their lives. But I took them into that. I led them into danger like a wolf mother who must teach her children to survive." This time, her voice shook. "Or to die."

"Dion . . ."

She shook her head angrily. "I'm not going to hide from the truth, Gamon. I have lived with the wolves for fifteen years, and I can't deny that it has changed me. What Aranur saw—what you see—as the 'Heart of Ariye,' I see as a heart of gray. I'm too close to the Gray Ones to have perspective. I'm not wolf enough to protect my children, and not human enough to keep them out of danger. My father and brother know that as well as they know me. They've told me that often enough." Her jaw tightened. "I can face my own blame now, Gamon. But I cannot face theirs, too."

"And going north will help with that?"

"It will give me some kind of purpose."

"Purpose, Dion? Or escape? Or punishment for the pain you feel you've caused? You think to reduce your life to atonement or run from every decision the elders ask you to make? You think you could live with yourself then? Look at Tehena. That's what she's become—a shell of a woman, so afraid to make decisions that she would rather be killed by the Gray Ones than decide herself how to force you to live. That's why she went to the wolves—to get them to make the decision instead, so she didn't risk hurting you herself. You are the only guide that woman trusts—the only person who gives her the hope that she should not herself be killed. She lives only because you do. She has direction, but it's your direction that guides her, not decisions of her own. You want to be like that? Running so far, so fast, for so long that you no longer have time to be human? That you've forgotten how to live? Dammit, Dion, you could run forever and not escape yourself. You *know* that."

Dion's eyes were shadowed, but her voice was steady. "Maybe I am escaping. And maybe I'm punishing myself. But let me ask you this, Gamon: Could you do any differently?"

He simply looked at her.

Dion made a sound, half snarl, half curse. "I'm empty, Gamon, except for old promises and goals. You want me to find purpose? To continue? To go on? I can do it only this way. I am no longer blind to who and what I am. And if I am too far from my humanity, and too close right now to the wolves, what better time to reach beyond myself, through the Gray Ones, to . . . to find out what could happen? At least that would have value."

"So you'll go where no human has rights to be. Where taking that path will put you in an icy grave that no one will ever find. Has my family not borne enough sorrow? Has there not been enough death?"

Dion didn't flinch from his gaze. Her own voice was so steady as to be almost hard. "And will there not be more, if no one ever does go north? What will happen when Ariye completes the work they've been doing? What will the response from the Aiueven be? The birdmen nearly destroyed the Ancients before. You can't believe that they will simply let your brother lead Ariye back to the stars without a fight. And as that date gets closer, so does the time of our reckoning. I cannot stay in your county, wandering about, blindly ignoring what will happen, while the lines of my family—our family, Gamon—sit, waiting to be crushed by another alien plague. You talk of the Heart of Ariye, of our hopes and dreams; I speak of our very future." She closed her eyes for a moment, and when she opened them, they were determined. "I have nothing here, Gamon. And all I will ever have again is what I leave behind for our family. What Ariye and Randonnen work for—it's a dream that will never be real unless someone goes to the north. Someone who can face the past through the memories of the wolves. Who can face the plague without fear, face Aiueven without forgiveness. I have no fear of death, Gamon. Who better to go than me?"

His voice was harsh. "It will be decades yet before we are ready to try to recover the Ancients' stars. If you want to die, let it be then, when there is a need for those without fear, for heroes and fantasies. Not now, while you still have a son in Ariye. Not now, Dion." The older man's jaw tightened into near-whiteness, and she realized slowly that his hard gray eyes glinted not with anger, but with fear. Fear for her. Fear for the grief she would leave him.

For a moment neither one spoke.

Finally, Gamon squeezed her hand. When he spoke, his voice was rough. "Your home is where your children are, and you belong with your family. Go where you must, do what you must, but remember that, Dion." He studied her face with his old gray eyes as if memorizing her features. Then he turned away.

"Gamon—" Her voice broke off.

He looked back.

"Tell Olarun and Tomi that I love them."

He nodded again. This time, when he rode away, no one spoke.

* * *

There were days when they made only a few kays; others when they made close to forty. The mountain route was sometimes smooth and protected, part of the major trade routes, and sometimes little more than deer paths that wound around the hills. And they stayed in inns more than campsites, and Dion didn't protest.

It took over a ninan to reach the northern border of Randonnen. There, from the pass, they could see to the edge of the mountains. The high desert that stretched across toward Ramaj Ariye was dry as Dion's eyes. At night, the line of tenor trees made a luminescent web, and Dion shivered as she eyed it, as though Aranur and his county spun those ghostly threads to catch her up again.

They had ridden through towns and villages, passed sheer stone walls, crossed lava flows that split the forests with washes of crumbled black rock. They camped in the common circles where the fire pits were well-used from summer and the stacks of cut wood were still full. And finally, they were met at the northeast border with a view of one of the Ancients' domes. Dion sat for a long time, gazing at it as if searching its broken facade for answers. Then she turned their dnu due north, past the Ancients' peak, toward Kiren, the abandoned county.

With the rising altitude, the nights were colder, and the air was crisp in the mornings. The wolves that paced the wolfwalker wore thicker pelts of gray. The snow that lay on the tops of the peaks crept down toward the lower forests, and the sky was filled with flocks of daybats migrating to the south.

It took ten days to skirt the edges of Ramaj Kiren. The skinny county would have taken three days to cross except that it was flooded. No one tried to cross that marsh if it was possible to go around it.

On the other side of Kiren, Dion eyed the northern peaks of Ramaj Kiaskari. Against the late-summer pale blue sky, the isolated peaks screamed their white, forbidden brilliance. She drew her cloak closer around her. Already the pull of the northern wolves was seeping into her consciousness. There was independence, not eagerness, in those voices, and something else that was cold and sharp. The gray voices that collected in the back of her skull were shadowed with other colors, and the yellow eyes that gleamed at her were somehow alien.

Something twisted in Dion's gut. Disturbed, she drew back from the packsong, then focused her mind and sent a shaft of need to the wolf she had left behind. Distantly, faintly, like a spider thread on the wind, the Gray One's voice came back . . . *Wolfwalker!*

And something else. She stared at the peaks and stretched, letting her mind spin out. There was depth there—she was sure of it. And life in those ice-covered mountains.

Then Tehena touched her arm, and she started. It was with difficulty that Dion turned away from that deadly, white-hard promise.

Ramaj Kiaskari was the opposite of Kiren. Where the county of Kiren had been smoothed and softened by mud slides and erosion, Kiaskari was hard and sharp. The settlements in this Ramaj were remote, linked by long, winding roads. The people didn't grow their houses here, but bermed them deeply into the ground and built their walls from cut woods and stone. The roads were also stone, lined with barrier bushes as thick as houses so that they appeared as rivers of green with a thread of white at their center.

Dion no longer ran with the wolves; crossing the barrier bushes meant running into worlags, and the northern beasts were smaller and faster, more vicious in the hunt. The Gray Ones who sang in Dion's mind stayed far from the barrier bushes, while the worlags scrabbled and chittered against the outer shrubs.

In the towns, she could see the touch of the Ancients everywhere—on this smooth street, on that pillared porch, within that set of bracings . . .

"Like a rast den," Tehena commented.

Dion nodded. After eight hundred years, the clusters of homes had grown into rough patches of color. Up and down the hillside, slab roads followed the contour of the steepening mountain slopes.

Kiyun eyed the quiet, hard-faced people who stopped to watch them ride by. He nodded at them, but none of them gave a greeting. "It's said that they are guards," he commented. "That they keep the Aiueven from the throats of the rest of us."

Tehena snorted. "They maintain the barrier bushes, nothing more. And it's for the Aiueven, not for us. The Ancients made a deal with those white-feathered aliens. And as the Kiaskari say, 'To hell with the plague, we'll keep our end of the bargain even if it kills us.' " She looked at Dion. "We'll stop here?"

"Only for supplies." Dion stared at the mountains that seemed to hunker over the town. "We're close," she said softly.

Tehena and Kiyun exchanged glances. "To the wolves?" the man asked.

She shook her head. "To the Aiueven."

"Dion . . ." Kiyun's voice trailed off.

She glanced at him, but her face was set. He shrugged, and they rode on.

It took two days to reach the northern end of the valley. There were only a few towns and isolated homes farther north, and half of those were vacant except in spring when the barrier bushes were tended.

The streets were stone, but all of these routes had been cut by the Ancients. They were white and smooth as if sanded down, even after eight centuries. The inns were empty, leaving them their pick of places and rooms. Dion chose one that looked toward the mountains.

For a long time, she simply stood at the open window to her room while the wind, like a hungry wolf, bit into her cheeks. The wolfsong, the wolves, and Aranur's voice rolled over and over through her head. The ledge was like the seawall; the drop like the fall to the rocks . . . The void hit her suddenly, and she almost cried out Aranur's name and Danton's.

Then Kiyun entered the room behind her, and Tehena muttered at the chill. Dion steeled herself, then shut the window, turned, and smiled at them.

They packed their clothes in bundles and stored them at a tanner's shop. In place of those lighter garments, they bought white fur parkas and fur-lined gloves, winter-weight shirts and socks. The outer layers of their pants and boots were made from the skin of glacier worms. They would keep out snow and ice and the worst of the wind while letting their bodies breathe.

At the foothills of the Blue Mountains, they traded their dnu for dnudu. The smaller beasts were more sure-footed, wiry, and agile, but their shorter gait also made their ride more uncomfortable. Kiyun's longer legs were so sore from the sharp-jointed jouncing that he cursed when he tried to get out of bed the first morning after they switched riding beasts.

At the last village north, Tehena bought the supplies. They spent the rest of the day packing so that each dnudu carried a combination of food, fuel, and gear. If one beast was lost, the riders could skimp but go on.

The first two days, they camped at the Kiaskari summer sites. A wolf pack Called Dion to run with them. The wolves shared a hunt so that she came back with a chunk of snowdeer, but also a sober expression from catching a glimpse of a pack of worlags that had been thirty strong. She stayed close to the fire that night.

Drawn by Dion's presence, the wolves crept close to the camp. They touched her thoughts and filled the back of her mind, pushing her gently so that she knew which road to take north or east, knew the places by which she should camp. They had read the Call from the southern wolves, and they came warily to run with her and howl her need to the moons.

The soil was poor, and the plants' roots thin along the road. Everywhere they could see where raging streams from snowmelt had eaten away at the mountainsides until huge slashes of stone jutted out. Fallen columns of granite lay where they had cracked and rolled. Only some were covered with the tenacious growth of the higher altitudes; others were bare except for the bright violet of summer fungus. At one point, the dnudu picked a path underneath an overhang of shattered columns, and the three riders were silent, listening nervously to the *click-click* of the riding beasts' feet echo off the rock overhang.

The third day, they reached the old snow line where leftover patches of last year's snowpack clung stubbornly to the ground. The fourth day, the wind blew cold, and the clouds that massed on the eastern horizon spoke of a coming storm. They found one of the summer Kiaskari caves, cold and open as a coffin, and holed up for two days while the sleet and the rain came down.

Kiyun eyed the muddy ground the morning after the storm. He slapped his arms to warm them up. "It's a fool thing we're doing, Dion. Autumn will settle down hard as a rock, and it's said in every other county that Kiaskari winters are greedy."

"Greedy?"

"To add bodies to their soils."

Dion bundled her bedroll and tied it onto the saddle. Her voice was flat. "Aiueven are more active in winter."

"Aye. 'Active' meaning that they'll be more aggressive should they find us within their reaches. There's a reason we maintain the barrier bushes between Kiaskari and these mountains." He eyed her expression. "By the moons, Dion, you can't really be thinking of contacting them."

Her voice was soft. "I need this purpose, Kiyun. I need this goal."

"Is that true, Dion? Or do you really know what you need?"

"You need art, Kiyun. It speaks to you, even if you cannot

describe it. It fills a void in you left by your life. This void in me—a painting might touch it; a sculpture might grasp for an instant what I feel. But no piece of art, no *thing*, no matter how complex, can fill my needs."

She gazed at him in silence. Then she turned away to the dnudu.

Kiyun stared after her, then pulled his shirt from the still-warm blankets and put it on.

Tehena watched him for a moment. "Why try to turn her from what she sees as the only path she's got?"

He shook his head mutely.

"It's not so bad," Tehena said. "At least here, she is working toward something."

"Toward suicide," he agreed. He stared after her. "I feel as though I should be able to talk to her—to talk sense into her if nothing else. But she looks through me half the time, Tehena. She answers me, but she's not listening. There's something else in her head."

"She doesn't see you, Kiyun," she returned. "You and I—we're like dreams to her. We don't exist to the wolves. What is in her eyes—what she sees night and day—is the ghost of Aranur."

"It's been two months. She's got to let him go."

"He was her life."

His voice was hard. "He'll be her death."

"No," Tehena returned. "In her own way, she's as stubborn as Asuli. But where that one looked only to herself, Dion searches elsewhere."

Kiyun's voice was low. "He told me to make sure she sought healing, not death. All I've done is help her turn her back on her own county, her own land."

"When there is no one left to hold you to the earth, why not seek the moons?"

"She has Olarun still, and Tomi. She has Gamon and you and me. Her own father and brother are still alive. She can't abandon them."

"She hasn't really abandoned them." Tehena's voice was thoughtful. "She's just changing the way she lives. I think she sees a way to make the future safer. To confront the one thing on this world that threatens the family she has left."

He shook his head. "What she seeks is still escape, Tehena. If death comes to her, she won't fight it now. She'll welcome it like a gift."

"I'm not so sure anymore." Tehena's hard voice was quiet. Absently, she rubbed at her forearms. "Something changed in her, back in that town, after the Gray Ones Called her. She's focused now. Before, they drew her—showed her the way. Now, I think she draws them. Whatever she sees when she stares at those peaks—it isn't part of the wolves. And Aranur's image might haunt her days, but it won't be that one who kills her. Out here, there are alien eyes to stalk her and alien deaths to find."

He followed her gaze toward the ragged peaks. "It is said that they are born like black demons, in the bowels of the earth. That as they grow, they change. By the time they're adult they are white as the snow over which they fly, and their wings encompass the heavens."

Tehena bundled up her bedroll. "There are no heavens near Aiueven. Dion at least knows that."

"Aye." But he said nothing more.

Two more days of slow, steep riding brought them to the Aiueven Wall. There they halted. It was like facing a forest of barrier bushes: The spiny shrubs were three meters tall and so thickly grown that their spines turned in upon themselves and pierced their own wiry branches. Dion fingered the edge of the bushes, twitching back as the sharp thorns pricked her hand. Like life, she thought, always drawing blood.

"Do we go through now, or camp here?" Tehena asked. Dion hesitated, and the other woman added, "The skies are clear—it will be cold tonight."

"If we stay on this side of the wall, we at least have the Kiaskari spring house to sleep in," Kiyun added.

"All right." Dion nodded. She rubbed at her gut.

Tehena's gaze followed the movement. "We've been eating off the land for days now, Dion, and the groundroots are getting thin as the soil. We won't be able to stay here for long."

"It won't take long to find them."

Kiyun gave her a thoughtful look. "For you to find them, or for them to find us?"

Dion shrugged. Kiyun and Tehena exchanged a long glance.

The night air was thin and cutting as paper, but the sky was thick with stars. They were washed out along the path the moons made and thick as curdled milk along the edges of the horizon. In the distance, a wolf pack raised its voice. Dion rose and went outside. She wrapped herself in her white parka and stood for a long time, listening.

Tehena, restless, got up to stand with her. The lanky woman pulled her cloak tightly around her as the night wind bit into their cheeks.

"Two days," Dion said softly in the dark. "As soon as we reach the snowpack I will see Aiueven."

"Are you sure?"

"There is something other than wolves in the packsong. I feel that, in my mind. Like Aranur's voice, only sharper. I asked, in that village, if they were ever sighted, and the people laughed and said yes."

"They laughed?"

Dion smiled without humor. "Every couple of years, they told me, some climber would dare the snowpacks. The few that have ever made it back—they lived only a few hours. They died with their bones soft as pudding. They had seen Aiueven, they would say. They had touched the wings that stripped their bodies like worms eating them out from inside."

Tehena drew her cloak more tightly around her.

Dion glanced at her. "Don't worry. They're sighted over the towns, too, but they never attack. They touch humans only if their dens are threatened—if the climbers get near the peaks."

"And that's what we intend to do."

The wolfwalker shrugged.

"Dion, you'll be the death of us."

"You could always stay behind."

The other woman snorted.

Dion's voice was soft. "I can Call them now."

"Through the wolves?"

"Through myself."

"Dion," Tehena said quietly. "You stopped drinking rou after Sidisport."

The wolfwalker didn't answer.

"And you stopped using brevven in your meatrolls."

Dion hesitated but still didn't speak.

Tehena prodded deliberately. "It's more than the rou and the brevven."

The wolfwalker almost sighed. Tehena waited, and finally, Dion said the words. "I'm pregnant."

Tehena nodded shortly, but her voice was cold as the air. "And you're out here, looking for likely death, instead of caring for your baby."

Dion's jaw tightened, and her own voice was hard. "It's too early to lose her."

"But not too early to lose yourself?"

Dion's silence was answer enough.

Tehena paused. "It's a she?"

She nodded.

"You're not one to jeopardize your child's future, Dion."

The wolfwalker's face tightened. "It is the future that I'm thinking of." She held up her hand, cutting off the other woman's reply. "What kind of future will my daughter have with the threat of Aiueven here? And Olarun—what of him? He's always had a bent for the sciences. Will I find him dead one day, with the mark of the Aiueven? Or will he find his own death in the wilderness from raiders or worlags or worse—because he has no other option of a place to live? Do I condemn my children to the life I lead because I can give them no other choice?"

"The Gray Ones—"

"The Gray Ones can't protect them—not from worlags or lepa or plague. Olarun has rejected the wolves already; he will never be a wolfwalker. But this baby . . . If she bonds with the Gray Ones, she'll just link herself with death in yet another way. I can't keep Ovousibas from her, not if she's my child. Even if she doesn't become a healer, she'll feel what I do and read it from the wolves' minds as easily as she'll read trails. And if she follows our sciences and strives for the stars, she'll be struck down by aliens the moment her work takes her up to the skies or it becomes recognizable to their sight or perceptions. All this hiding of our work . . . Aranur's goal be damned, Tehena. The aliens have ways of knowing that put all of us at risk. And how can I ignore what could happen to my children—the death that doesn't have to be? If I have the chance to act, how can I not act now?"

"Death now, death later—what's the difference? It's all the same in the end. A long path winding up to the moons or down to the seventh hell. All you can hope is that your children live well because of the things you have taught them."

Dion stared out at the stark line of snow against the green-black treeline. "My lessons were hard ones, then. Life and death, with little in between."

Tehena pointed with her chin at Dion's stomach. "You, at least, have another chance to change. How many people have that?"

Dion looked at her friend. For a moment, time flashed between them. Eyes flickered and blinked, and though they were yellow, what she saw were not the gazes of the wolves, but of alien eyes instead. She shook her head mutely, and Tehena didn't realize that it was not her words that Dion had answered, but the threat of Aiueven.

In the morning, they found one of the barrier channels and moved carefully through the forest of thorns to the other side of the wall. They built two shelters on the other side: one for them, and a lean-to for the dnudu. It took the entire day to build the structures, but as Kiyun said, better to be prepared to stay than find oneself out in the ice.

The next morning dawned with the sky light gray, covered in high, thin clouds. Only a faint line marked the spot where, kilometers away, the sky met the snow, and the massing clouds swirled above it. There was a cold wind sweeping down from the peaks, and it bit at their cheeks and hands. But Dion didn't hear the wind or the crackling of trees that waved in it; instead, it was Aranur's voice she heard.

She closed her eyes. It was as though his drive to bind her to his future had followed him into death. Eight hundred years of memories, and each year's images were harder to bear. The wolves, who had given her life itself, would not let her forget him. The dull sunlight turned her eyelids red inside; it was blood she smelled on the wind.

Wolfwalker! distant voices called.

I'm here, she returned.

She let her mind open, and the wolves surged in. With the wolves this close, the packsong swelled, and the Gray Ones howled. They were still gathering behind her, around her, drawn to her with her Call. Already, on the other side of the barrier bushes, three of them paced the wall of thorns. Within moments, some of the wolves braved the barrier and slunk through the narrow channel. When they appeared on the other side, they lifted their mental voices to the others, then raced toward Dion, flashing past her like streaks of gray. *Wolfwalker,* they howled in joy. *You seek our future. We run on your trail.*

Go back, she told them urgently.

Go back? You Call us. You hunt for us.

"Aye, I do." Her voice was low. "But I hunt this prey alone. There is alien death here that is swift like the claws of the lepa, and if it kills men as easily as they say, what would it do to you?"

But they didn't come back. Instead, they paused on an icy rise and waited for her to follow. Yellow eyes seemed to gleam in her head. *Run with us, Wolfwalker.*

"I'll follow you," she said softly. "Though it will likely mean my death."

We trade with you, life for life.

Dion's hand rubbed protectively across her belly.

The Gray Ones caught the sense of the baby and wove their words into her thoughts. *Your cubs are ours. We watch your litters as our own. They will run with our yearlings and sing with the pack. We promise this, Wolfwalker.*

Slowly, she nodded.

There were no roads on this side of the barrier; instead, they had to orient their trail to a hand-drawn map. It was slow, hard going, and they made only six kays that day. The next day they made only four. Early in the afternoon, one of the dnudu fell into a ravine and broke its neck. It took the rest of that day to get down that drop-off and recover their packs and gear.

The third day, they began to work their way out along one of the glacier valleys. At the edges, where the snow was too thin and the rocks too thick for snowshoes, they fell through the crusty, half-frozen drifts as often as they walked on the ice. The dnudu struggled with the weight of the packs. That night, they built no fire, but used their tiny fuel stoves for heating snow into water and soup. A chunk of dnudu made part of their repast and that of the wolves. Dion heard the Gray Ones worrying at the bones long into the night.

They were slow rising the next day, as though the cold kept them in their beds. When they finally started to pack up, it was midmorning, and the sun was bright behind the light-gray layer of clouds. The wolves had been close all night; the snow between the stunted trees was pocked with sleeping holes and marked with yellow urine. Dion looked back the way they had come. Their ragged, hoof-chopped path through the snow was like a brutal tear, as though some giant claw had reached down and ripped white land apart.

Dion stared into the distance. The hard, bright light made it difficult to see detail, but there was something in the sky. Kiyun shaded his eyes and followed her gaze. "Too big for a lepa," he muttered. "And the glide pattern's wrong . . ." But something crawled between his shoulders with his words, and he was already moving, picking up the packs and moving the dnudu under the thick trees. "Dion," he called sharply.

She didn't move with him. Instead, she crunched through the snow, sinking abruptly when her boots broke through the crust and fighting to continue forward till she stood out in the white expanse. Kiyun cursed and started after her, but she stopped him with a gesture. Dion held out her arms. In her white parka and leggings, her white boots and gloves, she should have been nearly invisible. But the shadow in the sky seemed to hesitate. Then it began to glide down.

Come, she cried out.

Something empty and vibrant hit her at the same time—some kind of power so vast that it filled her consciousness. Suddenly, there was a bigger void with the power than there was without it. Words, images struck her like a sledge.

(Child/youngling)?

The Gray Ones surged in Dion's head. She tried to check the

flow of gray that swept in on the tail of that voice. Instinctively, the wolves urged her to run, while instead she stood her ground. The wolves' fear of power almost blinded their minds to the promise they had used to Call her. But her promise was like a leash, strangling her terror, holding her in place through their need, while she wanted to flee.

The vastness seemed to sense her struggle. Like a blast of cold air, it swept across her mind. Slitted yellow eyes blinked.

(Child/youngling), it cried.

Come, she forced herself to send. *Come,* she said. *I am here.*

She saw the Aiueven as it closed on her and felt her chest freeze. She wanted to run, wanted to turn and flee in panic. She wanted to dive beneath the snowpack and burrow to some sort of safety. Gray voices howled at her in her head. Aranur's voice was sharp. Seek life, not death . . .

She stood her ground.

The alien dove at her like a rock. Its claws were long, like those of the lepa; its lips were more beak than teeth. Instead of a mouth, it had a gash, as if an ax had been taken to a smooth plane of metal. Instead of eyes, this creature had slits. Instead of a nose, its face was split by a ridge of silver spines. And where the lepa's color was a greasy black, the Aiueven's color was scaled and white as though its feathers were more like a solid surface. Its feet were more like hands, and there were tiny arms along the arch of its wings, with small hands at the midpoint of the arch.

Her jaw clenched as she fought her fear. *Come,* she called it to her.

It swooped. For an instant, she glimpsed Kiyun and Tehena staring out from the trees. Then the power struck like a furnace. Arrogant claws crushed her arms to her sides as she was lifted from the snow.

"Dion!" Kiyun screamed at her.

His voice was lost in the rush of air that followed her into the sky.

XXI

Skickitic kitlitic, Kin
  Winter brushing the tops of the trees
Stettitic siklitic, Stin
  Wind brushing my wings
Kitlis tik'klis abriklis, Kin
  Youth brushing the stars with its dreams
Skit'lettic kitlitin, Kin
  Our wings, brushing the stars

The birdman carried Dion like a lepa carries its prey. Its hand-like feet clutched her around her chest, and its legs drew her up against it. Colder than she would have thought possible, she clung to its talon-hands. Instinctive terror blinded her while the ground dropped farther away. At the same time, some obscure part of her mind marveled at the speed of its flight, and another part of her brain objectively and remorselessly calculated the time it would take to fall to the ground if the alien let her go.

Vast words rumbled through her head—questions and demands. Images she didn't understand blocked both her fear and her thoughts so that she could not even try to answer. *Why/what is your flight?* sent the birdman. *Where is your (mother/ancestry)? Why/name (name/image) wings?*

A rough hill skimmed up below, then fell away like water as they shot out on the other side of the crest. The bile rose in Dion's throat as even that tentative closeness thrust itself away while the wind whistled and cut like vicious, icy jets.

(Wings/name) your flight/why? (Color/name) your (mother/ breeding)? What/color your mind? Flight too (early/youth/cold). Why/why? The talon-hands gripped her ribs like a steel corset, then shifted, laying her body flatter to the wind. The deepness rolled on and the cold cut in closer. Her hands, without her gloves on, were already a purple white.

Dion, Dione, woman, healer, grief . . . Wings/name? Scout, Aranur, bitter, wolves, Dione. Her mind was too shocked from the blasts of ice-laden air to answer coherently.

301

Why are you (alone/cold/too-young)? Where is your (mother-debt/comfort/future)? Why (flight/freedom)?

"No mother," Dion gasped, not realizing that she instinctively projected her answer through her mind. "Don't have . . . mother. No flight."

The Aiueven seemed to understand her. *You are (cold/young) to try (freedom/future),* he returned. His sharp-gray voice sounded labored, but the impression of youth he sent to her hit Dion like a fist. She felt suddenly like the child he assumed her to be: wingless, immobilized by the cold. Child . . . Children . . . Her stomach muscles contracted as though the baby in her own belly reacted.

(Mother/mother/comfort/source/mother), the Aiueven returned, picking up her distress.

She tried to dig her fingers deeper into the Aiueven's leg. Her temples, barely covered by the fur-lined warcap, felt naked to the wind. They ached with pounding icy hammers, and her teeth burned with the freezing air. She could hardly feel her ears. The edges of her eyelids were freezing, a little at a time, from the tearing that the wind stripped from them, and all she could do was duck her head like a bird against her arms and chest.

It was the drop in altitude that made her raise her head again: The alien was descending. Two other Aiueven floated down in tight turns around the one who gripped her, and when she forced her eyes open to see their shapes, Dion's stomach spun at their conflicting motions.

They dove straight at an icy ledge. Fear clenched her mind. *Hishn—* she screamed. *Aranur . . .*

Gray voices howled back in her head. *Wolfwalkerwolfwalker . . .*

The instant of terror blurred into a tangle of white ice spires. Her stomach was slammed up into her throat as the ice gave way to a frigid cave, and that gave way in turn to an opening even larger. The Aiueven's wings spread open again. It soared back up, away from the bottom of the cave, flashing into another cavern. Blue-white light seemed to glow through the walls, and patches of green-blue fungi swarmed on the roof of the cave.

The Aiueven swooped into another cavern, still paced by the other two aliens. Below them, the ground was mostly ice, with only the darkness of glacier rock showing faintly through the frozen buildup. And there were shapes below her—white shapes, ovoid. Eyes—yellow, slitted eyes—looked up as she was carried overhead. There were more of them the farther in she was flown. First one, then three, then eight in the caverns through which they blasted. Then four figures slightly darker in shade, and one more even darker in the next ice cave on.

Suddenly, Dion's skin burned. Her cheeks were on fire, and her hands seemed covered with sparks, not skin. Some dull part of her mind realized that it was the temperature, not herself, that had changed. The air had warmed, and the wind that whistled past her ears was like a slap of shocking heat. They dropped lower, to a cave where a frigid stream of melted ice began to course over the floor. Another tunnel and another cave, and this one was empty except for a single alien squatting on the ice out of the water. Dion's teeth burned the other way now, as the temperature rose with each drop in altitude as they dove toward the bowels of the mountain.

Seconds—it felt like hours of frigid wind—later, the alien dropped her onto the rock that made up the floor of yet another cave. She fell to her frozen knees. The alien circled tightly, then landed. He seemed to stare at her as she huddled, shivering uncontrollably, on the rock. She didn't speak; she didn't move except to shiver. Her mind felt numb, as though her thoughts had frozen during their flight, and the warmth that should have been relief only made her chill seem worse. All she knew was that she was in a cave littered with what seemed like brown carcasses, and the three Aiueven who had flown her in stood like lepa over her cold, cringing body.

"Its wings have no name."

It was a voice, but not a voice. Clear as if it rang from a bell, the words/images shot into Dion's mind, rather than through her human ears. Yet where Hishn's images were muddied by the constant drone of the packsong, the alien's voice was crisp like frost. Some part of her mind was still cold with fear, but part of her mind leaped forward. That voice was power—it was what the Ancients had sought when they went to the aliens. Dion's hands, cold as they were, clenched with the thrill that jabbed her.

The male Aiueven who had dropped her regarded her dispassionately. The other two studied Dion in silence. With her arms crossed over her belly, she stared back, trying to read the expressions in their yellow-slitted eyes. It took long minutes to realize that it was not through their eyes at all that they saw her, but through their minds instead. She could hear them—on the edges of her mind, carefully not intruding but waiting for her to speak. There was a drone—it was similar to the fog of the wolf pack, but it was sharper too, as if she could hear individual voices more clearly. The young, she realized. She could hear the voices of the smaller aliens in nearby caves. The voices of the three adults were sharp, but the young alien voices were dull, as if their thoughts were not as formed. And the single dark-furred young alien who squatted in this cave had a voice even more dull than the others.

"Is it yours/ours?" asked one of the three adults. His voice was hard and dark gray like a wolf. "Does it (Know)?"

An image of consensus filled Dion's head, and she almost blanked out as the thoughts overwhelmed her and drove her own identity away. "It Knows. I (heard) it," returned the one who had brought her in, his voice a sharp white-gray.

"But it is so (young)," the first voice stated.

The third, softer voice eased its own question in. "It has no Name?"

"(Denial)." The first, hard-gray voice returned. "It is a (baby). It does not even dream of wings."

"Leave it then," the sharp voice said.

But the soft, yellow-bright voice hesitated. "If it tried to Fly on its own, it could be a (youth/dreamer) not a (baby/need/learner). It (possibility/indecision) is close to Naming."

"(Baby) or (youth), it was too (eager/reckless/ignorant), if it tried to Fly without a Name." The one that had brought Dion in seemed to study her more closely.

She stared at them. Their eyes didn't see her; their minds picked up her projections and folded her into the blend of their voices. They thought she was one of them.

"If it Knows, it can Fly. But it must be Named to Fly," agreed the dark gray voice that cut like paper across the other one. "And if it is close to Naming, who will (claim/mother-debt) it? You?"

"(Denial). Its coloring is too (soft) to be mine."

"All (babies) are (soft)," the yellow-bright voice said. "Their (teeth) have not yet hardened."

"(Agreement)."

The voices faded. Physically, the aliens spread their wings and leaped for the cavern opening. Mentally, they simply moved away, their thoughts echoing as they distanced themselves from the cave.

Dion stayed on her knees, shivering while the stone stripped more of her heat away. Alien. Aiueven. And she was here, a human. What would they do when they realized that she was not like them? Whatever idea she had had of confronting the aliens slipped away like water, and fear, which had settled into her guts, became as hard as a knot. She shivered.

Slowly, she realized the extent of her chill. Her face throbbed and burned with the heat of the air, and her nose was already dripping. Her teeth chattered louder. She tried to rub her hands on her belly to warm herself, but it took too much effort. Eventually, she simply huddled, arms wrapped around herself, on the stone.

Softly, the wolf pack echoed into her mind. Like a tiny stream, it flowed in after the aliens had left her. *Hishn* . . . She tried to project that name, but she didn't have the focus.

A wolf's voice echoed like a wisp of smoke. *Wolfwalker* . . .

She clung to that thought and staggered to her feet, dangerously cold. Roughly she bounced in place. She started gyrating, swinging her arms in wide circles and jumping from side to side. There was not enough focus in her to do more than force herself to move. Her muscles rebelled against the cold, jerking in unrhythmic patterns as her shivering began to lessen. But the blood was beginning to surge again. Finally, she slowed her gyrations. The chill still sat in her bones, but her lungs felt hot, and she could feel the heat seeping to her skin in that stage just before sweating.

How far had they flown? And how deep was this cave? There was a sense of pressure to the walls, as if the rocks and ice could collapse any time. And the air was not thin, as she had expected; rather, it was humid and cold. Survivable, though there was a taint to the air of gases—and a faint stench that reminded her of . . . lepa.

Those slitted eyes and hardened gums that served as teeth— they were lepalike also. And lepa, like Aiueven, used caves as breeding or feeding grounds. Dion eyed the young alien on the other side of the cavern. Bones turned to pudding . . .

But the creature was huddled in on itself, its light brown head tucked down on its breast and its darker wings by its side. Experimentally, Dion reached out to it with her mind. There was an instant of resistance, then a melting of what seemed like a transparent wall, and suddenly, Dion saw the alien outlined as though it was glowing. Startled, she blinked. The adult aliens had not had this faint aura . . . But that was not quite true, she realized. There had been several times when the aliens seemed to flash with energy. And there had been a constant, dull glow while flying.

She stared at the young alien before her. "Do you have a name?" she asked, projecting the question from her mind.

Yellow, slitted eyes seemed to see her. "(Namewings flight/not-flight)," the Aiueven returned.

Dion paused, then tried to shift her thoughts into the image patterns of the alien. "How far is this place from the entrance (cave/tunnel)?"

"(Denial/confusion. Cold/colder/cold.)"

"What is (down/back) that (way/down/there)?" she asked, pointing to the wide tunnel at the other end of the cave.

"(Joy/heat), but (too-young) place. Must learn (speed/time) (move/advance/flight/cold)."

Dion struggled to follow the alien's thoughts. Its images were not as clear as those of the adults. Even so, she could feel the pull of the little one's mind as it seemed to suck energy from her through her voice. Carefully, she drew back, holding her thoughts to herself.

She looked up toward the opening through which she had been brought. It was not on the cave floor but was perhaps fifteen meters up, along a sheer rock wall. Clumps of ice hung from the upper lip of the opening and dripped in tiny runnels down onto the floor of her cave. It was rough enough, she realized, even with the drips of ice. She could climb it if she had to, though the wet rock and ice-slick edge would be difficult.

She turned and moved toward the other tunnel, which seemed to drop away. It wasn't until she was right on the lip that she realized it wasn't a tunnel either, but another opening that dropped away steeply—perhaps twelve or thirteen meters—into another cavern. The lower cave was slightly larger than the one in which she stood, but it was empty as an old nest. Rough-hewn and as light as this one, it smelled more strongly of gases, and its walls were thick with fungus. But it was warmer down there—she could feel the humid draft, like a chinook.

Brooding, she paced the edge. Then she looked at the other short cliff. The young alien who was in the cave with her paid her no attention. Instead, it merely stared at the ice wall where the melting water dripped across the coiling fungus patterns. The patterns—for there were fractal patterns in both rock and ice—curled in and out of themselves. When Dion looked more closely, she realized that the patterns came first, not the fungi. Half the cave was covered in subtle designs, and the designs changed constantly, as though a thousand different ring-carvers had had their way with these walls. The Aiueven youngling stared at the wall before it, concentrating so hard that Dion could almost see in her own mind the focus of its tiny power. And each time it focused enough heat to melt an ice pattern, another patch of fungi was exposed to its hunger.

Cautiously, watching the young one for reaction, Dion drew a meatroll from one of her parka pockets. She ate it, softening it with water from one of the runnels that crossed the ground. Then she rose to her feet and went to the cliff that led to the outer tunnels.

It took her half an hour to scale that short cliff. With her bulky clothes and winter boots, she could get almost up to the top, but there she would hang, unable to find a way past the last two meters of ice. She finally used her knife to chip handholds in the frozen shelf so that she could get over the top. By the time she did it, she was trembling; her right leg was weak with strain.

She crawled away from the icy edge on her hands and knees, then huddled on the first patch of dry ground she found. It was colder here, and the walls were more ice than stone, but it was still warm enough that the floor of the cave was covered with a frigid stream. The sound of dripping water was constant, like the drone of the alien voices, but the melting ice did not obscure the patterns etched in either ice or stone.

She could still smell the faint scent of gases and lepa, and irritably, she wiped her nose and rubbed her hand on her parka.

One of the carcasses that lay in the empty cavern was close by, and she fingered it. It was nothing more than a pelt, half-feather, half-fur. It was not from a lepa—not the right feathering or shape, neither musky nor greasy enough. She couldn't help the flash of memory, though, and she flinched at the images. Spring, and a meadow full of grass . . . The flight of the lepa was hard and dark, as though it was made of blood. But the flight of Aiueven was neither dark nor light, but simply a sense of power. The alien that had taken her up—its wings were almost unimportant. It was the focus of its flight that had mattered.

Words crackled through her mind as she thought, warning her an instant before the aliens returned. Then they were swooping into the cave, dropping to the ice. The last images in her mind—of flying with the birdmen, of wings sprouting along her arm bones—seemed caught and pulled away.

"It has become (mature/colder)," a gray-blue voice said. "And listen—it (dreams/desires) flight."

Physically, they moved—she could see them: preening and shifting and perfecting the placement of furry feathers, picking at their mouths to clean those lines of hardened gum-teeth. But the voices they projected to her mind gave her the impression of motionlessness, as if they stood like statues, concentrating only on their thoughts. The gray wolf-fog, which had crept back with the aliens' absence, was shredded and blown away. In its place, the sharp gray of the aliens' words cut across her thoughts.

"It hears us," the sharp gray voice confirmed.

They seemed to move toward her. Automatically, she cried out, *Hishn!*

"It calls out," one of the creatures said sharply.

"For its (mother-debt/caring)?"

"It was a (baby) name it used," agreed the yellow-bright voice that had been there before. The voice seemed to be reluctant. "A (baby) would use a (baby/need) name for its (mother/comfort)."

"I have no mother," Dion said flatly, automatically.

Abruptly, there was silence. Then, "(Death/cessation/absence/grief). The (hole/void) in the mind. The (hole/void) of (unknowing/no-past)." A flurry of sensations swept over her. The voices spoke together—each one distinct like the patterns on the walls, yet soothing like a wash of warm water—and the weaving of image and sound filled the hollow part of her mind with twisting ribbons of nurturing. Abruptly, Dion began to cry.

Instantly, the aliens reacted. "No (mother-debt/past)? (Need/longing/absence/grief)." She was swamped with their concern. Yet she felt also the distance behind the concern, and it dried her tears like fire. She felt pulled emotionally, as if they toyed with her, but there was no sense of maliciousness, only an almost absently projected comfort while they continued their conversation. Angered, Dion struggled to shut them out.

The yellow-bright voice followed her withdrawal. "It draws away," the alien told the others. "It can (hear/read/understand) us."

"Then it did not belong with the (youth/dark/immature/heat)," the gray-sharp voice agreed. "It is (old-enough/better) here. It (proves/agrees) that by moving itself."

A golden red voice answered. "If it can read us so (easily/clearly), it may already have begun to grow its (wings/freedom/future)."

"(Denial)," shot back a thunder voice tinged with purple. "Listen to its thoughts. It has no (direction/depth) of a Name. I cannot even read its youth image. Without a youth Name, it cannot grow its (adult/complete/soaring/future) Name. Without its (adult/home) Name, it cannot grow its wings. Without wings, it cannot Fly. Even if it has reached this (mature/cold), it will not grow enough before Last Storm to survive the flight to (home/ship)."

Images followed the voice like a swarm of angry needlers: Flying dangerously slow so the newly winged could keep up. Expending power to feed starving cells against the icy jet streams. Getting caught in the whirling snow and ice bullets of Last Storm before making it to their (home/ship/stars) because they must wait for the weather to bring on the Naming . . .

"Stars," Dion whispered. "You still go to the stars."

One of the slitted pairs of eyes seemed to turn to her. "It (hears/desires/dreams) again. It can (comprehend/future)."

The yellow-bright voice was thoughtful. "It has taken dream-debt then. We cannot (leave/abandon) it."

The golden red voice agreed. "We already (debt/owe) it the (future/stars)."

The thunder voice was adamant. "(Denial). It is too (baby/young) for the (future/stars). And if it is too young, it was (badly/incompletely) made. It lost its (mother/ancestry/history) too soon. It will never reach (stars/future/home)." The dark voice dismissed her.

Dion felt his slitted eyes in her mind, but the impression they left was of an ancient time. She shivered. Was this how the aliens had assessed the Ancients before they sent the plague? She felt her anger stir. If she could not reach the stars, whose fault was that? How many humans had already died because of alien plague?

The Aiueven seemed to stare at her. The sharp-gray voice said speculatively. "It knows (anger/rebellion). It understands (death/cessation/end). It is already part of our (flight/past-debt/future-debt). (Abandonment/loss) will stay in our (minds/memories/stigma) for generations. Even if it is too (young/baby), we cannot (dismiss/leave) it here."

"(Agreement)."

They seemed to pause.

Then the yellow-bright voice said, "What if it is a (throwback/ancestor)?"

There was a questioning sense, as though the others waited for more. The yellow-bright voice added softly, "(Throwbacks/ancestors) are slow to mature, yet they are a joy in flight. If this one was Named, it might survive. It might be able to make the Flight to the (ship/home)."

The gray-blue voice acceded. "Eastwind-rider-across-the-rocks said it (now/already) Knew. Naming is not so difficult once a youth (dream/future-debt) Knows."

The voices paused, and the mesh of images was more than Dion could sort out. Finally, the blue-gray voice interjected, quieting the hum. "If it Knows now, it can learn to (chill/focus) here and to Fly during Last Storm. Then, if it cannot make it to (home/ship/stars), it will be our (loss/cessation/loss), but not our (stigma/memory/grief) and (life-debt/name-debt)."

"(Agreement). Let it be Named before we go."

The thunder voice seemed to compromise to the hard golden red voice. "(Eastwind-rider-across-the-rocks) carried it here. He can Name it."

"His coloring is too (sharp/hard) for it," the yellow voice inter-jected. "(Sweeper-of-ice-ridges-sharp-on-the-horizon) is closer, but still too acute. Listen to how soft it is. We should know its youth Name first, before offering (Name/future/flight)."

The blue-gray voice agreed. "Ask it for its youth Name."

Instinctively, Dion braced herself, but there was a pause. Then there was a merging of colors and sounds that became dark—almost completely black with the solid blend of voices. There was the angry-thunder voice. There was the grayish blue voice that was softer and protesting—like a wolf pack swirling in her head. The sharp but clear gray voice—like water too cold for ice. The yellow-bright voice, cutting but not unkind. Impatient? She couldn't tell. And the golden red voice, like heat in her mind. Finally, a silver-white voice swirled to the front. "What Name your (ground/unwinged)?"

Dion hesitated. The question had not been simple, as she had expected, but layered, as though there were meanings upon meanings—like the memories of the wolves. Gray layers, gray fog—a thousand answers that made a single response ... Instinctively, she knew what it required: a definition of self.

She shrank from that.

They stared at her. She didn't move. But the question stuck in her mind, hanging like a sword: What was her name—her definition? Was she her past? Or Aranur's future? Was there nothing more than duty in her, that she had come here at all? Or was she grief—and through that a drive to connect to her mate through her demand on the aliens, and to connect to her sons through her death?

She felt her hands clench, and she couldn't help the anger that built within her. She was a tool, she thought. A blade of gray. A salve to the wounds of her county. She was the feelings she rejected, and the rage she contained. She was light and dark, life and death. She was a wolfsong without voice. And in the end, she realized, she was nothing more than a driving desire to end death with life—to resolve the Ancient's debt of plague with payments on the debts she created: Danton's debt—of death and loss, Aranur's debt of duty ... The debt to her mother who died at her birth. The debt of love her mate had stolen when he took his path to the moons ... And the life-debt from the wolves—that promise, which demanded life in return—the demand that an old death be settled.

Something stirred in her heart. She still lived, she knew, deep inside herself, behind the walls of emptiness and the void that death had brought. She just didn't want to face herself for fear she could not live with her own truths. But the aliens waited, and the wolves died outside. Abruptly, rage tightened her throat. Grief, fury, longing, loss; love and joy and dreaming . . . They whirled together in a maelstrom, slamming about until they wove their patterns into the sound she projected at the waiting Aiueven.

I am Ember Dione maMarin.

A burst of energy flashed back like a splash of water. She flinched. But it had not been painful. It had been dizzying—as if she had somehow begun Ovousibas and had jerked back out as soon as the thought was formed.

"There are no (teeth) in its name," the soft one protested. "Is it Named correctly?"

"(Affirmation). It is a baby, not a yearling. It has a baby Name. But it (hears/understands) us. It speaks (clearly/maturely) with depth to its tone. It has lived. We can hear the (future-debt) of a binding in its Name. It has taken life-debt from one of us."

The golden red voice agreed. "You saw (true/future). It Knows."

"It learns quickly," the sharp-gray voice put in. "I have heard its voice before, as it learned to (move/change) its own energy. It was alone, I think, even then."

"But if it does not learn enough to Fly before the Last Storm, it must be left behind."

"It is confused from the (wolves)," the gray voice returned. "I heard (wolves/gray/aliens) in its recognition of the (patterns/layers) of the question. It could have been damaged from that contact."

"(Affirmation). Did Eastwind-rider-across-the-rocks chase off the (wolves/gray) when he took the (baby/youngling) back?"

"He is in (Ves) phase, and the storms are already rising," returned another voice. "Bringing the baby here was hard on him. He had nothing left with which to chase off the (wolves/aliens)." The golden red voice paused and regarded Dion's voice. "He could not Name it anyway; its coloring is too different than his. Its coloring is much like yours, however," it said to the gray-blue alien.

The alien seemed to turn to Dion. Yellow, slitted eyes blinked, and in that instant a wash of despair flooded her mind. She gasped. It was as though every instant of grief she had ever felt was concentrated into a single thrust of mental energy.

It was gone as suddenly as it came, but Dion was frozen on the rock.

The blue-gray voice seemed to consider the others' images. "Has it shown any other (eagerness/desire/dreams) to Fly?"

"(Denial). The single dream, (unfocused/fear), that you heard when you arrived, and that single desire for the (home/stars/freedom). But it has seen (time/ancestors). Throwbacks can reach (time/back) like that."

"If it is a throwback, it will learn differently than we (expect)," the other one agreed. "Throwbacks are more (unstructured/creative) than we (structured) when young."

"Throwback or structured—it doesn't matter. It must Fly or die."

"But it must be Named to Fly," the yellow-bright voice retorted.

The purple-dark voice rounded on the last voice. "Then find it a (mother-debt/guardian/teacher). I will not do for it. It doesn't feel (right/smooth/timed) to me. Its (thoughts/self) feels awkward and (wrong/rebellious/accusing)."

"Perhaps it is (linked/debted) to your (ancestor/stigma)."

There was a general agreement. Finally, the blue-gray one spoke again, slowly, as if to convince itself of what it said. "It feels (strange/clumsy/confused) to me," the alien projected, "but its (gracelessness) will disappear with (cold/growth/familiarity)."

"Do you claim it to Name it, then?" the sharp-blue one demanded. "You accept its (mother-debt)?"

"Your (child-debt/grief/loss) is still strong," another said. "Its (mother-loss/grief) is as harsh. It will compound your (cessation/no-future/grief) and color all our voices."

"It has already touched us with its (grief/loss). You heard it call for (life-debt/payment/resolve). If it is to learn to (power/

focus) any other (emotion/vision), one of us must (mother-debt/guide) it soon."

Their voices linked and blended, and Dion realized that the sense of debt that pervaded their words was a symbiotic sense. Each one was tied to the next one through its actions and words. She felt the power they focused between each other and studied those links. It was Ovousibas they used—the sense of it was the same as the power she had learned from the wolves. But linking and communicating like this—it was something she had not considered, that energy could be used in ways other than healing. She followed their links, watched the mesh of their voices and the way each one projected to and fed off the pattern. Like the designs in the cave walls, the words between them were a weave of intent and emotion, history and future, guide and focus. And in the tapestry they wove together, each one's voice blended perfectly, yet was distinct and minutely detailed. Like a packsong, she thought, only where the wolves howled together to blend into a single group—like long grass twisted into a single rope—the aliens sang together yet remained separate— like the grass in a meadow when the wind blows through. And as she studied their images, a single question rose in her mind: If they could aim a voice at another, why couldn't she do the same?

Quietly, she let her mind shift to the left and down. But instead of slipping into her own body, she let the focus of her mind hang for a moment in thought. Then, gathering herself into a sense of direction, she projected it out beyond the caves and south toward the lower snowpacks. *KiyunTehenaKiyunTehenaKiyun* . . .

The aliens' voices silenced. Abruptly, Dion stopped.

"Listen," the bright yellow voice broke in. "Did it Name itself?"

"(Denial)," the sharp, ice-blue voice said. "It was calling. Did you (see) the narrowness of its voice? There was direction to its call."

"(Uncertainty/possibility)," the yellow voice protested. "Hear the rhythm—it is almost a flight pattern," she said. "Kiuntihin' kiuntihin'kiun."

"It is still too (soft/babyish)," the other one scoffed. "Even my first pattern had twice as many (teeth) as that: Kikliti'clintikin."

"It is much (younger) than you when you learned to Fly," the gray-blue voice admonished. "Its Name, like yours, will harden with (age). As a (throwback/ancestor), it will need more (time/ mother-debt) to harden its (teeth)."

"Do you Name it then? Do you give (mother-debt)?"

Whose-wings-make-the-grass-flow hesitated. Then the alien seemed to solidify its thoughts. "(Agreement)," it said quietly. "I will Name it. It will be my (child-debt/child)."

Dion eyed them warily. Unconsciously, she edged back on the ice, but her back was already against the wall. A drip from the roof of the cave hit the back of her neck, but the chill was nothing compared to the sense that hit her stomach. There were no Ancient legends about naming each other—only of trading science for the right to stay on this world. Or of being killed. And there were no stories of humans being linked to Aiueven . . .

The hum was subsonic at first, but it grew into her sternum within seconds. The humming rose, and the bones in her chest and thighs began to vibrate. The noise became a sound that demanded her attention like a pounding that breaks down doors. She opened her mouth, but her voice involuntarily added to the song of tension. Her vocal cords shivered together. The Aiueven riveted on her, and under the impact, her mind fractured like an egg.

Their thoughts spun together and dropped to the left. Dion was dragged along. Need blended with need; grief understood grief; their losses bound them like steel. Dion gasped with the sudden flush of strength that came with that into her mind. Then their mental voices caught at each other and formed a resonance.

> *Kiuntihin'kiuntihin'kiun. Soft, for it lacks teeth.*
> *Kiuntihin'kiuntihin'kiun. Young, since it lacks age.*
> *Kiuntihin'kiuntihin'kiun. Wise, though it lacks*
> *wings.*
> *Kiuntihin'kiuntihin'kiun.*

It was a river of sound that, once unleashed, could not be stopped from its pattern. It spilled over Dion's mind, locking her thoughts into that of the alien, and binding the alien back.

The blue-gray touch dipped into her body and bones, and wondered at the solidity of them before it found her unborn child. Grief and need became a set of teeth that tore into Dion's mind, even as the alien (greedily/urgently) bound itself to her unborn daughter. Purple light flashed without being seen. Sound without sound slammed between them. Child-debt, mother-debt became the same. The alien cried out, and it was Dion who instinctively soothed her.

> *Kiuntihin'kiuntihin'kiun. Fast, for its dreams soar.*
> *Kiuntihin'kiuntihin'kiun. Heavy, since it makes a*
>   *(child).*
>   *Kiuntihin'kiuntihin'kiun. Strong, not one, but*
>   *two.*
> *Kiuntihin'kiuntihin'kiun.*

The alien swept deeper into Dion's mind, finding the core of her thoughts. Like a thousand links to a thousand wolves, their voices meshed together. The past became the possibility of a future, the link between them a line of continuity that ran in both directions. Human, alien touched. Dion screamed. The alien froze, but it was too late to go back. The sense of Dion's humanness flashed along her Name.

> *Kiuntihin'kiuntihin'kiun. Earthbound.*
> *Kiuntihin'kiuntihin'kiun. Skybound.*
> *Kiuntihin'kiuntihin'kiun. Named.*

Abruptly the air filled with rage. Purple shouted with blue and gray, tinging into black. Red-orange burned like a piece of the sun falling through the sky. The noise was real, and Dion fell to her knees while talons chipped the air above her. Mouths gnashed. And all the while, there was one image clear above the rest: Human.

XXII

Kek'kallic krast
The plague of the past
Te'etrellic ek'kit
The death-debt

There were suddenly more Aiueven there. Ten, twelve, two dozen ... She couldn't tell. The din in her head was vicious, slamming back and forth. The alien who had Named her was close, almost touching, yet its mind recoiled in a flash.

"Not (Aiueven/us/pure). (Loathing/horror) Human!"

"(Distress). I did not know—"

"Human!"

"What (abomination) have we done? To spit out the (Song/future) for wings—how could it Know?"

"(Kill/destroy) it."

"Kill it (now)."

"Stop!" Dion screamed, cowering. She did not realize that none of them had moved.

The din ceased instantly.

Dion's fists clenched. "I am Named. I can speak for myself."

"Human," hissed the cold, ice-blue voice. "You cannot speak."

"I have a Name."

"It is Named," the birdwoman said sharply, the horror in her voice clanging like an off-key metal bar on stone. "(It/my-youth/child-debt) can speak."

Two of them looked at Dion's (mother-debt/bond). "Is it bonded?"

As though her head bowed and her wings melted before them, Whose-wings-make-the-grass-flow agreed. "It is my (youth/child-debt) now."

"Human (youth)?" The sharp-blue voice seemed to coil in on itself in a vile sense. "(Pity). (Horror)."

"Take back its Name," another one said hotly, fired with its own fervor. Dion could almost feel its claws reach for her throat.

"My Name is myself," Dion snarled back. "You can kill me, but you cannot destroy that. And I understand enough to know that I am in your history now, no matter what you do."

"A Human cannot be Named," the young one spat. "A Human cannot have wings."

"No? We soared the skies and stars like you—"

"You (crawl/ground-dwell) now."

"You made us this way."

"You cannot even (dream/know) flight."

Abruptly, Dion stood. She faced them, and their slitted eyes stared back at her. Their minds were like badgerbears, poised to strike. "My wings are here," she said vehemently, and in her mind, behind her, curling out of her shoulders like moths hatching from their cocoons, she imagined a set of wings.

"Human," gnashed Sweeper-of-ice-ridges-sharp-on-the-horizon. "You mock us. Your wings are not (power/truth)."

"Are these better?" she snarled. Her image changed, and she projected the skycars as she had seen them in Ancient places. She took the image and let the skycar soar into the sky, floating down on its extended wings. "Or this?" She projected the picture of spacecraft she had seen in the Ancient texts in Ariye. "We had flight. We owned the stars like you."

"They are not (real/power). They are no longer (truth). It mocks us with these (images)."

"Can any Human make light of us?" Dion's (mother) dismissed the other's claim. But the birdcreature's voice was filled with a loathing that was directed half at herself. "They are wings, even if they are not (truth)."

"(Denial)." The answer was a sharp, slashing note. "There is a debt building here. (Intrusion-debt), (Naming-debt)—"

Dion cut them off. Her voice, thin compared to theirs, was sharp as a knife. "You want to talk about debt?" she snapped. "Who owes what to whom? We bore thousands of deaths from the plague you sent when you broke your bargain with us. We built your barriers, kept the worlags from your dens, but you killed us anyway—" Her voice broke off.

Suddenly, she knew what she had seen, so long ago in the wolves. The voices, the colors, the shifts of alien thoughts . . . Something turned over in her gut. "It was you," she breathed, turning to the purple-dark voice. "It was you who sent the plague." Stunned, she stared through her eyes as well as her mind. "It wasn't all of you together," she whispered. "It was you alone who did it—the ones that were colored like you. I saw your eyes—I saw them through the wolves. And I heard your voices in the packsong. Their memories were clear. Eight hundred years, and you haven't changed. Your colors are the same."

The purple-dark voice went still.

"It has (called/recognized) you," the golden red voice said harshly to the other.

"It is your (stigma/ancestry)," said another to the purple-dark voice. "As with us, (it/human) (thought/memory/debt) does not (fade/forgive) from their minds."

"(Denial). It is (insight/more) than that," countered the cold, blue voice.

The sharp-gray voice seemed to whisper agreement. "It claims (life-debt/death-debt) from us."

The purple-dark voice shivered. "(Denial/impossible)."

"I saw you," Dion repeated. "I saw your voice. The shades—they were the same. Even now the wolves carry your plague, dormant in their bodies. A single trigger, and they die like the Ancients. Like the wolves you first killed yourself."

"It (sees/perceives) the (stigma/history)," said the cold, blue voice. "It brings it back—enters it into the (line/matrix/all-of-us)."

"Then I must (kill/cessation) it," the other returned. "Or it will contaminate us all."

The others agreed. "The Naming pact is broken. Kill it."

"Kill it," the hard voice agreed.

Dion stood her ground. "You can't kill me," she said harshly. "You owe me my life and the lives of the thousands you killed. You owe my people the future you stripped away from us."

"(Denial)!"

"You owe me (blood-debt/life-debt)," she repeated, using their own images back at them.

"(Blood-debt?) There can be no (debt) with Humans." The soft, yellow-bright voice was like a fingernail scraped across slate.

"Death is always a debt," she snarled back. "Look at what you have done." The images of the scattered dead from an Ancient city-dome spilled into her mind. The skeletons, bare and twisted, lay where their bodies had fallen, eight hundred years ago. Dion pulled on the threads that bound her to the wolves, and death howled back out of the packsong. Images she herself had seen and images eight centuries old mixed and projected like blades into the minds of Aiueven. "(Blood-debt)," Dion said harshly. "(Blood-debt/life-debt) and (payment/retribution)."

"We (traded/agreed) with Humans long ago," one of the aliens projected. "But there was no debt between us."

"(Agreement)," another said. "Knowledge was (traded/paid-for) for the safety of the dens. We have no other agreement."

"You reneged on the one agreement you had," Dion snapped back at them. Her eyes were open, but she could see only with her mind, and the swooping, tearing of the Aiueven's mental talons pitched her fear higher than a physical tear could ever have done. "You flew (death/pain) into the (bargain/trade) so that the knowledge was (destroyed/lost) after being given." She had had the fever herself, and she had touched it in others. Now she stretched into the memories of the wolves and let them fill her mind. Like a soiled stream flowing beneath a heavy sky, the memories streaked in. Old death stank in Dion's mind. Fevers burned and convulsions broke bones. Minds shattered as hearts burst. Hallways filled with fallen men and women, and the tiny bodies of a thousand children twisted in the throes of the plague. The Gray Ones' grief, the Ancients' grief, Dion's own grief splashed into alien minds. And the death mounds rose, and the white stones grew, and the smoke lingered on the funeral pyres.

Even the Aiueven shuddered.

"It knows grief," Whose-wings-make-the-grass-flow said softly. "It brings that (grief/debt) to us."

The yellow-bright alien stirred. "That is your (father's father's mother's) debt," it said to the purple-dark voice. "It is your (honor/stigma) to clear."

"(DENIAL)!"

One of the others raised his wing, and the icy blast it sent shut the other up. He sent a shaft of demanding (rage/skepticism) to Dion's (mother).

"It is Named. It cannot lie," Whose-wings-make-the-grass-flow said in a determined voice.

There was silence.

"Then there is debt," the silver-ice voice said finally. "The Human must be paid."

The purple-dark voice was thunderous. "Balance cannot be found in this, no matter what debt is paid. Kill it and the debt is gone, lost in the centuries."

The others hesitated.

"The debt died long ago," urged the purple-dark voice. "Let this ... (Human/horror) live, and the debt (grows/reaffirms) again." His images were clear.

"Kill it ..." The sharp-blue voice seemed to roll the idea around between them. The horror that had hit them with their realization of her was suddenly a prod. "Kill it?"

The dark, purple voice said almost softly, "Kill it."

The Aiueven seemed to converge. Death seemed to center in their minds, and the power they focused shook her.

"(Mother)!" Dion screamed. She threw up one arm, the other protecting her belly.

Abruptly, their movement stopped.

Dion opened her eyes. Whose-wings-make-the-grass-flow was in front of her. The alien's slender white arms stretched away from her wings, leaving a hollow among the furred feathers. And the mother-creature blocked the talons of the others.

"Do not touch it," the Aiueven warned, her soft, gray-blue voice like steel. "If it is to die, then I will do it. My own (youth/horror/child-debt) betrays me, so I must (betray/kill) myself."

"(Contrition)." The sharp-gray voice acceded.

"(Agreement). (Contrition)," voiced the others. The Aiueven stepped back.

The mother-creature turned to face her, and Dion's chill did not lessen. "You would kill me to (hide/deny) your debt?" she threw out desperately. "What stigma does that create?"

The blue-gray voice hesitated.

Dion stared at the talons that seemed poised before her and

waited for them to strike. It didn't matter that the talons were small—almost delicate to her. It didn't matter that they were no longer than her fingers. The sense of power they radiated was enough to tear her without touching her flesh, and she knew suddenly how other humans died.

Yet the alien still stood without moving.

Dion stared at her, stared deep into yellow eyes. Like knives, each pierced the other's mind. Hurts and dreams and joys and griefs swam together in a howling sea. They bit at each other, then blended. They cut at each other, then melted together. And in a flash, Dion understood. The link between her and the mother-creature was already fixed, like a twenty-year bond with a wolf.

Her voice was quiet. "You can kill me, but not who I am," she said. "I am too strong in your mind already. And no matter how quickly you do it now, my death won't hide your debt."

Dion's words echoed into their minds and hung there like ice.

"It calls for honor," said the sharp-gray voice finally.

"It is Human," the dark one returned.

"Still, it calls for honor."

The purple-dark alien shoved the shock out of his voice with so much effort that the air shook around him. It was minutes before he controlled the enraged flashes of power. "Human," he said rigidly. "What is your payment?"

"Knowledge." Dion's voice shook. She steadied it carefully. "Knowledge (equal) to that (lost/taken) by your plague."

"It is too much!" The furious clamor rose instantly. "How can it ask for such from us?" And, "How can it be worthy, this Human?"

At the last voice, the others fell silent. The sharp-blue voice added, "There is debt, and the (debt-price/repayment) is within honor, except that it is paid to a Human. How can it be (worthy) of such knowledge which was already given in trade?"

"Paid for, then stolen back by death," Dion said harshly.

"My (youth) is right," her mother agreed unwillingly. "The bargain was never honored."

"So I must honor it to a Human like this—one with no flight at all?" The purple-dark birdman spat at her feet. "At least her (father's father's ancestors) could fly with us to (talk/trade). Show me that it can Fly, and then I will pay the debt-price."

"That is right, (too)." The consensus was relieved, as if a test of flight would put them in balance again.

"(Mother)," Dion protested. "(We/humans) have already paid the price. Why should I prove (myself/us) again?"

"The price was paid by Humans who had flight," the alien returned. There was still loathing in her voice. "You have no flight. You must prove your (worth/flight/ability), or the debt will be paid to a—" Her voice faltered. "—Human that can Fly."

"(Agreement)," the purple-dark voice said. "Show that (it/ human/primitive) can Fly, and I will balance the debt."

Dion's voice was desperate. "Mother?"

The gray-blue Aiueven looked at her a long moment, its slitted eyes blind to Dion's physical body. "It is Human," she said finally. "Its wings are not real. It cannot be tested with Flight."

"But it must still be tested," others argued. There was grim determination in their tones. "If it has no wings, why should it be given full (power/knowledge/past)?"

"Do you claim its (proof/flight) for it?" the strong, silver voice demanded.

"(Denial)." The Aiueven, repulsed by the idea that she was bonded to the Human, was shocked at the suggestion.

"(Pity)," the silver-voiced birdman sent to Dion's mother, recognizing the other's horror. To have to defend a Human to keep one's own voice clear of the darkness that colored another's tones . . . "Let it prove itself if it wants the debt paid. But let the proof be within (honor/balance) or we will pay again (later/ descendants)." The image of plague and blood coloring the purple-dark voice was clear.

"When I brought it," Eastwind-rider-across-the-rocks cut in slowly, "it said it was a (healer)."

"Then I will test its (healing)," the purple-dark voice snarled.

Before Dion's unfocused eyes registered what happened, he moved blindingly fast. A tearing, indescribably burning pain shrieked through her body. Dion froze, unable to move. And she looked down to see her parka torn from one side to the other. Blood gushed out over her hands.

It was then that she finally screamed.

XXIII

What gift is given that has no giver?
What glass returns a stranger?
What song has words of honesty?
What lesson is a thief?

—Second Riddle of the Ages

"It makes sound," Sweeper-of-ice-ridges-sharp-on-the-horizon said with satisfaction. "It doesn't (heal) itself. It thought itself (worthy)."

Dion strangled on her shriek. In the back of her mind, the gray wolves surged, slipping past the voices. Her child, her daughter . . . The last of Aranur . . . She tried to feel her womb.

"(Distress). It is dying," said her (mother). "Look how it centers itself away from the gash and onto its own (child/future). It cannot stop its (blood/life)."

"It uses (skin/fur/crude) to stop its (blood)," disparaged the purple-dark voice.

Dion heard their voices as if in a fog. The blood on her hands; the sudden frigid touch of air inside her body. The sense of the mother-alien was heavy in her mind, but it was watching, taking up her thoughts without helping her to be strong. Dion fell to her knees. The jarring spurted more blood into her parka, soaking the front of the coat.

"Hishn," she whispered. "Aranur . . ."

It was the shock of the ice that focused her. The alien mother did not seem to touch her, but still, its strength was part of her. A bond, she thought, like the one with the wolves. A link to power . . . She grasped the sense of the Aiueven and used it as she used the Gray Ones. She felt her own heart and slowed it; felt for the blood and stopped it. The slash had not torn her womb, but the child within her struggled for more of her blood.

"It is dying," the hard, gray voice said.

A silver voice seemed to frown. "(Denial)," it answered the other. "It is just slower than you wish. It is stopping the (blood/life-flow) now."

"But it does not (even) try to (regenerate/heal)."

The gray-blue voice of Dion's (mother) was a knife that twisted in her mind. She shuddered and tried to cling to it, but the alien seemed to back away. The Aiueven shifted from foot to foot as she tried to condemn and yet defend the bond into which she was locked herself.

"It is Human," the silver voice attempted to comfort. "They do not have the (ability) in their bodies."

"But see how it (protects/life-debt) its (baby/child-debt)," her mother said in despair. "It makes honor-pact with its own (child-debt/future)."

The ice-blue voice snorted. "It is Human. It knows no honor-pact."

"(Denial). It has (youth) in it now."

"How can this be? It is a (yearling) itself."

"It is Human," the orange-red voice snapped. "They (pro-create) like rasts."

"Does it (really/disbelief) pact with its (young)?"

"(Affirmation)." Dion's (mother)'s wings beat as if to clear the air for them to see.

One of the others looked closely. "You are right," he said with resignation. "It has (youth)."

"(Despair/pity)."

With a shudder, the Aiueven mother reached out to Dion's hands.

"(Denial)!" the purple-dark voice snarled. The alien snapped his lips so that flashes burst back in the recesses of his mouth. "It cannot (heal/future) itself, so let it (die/stop/end-debt) like it should."

"It has honor-pact with its own (young)," the birdwoman spat. "Do you break this pact as your (father's father's mother) broke the one you test now?"

"(Shame). (Hate)."

"(Agreement). But it is frail and weak and confused by its

dreams. And it is now my—" She shuddered. "—(youth/child-debt)." She watched while Dion tried to protect her baby. "(Look) at it."

There was shock in her body—Dion could feel it. The cold crept up from her legs. She had to struggle to control her heart-beat now, to force her lungs to breathe.

"Human." The birdwoman shuddered again. She turned to the others. "This place is (contaminated/dead). Take our (children/future) and go. There are other dens in which to (live/grow/dream). I will see you at (home/ship) before the storm rides me down."

"(Relief). (Lingering loathing)." As one, all but the mother-debt alien rose and flew from the cave, their voices calling, urging, commanding the young to listen. Two flew back toward the warmer, lower cave to grab up the brown-furred youth. A few seconds later, those two flashed through the cave, following the others, and the sound of collapsing stone shuddered up from below. Icicles snapped and crashed to the floor of the cave, spattering Dion with slivers. She could hardly see through the fog. The white walls around her blurred with her shock, and she couldn't think anymore. The cold reached through her like talons. There was no energy for her to suck from the wolves, so she sucked off herself instead. But her focus faded like an old man's sight, and the blood kept weeping out.

The Aiueven's eyes were slits, blank and waiting.

The pain grew and lessened, pulsing with what was left of Dion's blood. "Mother!" she cried out finally. "Help me or hurt me, but don't just watch me die."

"(Distress). (Denial)."

"Does my Name mean nothing? Can you not accept anything outside yourself?"

"That is a Human thing."

"We're bonded now—your voice is meshed in my thoughts. Can you deny that you are part human too?"

A tearing, screeching sound bit at Dion's ears. The wolf-walker cried out.

The Aiueven's voice was horrible in its own shock and anger. "Do you (stigma/curse) me too? What (life-debt) must I owe you?"

Dion stared up from the ice. Her bloody hands clutched her belly. "If you are my mother, then this is also your child."

"(Denial)."

"But we are bonded—I can feel you in my thoughts."

"(Affirmation/distress)."

"I felt your grief; it was the same as mine, multiplied by thousands."

"(Grief/loss) cannot be replaced. The child-debt is my future. Without it, I am as one who is dead, but still in the land of the living."

Dion felt a deep shudder catch her. She had not stopped her bleeding. She tried to focus on her own tissues, but she didn't have the strength. "Feel me," she said hoarsely. "Feel this child. It is yours now as much as mine."

"There can be no (love/future) like that between us."

"It is already there."

"(Denial)!"

"Feel it. You are part of me now. I must love you as myself."

"(Denial)!" This time it was stronger. The yellow, slitted eyes glared in the back of her head.

"Is it better to be without a child—without a future—for the sake of empty pride?"

"Generations cannot be shared."

"With us, that isn't true."

The alien hesitated. One of its slender arms seemed to reach out, and Dion no longer knew if she saw it or if it was in her mind. Cold touched her belly, and she knew that the shock was growing. The numbness spread faster now. "My child," she cried out. She sank to the ground.

The alien mother seemed torn. "You have a (choice/future): Live or die."

"I want to live," Dion whispered.

The Aiueven was silent for a moment. "You (bind/condemn) us both," she said finally, softly.

The alien mother stretched out a wing, and a clawlike hand touched Dion's frigid skin. Then the alien mother made a sound, and some part of Dion's mind realized that the sound was real— in her ears. Her mind began to blur. A hot vibration started deep in her bones, and crawled out to her muscles and skin.

White fur brushed her face. Blue and gray tones washed through her thoughts, and the sounds were loud without sound. Wolf minds blended with alien thoughts; the howling became alien tones. Something shifted inside her, as though water rushing through a broken dam was suddenly slowed and stopped. Pain sagged momentarily. Then it faded away.

Dion stared at her (mother). She could hear the echo of Hishn and a hundred other wolves. She could feel the ice against her parka; she could feel the cold again in her guts. But the life of her child was strong, and the numbness was gone. She touched her belly. It was closed. There was an ache inside and along the gash, but the flesh was smoothly seamed.

Whose-wings-make-the-grass-flow eyed her from the icy cave. "The debt is paid," she said.

Wait. Dion tried to speak. A shiver hit her, and it took a moment to realize that it was the cave, not herself, that shook. "Wait," she projected. "Take me back. Take me back to my (family/friends/barrier). Then, the debt is paid."

"I will not reach (next-home/den) in time. This den will collapse as the rock pressure releases, and the storm now gathers outside."

"Then take me as far as honor demands."

The alien seemed to stare at her for eternity. The slender arm shifted away from its wing to point at Dion's belly. "This (child) is mine, as much as you are now mine."

"Aye," Dion breathed.

Abruptly, the birdwoman clutched her. Automatically, it grasped her close to its body, then shivered and tried to hold her away so that there was no body-to-body contact. But as its wings gathered power and it lifted from the cave, it had to draw Dion close again to fly through the icy opening. *Ahhh* . . . It tried to hide its loathing—the mental voice was clear. But its horror mixed with something else, and the alien did not let go.

Through the next cavern and the next, up into thicker ice . . . The caves grew cold, then frigid as the walls became solid ice, then began to glow blue-green again with natural light instead of glowing fungus. Massive icicles lay on the floors of the caverns—and more shook down as they flew through—and the walls blurred as the depths of the mountain collapsed. But the alien mother swept like a lance, driving toward the outside air till she burst out into the sky between the ice spires. There was a moment of blinding glare, then the shades of white and gray that made up land and sky saturated her sight.

Air sucked into Dion's mouth. She barely glimpsed the depths they dropped into before the wind caught the birdwoman's wings and they swooped sickeningly to a more even flight. A jagged ridge rose up like twisted teeth, then fell away as if it had snapped at, then missed, their feet. The slash in her parka hung open, and the blood there froze in seconds into a rock-hard slab. They swooped sickeningly lower, across a steep expanse of snow, and the wind bit into her body, then her frozen cheeks, like a hundred tiny mouths.

In her mind, Dion could see the ring of light that seemed to surround the Aiueven. She could feel the mental laboring of the creature against the rising winds, and the rock-hard strength of its physical body as it hugged her to its breast. She could feel the strain grow like grief. Her mind flashed to Aranur, to Danton, to Hishn, and the gray tide in the back of her head swelled as it sensed her.

Wolfwalker! The howl hit her, and she felt the dim strength of their bond. It was full and rich, even at that distance, and it made the strain of the Aiueven seem thin. Tentatively, she touched the alien's mind. "Mother?"

"(Child-debt/youngling)." But there was still horror in its voice, and it tried to keep its mental distance.

"You are straining. Take strength from me. From the wolves."

"(Denial)."

The alien swooped across a rounded shoulder of the mountain, and Dion swallowed against her stomach as it rose into her throat. The wind, which had seemed strong before, hit them like a sledge. The Aiueven strained, and Dion could feel its strength pouring out as it held her weight aloft.

They flew back along a ridge where the clouds boiled on the other side of the rock. Dion's weight dragged the alien down. The Aiueven's breath became labored, and the power that seemed to cling to its wings faded to a dull glow. As they dropped lower into the edge of the glacier valley, the wind surged, then struck violently. They were buffeted back up, then slammed down toward the ice. The Aiueven mother was grim.

"I can go no farther," she said, stalling so that they fell quickly. "You must go the rest of the way on your own."

The alien struck the ground heavily, as if she did not have the control to land well, and Dion hit the ice hard. She rolled meters across bumpy, sharp ice, and lay for a moment breathless. Slowly, she crawled to her knees. She hugged her arms tightly around her. "Mother," she whispered.

Kiuntihin'kiuntihin'kiun, the other sent. The Aiueven leaped into the air. The cold, biting wind caught the mother-creature and lifted her so that she shot up, then away, fading into the swirling white. The sense of power was weaker now, as though it dissipated as the distance between them grew.

Dion didn't notice her hand stretching out. "Mother," she cried out. "What Name have you given me? What does my Name mean?"

From the distance, the voice returned. It was sharp in her head, in a way that the wolves never were, and it resonated with the focus of alien power. *Human*, it returned. *You have no right. We are bound, but not so tightly yet. This (stigma/horror) may still fade.*

"You Named me," Dion called steadily, light-headed and almost numb. "You (mother-debt) me. And we share this child and our futures."

Whose-wings-make-the-grass-flow hesitated, and Dion could almost feel the expenditure of energy that the alien put forth. The winds had strengthened, even in the few minutes that lay now between them, and the front that was moving across the valley thickened and darkened the sky. The blue-gray voice, when Dion heard it, was quiet. *(Mother-debt/child-debt). The Naming is between us.* There was a pause, as if the alien gathered her grief and set it aside, then put Dion in that mental space. *It has (bright/dreams) images,* the alien sent finally. *It has (grief/strength) meaning. It is (constant/inevitable) and (changes/softens/sharpens) its (edge/meaning) with time. It is The-winter-that-cuts-the-ice.*

"Mother," Dion whispered.

The debt is paid, (youngling/Human). We are bound, but your (life/future) is your own.

Dion stared into the sky. She could no longer see the alien. The dry flakes that began to whirl into her eyes made her dizzy, but she still strained to find that speck of motion. "You bind me to you," she cried out. "Then you give me up?"

You are Human.

"And part of you."

(Denial). I am (unwhole/destroyed).

"You are more than you were before. How can that be destruction?"

The wind cut viciously, as if in rebuttal, and Dion hunched her shoulders against it. She stared across the snow: It was a massive expanse, and she was alone upon it. It had looked smooth at a distance, but close up it was covered with humps and ridges where shrubs lay hidden beneath the surface, and rocks and old ice created irregular lines. Far in the distance, kays away across the expanse, there were dark patches of trees. There were wolves somewhere there—they were a faint din compared to the Aiueven—and Kiyun and Tehena were with them. But the clouds were hunkering down even now, and the tiny, dry snow was coming down harder.

The wind whipped the frozen edge of her parka, but Dion turned into it, searching for a trace of the mother-alien's flight. She thought she saw the speck of the creature, struggling against the wind. She stretched, and the link between them seemed to shiver. Loathing, disgust . . . And yet there were other things too. The empathy of one for the other's grief . . . The need filled, one by the other . . . And the Naming, which bound them in each other's mind . . .

The winds hit Dion hard on the right, and she staggered before she realized that it was not her body that had felt the gust, but the Aiueven who had faltered. "Mother!" she cried out.

The voice swept back. *(Child/youngling).*

But the winds cut, and Dion's cheeks, white and chapped, felt a cold that was more alien than hers. *Mother!* she shouted. *Mother, if you need my strength, take it.*

No more debts, Human. But the voice was faint and weakening. *No debt. I give it freely.*

Human. You have no (concept/knowledge/vision) of freedom.

Imagery was not enough, and Dion found herself straining with her voice to convince the Aiueven. "You made yourself my mother," she said fiercely. "Your flight is now my own."

No power can be given over (time/distance). It is not the way.

"I am human," she acknowledged. "So I do not know the way. But you are in (need/hungry/failing). Let me send this to you."

At the risk of (your/my/our) own (baby)?

"I am human, not Aiueven. I do not risk our child in this."

There was a hesitation in the alien, and Dion could feel her own mind crawling, as if the Aiueven somehow searched her for truth.

But it was not the truth of her statement of risk, but the truth that the child was both hers and the alien mother's. The emotional void in the Aiueven swamped Dion like night, and Dion saw the death of the alien's child. The heated gases of volcanic vents . . . The shiver deep in the mountain . . . The fractured stone, crushing down . . . The loss that tore at her guts like lepa. The alien's need meshed with Dion's; their grief screamed out together. And the child within Dion became a light between them.

The alien's voice was faint in her mind. *Our (children)?* the alien asked. *Our (child-debt)?*

Dion caught her breath, and the cold air cut her throat, but she returned steadily, "Mother of myself. Mother of my own."

Then we are (bound/family/timeless).

"Aye." Dion's voice was a whisper. She didn't ask again if she could send the internal power across the sky to the other. Instead, resolutely, she gathered what was left of her strength into a fist of heat within her. And as if they had been waiting for her voice to Call, the wolves howled in the back of her mind. They were still faint compared to the alien, but it didn't matter to Dion.

She pulled at them, sucking their packsong into her voice. Eagerly, they swept into her head. Energy flowed in—from her mouth with every breath, from her hands with every shiver, from her chest with every gust of wind. Greedily, she clutched at the wolfsong. Images, strength, warmth—they were thrust into her mind in a tide of gray.

She loosed that heat in a single burst, like a silver-blue arrow shot through the clouds. It sought the Aiueven like a hunter.

There was a moment of rejection. Then their voices merged. Dion could feel the alien, could feel the focusing of the power that the Aiueven controlled. Some part of her mind studied that while another part of her pushed her strength toward it. Emotions flared, clashed, clung. Something comforting and wise, distant and cold clicked into Dion's mind. And in the alien's mind, something determined and unyielding, as raw as youth and as uncontrolled, hot as bloodlust and powerful as love, slid into Aiueven patterns. Dion's mouth was open, but she couldn't tell if it was she or the alien mother who screamed. But it was not a scream of horror or anger or pain. It was a scream of recognition, as though a child were returned, or a mother found.

Wind seemed to cut through Dion's mind, but it was no longer full of ice. Thin air screamed into her lungs, but it was no longer freezing her throat. The horror faded between them, and something else replaced it.

Kiuntihin'kiuntihin'kiun! The alien's voice was suddenly strong.

Mother! Dion cried.

Then the blue-gray voice faded, and the snow thickened, and Dion stood alone.

She stared at the sky, blinking as the dry snow hit her face. Wind chapped her lips. She didn't realize that she sank to her knees, her legs weak as grass. For a moment—for less than a moment—her eyes had been filled with a vision of darkness that went beyond night. Of a light that went beyond brightness. It was a star seen not through atmosphere, but from the vastness of space itself. It had been the alien's future that she had felt, for the barest of an instant.

She stared up at the sky, heedless of the snow. Stars . . . Aranur's dream was as close as that—as close as an alien's ship. The link to the past that he had sought to strengthen—that would never be enough. It was a link to the future that was needed.

She looked at her fingers, still stained with blood and now blue-white with the chill. She had touched something beyond herself—something alien, but also something more than that. As though Danton's death had destroyed her vision, and Aranur's had destroyed her future, she had forgotten that her own life was power, and power harnessed was hope. The plague in the wolves, the death in the domes . . . Power had created those, so power could find a cure. And she now knew that power.

She touched the parka where the slab of blood-ice covered her belly. The bond between mother and child was not something either she or the alien could deny. There was a power now between them that stretched through distance and time. And the energy brought with it a realization more clear than winter water. It wasn't her humanity she had lost, but that sense of strength— of what she could do to create the future she sought. Not Aranur's future, but her own. Her future, Olarun's future, the future of the wolves . . . Aranur's dreams had been his, not hers; she had to find her own. "My sons," she whispered. "My daughter."

She looked out over the ice. In the distance, she could see the shapes of the wolves who ran through the snow to meet her. *Wolfwalker!* they called.

Their song filled her head. She got to her feet and swayed. She took a step and staggered, then gathered her focus as she had seen the aliens do. Her legs stiffened, then strengthened as they accepted the energy. Her skin became suddenly warm. The wolves howled again, Calling her as they felt her mental voice strengthen. Her voice had changed, she realized. It was tinted with blues, not just gray, and the vision she projected was not just of the wolves, but of cold and starry futures.

She threw out her arms and spun, cold-clumsy on the ice. This time, when they Called, she sang her name back. For a moment the packsong was stilled. Then the wolves surged deeply into her head, seeking the voice they had known. They spun memories and flung them into the back of her skull. They dragged at her consciousness. What they found was not simply Dion, but something also Aiueven. Slitted eyes met lupine ones; promises met and merged. Histories blended so that time was a coil that touched itself through the ages.

Dion let the sense of the wolves strengthen in her mind. Hishn, so distant, clung to her, blurring her eyes and yet leaving her eyesight clear. Thick with the wolves, clear as Aiueven . . . She sang her name again to the wolves, and this time when she touched their gray-shadowed minds, they howled hauntingly with her.

XXIV

What do you have but yourself?
What do you face but yourself?
What do you hear but your voice in the night?
Whom do you know but yourself?

—*Answer to the* Second Riddle of the Ages

The three of them stopped at the barrier bushes beneath a blue-gray sky. Dion turned back and searched the clouds for a glimpse of a winged shape, but knew she wouldn't see one. The Aiueven were far away, in deeper, stranger caves. There were still wolves around her—she could feel them waiting on the other side of the wall.

Slowly, while Tehena and Kiyun watched her, she stepped forward and touched the thorns. They pricked her skin, just as before, but this time, she didn't flinch. In her mind, her body focused, the wolves howled softly, and the power flowed. The trickle of blood was stopped. The child in her belly turned. Her child, Aranur's child. And now, too, an Aiueven youngling . . .

Dion turned to Kiyun and stopped him from automatically tightening the lashings of his pack. She opened the bundles on his dnudu and drew out a small shape, then took the wrapped sword from his saddlebags. "These, I think, are mine," she said.

She unwrapped her healer's circlet. For a moment, she simply held it in the light and let her fingers trace the carving of the silver. There were lines of ancient symbolism twined with lines of newer hopes; twists and metal coils that curled like wolfsongs against a silver sea. "This was my mother's," she murmured, to ears that could not hear and yellow, slitted eyes that could. "And now, through you, it is my mother's, again." She settled the circlet on her head. Then she buckled on her sword.

Tehena moved beside her, searching her face with those flat, faded eyes. Dion had not spoken when she returned, and the days coming back had been silent. Now, as Tehena watched Dion take back her things, the woman cleared her throat. "You found it, then? What you were looking for? The cure for the plague in the wolves?" The cure for yourself, she wanted to ask. Her hard voice had been carefully neutral, and Dion missed the flicker of desperation in the other woman's eyes as Tehena rubbed at her forearms.

For a moment, Dion didn't answer. She should have bought that painting back in Vreston, she thought, as she caught the worry on Kiyun's face—or the one in Sidisport. He would have liked the blending and rawness those paintings had portrayed. And there had been that inlaid drum that Olarun would have jumped at. And Tehena . . . Dion wished she could share the strength of the Aiueven—the power and depth of that contact.

The wolves growled in the back of her head, and Dion's eyes became unfocused. The bond between her and Hishn was strong, but the other wolves had entered it now, as had the alien mother. There was a richness in the gray din that went beyond any single voice. She felt it curl around her thoughts, around Aranur's voice and Danton's silence. Felt it touch the silver and steel and fold them into her heart like gifts. She fingered the circlet absently. The weight of it was no longer on her shoulders, she realized, but in her heart, as if she finally understood it was her own needs that drove her, not the pushing of other people.

Her fingers traced the circlet's designs, remembering other, icy patterns. Her voice was quiet. "I failed. And yet I could not win. And still, I live—I breathe." She looked up. "I found no cure," she answered. "The moons left me that, as a goal—" Dion gave a faint, twisted smile. "—or a punishment." She looked back toward the mountains. They were hung with a new shroud of white that looked clean against the half-gray, half-blue sky. There were no wings to break that cold expanse, no speck of motion soaring between the peaks. Her voice dropped, as if she spoke more to herself. "But it is a goal, and one that I can work toward." Her hand rested against her belly, and she stretched through the wolves to the life that grew within her. "And if I do not reach that goal myself, my children will take up that burden. The wolves won't let them forget the promises to which I've bound them."

"You didn't even find what you were looking for?" This time, the desperate taint was stronger in Tehena's voice, and Dion didn't miss it.

She met Tehena's eyes steadily. "No," she said. "But I found what was needed. And in the end, that is all that matters."

Tehena let out an imperceptible breath, but all that showed was that the lanky woman nodded.

For a moment, Dion looked down at her hands. There was no trembling in her fingers. She stretched, and as if her strength had grown, not simply been sharpened by the touch of Aiueven, she could hear Hishn's voice clearly. The Gray Wolf of Randonnen. The Heart of Ariye . . . She looked at Kiyun and Tehena, then glanced back only once at the mountains. Then, as one, they mounted and rode into the barrier bushes.

As she passed through the channel, in the back of her mind, the yellow, slitted eyes blinked, and a gray-blue voice brushed the wolfsong. Soft, it was there for no more than an instant, but Dion felt it cleanly. And around her, on the wind, her hope seemed to lift, like a pair of alien wings.

Epilogue

Heart of Ariye

Sevlit arranged the sticks in the fire pit as the children began to gather near his wagon. The evening was full of soft noise: wood creaking, dnu stamping their feet, a dozen families murmuring as they set up evening camp. The light dust of three dozen kays clung to his teeth, and his muscles ached from riding. But this was his hour, when the world hung on his voice and the tiredness of others could be forgotten within the realms of stories. So he accepted more sticks from another young pair of arms and built the wood fire higher.

He studied the group as he arranged the branches, watching the youths who pushed each other eagerly for a seat near the fire pit, and then those who showed more sober faces: the boy with the large brown eyes and stringy blond hair; the two sisters who never let go of each other's hands, even when they sat down; the young man whose sharp voice stilled his brother; the girl with the loose black braid . . .

Sevlit let his eyes linger on the black-haired girl. She was young—nine or ten, perhaps—and her riding boots had seen more wear than this caravan had provided, but her slender frame was already muscled, rather than simply lanky. She did not smile, but in the dusk her dark eyes glinted with anticipation at his words, and her gaze followed his movements like a wolf stalking prey. She rode with her parents sometimes, away from the rest of the caravan, and other times alone, beside neBukua's wagon. She seemed a quiet child, but Sevlit had heard her laugh and sing as noisily as the rest when she thought she was alone.

She had not yet lost her dreams, though she already had the eyes of the Gray Ones, far-seeing, deep-reaching, and wary.

The future, he thought, in the hands of such a child . . .

He nodded to himself, then waited for the small crowd to settle. Waited while the parents provided their last admonishments before moving off to prepare the suppers. Waited while the scouts set watches around the camp, and the older youths began to split wood to replace what they would use that night. Waited for the noises and voices to become a background hum, until his patience itself became intriguing.

"Heart of Ariye," he said softly. The group stilled. The evening seemed to deepen as though, with those three words, his breath drew the darkness close like a curtain across the day. The glowing wood sparked, and Sevlit spread his hands, smoothing air and fire into palette and paint for his story.

> Where is hope, that you might find it?
> Where are dreams that you might see them?
> What is life, that it continues?
> Who is the Heart of Ariye?
> Wolfwalkers run the trails at night
> They scout our borders, watch our homes
> And one among them stands alone:
> The Gray Wolf of Ramaj Randonnen,
> The gray Heart of Ariye.

The firelight caught the words like tree sprits, playing his questions back in the children's eyes as the yellow-bright flames began to consume the wood. He felt the familiar anticipation, the catch in his own breath. Each story had its own life, its own passions, but this one had made his own pulse pound ever since he first heard it. He nodded at the children, pulling their gazes with him. And within the lines of the story, the sound of the fire crackling became a rhythm of its own.

> Ariyens work in secret, silence,
> Recovering the ancient skills;
> That once again, we'll touch the stars
> And skies of other worlds.

But next month, next year, next century—
They hang like threats, dissolving time,
Till past and future merge once more,
And ancient plagues, which killed before,
Are roused to kill again.

What would you do to keep your hopes?
How long will you struggle to dream?
How far ahead will a wolf-mother run
To built a future for her sons?
To protect her wolf-spun children?

Sevlit let his gaze take in the group, as though he was asking the questions of each child. The fire, still gaining strength as it ate the surface of new wood, threw off only thin tendrils of smoke, while the flames themselves were quiet. The storyteller nodded, as if he had heard the answer he wanted within the children's silence.

Aranur's Heart looked long ahead
And taught her wolf-sons how to seek:
So as they learned the trails here
They set their feet on older roads—
On paths to Ancient stars.

She took them with the wolfpack, hunting,
To Still Meadow's heavy grass.
Hidden eyes sought out their footsteps;
Hidden minds saw what she taught:
Saw the Heart of Ariye.

Sevlit's hand fluttered like wings, and the blackness of the lepa beasts came alive. Birdbeast eyes were the sparks that snapped up into the smoke; his fingers were talons as he clutched the images before him. His shoulders tensed as if it were his hands on the knife, his hands that fought to hold on to his son, his fists that clutched the earth as he lay, finally, dying.

He let his hands fall. The coals hissed, but did not spark. His voice was tight. He let the tears blur his eyes and catch in his throat; he let his hands curl into fists as though he drew emotion, not simply from himself, but from the listeners instead. Someone stirred at the edge of the shadows, and he knew the parents were gathering. His voice gained strength.

> But Ariyen love is strong as steel—
> Binding, bending, never breaking;
> And Aranur could not release
> The gray Heart of Ariye.
>
> He Called the wolves and forced them in;
> Bid them tear into her soul;
> Bid them find her, bind her to him.
> Commanded them to hold her:
> The gray Heart of Ariye.
>
> The wolf packs Answered, gathered to him;
> Held his mate where love could not.
> Swept her on a tide of gray;
> Forced her once-stilled heart to stay;
> Claimed the Heart of Ariye.
>
> What price of him who Called the wolves?
> Who dared cold death to save our dreams?
> What seized the moons in payment for
> The Heart of our Ariye?
>
> He offered life in place of hers,
> That she continue with the wolves,
> Teaching courage, vision, hope—
> The Heart of our Ariye.

Sevlit let his eyes roam the crowd. His voice was sober yet compelling, and his hands, half open, were suspended above the flames, as though they captured and reshaped each word he loosed into the air.

> And yet, Ariyen love still bound her
> Aranur still touched her soul.

And from the moons, he urged her on,
Through the packsong, through the wolves.
His heart, the Heart of Ariye.

He led her north, to icy mountains,
Where once Ariyens dared the stars,
Where different wings swept frigid peaks
And saw the Heart of Ariye. And
Took the Heart of Ariye.

Aiueven, distant, mind-cold, eerie,
Icy-white and glowing cold,
Jealous of their wings of moonlight,
Wary of Ariyen goals.

They challenged her to find our future;
Challenged her to reach their stars;
Flaunted space and flight before her;
Dared the Heart of Ariye.

Ariyen-driven; gray-wolf owned,
She set one pact against another:
Debt to debt, and life to life.
She bound them with her unborn children;
Bound our futures with her blood:
Aiueven and Human.

Sevlit's clenched hands crossed his chest, holding that binding within himself. Then he forced his voice to warm, releasing the tension with the flaring of the fire at his feet.

We who work in hopeful silence,
Hiding science in our homes,
Stretching dreams toward night-dark skies,
Gazing at forbidden moons;

We strive to spread our arms in flight,
Like hawks that rise on distant worlds,

On wings, that with our blood was bought,
By one whose vision was returned.

Where is that hope, that you might find it?
Look you to the forest night;
Listen for the Gray One's howling;
Look you to your own self's heart.

Aranur, whose strength and faith
Held off the grip of icy death;
Who offered life for one more chance,
To touch the Ancients' Earth.

And the Gray Wolf of Ramaj Randonnen,
Who fought to keep an ancient pledge—
Took our goals and paid their price,
And gave to us our future.

Where is hope, that you might find it?
Where are dreams, that you might see them?
What is life, that it continues?
Who is the Heart of Ariye?
Who is the Heart of Ariye?

Sevlit's words hung in the air like tiny, foreign suns, spinning out above the fire. In the pit, the flames crackled softly; the coals glistened like gold. The sparks that snapped up with the smoke circled in the thready vortex before whispering into the night.

Finally, a boy with skinned elbows and a smudged face shifted uncomfortably. His young voice broke the suspense that had continued to hold, and the storyteller hid his smile as the child smudged the dirt further when he rubbed at his cheek. "Who is the Heart of Ariye?" the boy asked. "Where is it now?"

The storyteller spread his hands, as if to encompass the group. This was what he loved best—the afterward, when he could shape each child by his answers. It was those gems that sparkled in the eye long after his other words faded. He looked at the boy, but let his expression take in the group. "The Heart?" he echoed. "The Heart of Ariye is in you."

"In me?" the boy asked, surprised. "Just me?"

"No," Sevlit smiled. "It is in each of you—in you and you and you." He pointed. "The Heart of Ariye—it means that you are your own center. You are what you make yourself: brave, skilled, determined, wise. Like Aranur—or the wolfwalker." He caught the child's gaze again. "You are the Heart," he said. "You are the future. Carry that well, boy, and you can carry the world."

The young boy stared back, his eyes wide. He almost missed his brother tugging at his sleeve, urging him to return to their wagon as the group broke up. Parents came to retrieve their families; older siblings ordered smaller ones about. The smells of dinners warming and roasting tugged at Sevlit's nose. But he was not yet alone at the fire. The black-haired girl still waited, even as the others left. He knew she could take herself back to neBukua's wagon had she wished it, but she lingered, her gaze following his movements as he tucked another stick in the flames.

"What is it, child?" he asked quietly.

She studied him for a moment, and he could almost see the thoughts turning over in her mind. Then she said, "The story is about Aranur. Who did he love so much back then? Who is the Heart of Ariye?"

The lines of Sevlit's face, which had wrinkled and stretched and held so much emotion as he had told the story, became still and sober. Someone shifted at the edge of the firelight, and he looked over the girl's shoulder to the single figure who melted out of the trees. For a moment, he met the wolfwalker's gaze. The Wolfwalker had heard the question—he saw it in her face. But even as he saw the shadows gather in those violet eyes, he knew what he would say. And even as he saw her beg him silently not to answer, even as he saw her expression grow bleak with the words that rose to his lips, even as he knew he would forever change the girl's life, he said, "Child, she is your mother."

He held out his hand to the shadows, and the woman moved into the firelight. She and Sevlit exchanged1 a long glance, until the storyteller inclined his head and looked away. The woman took Noriani's hand and tucked it gently in the grip of her scarred fingers. And as they walked away, he heard the little girl ask, "Momma, what is your name?"

DEL REY® ONLINE!

The Del Rey Internet Newsletter...

A monthly electronic publication, posted on the Internet, GEnie, CompuServe, BIX, various BBSs, and the Panix gopher (gopher.panix.com). It features hype-free descriptions of books that are new in the stores, a list of our upcoming books, special announcements, a signing/reading/convention-attendance schedule for Del Rey authors, "In Depth" essays in which professionals in the field (authors, artists, designers, salespeople, etc.) talk about their jobs in science fiction, a question-and-answer section, behind-the-scenes looks at sf publishing, and more!

Internet information source!

A lot of Del Rey material is available to the Internet on our Web site and on a gopher server: all back issues and the current issue of the Del Rey Internet Newsletter, sample chapters of upcoming or current books (readable or downloadable for free), submission requirements, mail-order information, and much more. We will be adding more items of all sorts (mostly new DRINs and sample chapters) regularly. The Web site is http://www.randomhouse.com/delrey/ and the address of the gopher is gopher.panix.com

Why? We at Del Rey realize that the networks are the medium of the future. That's where you'll find us promoting our books, socializing with others in the sf field, and—most important—making contact and sharing information with sf readers.

Online editorial presence: Many of the Del Rey editors are online, on the Internet, GEnie, CompuServe, America Online, and Delphi. There is a Del Rey topic on GEnie and a Del Rey folder on America Online.

Our official e-mail address for Del Rey Books is delrey@randomhouse.com (though it sometimes takes us a while to answer).